MW01640091

For Megan

Happily Ever After ~

THE PAGES in Between

A story of love, life & cocktails...

RENAY JORDAN

Have Happy Every Day

Renay Jordan

Print ISBN: 978-1-54391-964-6

eBook ISBN: 978-1-54391-965-3

For Jacob, Caleb,

Savannah and Susan

So many stories, so little time…

And Kevin

For making all my dreams come true

Tristan

I had high expectations when I moved to Woodlawn. I thought it would be simple because everything about it screamed small town mentality. I'm used to big cities with people who have big city thoughts, aspirations, and attitudes. Woodlawn isn't that place. I was told small towns are places full of people who never dream of leaving them, close knit families and circles of friends who have known each other their entire lives – none of which I'd ever had.

I did have my sister, Tiffany, who was not just my sister but my twin sister. Her and I have a connection unlike other brothers and sisters because we can read each other's minds. My mother used to say it wasn't because we were twins but because we were both wicked. Having Tiff with me when I went to Woodlawn was a comfort but not necessarily a promise that everything would turn out okay.

I could adapt to any kind of environment but then pretending came easy for me and Tiff because in the past if we showed weakness it meant we needed a therapist. Trust me when I say going to see a therapist to talk about things you'd rather forget is like poking an alcohol soaked cotton swab into an open wound.

I am a smart guy. I don't mean to be tooting my own horn, but I don't consider saying I'm smarter than most people to be conceited. There aren't many things I can't eventually figure out. Although I will be honest and tell you upfront I cannot solve a Rubik's Cube. My mother used to tell my dad he wasn't a professional at anything but an amateur in everything. I'm still not sure if that was a compliment or an insult.

Despite my upbringing I'd somehow managed to stay on the honor roll at every school I'd ever attended. It doesn't mean I haven't had my share of difficulties but that is coming purely from a behavioral standpoint. I have a penchant for not following the rules. I am fully aware that using pot at school every now and then to calm my nerves is not allowed, which come to think of it is probably how I ended up where I am now.

Tiffany and I haven't had parents in a very long time. Well, I take that back. We've had a lot of foster parents and lived in a lot of various places. I feared living in Woodlawn was going to be a major lifestyle change, not only because it was a small town but because we were going to be living with a retired couple who had no other children. Under normal circumstances that might have meant we'd be treated like adults who could do whatever they wanted or like three-year- old's who had to be checked on every ten minutes. There was never any way to predict how people would treat you.

Over the years I had researched towns, schools, how many restaurants and bars were within walking distance of my new home and what my cell phone service would be like once I got there, but one thing I couldn't research was human nature. General psychology, yes. Individual human nature, no. If you've ever moved to a new town you know how helpful that would be but, alas, people will always be unpredictable. They will also be unreasonable, irrational, irreverent and generally unreliable. I usually know what people are going to do. I just don't know when they are going to do it.

I've been spoiled rotten, treated like an indentured servant and once, hit on by a very sexy foster "mom" who told me I looked like Aladdin. Tiffany and I had been told by every kid in every school we'd ever attended that we were what everyone called "the beautiful people." I don't know if it's because we have perpetual tans, jet black hair or incredibly long eyelashes but it gets old after a while. Along with it comes the expectation that we are perfect which couldn't be any further from the truth. It should be a sin for God to give beautiful children to such shitty parents.

The difference between me and Tiff is that her looks took her places. Mine never did. Tiffany could have been sent to another country where no one spoke English and she'd still have fifty friends by nightfall. It is conceivable to think that she may be able to cast spells. When nothing else works she is always my back-up plan.

A weird fact about Tiffany? She reads her Bible every day. I don't know why because she never retains what she reads. I know this because of what she does. I guess she believes in forgiveness except she asks for the same forgiveness every day. Somehow, I don't think that is the way God intended it. But don't ask me. I know nothing – or so she says.

I am not religious although I could recite the Bible backward and forward and upside down if someone tried to waterboard me over it. I stay away from churches simply because our parents practically made us live in one. I believe in God. I just don't want people trying to tell me how to live my life. I don't need someone telling me how I need to repent or how I'm going to live in eternal hellfire if I don't. Plus, I don't like people knowing my twisted spiritual history because I don't want them to judge me by it. Religious people tend to do that, yet they seem to not understand that it is one of the worst sins you can commit. (I can give you the book, chapter, and verse if you're interested.)

I never expected a complication of the magnitude I experienced while I was in Woodlawn. There is no guidebook that tells you what to do when you put yourself in the kind of predicament I did. If there is, I'd like to read it. Although now it is much too late to make any changes that would matter.

When I first met Lilah, I thought she was the most beautiful woman I'd ever seen. I'd never met another woman like her, but I instantly knew she'd been judged, which was why developing a friendship with her was a problem. She was so beautiful I forgot what I was supposed to be doing and that ended up getting me into a lot of trouble. I had never had a split lip until I met Lilah. I'd had a lot of other injuries but never a split lip and let me tell you right now, it hurts like hell.

I had also never met anyone like Isabel, who still to this day makes me want to hit something. Not in a destructive or hurtful way, just in an exasperating way. Or maybe infuriating would be a better word. I don't blame Isabel for anything she does or says – she does it all in Lilah's defense because apparently Lilah doesn't know how to defend herself which is partially true - but it is still incredibly unnecessary.

I won't claim the people in Woodlawn are down-to-earth, but they are good, honest people. Once you earn their trust they will never turn their back on you. They are proof that friendships can develop between the most unlikely people. I still don't understand what I did to deserve that friendship, but I guess when you care about people the why of it doesn't have to make sense.

Because Lilah and I were so different, from diverse backgrounds and in various parts of our lives, our relationship was a little complicated. Eventually I had to tell her the truth – because you can't hide the truth from someone you love and in most cases, you don't want to be lying in the first place.

You don't have time to think when someone points a gun at you. You do what comes naturally. You protect yourself. When someone threatens to come between you and the people you love, you use commonsense. You shoot.

"As the Scriptures say: There is no one who always does what is right, not even one."

Romans 3:10 (NCV)

Lilah

As soon as I woke up I could hear the children fighting in the bathroom, but I didn't have the energy to go in there and play referee. Anyhow, my husband could do it. And he would do it. Because he knew more than likely I wasn't going to get out of bed. I felt guilty but not guilty enough to do anything about it. I should have gotten up and been a mother to my children. But I didn't. Instead, I rolled over and pulled the comforter up closer around me.

It wasn't long before I heard the ramble of footsteps going down the stairs that told me everyone had dressed and was ready for school. Everyone except my youngest daughter, Maria, who had just turned five. She was old enough to feed herself and take herself to the bathroom, so I rationalized she didn't really need me either. At least not until my husband went to work and left her in front of the television watching whatever her favorite cartoon happened to be at the time. I couldn't keep up with all the Disney shows anymore and it didn't matter anyway because Maria was a good child. She would watch anything if our poodle, Max, was by her side. I was glad she had him because at the time she sure didn't have me.

My husband, Eric, came into our bedroom to tell me everyone had eaten breakfast and was waiting for the school bus at the end of the driveway. I briefly thought about how I should have packed them all a healthy lunch, but I dismissed it quickly by convincing myself they would rather buy their lunch in the school cafeteria. It may or may not have been the truth.

"You need to get up," Eric said. "Maria is downstairs watching TV and I have to go to work."

"I know," I said sitting up. I threw my legs over the edge of the bed and he squatted down in front of me.

"You can do this Lilah," he said putting his hands on my knees." It's going to be a good day." He kissed me on the cheek. "But brush your teeth."

I smiled. I'm not sure any other husband would have taken on all the responsibilities I failed at every day without resentment. Eric understood my depression and he didn't blame me for it. There were certainly plenty of times he played the tough love card. But Eric knew he couldn't play that card every day without showing compassion on other days. I got up and threw on a pair of pajama bottoms with my t-shirt and ambled down the staircase. When I got the bottom, Maria ran over and hugged my legs.

"Mommy," she said. "Guess what?"

I laid my hand on top of her head and ran my fingers through her thick blonde hair. Everyone said she looked like me at that age. Her face was full where mine was more angled, but she had my green eyes and ash blonde hair.

"What honey?"

"Guess," she said excitedly.

We started walking toward the kitchen together. She still had on her princess nightgown and the purple socks she had worn the day before. Today I would have to give her a bath and wash her hair. I saw the open container of strawberries sitting on the counter.

"Um," I pretended to think. "Daddy cut up strawberries for your cereal this morning."

"With sugar," she said as I leaned down to pick her up. I kissed her temple. "Don't be mad at him. You promise?" I smiled.

"I promise, honey."

Max sat at my feet, tail wagging.

"Do you want to give Max his food?" I asked putting Maria down.

"Yes!" Her enthusiasm amazed me.

Max followed her as she headed toward the utility room. I poured myself a cup of coffee. That dog had been Maria's shadow since the day she was born. Eric had given Max to me for my birthday that same year. A poodle puppy in April. A new baby in September. At the time I had asked Eric how the hell he rationalized giving me a poodle puppy when I was four months pregnant.

"Because you said you always wanted a poodle," he said.

"Not now!" I said. "What am I going to do with a puppy and a baby together?" He smiled.

"I'm sure you'll figure it out."

This was the same question I had asked my obstetrician at my next appointment. She had known Eric and I for years and had delivered all our children. She had helped me through the post-partum depression that set in after I had Ben and eventually referred me to my psychiatrist, Dr. Stone.

"I think a puppy is a wonderful idea," she said.

"Yeah," I replied. "Because you don't have to deal with it." She laughed.

"What am I going to do with him after the baby is born? He sleeps in the bed with me every night. He worships the ground I walk on. What if he is jealous and wants to kill her?"

"The baby?" my doctor asked, surprised.

"Yes."

As it turned out Max loved Maria. From the day we brought Maria home from the hospital Max attached himself to her. He sat beside her carrier, he laid beside her when she was on the floor on a blanket. He watched over her when she was sleeping. If she cried and I wasn't around, he came to get me. We hadn't been able to separate them since and that was perfectly fine with me. Max was such a loyal dog, not only to Maria but to everyone in our family.

I heard a crash from the utility room, so I sat my coffee down on the counter and hurried across the hall. Maria was sitting on the floor surrounded by dog food while Max ate off the floor around her. She was laughing.

"What happened?" I asked then noticed the bag of dogfood on top of the washing machine, just out of Maria's reach.

"I tried to get it down," she said pointing to the bag of food. "But it spilled. It's okay Mommy. Max is eating it anyway." I squatted beside her.

"Yes, he is." I patted Max on the head and he briefly turned my way. "Maybe we can sweep this up with the broom and put it in Max's bowl." I stood up to grab the broom in the corner.

"No!" Maria said adamantly. "Then Max will have dirt in his bowl with his food." Very perceptive, this child was. "I'm going to pick it all up and put it in there." I sat the broom back in the corner.

"Okay," I said. "If you insist."

I went back into the kitchen and sat down at the table with my coffee. There was a half empty bag of doughnuts in the middle of it and I reached for them. That would be my breakfast. A doughnut and coffee. It would also be my lunch and dinner. I wasn't very hungry most days. I usually only ate so people would leave me alone. I heard the front door open. Living in a small town we rarely locked it. There really was no point. I stayed at the table. Whoever it was would find me.

My best friend, Isabel, poked her head around the corner. She had just taken her youngest sons, Matt and Abe to school.

"Why are you still in your pajamas?" I only stared at her while I ate my doughnut. She held up her hand. "Wait! I want to rephrase my question. Why are you still wearing the shirt you wore yesterday with pajama bottoms?"

"Because this is what I slept in." I reached for another doughnut and she grabbed the bag out of my hand. "Why are *you* not at work?" I asked.

"Because I called in sick," she said. "I needed a mental health day."

"*You* needed a mental health day?? That's funny. Your life is practically perfect."

"...in every way," she sang. "Are you kidding? You haven't been over to the house lately to know it is filthy, I have about 110 midterms to grade and I spilled a cup of coffee into my bra this morning."

"Ouch," I said.

"Yeah." She turned away from me and opened the refrigerator door. "I'm making scrambled eggs." She searched around inside looking for the eggs. "Do you have eggs? And where is Maria?"

"She's in the utility room cleaning up dog food," I said taking a sip of my coffee.

"What?" Isabel asked. "Why? Because you're too lazy to do it?"

I thought at that moment everyone needed a friend like Isabel. She was my comic relief and always tough love. She wouldn't tolerate me feeling sorry for myself unless I had a legitimate reason and there weren't very many legitimate reasons with Isabel.

"No," I said in my defense. "Somebody put Max's food on top of the washer and she wanted to feed him, but she couldn't reach it so when she grabbed it, it tipped over and spilled onto the floor. I was going to sweep it up, but she insisted she was going to pick up each piece and put in Max's bowl because she didn't want Max to have dirt in his food."

"Smart girl," Isabel replied. She mixed up the eggs and poured them into a frying pan.

"I can't eat eggs today," I said.

"Yes, you can. I put cheese in them. You love cheese." I sighed.

"Okay." She turned from the stove.

"What's your plan today?"

"I have no plan." Maria walked through the kitchen door and over to me. I pulled her up into my lap.

"Hi Isabel," she said. "How are you today?" Sometimes she said things you wouldn't expect to come out of a five-year old's mouth.

"I am very good, Miss. Maria." Isabel kissed the top of her head. "What do you want to do today?"

"Let's go ice skating!" she said. "The pond is frozen!"

"The pond might be frozen honey," I said. "But that doesn't mean we can ice skate on it. We might fall through."

Isabel sat the scrambled eggs down in front of me and handed me a fork. I fed most of them to Maria until she realized what I was doing.

"Did you have breakfast this morning?" she asked Maria.

"Yes! I had cereal with strawberries!"

"Yum," Isabel said. "I wanted to make sure you'd eaten. Do you really want to go ice skating?"

Maria jumped off my lap and started jumping up and down.

"Yes, yes, yes!" she said to Isabel.

I took a deep breath and shook my head no.

"Well, we're going," she said to Maria excitedly, but I knew it was aimed more at me. "We'll go to the one in the West End. It's a Tuesday. No one will be there."

Maria was beside herself with excitement. At that point my unwillingness was the only reason Isabel insisted we go.

"Well, go get ready," Isabel said.

"Yay!" she shouted as she ran out of the room. I heard her scampering up the stairs.

"She needs a bath," I said to Isabel. She poured herself a cup of coffee.

"Well, go give her one," she said. "And then we'll go."

"I don't want to," I said. "I'm tired and I don't feel like it."

"You do feel like it," she said. "We think; therefore, we feel." She took my hand as if I needed help standing up. "Get up."

I begrudgingly got up from my chair and poured myself more coffee.

"Seriously, Isabel. I don't feel like it and I have a headache."

She reached for her bag on the table and pulled out a bottle of aspirin. She opened it, poured some into her hand and held it out to me.

"Aspirin is good for headaches," she said. "Down them and we're going. You go get yourself dressed and I'll give Maria a quick bath." I scratched my forehead. "Go!" she said.

I trudged up the stairs and heard Isabel loading the dishwasher. She yelled after me.

"Start Maria's bath water. I'll be right up."

I found Maria standing in the hallway naked at the top of the stairs. She had heard me say she needed a bath which meant she'd also heard me say I didn't want to go ice skating with her – more than once. I'm sure she'd heard plenty of things in her short life she shouldn't have but the ones that upset me the most were the ones I knew hurt her feelings.

"I see you're ready for your bath," I said. She took me by the hand.

"Mommy," she said looking up at me. "I know you're tired and you have a headache. Thank you for going with me to skate today anyway."

"You're welcome honey."

I squatted down beside her and wrapped my arms around her tiny body. She still smelled like a baby. Baby shampoo. Baby lotion. I broke down and started to cry. Maria pulled back and wiped away the tears rolling down my face.

"Don't cry Mommy," she said. "Everything will be okay."

This made me cry even more. A five-year-old little girl should not be comforting her mommy. Her mommy should be comforting her.

Most people don't understand depression. It is not unhappiness and sadness every minute of every day. I think people see you and think, what's wrong with her? She looks fine to me. Well, for one, I am not fine. I may look fine but that is me pretending to be fine because I don't want other people nosing into my business. I don't want people feeling sorry for me or constantly asking if I'm okay. I'm not okay but I don't need you to remind me of it.

Everyone always thinks they are being nice and I'm sure that is their intention but it's like telling someone whose family member died that you understand and that everything will be alright. Let me tell you that those people don't understand, and things may or may not be alright.

One of the hardest parts of depression is wanting to do better. I wanted to please the people in my life, but I knew I constantly let them down when I didn't do any of the things I said I was going to do. I have good days and bad days. On the bad days I wish I could make myself get out of bed, clean the house, and cook my family dinner but on those days, I can't. There is no energy but mostly there is no desire and that makes me feel guilty because I should feel SOMETHING. Shouldn't I?

I often wonder if losing that desire is the only thing that will happen to me. Will I lose my mind completely and not be able to think at all anymore? Or not know my name? These are actual things that go through my mind on a regular basis.

Isabel is one of those persons who gets it. I'm not going to go as far as saying she completely understands because I don't think unless you've been through psychiatry school you truly understand. It's a hard concept to grasp. There are no physical explanations for depression. I can't point to a spot on my head and say, 'it hurts right there.' It hurts inside my soul. It hurts my heart.

I think Isabel does what she does because she loves me and my children. Sometimes she loves Eric but not usually because she is mad at him for not doing more to help me. I always try to explain he has a demanding job and does what he can. Isabel doesn't pursue that train of thought. She just nods and says okay.

Isabel likes to be the heroine. She is the type of person who likes to save the day and get credit for it later. I don't see this as a bad aspect of her personality. I think it makes her feel good about herself and that's okay. Everyone needs to feel needed.

Isabel was definitely needed. Not only by me but by her children. Between the two of us we had seven children. I had four and she had three. They were the same ages and because we lived so close together – a few blocks – they were always back and forth between the two houses.

If it could be said my children had a second mother, it would be Isabel. She picked up the pieces when I didn't even recognize the puzzle and I'd like to think despite my loss of ambition and restlessness her children thought of me as their second mother, too. They loved me despite my unpredictable moods and that made me feel good. Outside of my family it made me feel needed and every person who suffers from depression needs to feel needed somehow.

My friendship with Isabel worked because we had the same parenting philosophies. Some people in our small town simply called it bad parenting philosophies. We called it life skills. We believed our children could face the reality of life now or face it later but undoubtedly, they *would* face it – sex, drugs, movies rated NC-17. Other parents acted like their kids didn't already know these things – like they were protecting them from something evil. Isabel and I believed it didn't matter whether you protected your children from these things because if they wanted to know about something and you didn't tell them, someone else would.

We didn't hit the fast-forward button when there was a nude love scene or a zombie attack (pretty much the same thing) in a movie. Our kids thought all the other kids were the weird ones when they found out their parents had blocked certain TV channels, or they didn't have them at all. We didn't advocate those channels, but we didn't worry ourselves to death over whether the kids were watching them either. We noted when our kids didn't get in trouble for watching them they didn't want to watch them anymore. Occasionally the younger ones were interested but that never lasted very long.

Several months ago, while I was in the kitchen cooking dinner I overheard Maria tell one of her friends, "It's just a penis." Of course, I received a phone call from said friend's mother the following day asking me why I let her daughter watch a movie with a man's penis in it. I told her I had no idea what she was talking about and that everyone in our house walked around naked so maybe it wasn't a movie. Isabel and I laughed about that for days.

Winter was always a tough time for me. I wasn't afraid of the dark, but I loathed it because darkness is depressing. I waited patiently for Spring every year and when it arrived Isabel and I always took advantage of the warmer weather.

One night in early Spring that year, Isabel showed up unexpectedly and sat down at my kitchen table while I loaded the dishwasher. It was warmer than usual at that time and I had the windows open. It drove Eric crazy because of his allergies and he was always going around putting them down one by one.

"I have a mission you have to help me with," Isabel said.

"Oh no," I said turning around from the sink because Isabel's "missions" almost always ended badly.

"Isaac..." This was her oldest son. He was 17. "...started working at the garden shop last week."

"Joe's garden shop?"

"Yes," she replied. "Anyhow, he said Joe had put all the un-sellable plants around the back."

"What is an un-sellable plant?" I asked.

"You know," she said. "The ones that didn't quite make it." I raised my eyebrows.

"So, dead plants."

"No," she said. "Would you listen to me??"

Isabel never worried about whether she hurt my feelings enough to send me into a downward spiral of unrelenting depression.

"I'm listening!" I insisted.

She got up from the table and went to my refrigerator. She opened it and took out the milk then reached into the cabinet above and got down the vodka I hid from the children. She proceeded to make us a cocktail even though I hadn't asked for one.

"Isaac said he thinks the plants are free to the public, so I thought we'd go over there tonight and get some." She handed me my drink.

"What is this?" I asked because Isabel was famous for her cocktails. Most often she made them up as she went along. She was pretty good at it but not always.

"This...," she said holding up her glass, "...is a ***Snowy Night.*** We're not going to have any more of these this year so enjoy this one." I smiled and shook my head.

"I hope you're right," I said as I touched my glass to hers.

"I am. I got my Farmer's Almanac today. I think I'm going to plant corn this year."

This was an insane aspiration on Isabel's part. She would never plant corn.

"Lord," I said. "You and your Farmer's Almanac. Speaking of planting, I highly doubt those plants at the garden shop are free to the public." I took a sip of my drink.

"Me too," she said conspiratorially. "But let's go get some anyway."

Isabel had no fear of the law. I had gotten to the point where I didn't either. Not just because most of the time I had no feelings in general but because Isabel's uncle was the town sheriff. We had gotten ourselves into a few pickles over the years and we'd never gotten anything more than a warning.

Eric maintained Isabel was a bad influence on me, but I thought the opposite because Isabel was full of life and fun and good times. Lord knows when it came to needing a little fun and excitement in my life she never failed to deliver. She always had good intentions but every now and then we did or said something that backfired and got us into trouble with our husbands. Hence, Isabel's divorce. I would rather not get into the specifics of what happened between her and Tom but suffice it to say that over the years Isabel and I had somehow convinced each other it was okay to have a little fling every now and then if we were bored.

Our idea with the plants was to give them to our mothers and other friends who would nurse them back to health and in turn not have to buy their own summer annuals from the store. This in fact *was* stealing as we found out by one of the local deputies while we were putting them in the back of Isabel's SUV.

"You can't just take the plants Joe puts out back," Roy said. "They are not your property and you are trespassing."

"But we thought since Joe put them out back they were free to the public," Isabel said.

She yanked her t-shirt down a little further, so her boobs would spill out of the top. Even if Roy wrote her a ticket, which he wouldn't because his boss was her uncle, she would get out of it, so I never understood it when she tried to seduce him. I had learned over the years not to question Isabel's motives. She could always justify her actions somehow. Except for her divorce with Tom. There was no justification for a picture of her naked with another man.

"Who told you they were free to the public?" Roy asked.

Of course, this entire scene was witnessed by whatever townspeople happened to drive by during the inquisition and who, undoubtedly, recognized Isabel's SUV as we stood in the parking lot talking with Roy while he shined his flashlight into our eyes.

"I can't tell you that," Isabel said. "I don't want to get him in trouble."

"Him?" Roy inquired.

We were silent.

"Okay, look," he said. "I'm going let you go. Because you know I could charge you with trespassing and breaking and entering."

"There was nothing to break," Isabel said. "The gate was open."

"Shut up Isabel," I said from behind her.

"Just because the chain isn't locked does not mean the gate is open," Roy pointed out. "Now get out of here before I change my mind."

We stood there for a few minutes until Roy had gotten into his car and pulled out of the parking lot. As soon as he was out of sight Isabel and I slammed the door of the SUV – with all the plants inside and left at once.

Our next stop was the liquor store. We had to pick up some good gin, so Isabel could make us a drink when we got home. We followed all our escapades with a drink, but someone had stolen Isabel's bottle of gin and she wanted to make this gin martini she had found on the internet. There was no question one of our children or one of our children's friends had stolen the gin, but we didn't make a big deal out of it. They knew we knew and oddly that was enough. Sometimes. When we got back to Isabel's house we decided we should hide the plants in the garage until we could transplant them into other pots. I grabbed the bag from the liquor store.

Isabel's house was one of those midcentury modern homes built around an inground pool. She wasn't fond of the design, but her children loved it. So once the divorce was final and despite her misgivings she decided to stay. She admitted to me afterward it wasn't all about the design but about whether she could forget the memories she'd made there with Tom. Plus, she said, moving would break the children's hearts. That may or may not have been true, but I didn't believe it would break their hearts for any sentimental reason. I believed it would break their hearts because every bedroom in the house had sliding glass doors that opened onto the patio of the pool. I didn't think there was a teenager on the face of the earth who would want to leave that set-up.

The first winter after Tom left the kids were a little wild. Isabel was paying even less attention than she normally did because the divorce proceedings were a major distraction. During that time her boys drained part of the water out of the pool and used it as a skating rink for themselves and all their friends. Isabel's children were not only mischievous but clever. She took that into consideration when doling out punishments which meant they usually got away with their shenanigans. For that very reason every child in the neighborhood wanted to be at Isabel's house. Isabel's kids may have been a little reckless, and most of the neighbors thought they were totally out of control but they respected their mother. Isabel did not tolerate disrespect. She caught up with me on the front sidewalk and bumped her shoulder into mine.

"What do you say we have a drink to celebrate our undercover mission?"

"Well, duh."

"Kids," she yelled as she walked through the front door. "Where are you??"

Five of our kids came out of various rooms and into the kitchen. Isabel's middle son, Matt, took the bag with the liquor out of my hands. He pulled the bottles out and sat them on the table.

"Nice," he said.

Isabel slapped him on the back of his head. We agreed if you let teenage boys think for one minute you weren't in control they would take complete advantage of you.

"No," she said. "Go watch a movie."

"You called me in here!" He said leaning against the counter, a smirk on his face.

"Okay," she said thoughtfully as she pulled the bottle of sour mix out of the refrigerator. "Then, hmmm… go watch a movie. Nothing X-rated."

"We have X-rated movies?" he asked. He was fifteen. Of course, he asked.

"No, you dummy," Abe said. He was thirteen. "She means the French porno's."

"You have French porno's?" I asked. "How do I not know about this?"

"They're not really porno's," she said. "They're just French. You know they show *everything*." What she really meant was that they *did* everything. I shrugged.

"Well, yeah."

Even we had *some* limits.

Our children were curious about *everything*. Even the things most children would not have cared or tried to do. How many people can we get in the jon boat before it tips over and we all must swim to shore? What happens when we mix bleach with vinegar? (Because our teacher told us NOT to do this.) Can we make it to the other side of the woods in the middle of the night on the four-wheelers with no headlights? And how fast can we do that without killing ourselves? What if we slide down the laundry shoot? Or powder the cat? They had once given the dog breath strips because they said he had bad breath. They weren't wrong.

When our children got together we never knew what might happen. We didn't believe any of our kids had an ounce of fear. We knew this because they had defied death too many times. On occasion Isabel and I were paying attention. Most of the time, though, it was just the grace of God.

Isabel and I sat down at the counter bar in her kitchen with our drinks.

"I have a question for you," I said.

"The answer is no."

"You don't even know the question yet!" I protested.

"Well, ask away."

I took a sip of my drink.

"Gosh, this is strong."

"A Peaceful Acquisition."

"What?"

"That's what I named it." I raised my eyebrows in question. "You know, like, the plants were a peaceful acquisition?" I laughed.

"Seriously, Isabel?" She smiled and held up her glass.

"It's got extra gin in it."

"I shouldn't even be drinking," I said as I took a sip. "You know alcohol interferes with my medication."

"Okay, Eric." I frowned at her.

Eric and Isabel disagreed on my drinking habits. Eric said alcohol aggravated my medicine and, therefore, my depression. Isabel rationalized my medicine didn't work in the first place so what difference did it make if I had drink every now and then? Personally, I thought Isabel might be right.

"This new kid whose been showing up at our houses," I said thoughtfully.

"Tristan?"

"Yes. Who is he and where did he come from? It's like he appeared out of nowhere."

"He's a foster kid. He lives with Mrs. Jenkins."

Mrs. Jenkins lived on the other side of the woods behind me. I occasionally saw her at the grocery store. She and her husband took in foster kids for years, but it was a while since they'd had one. They didn't have any children of their own so I'm sure it made their house a little more interesting.

"He has a twin sister, Tiffany," Isabel continued. "I heard their parents were killed in an accident."

"What kind of accident?" She shrugged.

"I'm not sure."

"Oh my gosh," I said. "That's horrible."

"Yeah," she said as she cut up a lime. "I can look it up at school."

"Isabel," I warned. "That's a probably not a good idea."

Somehow over the years of our friendship Isabel and I had become each other's moral compass. It is obvious our moral compasses are a little off base. Okay, a lot off base.

After Isabel's husband left she had gone back to teaching school because she needed the money. She now taught high school biology, chemistry, and physics. You would never know Isabel was that smart. That's a horrible thing to say about your best friend but it was true.

One day while she was in the teacher's lounge she saw the assistant principal at the computer and only moments later saw him entering his personal identification code into the password box. Of course, the assistant principal has access to everything in the student files, unlike the teachers, who are only privy to less personal information.

Isabel is one of those people who sometimes can't stop herself from doing things she knows she shouldn't be doing. The next thing you know she's at the computer on her lunch break looking up kid's files using the assistant principal's code. Ever since then she'd been addicted to snooping on people. She always looked up our children's classmates or anyone involved with them to see if they had, what she called, a 'mental defect.'

"I've done it a million times," she said. "You know that."

"And one day you're going to get caught."

"I don't know what you're so worried about," she said. "It won't affect you."

"Yes, it will," I said. "Anything that affects you affects me." She leaned over and rubbed my arm.

"Aw thanks honey. That's so sweet." She took another sip of her drink. "You know I'm going to do it anyway."

"I didn't ask you because I wanted you to look up his file," I reminded her. "Although I'm surprised you haven't already done it since he's been hanging around our houses so much lately." I picked up a slice of lime and squeezed it into my glass. "I only wanted to know if you'd heard anything about him at school."

"I've told you what I know," she said. "But now I'm going to find out the real story." She winked at me.

I hated it when she did that.

Isabel and I spent most our afternoons together having what we called "Happy Hour." Eric called them "happier" hours. I must admit we sometimes got a little silly but today was a difficult day and I didn't really feel like a happy hour. Isabel could always sense this even before she talked to me.

"What happened?" she asked when she walked into my living room after school. "You had such a good day yesterday."

"I know," I said softly.

We were sitting in my living room in front of the fireplace where we usually sat on winter afternoons, but it was Spring, and we should have been outside. The sun was out, and it was nearly eighty degrees. We should have been sitting at the bar beside Isabel's pool, but I didn't feel like it. I didn't even feel like leaving the house.

"When are you going to open the pool?" I asked taking a sip of the wine Isabel had poured me.

"I don't know," she said. "I know traditionally I'm supposed to open it Memorial Day weekend but that's over a month away and the kids are driving me nuts about it. I don't think I can take much more."

"Is the cover still on?" I asked.

"No. Isaac and Abe took it off the other day. It's so nasty inside. I should clean it."

"Make them clean it," I said. "That's why we have children."

"Ha."

My son, Ben, walked into the living room and plopped down at the table where the kids always did their homework.

"Hi," I said. "What's up?"

"I have a huge chemistry test tomorrow," he said. "I'm going to fail it."

"Why?" Isabel asked.

While Isabel taught chemistry and Ben was taking it, I'd requested he have a different teacher. It seemed like a conflict of interest to me.

"Because Mr. Watson is a dick."

"Ben!" I said. "That was uncalled for."

"It's true," Isabel said. "He is a dick. He saw me the other day in the cafeteria and whistled at me."

"Eeww," I said. "Who does that anymore?"

"Mr. Watson," Ben said without looking up.

I had a tough time thinking Isabel hadn't provoked that whistle. She just had this way about her that made men crazy. My other son, Michael, said it was because she had a nice torso. I had looked at him sideways, but he didn't elaborate.

Despite Isabel being like a second mom I knew Ben and Michael thought she was gorgeous but that was okay. They would grow out of it. It hadn't helped the night Isabel was drunk and kissed Ben on the mouth. Mind you she was *drunk* and didn't even remember it the next morning. Afterward she was mortified. Ben, on the other hand, wasn't mortified. He was infatuated. I had to threaten him the next day not to tell anyone. He told me he'd just put it in his spank tank. I had let that go because at the time I did not know the definition of a spank tank and I wasn't up for asking. I had a tendency not to ask questions when I didn't necessarily want to know the answers.

"Come on," Isabel said as she stood up. She came over to my chair and grabbed my arm. "Let's go clean out the pool."

"Oh Isabel," I said. "I don't feel like it."

"You don't FEEL like doing anything."

"That's true," Ben said. "You should go Mom. I'll be over in a little bit and I'll bring Maria."

"No," Vonnie said waltzing into the room. She was sixteen and wearing a neon yellow bikini. "I'll take Maria with me."

"You look like a traffic light." Ben replied.

"Shut up, Ben."

"Why on earth do you have on a bikini?" I asked.

"I haven't opened the pool yet," Isabel chimed in.

"I thought Isaac said you took the top off."

"No. *He* took the top off and it hasn't been cleaned yet so it's nasty."

"I don't care," she said. "I wasn't planning on getting in it anyhow." She had a beach towel thrown over one arm and my tanning oil in her hand. "I'm only going over there to lay in the sun with Tiffany."

Isabel and I looked at each other. Up until this point Tristan's sister, Tiffany, was an enigma. We knew she existed, but I'd never seen her. Isabel had seen her at school, but only from a distance. She hadn't been to either of our houses. Until now, when she was apparently scheduled to show up.

"I haven't met Tiffany," I offered as I looked over to Isabel. "Who is she?"

Vonnie walked into the kitchen and grabbed a diet coke out of the refrigerator.

"She's Tristan's sister. She's been here."

"She has?" I asked. "I don't recall her being here."

Vonnie came back into the living room.

"You were probably in bed," she said as she kept walking. "You're always in bed."

Certainly not what I wanted to hear but true nonetheless. I worried about my children when it came to my depression. Sometimes it seemed they understood, like the day Maria said she knew I was always tired. Of course, she was five, but it made me feel better anyhow. She wasn't old enough to understand why I was always tired. She may have realized her Mommy wasn't like other Mommies, but she didn't seem to love me any less. At least, I didn't think so. Vonnie, on the other hand, could be quite scathing sometimes. I'm sure there were times when she felt abandoned, when everyone else's Mom was at the Prom taking pictures or serving cake at birthday parties. I'm sure it embarrassed her when I didn't go with her to the picnic at the park on Mother-Daughter day. Those were the times I felt like the worst mother in the world and while I knew on some level Vonnie understood it all it didn't make it any easier for her. How was she supposed to explain my condition to her friends? I couldn't explain it to myself. So, when she made cruel comments about me I tried not to take them personally.

"Don't listen to her," Ben said to me now as I sat my wine glass on the counter.

"Are you coming or not?" Isabel said slipping on her flipflops at the front door.

"She's coming," Ben said and looked at me. "You're going…go."

It surprised me how warm it was outside when I walked out onto the porch.

"Wow," I said taking off my sweatshirt. "It's kind of hot out here."

"And there you are," Isabel said as we walked toward her house. "Cooped up in the living room with the air-conditioning turned up so high you have to wear a parka."

"That's Eric," I said. "You know I'd have all the windows open if he'd let me." She rolled her eyes.

"Don't get me started."

It was near five when we settled at the pool bar. We had decided it was too late in the day to get into cleaning the pool. That job took hours and more people than only us. It was a good reason to have a cookout the following Saturday and invite all the kids' friends. That way Isabel and I could sit at the bar and drink while we told the kids what to do. That was our plan most of the time. Drink and give directions.

So, the following Saturday that's exactly what we did. By three o'clock that day the pool was clean and full of water and we hadn't lifted a finger. A very strong scent of chlorine hung in the air.

"I always think I'm putting too much in there," Isabel said. "But I think about all the germs and all the kids and crap. I mean, who knows what they do in there." She shook the cocktail shaker over her head and strained it into two glasses.

"Voila! ***A Sophisticated Lady.***" She clinked her glass up against mine and sat down on the chaise lounge beside me. "This is a really cool one. Are you listening to me?"

"Uh, no." I looked back to her from where our boys were standing out in the yard.

"What is it?" She turned around and looked their way. "Are they smoking something weird?"

It wasn't so much an accusation as it was a concerned question. Although we didn't normally worry when the boys smoked pot. It was smoking regular cigarettes that bothered us. Well, it bothered

Isabel because she was addicted to cigarettes and determined her boys wouldn't be. With teenagers you had to pick your battles.

"Not that I can tell," I said distractedly. "But I feel like someone's watching me. Do you ever get that feeling?"

Isabel started singing the 80' s song, "I always feel like, somebody's watching me..." and looked over her shoulder to the boys again.

"Don't think what you're thinking," she said looking back to me.

"What am I thinking?" I asked.

"Tristan," she said. "That's why you asked me about him the other day. You think he's hot."

"No, I don't."

"Don't kid yourself," she said. "That long dark hair he keeps running his hand through. Those muscles."

"Isabel!"

"What?" she asked. "It's true." She stirred her drink with her finger. "But he is off limits."

"Well, I know but it's kind of hard not to look at him." I glanced over at him again. "Don't you think? He's..."

"Young," Isabel finished. "He's young."

"He's coming over here," I said.

"What?" Isabel turned around to find him headed our way. He opened the gate between the yard and the pool and came over to us.

"Hi," he said extending his hand to her. "I'm Tristan. I just wanted to come over and introduce myself. I don't believe we've ever officially met." Isabel took his hand.

"Hi," she said. "No, I don't think we have. I'm Isabel. Call me Isabel. Anything else makes me feel old." She hesitated. "Except at school. You must call me Mrs. Lund at school." Tristan smiled.

"Well, you absolutely don't look old." Isabel ignored his compliment and turned to me.

"This is Lilah, Ben and Michael's mom."

"And Vonnie," I added.

"Oh sorry," Isabel said. "Sometimes I block her out because she's so mean." I glared at her.

"She's just kidding," I said to Tristan.

"Oh," he said extending his hand to mine. I took it and then he looked back to Isabel. "I didn't mean to interrupt your conversation." He motioned over his shoulder. "I should probably get back out there with the guys."

He reached up and ran his hand through his hair. I'd noticed he did that a lot. I'm not sure if he did it for a desired effect or because it was hanging in his eyes.

"I just wanted to say hi and thank you for having me here," he said.

"You're welcome," Isabel replied.

"It was nice to meet you…Lilah," he said as he backed away.

Isabel stared at me and I tilted my head and stared back.

When Tristan was out of hearing range she leaned toward me. "Do not touch him," she said. "Ever."

I am not one of those women who is insulted or offended when my husband watches porn, so I don't understand women who think porn is a threat to them. I suppose some women think porn increases their partner's desire to cheat. It certainly increases their desire, but I don't think porn is the reason men cheat.

Men cheat because they aren't getting what they need from their partner. Maybe they ask, and their partner continually says no, or they aren't asking at all and are just jerks. Keep in mind I am not solely talking about sex. A man needs a lot of things. Sex is only one of them.

And please don't slip into the thought pattern that porn turns men into incorrigible monsters because let's face it, if it did we'd be having a zombie apocalypse. Men who say they don't watch porn are like men who say they don't masturbate. Non-existent.

This whole rant is not really about porn. It is about what Ben called a spank tank which I assume normally gleans its contents *from* porn. Obviously, I am not a sex expert and I couldn't care less about whether my boys watch porn, or have spank tanks. I am only concerned about spank tanks when I think I might be in one. This came as quite a surprise to me because all the boys' friends usually want Isabel. Why? Because Isabel looks like a Barbie doll.

"*You* wear bikini's," Isabel said. "What's wrong with it?"

"I didn't say there was anything wrong with it. I'm just saying the boys' friends like to look at you and maybe it should be a little less skimpy."

"You're making me feel creepy," Isabel replied. "Should I be feeling creepy?"

"No," I said.

"This isn't really about me. Is it?" she asked.

"I wanted to talk to you about something."

"That's what I figured. Can we pour some wine first? Because I'm parched."

"Wine is not a thirst quencher," I pointed out. "Wine dehydrates you."

"Okay," she said. "Let me rephrase that question. Can we pour some wine first? Because I'm an alcoholic and I need some."

"Funny."

We walked into my kitchen from the living room and Isabel pulled a bottle of red wine out of the wine refrigerator in the corner. Eric had given me that refrigerator for Mother's Day a few years back. It seemed like an odd sort of gift for Mother's Day, but Eric was prone to giving me what I wanted without asking any questions. It was probably why we'd been married for so long.

Isabel poured two glasses and we took them back into the living room. I sat in my favorite overstuffed chair and Isabel sat in the matching one on the other side of the room. She tucked her feet up underneath of her.

"Damn, it's cold in here," she said. "What is the thermostat set on?

"I don't know," I said covering myself with a throw. "It feels like fifty."

"What did you want to talk to me about?" she asked.

"Never mind. It's not important."

"Lilah," she said. "We don't do that to each other. We never have – you can't say you want to talk about something and then change your mind. Spill it."

"Remember when Tristan came over and introduced himself to us the other day?" She looked at me suspiciously.

"Yes."

"Well." I shifted in my chair. "I think he has a thing for me."

"What?" she said. "Why?"

"He talks to me."

"What do you mean he talks to you?" she asked. "What does he talk to you about?"

"He told me about his parents being killed in a car accident."

"Okaay," she said dragging out the word and holding out her hand to stop me from talking.

"No wait," I persisted. "Let me finish." She conceded. "Sometimes he just walks into the house and starts talking to me. He talks about Tiffany, the way things are at the Jenkins' house, lots of stuff."

"And how many times have you talked to him?"

"I don't know," I said. "A few."

"A few as in what a few means…which is three…or a few as in you don't remember?"

"I don't remember."

"Uh-huh," she said. "Lilah, I think this is bad. You should stop talking to him."

"How? What am I going to say?" I asked. "Sorry Tristan, I can't talk to you today even though I've talked to you a million times before?" She stayed straight faced.

"A million is a lot more than a few. Take a sip of your wine because I have something to tell you about him."

"Oh no," I said. "What?"

"I looked up his file. His parents were not killed in a car accident."

This was when she was likely to tell me something abnormal or twisted had happened to his family and scare the living daylights out of me. It was possible I was talking to a sociopath who was just waiting to get me alone long enough to kill me. She had looked up kids at school before who were suspected sociopaths so this wasn't entirely out of the question.

"His parents were evangelical Christians," she said in her typical storybook fashion. "His father was a preacher. They traveled all over the country doing tent revival meetings. He and Tiffany were supposedly homeschooled until the state took them away."

"Which state?"

"This one I guess. It didn't say."

"Maybe he's embarrassed by that," I said thoughtfully. "Who does tent meetings anymore?" She shrugged then got up to get us more wine.

"Do tent meeting people do stuff with snakes?" she asked. "Because I've seen shit like that on the Discovery channel."

Isabel was not religious. Although there was the time she'd started going to this strange church right after her divorce and thought Ben had a demon inside of him. He didn't, of course. He was just being a typical teenager.

"Don't be weird," I said. "What happened to his parents after that?"

"They were arrested for felony child neglect, convicted and put in jail."

"How long ago was this?"

"I don't know."

"You didn't look that up? It seems kind of important."

"I had a time limit," she said. "It's not like I can sit there all day and read the entire file. I have to look for the good stuff."

"Jeez Isabel," I said. "Why haven't you told me all of this before now? It may have been helpful."

"Because I was hoping this wouldn't be an issue."

"It's not really an issue.

"If he is telling you personal things about himself especially when they aren't true, it is an issue," she insisted.

"It's not," I said adamantly.

"Maybe he has a thing for older women. Mother figures."

I stared at her because that was a crazy conclusion to make on his part.

"You know," she said casually. "Since he didn't have one."

"That is insane," I said.

Isabel held up her hands like she was waiving away any kind of responsibility for anything that might happen going forward.

I picked up my wine and downed what was left in one swallow. Unfortunately, Isabel could be quite prophetic at times.

It always seemed like Tristan showed up when you least expected him. I never knew if he was at my house because he came to see one of the kids or if he came to see me. He'd just walk into the kitchen and start talking to me. We talked about the weather, what I was cooking for dinner, if I thought the chemistry test he and Ben took the day before was "fair."

He told me he worried about Tiffany and the reputation she was establishing for herself at school. I didn't ask what kind of reputation he was referring to because I, as Isabel had suggested, was trying to limit our conversations as much as possible. Vonnie told me all the boys at school thought Tiffany was hot and wanted to "get with" her. I assumed that meant they wanted to sleep with her. I had only seen Tiffany once, so I couldn't make a fair evaluation. When I asked Vonnie what all the girls thought about Tristan, she told me he was "okay."

"I don't think he's that good-looking. I mean, he's cute and all but…"

"Who's good-looking?" Ben asked as he strode into the kitchen. Vonnie turned around from the sink.

"Was I talking to you?" she asked.

"No," Ben said as he downed the last of the orange juice from the carton. He shut the refrigerator door. "But you can tell me anyway."

"She's talking about Tristan," I interjected.

"You like Tristan??" he asked Vonnie.

"No, you dummy. I was telling Mom how I didn't think he was that cute."

"So, you like him?" Ben said teasingly.

Vonnie threw down the dish towel she was using to dry the dishes onto the counter and stormed out of the kitchen.

"I hate you," she yelled back to Ben.

Ben ignored her. She told him at least once a day she hated him. She didn't, of course.

"Do you think Tristan's good-looking?"

"Me?" I pointed to myself.

"Yeah."

"Oh, I don't know. I can see how all the girls would like him."

"I'm gonna tell him you said that," he said, laughing.

My heart pounded.

"What?"

"That my mother thinks he's hot."

"That is not what I said!"

"I'm joking, Mom. Chill out."

I couldn't let anyone – even Isabel – know I was somewhat infatuated with Tristan. It was wrong, and I should have been ashamed of myself. I kept rationalizing it was just a safe little fantasy I thought about when I was bored. I also thought about it when I wasn't bored. Isabel was right. I needed to stop talking to him.

I think Vonnie was an anomaly because she was never attracted to the good-looking guys. Not that attraction to someone should be solely based on looks – because granted, there was a lot more to a person than their looks. Someone could be gorgeous but be a complete jerk – and when you found out what a jerk they were, they weren't gorgeous anymore. They were just a jerk. Or someone not so attractive could be hilariously funny – which would make them more attractive – to me, anyway.

Tristan was good-looking. He didn't need any other redeeming qualities but one thing I had noticed was that whenever he left a room it always smelled like chocolate chip cookies. You know the cookies baking in the oven smell? Yeah, that's the one. When I told this to Isabel, she said I shouldn't be going around smelling teenage boys.

Despite Isabel telling me to limit my conversations with Tristan, there were times when he would ask my opinion on controversial topics like the death penalty or gun control or the legalization of marijuana. One day he asked me if I believed in karma.

"I think so," I said as I wiped off the kitchen table. "I think you get what you give."

He leaned up against the doorframe and smiled.

"That's karma."

"Okay, then yes."

Tristan had the type of smile that made you think he knew something you didn't. Everyone seemed entranced whenever he spoke.

He had that gravelly voice that sparked curiosity. When Tristan said something to you, you moved a little closer to him. Talking to him was not like talking to any other of my boys' friends. He was smart and articulate and well, his jeans fit just right.

On a Sunday morning, after which I hadn't slept at all the night before, I finally gave up and went downstairs to make a pot of coffee. I decided to carry a cup down to the pond to watch the sunrise. Eric had bought me two Adirondack chairs several years before and it was the perfect place for it. It was dark and still a little chilly, so I grabbed a sweater off the hook by the back door. I had only been sitting there for a few minutes when I heard someone walk up behind me. I assumed it was Eric. He often got up with me when I couldn't sleep, and I thought he was coming down to the pond to watch the sunrise with me.

"Lilah?"

I looked over my shoulder. As always, like an apparition, Tristan was there when he shouldn't have been. Hearing his voice gave me the same feeling I had after I'd crested the top of the highest roller coaster in the park and was on my way down the other side. He had on a holey pair of jeans and a black t-shirt with the RVA logo on the top left side. He had nothing with him. He wasn't carrying his phone or a cup of coffee or anything else. I couldn't help but wonder why he was wandering around in the dark. Especially in the field behind my house. He was barefoot.

"*What are you doing here*?" I asked in disbelief.

"What are *you* doing here?" he asked as if he were amused. "Escaping reality?"

"Aren't we all?" I answered. I took a sip of my coffee. "But I do live here."

"Very true," he said as he stuffed his hands into his pockets. "This pond is amazing."

"Yes," I replied. "It is."

He didn't offer to tell me why he was there, and I didn't ask him. If I hadn't already had several conversations with him his presence would have seemed almost sinister but if there was anything sinister about Tristan and there was a record of it *anywhere* Isabel would have found it by now. She would have told me about it, along with how we should keep him away from our children before something catastrophic happened.

"You can sit down if you want." I gestured to the chair beside me.

He looked past me, out over the pond. We had several geese and they had congregated on the bank on the other side. The sky had gradually lightened and the sun cast an orangey glow over the water.

"It's a beautiful sunrise. Isn't it?"

"Yes," I said. "I would offer you some coffee but obviously…"

"It's fine," he said shaking his head. He sat down beside me. "I don't really drink coffee."

We sat in silence for a moment. It should've been awkward, but it wasn't.

"Tell me about your husband," he finally said.

I turned to him, surprised. It seemed an odd question.

"Why?"

"I don't know." He shrugged. "I'm curious, I guess."

"About Eric?"

"Yeah," he said.

"What do you want to know?"

"How long have you been married?"

"A long time," I said. "Why would you ask me that?"

"Why would I not?" he asked. "You guys don't seem very close."

"How often have you been around Eric and I to know whether we're close?"

He took a deep breath and leaned forward on his knees. I wondered what he could possibly be thinking. It was a few minutes before he spoke again.

"Have you told him you don't love him anymore?" he asked as he looked out across the water.

"Excuse me?"

He looked over to me and tucked a lock of hair behind his ear. I sat up a little straighter in my chair, so I could see his face.

"Does he know you don't love him anymore?" he asked again as he stood up.

I stood up beside him because I didn't want him towering over me. As I did my coffee spilled down the front of my t-shirt. He reached over and took the coffee cup out of my hand while I blotted my shirt with my napkin.

"I didn't mean to upset you," he said. "I guess it's really none of my business." He handed the coffee cup back to me.

"No. It isn't," I said. He turned to walk away then stopped and looked back to me.

"All I'm saying is if you didn't love me anymore…" He put his hands on his chest. "I would want to know."

I didn't say anything.

"Wouldn't you want to know?" he asked. "If you were him, I mean."

Isabel and I were sitting in the overstuffed chairs in my living room, drinking what she told me was a ***Bumblebee***. It was for Spring, she said. It was whiskey and honey and some other ingredient I had missed while we were talking.

I'd been thinking about the conversation with Tristan at the pond all day and ruminating on whether I had handled it the right way. I hadn't. I should have defended my relationship with Eric. I should have told Tristan I did love my husband. The problem was I didn't love Eric the traditional way a wife should love her husband. I loved him because he made me feel financially secure and helped me take care of our children. I wanted to feel more for him but what I'd had with him in the beginning was gone and it had been gone for quite some time now.

"DO NOT talk to him about your relationship with Eric," Isabel practically yelled at me. "What is wrong with you?"

"I'm not the one who brought it up," I countered. I leaned back in my chair and pulled my feet up underneath me. "He did."

"Who cares?" she asked. "It's none of his business and he shouldn't be asking you those kinds of questions."

"He said it was none of his business."

"Why do I feel like I'm having this conversation with a three-year-old? You don't have to justify your actions to me, Lilah. Personally, I don't care what you talk to Tristan about, but I think you're playing with fire. I don't think Eric would be very happy if he knew you were talking about your marriage with other people, much less a teenager."

"Since when are you on Eric's side?" I asked taking a sip of my drink. "You hate Eric."

"I don't hate Eric," she said. "I just think he's weird and I have never totally understood what you see in him but that is an entirely different topic." She hesitated. "Hon, I love you like a sister and I don't want to see this..." She swiveled her hand around in front of her like she was trying to imitate what I thought must be a tornado. "...turning into something it shouldn't."

"Like what?" I asked.

"I don't know," she said as she sat back in her chair. "It sounds like Tristan is somewhat infatuated with you. Maybe you should try to discourage that."

"How?" I asked. "How do you discourage teenagers from putting you in their spank tanks?" Isabel laughed out loud.

"I didn't even know you knew what a spank tank was."

"I didn't," I admitted. "Ben told me."

"I hope you're kidding." I shook my head. "Since when are you talking to your son about spank tanks?"

"It wasn't about *his* spank tank," I said defensively. "That's disgusting. It was just about the fact that guys have them."

"And apparently, you're in Tristan's," Isabel said winking at me. "You should think about wearing a one piece this year."

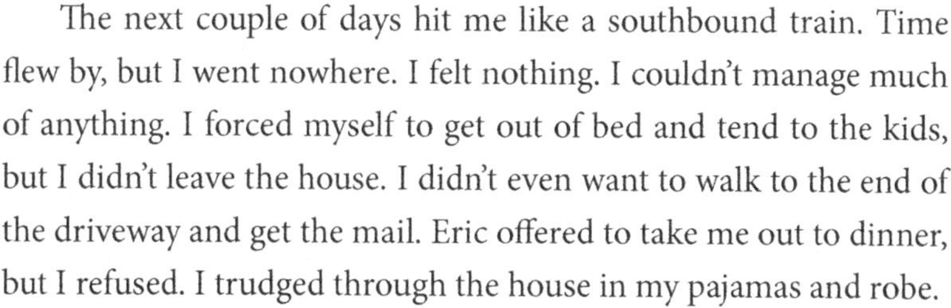

The next couple of days hit me like a southbound train. Time flew by, but I went nowhere. I felt nothing. I couldn't manage much of anything. I forced myself to get out of bed and tend to the kids, but I didn't leave the house. I didn't even want to walk to the end of the driveway and get the mail. Eric offered to take me out to dinner, but I refused. I trudged through the house in my pajamas and robe.

After about three days I finally took a shower because Vonnie told me my hair was dirty and that I smelled. It had to be bad if Vonnie addressed my appearance. She knew when I was in my right mind I was vain and that appearances meant everything to me. Although lately I looked in the mirror and saw nothing I liked in its reflection. My clothes didn't fit right. My hair curled the wrong way. I didn't have a tan. The list could go on and on until something or someone finally snapped me out of it.

Currently my hair needed coloring and I drastically needed a manicure. It would also be a good idea to take off the chipped nail polish on my toes. What I should have learned over the years was that a bath, a little sunless tanner, and about fifteen minutes with a curling iron made me feel more confident and beautiful which, in turn, affected my mood. That was what I needed. A deep tub full of hot water to sink into and a glass of wine to soothe my soul.

It dawned on me at that moment that Isabel had a huge, garden tub in her master suite and that I had a key to her house. She wouldn't care one way or the other whether I used her tub plus she had a date after school that could last anywhere from an hour to half the night. It depended solely on whether she decided to sleep with him.

Eric had planned a play date for Maria. I'm sure he was hoping I would get myself together if I didn't have to think about anything except getting better. He knew when I got into this cycle any level of stress could push me further over the edge.

I gathered all my things together in a tote bag and quietly slipped out the front door. I wasn't trying to be sneaky. Whenever I wasn't home everyone assumed Maria and I had gone somewhere with Isabel. Eric never asked where I was going or where I'd been. He wouldn't even notice I was gone. No one would notice I was gone.

I didn't intend on leaving my cell phone at home, but I did. I was always laying it down somewhere and not remembering where I'd put it. That afternoon I left it sitting on the bedside table in my room, so later when it rang repeatedly I wasn't there to answer it.

Isabel

It was hot as hell when I got home from my date that night. You'd think as the sun went down so would the temperature but oh no. It was much too hot for April and if the weather was any sign of what the summer was going to bring, God help us all.

The house was dark except for a few lamps scattered across the front windows. Lilah said the front of my house looked like what you'd want your mother-in-law to see while the back looked more like your husband's best friend standing in your bedroom doorway with his pants unzipped. Lilah was famous for her metaphors. Sometimes they were funny.

I knew the darkness of the house which would normally mean a peaceful night was an illusion after seeing all the cars and trucks parked in my driveway. The bass of Usher's *"Yeah!"* reverberating through the air was also a significant clue. I knew then my children were going to be grounded for the rest of the school year and possibly the entirety of the summer.

I opened the front door. The volume of the music felt like a physical blow. Across the foyer, the sliding glass doors to the back patio were open. I walked straight through searching for Isaac. I didn't see him, but I spotted Ben and his girlfriend, Rianne, sitting on the steps at the shallow end of the pool. Rianne was smoking a cigarette.

"Where's your mother?" I asked Ben as I took the cigarette out of Rianne's mouth. She startled. I took a drag and handed it back to her. Ben shrugged so I blew the smoke back out into his face. "Where?!?"

"Jeez Isabel," he said. "Calm down. I don't know."

"I have called and called and called. You don't know where she is?"

"Is her car at home?" He answered my question with one of his own.

"Can you not help me out a little?" I asked as I stood up.

"I don't know what to tell you. I haven't seen her. I don't know where she is."

I saw Isaac and Vonnie out of the corner of my eye with two other girls in very skimpy bikinis. The only one I knew, Lindsey, was missing her top. He was holding my bottle of Grey Goose vodka.

"Oh, hey Mom," he said when he saw me.

He didn't seem worried about whether I was going to walk over and rip it out of his hand which told me beyond any doubt that he was drunk.

"What is going on?" I yelled over the music.

"It's a party," he said. "What are you doing here? I thought you had a date."

"I am going to strangle you," I said. "Who cares whether or not I had a date? What the hell were you thinking? I don't even know half of these people!" He looked at his feet.

"I'm sorry," he said.

"I think it's a little late for I'm sorry right now. Do you know where Lilah is?" He looked around.

"Umm…I'm not sure. She was just here."

"She was here?" I asked pointing down.

"Yeah. I'm pretty sure it was her."

"With who?"

"What?"

"WHO WAS SHE WITH??"

Tristan walked up behind me. When I turned to face him, he handed me a glass of wine.

"You look distressed," he said as an explanation.

I wanted to throw it back in his face because it pissed me off so bad he knew I needed it. I took a few swallows instead.

"Do you know where Lilah is?"

"No," he said.

I threw back the rest of the wine like it was a shot.

"But relax. It's just a party."

"Why do I feel like you are somehow involved in all this?" I asked waving my empty glass around.

"I'm not," he said.

I'm sure it was obvious to him this wasn't the first drink I'd had over the course of the evening. He took the empty glass away from me and sat it on the patio table behind him. Something was not right. I could feel it. I moved through the crowd looking for Lilah. When I had come around the pool full circle I met up with Tristan again.

"I think you're freaking out for no reason," he said. "I'm sure Lilah is around here somewhere. Chill out."

The fact that he said, 'chill out' infuriated me. I doubt I would have gone off the deep end on him if I hadn't recently had twelve

Mojitos with a chubby Jewish man who thought he was God's gift to humanity.

"You have no idea what you're talking about," I spat back at him. "You think you know Lilah because you have these little "talks" with her but you don't know anything about Lilah. She's a good pretender."

"Me, too." I ignored his comment.

"Lilah makes you think everything is fine when it is not fine. I know everything is not fine right now because I have been calling her all afternoon and she isn't answering her phone. She always answers me so get out of my way, so I can find her."

He held up his arms as if he had given up on trying to appease me. I ran back into the house, directly down the hallway toward my bedroom. I don't know what made me think she was in my room unless it was divine intervention. The door was locked. I banged on it but there was no answer. I went around the spiral staircase to the sitting room on the other side and banged on the door between it and my bedroom. It took me a few minutes to realize it was unlocked. I flung the door open, yelling Lilah's name as I went through to the bathroom.

As I rounded the corner I slipped on the wet floor and caught myself on the open linen closet door. Lilah was in the enormous jacuzzi tub in the center of the room, her face just under the surface of the water. I fell into the tub and grabbed her underneath her arms, pulling her into my lap.

"Lilah!!" I shook her and grasp her wrist in my hand trying to feel for a pulse.

Tristan walked through the doors of the patio into my room and realizing what had happened, ran into the bathroom, and jumped over into the tub. He shoved me out of the way and picked up Lilah, taking her out of the tub and laying her down on the cool tile. I crawled out beside her. He put his fingers against her neck and felt for a pulse. When he couldn't find it, he picked up her arm and felt her wrist.

"Call an ambulance," he yelled and when I just sat there, "Now!"

I pulled my cell phone out of my back pocket, forgetting it'd been underwater. I was shaking so much I could barely get up. Tristan started CPR and I snatched the house phone off the nightstand. I talked to the emergency dispatcher, but I don't remember what I said.

I threw the fur coverlet from my bed over Lilah just before Isaac and Ben ran through the sliding glass doors. I grabbed Ben and pulled him back, away from his mother, but he was too strong for me and I had to let him go. Isaac realized what was going on and took Ben's arm and pulled him backward, taking him back out onto the patio. I could hear Tristan counting to himself as he lifted his head away from Lilah's face. The stereo still beat in the background and Lilah coughed up water. Tristan turned her head to the side and she gulped in air. She looked back to him and raised her arm trying to slap him, but he grabbed her wrist before it made contact with his face. I knelt on the floor beside him. We were all soaking wet. I took Lilah's hand in mine.

"What the hell do you have to do to die around here?" she asked jerking her hand away from me. "And what the hell is this on me? Rabbit fur?"

She threw the coverlet off and I grabbed it and tried to pull it back over her. She didn't seem to care that she was naked which told me she wasn't in her right mind. She continued trying to rip the blanket off, so I finally just straddled her while she twisted and turned beneath me.

"So, is the Lilah you were talking about?" Tristan asked me as he grabbed her other wrist in his hand.

"Yes," I said. "The one you *think* you know.

"Stop talking about me like I'm not here!" Lilah screamed.

"What did you take?" Tristan asked her quietly.

"Fuck you," she yelled at him.

"They're going to pump your stomach out if you don't tell me."

I didn't understand how Tristan could be so calm when I felt like a ticking time bomb.

"Thank you," I said to him.

"Sure."

He was still holding Lilah's wrists in his hands, but she had given up on fighting him. When he let go Lilah began to sob uncontrollably.

"Hey," he said to her. "Look at me."

She looked up to him as tears rolled down her cheeks. He talked to her as if he knew her intimately when I knew, beyond any doubt, he did not.

"I'm gonna need a thank you note for this."

A small smile escaped her lips.

"Don't hold your breath," she said.

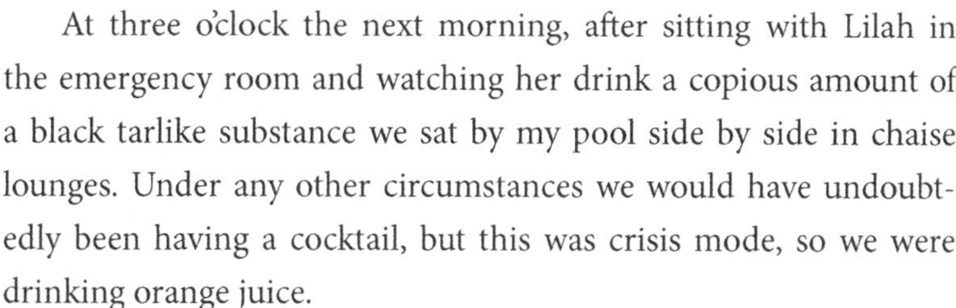

At three o'clock the next morning, after sitting with Lilah in the emergency room and watching her drink a copious amount of a black tarlike substance we sat by my pool side by side in chaise lounges. Under any other circumstances we would have undoubtedly been having a cocktail, but this was crisis mode, so we were drinking orange juice.

"This would be better with vodka in it," Lilah said holding up her glass.

"It would," I agreed. "But not when you're already looped on twenty-seven Xanax."

"The nurse at the hospital told me if I wanted to kill myself I would have to take more next time." I looked over to her.

"How thoughtful of her."

"That was after she told me what cute jeans I had on."

"That was me," I said. "And those are my jeans."

Lilah looked down as if she were trying to remember. There is no way to remember when you've taken twenty-seven Xanax.

"The ones I still have on? Right?"

"I want them back," I said as I got up to retrieve more orange juice. "Just because you tried to kill yourself doesn't mean you get to keep them."

"I love you, too."

I plopped down in the chaise lounge beside her and offered her more juice. She held out her glass.

"We need to talk about this Lilah," I said more seriously. "If Tristan hadn't come to find me last night I doubt you would be here right now."

"That makes me so mad I want to spit," she said.

"What? That he saved your life?"

"Kind of," she admitted. "But mostly just that it was him."

"Why? I thought you would have liked it since you're so infatuated with him."

"I am not!" she exclaimed. "He's not even old enough to drink."

"That doesn't mean you can't be infatuated with him."

"Well, I'm not."

"So, you say. I think you should write him that thank you note." She turned to me.

"Now you're being facetious." I laughed.

"No thank you note?"

"The fact that I have to look him in the face again is mortifying enough."

"He doesn't seem like the kind of person who will hold it against you."

"I mean that he saw me naked."

"Lots of guys have seen you naked. What's one more?"

"Not funny." She hesitated. "What will everyone say?"

"About what?"

"About Tristan?"

"Could you be a little more specific?"

"About him saving me?"

"I would imagine most people would be grateful."

"I don't want anyone to know it was him." This was confusing to me.

"Why not?"

"It's kind of a personal thing. Don't you think?"

"Lilah, tell me what you're *really* thinking." She bowed her head.

"I don't want people to think he has a crush on me."

"I don't think resuscitation is considered flirting." Lilah blushed. "But okay." I threw my legs over the side of the chair and turned to her. "Lilah, talk to me. Tell me what's going on."

She sat her glass on the table between us and brought her hands to her face. She shook her head back and forth and I reached over and put my hand on her arm.

"I wake up every morning," she cried. "And I don't want to be there.

"Be where, honey?" I asked. "At home or here on earth in general?"

"Anywhere," she answered.

"Why?" I asked.

"Because I am a terrible mother and a worse wife."

"No, you aren't," I reassured her. "You are an amazing mother and Eric loves you very much."

"But I don't love him," she whispered, almost to herself.

"What?" I asked because I wasn't sure if I had heard her correctly. She looked over to me.

"I don't love him anymore," she said softly.

"Well, no two people love each other all the time," I said trying to make light of the conversation. "All marriages have their difficulties. None of us are perfect."

"I don't think I can possibly love him anymore."

"Why not?" I asked. "You've been together since the beginning of time."

"It's not that," she said.

"Then what?"

I could tell she was viciously processing something. Something that more than likely she wasn't sure whether she should tell me or not.

"You fell in love with another man, didn't you?" she finally asked.

"Well, technically, I wouldn't call it love."

"Okay," she said. "Well, you fell in infatuation."

"That's giving it a lot more credit than it deserves as well. It was more like just good sex."

"I don't know what to do," she said turning to me. "What if he can tell?"

I knew at once she wasn't talking about whether Eric knew she didn't love him anymore but whether Tristan knew she fantasized about him all the time.

"I don't think he knows," I said. "Has something happened that makes you feel like he does?"

She didn't answer me and to prod her further would have been a mistake. Even though there were a million things that still needed to be said it was nearing four in the morning. At eight she had to go back to the hospital.

A few hours ago, Eric and I had agreed that to force Lilah to stay at the hospital against her will would have been devastating to her. She would never forgive either of us and she would hold me just as much accountable as she did him.

Although she was not entirely aware at the time, Lilah had agreed to return to my house and go back to the hospital the next morning. I wasn't sure if she still remembered that decision. It was very likely she did not, and I was a little concerned about what was going to happen when I reminded her.

I thought I only knew one person other than myself whose opinion mattered to her at that moment. Tristan's. The only reason I knew this was because as much as I'd tried to discourage their little talks, I now knew those talks meant something to Lilah.

I couldn't think of anything I wanted to do less than call Tristan Collins but when Lilah went into this headlong spiral of depression you had to take advantage of whatever tools God gave you.

She would eventually forgive me.

"Don't say la-la land to your mother," I told Vonnie one day when she had made the same mistake I did. "She is simply having an off day."

"Right," she said as she walked out of the room.

I wanted to smack her in the face sometimes, but she wasn't mine, so I couldn't.

I didn't say la-la land to Lilah anymore because it was the equivalent of poking her in the eye with a pair of scissors. She went ballistic. With Lilah you just tried to go with the flow. Sometimes the flow was a lot more difficult than other times. I had a feeling this was going to be one of those difficult times so when she got up to go the bathroom I searched her phone for Tristan's number. I knew if I asked for it she would tell me she didn't have it, but I knew she did. When Tristan answered the phone, he sounded as if he had just woken from a coma.

"Did I wake you?" He cleared his throat.

"Who is this?"

"It's Isabel."

"Oh, hi."

Not what I was expecting. I was expecting, 'Why in the hell are you calling me at five o'clock in the morning?'

"I need a favor." He was silent for a moment, so I added, "For Lilah."

"I think I already did Lilah a favor."

"Don't be a smartass."

No response.

"I'm going to try to make this as succinct as possible."

"Okay."

"They discharged Lilah from the hospital last night but only with the requirement that she return at eight this morning. She may or may not remember signing the release papers and when I tell her she is likely going to go off the deep end."

He cleared his throat again.

"Like last night deep end?"

"Mm…probably not that bad."

"So, what's the favor?"

"I need you to come over here and talk to her."

"Now??"

"Yeah."

He sighed.

"You know I have a hangover, right?"

"I assumed."

"I might even still be drunk. I'm not awake enough to figure that out yet."

"You're hilarious."

"Don't you have a hangover?"

"Kinda."

"Okay." I could hear his sheets rustle as he got out of bed. "Give me, like, ten minutes."

Lilah

Tristan's hair was wet when he walked out of the sliding glass doors of Isabel's kitchen. When I saw him, I knew what she had done. I wasn't mad. I was only resigned. Nothing he said convinced me I needed to go back to the hospital. It was the way he looked at me. That, plus he wasn't very nice.

"Do you know why my hair is wet?" he asked me when I just stared at him. I looked over to Isabel.

"I think he's talking to you," she said.

I still didn't answer. He came over and sat beside me on the chaise lounge.

"It's wet because I literally got out of the shower five minutes ago." He paused. "You know what Mrs. Jenkins said to me?"

"No, but you're going to tell me."

"I am. She told me if I went outside with my hair wet I would 'catch my death.' If she's right, I'm going to be dead soon." Isabel chuckled. He leaned over, his elbows on his knees. "You gave me no choice last night, Lilah." He paused again. "Did you know I had no choice?"

"You should have let me die."

"I should've." He paused. "But I didn't." I turned to him.

"Why are you here?"

"Isabel didn't think she could wrangle you into the car by herself." He had this little smile playing on his lips and I turned away.

"That's funny. Do I look like I need to be wrangled?"

"I don't know," he said. "Do you? Given what I saw last night I think it's possible. Are you going to the hospital?"

I said nothing, so he leaned over further to see my face.

"Lilah?"

"What?" I asked because I knew if I didn't answer he wouldn't leave me alone.

"Are you going to the hospital?"

"Yes," I said reluctantly. "Jeez."

He smacked the tops of his legs with his hands and stood up.

"Okay, my job is done." He turned to Isabel. "I'm going back to bed. Call me if she gets too crazy and I'll bring over the tranquilizer gun." She laughed. I don't know why because it wasn't funny.

"Okay," she agreed and then, "Hey, Tristan?"

"Yeah?" he said as he turned around.

"Thank you."

"Yep."

"He's a jerk," I said as soon as he'd walked back into the house. "I can't believe you called him."

"Does that mean he's less sexy now?" She smiled. "Because I thought he looked pretty hot with the wet hair." I looked over to her.

"I hate you, Isabel. I'm going to the hospital but only for one reason.

"What's that?" she asked.

"So, I can get away from you."

"Okay."

"And don't you dare let him come to the hospital while I'm there. I don't want him anywhere around me. Either one of you. Both of you can go to hell."

There was only one reason I didn't resist going into "the ward" - that's what everyone who has ever been in there called it - because I knew it was of no use. After I got over the initial fury of being put into this place against my will - I say against my will because I do not remember signing that paper - I realized that despite my anger it was for my own good. I didn't understand why all my medication needed changing but I did recognize that what I was now taking wasn't working. It wasn't the alcohol because I had been drinking for years and up until recently I was fine. I had never had all my medicines changed at the same time, so I had no idea what to expect.

Dr. Stone warned me there would be withdrawal symptoms and to accurately monitor them I would need to be in the hospital in case of an emergency. It scared me a little. What on earth could happen that would constitute an emergency of that proportion? She sat on the edge of my bed and explained how they would check my heart rate and other vitals until there were no other withdrawal symptoms and I could do one of two things:

"You can sweat it out," she said. "Or you can let me prescribe something that will help."

"What are the symptoms?" I asked.

"Typical drug withdrawal," she said. "Vomiting, diarrhea, hot and cold spells, etc."

She acted as if those things happened every day. Maybe in her world they did.

"Can I ask a question?" I asked. She smiled.

"You just did." I took a deep breath.

"Why am I on medication that is so addictive?"

"It's not so much addictive as it is essential for your body to function normally now. It's changed the receptors in your brain and, in turn, it's changed the way your body responds."

"So, when my body doesn't have it anymore it rebels?" I asked.

"Yes," she said. "I wouldn't have put it that way but yes."

"What will happen if you prescribe something for me to help with it?"

"It won't lessen the symptoms. It will only lessen how much you care about the symptoms." She paused. "And knock you out." I put my hands over my face.

"Oh God," I said. "I don't know what to do."

"I suggest taking the prescription."

"And if I don't?"

"You'll wish you had taken the prescription."

"Okay," I said quietly. "Then I guess I'll do it."

"Good." She patted my hand and stood up. "Go out into the commons room and have dinner with everyone."

"Do I have to?"

"Yes," she said. "And at bedtime we'll start you on the meds."

I felt raw. I was still in the hospital gown they had put on me after my bath. It's not actually a bath. It's more like an assault. After I was admitted and brought upstairs they took me into a washroom and made me take off all my clothes. It was a stand-up shower, like in a men's locker room, and one of the nurses held the sprayer while the other one scrubbed me down with a soapy brush. It wasn't quite as humiliating as the first time because I had known it was in my foreseeable, inevitable future.

They washed my hair and checked every crevice of my body to make sure I wasn't sneaking in any contraband items. In case you're wondering, a contraband item is everything you own. They had taken all my jewelry, even my wedding rings and the pearl earrings that stayed in my ears twenty-four hours a day.

The hospital gave me deodorant and essentials. I could put on my jeans and t-shirt when I was up and walking around but the nurse patted me down every time I went back into my room. Every time.

I had succumbed to these procedures. I knew I couldn't go to the bathroom by myself. I knew I couldn't shave my legs (or anything else) without a nurse watching me do it. I knew I couldn't wear makeup or perfume and they had already taken the polish off my fingers and toes. There was only one luxury allowed. Lip balm. And I had to go to the nurse's station to use it.

No one could have anything except a plastic "spork" when they brought our meals. It was a combination of a fork and a spoon which I was told was the least likely utensil to use if you wanted to kill yourself or someone else.

Every morning and evening everyone would line up in front of the medicine cart and a nurse would give us our pills in a paper container and watch while we took them.

Apparently, there were instances where people would put the pills under their tongue and spit them out after they left the cart so now they made you open your mouth after you handed the water cup back to them.

That first evening after dinner I went into the day room (different from the commons room) where they did the group therapy and picked up some of the drawings and colored pencils they offered for us to color. Coloring was a type of therapy, they told us. And they were right. When you were coloring you didn't think about anything except coloring. It worked but when you finished coloring all your issues came back and you were at square one again.

After I colored I went back into the commons rooms to get a cup of juice. There was a snack room where we could get coffee, other drinks, and basic snacks. Nurse's aides who seemed to be more sympathetic to your state of mind than the regular nurses regularly patrolled that, too.

"Hi," I said to her as I walked out of the door with my juice. She stood up.

"I'm sorry, Mrs. Trenton but you can't have any juice tonight."

"Why?" I asked as she took it from me.

"Because of the medicine you'll be taking at bedtime. You aren't allowed to have anything after eight."

"Why?"

"You should ask the medication nurse that question," she said. "I'm not really sure."

I strode over to the nurse's station.

"Why can't I have juice?" She stared at me for a moment.

"And who might you be?"

"Lilah," I said and when she continued to stare at me, "Lilah Trenton." She looked at her chart.

"Because the medicine you are about to take will take you through your withdrawal and the less you have in your stomach the better." I took a deep breath.

"Okay," I said because it was senseless to argue. "Can I have it now?"

"Are you ready to go to bed?" she asked.

"Sure," I said. "There's nothing else to do."

She pulled out several drawers and retrieved the pills. There were three of them and each one was in a plastic bubble. She punched them all out, put them in the little paper cup and handed it to me. I took them all at once because they were so tiny. I handed the paper cup back to her.

"Open your mouth," she said.

She shined a little flashlight into my mouth.

"Move your tongue to the side." I did. "Okay. You can go."

There was no love lost during that transaction.

I walked back over to one of the tables in the middle of the room. I was hoping someone would come talk to me, but no one did. Bored out of my mind, I laid my head over on the table. The nurse called my name.

"Lilah," she said. "Are you okay?" I lifted my head and looked her way.

"Yes."

"You should probably go to bed before you pass out. That little cocktail of drugs you took is pretty potent."

"Great."

Once again, pointless to argue.

"Do you need any help?"

"No."

"I'll be in to check on you in a minute," she said which really meant she would come in and search me in a minute.

I walked into my room. There were two twin beds, but I didn't have a roommate. It was a warm Spring night and I longed to be sitting by Isabel's pool with a cocktail in my hand. It didn't even matter what kind of cocktail as long as it was a cocktail. I don't remember much after going to bed that night. It was a Tuesday night and when I woke up again it was Friday.

"Have I been asleep that long?" I asked as the nurse plumped my pillow.

"What do you mean?" she asked. "How long?"

"Since Tuesday?'

"Oh no," she said. "You don't remember coming out for lunch or dinner yesterday?"

"No." She sighed and patted my arm.

"Don't worry," she said. "Sometimes that happens."

I laid my head back on the pillow and brought my hands to my face. That was when I realized I had an i.v. in my arm. The tears came even though I had told myself I wasn't going to cry.

Another nurse popped her head around the corner.

"You have a visitor," she said.

I knew right away it was Isabel. She was always my saving grace.

"Hey, hey, hey," she said with a flourish on the end.

"Hey."

"That was poor," she commented. "Again."

"Hey, hey, hey," I said blandly.

"Better but I still think Dwayne would be disappointed."

She meant Dwayne from *What's Happening*. It had always been her favorite show when we were growing up. It wasn't my favorite show, but she insisted I say it anyhow.

"What's up, girl?" she asked as she came over and sat on the edge of my bed. "I see they've still got you hooked up to an i.v."

"Thanks for reminding me."

"Have they started your new medicine yet?

"I just woke up. Your timing is impeccable."

"So, how's it going?" she asked. "How long are you in for?"

"You make it sound like I'm in jail."

"Aren't you? I had to go through three security systems to get in here." I rolled my eyes.

"Of course, you did."

"Has Eric showed up yet?"

"What do you think?"

"Umm." She pretended to think. "No?"

"No. Nobody has come to see me except you."

"Well, if it makes you feel any better, Tristan has asked about you twice."

"What am I going to do about that?" I lamented.

"What do you want to do about it?" I shrugged.

"Well, let's not think about it right now," she said patting my leg. "Let's just get you better and home again."

I laid my head back on my pillow and rolled over, this time successfully pulling the i.v. completely out of my arm. I wanted to think about Tristan, but I didn't want to think about him either.

"Perfect," I said out loud as Isabel reached for me.

The alarm in my room went off and two nurses came running in to check on me. Much to my dismay, within minutes, the i.v. was back in my arm.

"I can't even imagine what he must think of me," I said to Isabel afterward.

"Who?"

I didn't want to say his name out loud. I felt guilty about feeling the way I did, embarrassed even. I most certainly didn't want to think about what Ben would say if he knew the thoughts I was having about one of his best friends. I thought about all my children and even Isabel's children, but it didn't dawn on me until much later that Eric never entered my mind.

I was in the hospital for another four days, long enough for Dr. Stone to make sure my body wasn't going to shut down from all the drugs I had taken over the last week. At least that's what she said. She came into my room the day before I was to leave the next morning.

"How are you feeling?" she asked me with a smile.

"Good, I guess."

"No nausea, vomiting, diarrhea, headaches, general inertia?"

"No. I'm good."

"You sound worried." She knew me so well. "What are you worried about?"

"My kids," I lied.

There was no way, even though Dr. Stone had been my doctor forever, I could bring myself to tell her about Tristan. I was going to have to deal with him on my own. Hopefully, with a little help from Isabel.

Still, I felt like I was on an inevitable course of destruction. Yet I had lived! Yay me. I thought there must be some reason I had lived but I was certain it wasn't to have an affair with a teenager. Maybe

Isabel was right. Maybe I needed to concentrate on getting better and worry about Tristan later.

"What about your kids?" Dr. Stone asked.

"I worry about them," I lied again. "Having a mother like me." She sniffed.

"Like you? What is that supposed to mean?"

"Me being crazy and all. I know it embarrasses them I'm this way."

"Okay," she said. "First, you are not crazy, and I don't want to hear you say that word ever again, alright?"

"Okay."

"And secondly, we're going to talk about your treatment plan."

"Okay."

"Lilah, I've put you on a mood stabilizer drug. I've looked over your chart and I think your moods go up and down a lot more than you realize. I think you may be bi-polar."

"That's bad, isn't it?"

"It's not bad," she said. "Sometimes it causes you to do things you wouldn't normally do but it's not bad. The good thing about psychiatric drugs now is that we can make it better. I'm going to try you on this drug and we're going to see if it makes a difference in how you feel, okay?"

"Okay, but what will it do?"

"It will help stabilize your moods. You won't feel so up and down all the time."

"What if it doesn't work?"

"Well, that's part of the treatment plan. We'll have to see what happens. If it doesn't work, then we'll try something else. But let's give it time to work, okay? Let's give it a few months and see how you feel." She looked down at my chart. "I want you to check in with me next week. The hospital will make an appointment for you before you leave. Do you have any other questions?"

"I don't think so." She stood up.

"I think this is going to be good for you, Lilah. I think this is going to make a substantial difference in your life. Pay attention to how you feel, okay? And if you have any problems between now and next week, give me a call."

"Okay."

I didn't give Dr. Stone a call that week or any other week even though I went faithfully to every appointment. We moved our scheduled times from once a week to once every other week. I was busy and the appointments into the city to see Dr. Stone took up even more of my time. As if being a mother of four isn't enough.

There was soccer practice and orthodontist appointments and ballet for Maria. Michael wanted to do fencing but I talked him out of it for fear he would lose a limb. He wasn't the most coordinated child you'd ever seen. Vonnie, on the other hand, was completely the opposite of him and was now in Advanced Gymnastics.

Given all my obligations Tristan and I barely saw one another. I'm not sure if it was because both of us were busy doing other things or that we were afraid someone would somehow sense the energy between us.

He had dinner with us twice during that time. Each time he looked at me across the table as if we'd never had a conversation about how I didn't love my husband or the fact that he had saved my life. He looked at me as if those moments had never existed. All I could do was think about those moments.

One night after one of those dinners I stood in front of the mirror in my bathroom, naked, wondering what in the world had happened to me. Where had these feelings come from?

This is not who you decided you were going to be when you married Eric. You are a mother, a wife, a daughter. Stop thinking about him, I chastised myself. But I didn't want to stop thinking about him, so I ignored that voice inside of me. I convinced myself whatever happened would happen and that I had no control over it. I knew very well that everyone had control over their own thoughts and actions. I just didn't want to take responsibility for mine. Isabel said I was having a mid-life crisis. It was lust, she said, and I should take up a hobby. She suggested needlepoint because she said it took a lot of concentration.

I began to see Tristan more. He was always with our boys watching movies or whatever it is boys do when they get together. They always stopped talking whenever I walked into the room. I realized whenever Tristan was around I forgot what I was doing.

That night Ben and Tristan were in the basement playing pool and Vonnie was painting Maria's nails at the kitchen table. I was cleaning up the kitchen from the extravagant meal I had spontaneously cooked for dinner when I heard them coming up the back stairs. I looked up as Ben walked around the corner.

As Tristan walked behind me he brushed his fingers lightly across my waist. I sucked in my breath. A wave went coursing through me, sending an instant rush of adrenaline over my body. I walked out onto the back porch for some cool air.

I comforted myself by taking a deep breath. I ran my hands through my hair. You stupid, stupid woman, I thought. Why would a guy like Tristan be interested in someone like you? It's crazy, I told myself. He cannot possibly want me *that* way. But from the moment he touched me, I knew he did.

The following Saturday while Isabel and I sat by the pool in her back yard I finally broke down and admitted how I felt about Tristan. I told her about what he had done. She asked me if I had started my needlework project yet.

"Very funny," I replied. "No."

She turned in her lounge chair toward me and propped herself up on her elbow.

"Let's go out tonight!" she said. "It's Saturday. There will be a million people at the club. It'll take your mind off everything." I ignored her.

"Please," she whined. "Please…please…please…" I raised my sunglasses as I looked toward her.

"We're getting too old for this," I said.

"Maybe *you* are." She reached out and touched my arm. "C'mon Lilah. Live a little."

It's hard to say no to Isabel when she begs. It'd been years since we'd been downtown together. Maybe because we always got into trouble when we did.

"Please!" I threw my magazine down onto the patio.

"Okay. Fine. We'll go."

I told Eric we were going to the movies. Instead I met Isabel at her house for a few drinks and we went through her closet until we found something that made us look younger than we were.

"I haven't worn heels this high in years," I said as I walked around her bedroom.

I stood in front of the floor length mirror on the back of Isabel's bathroom door. I knew I had lost weight, but I didn't realize how much until I turned sideways.

"You look amazing," she said as she grabbed my arm and her clutch off the bedside table. "Let's go get Tristan out of your system."

"Isabel!" I said following her through the house. "It's not that bad."

"It is. Let's go."

His name was Cabot. I'll never forget that because it made me think of a man who used to be on my mother's favorite soap opera. I had never heard of anyone else named Cabot. When we started dancing together I wasn't drunk, only buzzed, but then we had a couple more drinks and we danced again. Then I was drunk.

I looked around for Isabel, but I didn't see her. The club wasn't that big, but I didn't panic because we had made a promise never to leave the club without each other. I knew even if Isabel was more plastered than I was she would still not leave without me. Therefore, I concluded she must have been in the bathroom.

Cabot took me back to his table where he was sitting with another couple. I glanced at the girl's hand and noticed she was wearing a wedding band. I momentarily thought about how blatant it was that she would wear her ring when she was with another man but then I realized the man at the table was her husband. She leaned over to me.

"You should feel honored," she yelled into my ear. The music was so loud she had no other choice if she wanted me to hear her.

"Why is that?" I yelled back.

"Because we come in here every weekend and he never dances with anyone."

"Oh..."

"He must think you're really beautiful," she continued. "You are beautiful, and I like your necklace."

When she reached out to grab it I knew without a doubt there was at least one other person in the club drunker than me. Over years of having happy hour every day with Isabel I had built up quite a tolerance. It didn't mean I got any less drunk, only that I was better at handling it than most people. It wasn't necessarily a good thing.

"Cabot is very picky," she said as if it was a secret. "We used to think he was gay." She laughed.

"Is he?" I asked.

"No," she said. "...finitely not."

Cabot reached over and put his hand on my knee under the table and slowly ran his finger up and down my thigh. I took a deep breath. All the thinking I'd done about Tristan lately had stirred feelings in me I hadn't had in a while. I put my hand over Cabot's and squeezed it. He leaned toward me. I thought he was going to say something, but his lips just grazed the back of my ear. I squeezed his hand harder.

"Let's get out of here," he said. I shook my head no.

"Why?" he asked. No type of coercion. Just a simple question.

"Because my friend is here somewhere, and I can't leave without her."

"Well, let's go find her," he said pulling me off my stool. He grabbed my hand.

We found Isabel, unsurprisingly, in the VIP section. She wasn't anywhere near as drunk as me. I wasn't even sure she was drunk.

"Come on in," she waved. I motioned for her to come over to the rope.

"What?" she said when she got to me.

"This is Cabot," I said. Isabel glanced at him then looked back to me.

"Nice to meet you Cabot. What is going on?" And when I didn't say anything, "Really?"

Her eyes widened, and I nodded.

Once outside the VIP section Isabel offered to take Cabot home. This was also a plan hatched by us several years ago to accommodate one another if we wanted to be with a guy alone. We had never acted on it before but there was always a first time for everything. We left Cabot by the bar, so we could go the bathroom.

"I'll wait here," he said. Isabel pulled me toward the line for the bathroom. There was always a line for the bathroom.

"If he's there when we get back you can have him," she said.

"What does that have to do with anything??"

"See if he's serious or if he's just messing with you." I shrugged.

When we walked back out of the bathroom, there he was, standing at the end of the bar still waiting. I guessed guys didn't feel they needed a friend to chaperone them the way girls did. He didn't seem to even think twice about going with us and leaving his friends. He directed Isabel into a quiet neighborhood about fifteen minutes from the club. The house was humongous.

"Is this your house?" I asked. He shook his head.

"No," he said. "My parents but they're on their boat this weekend."

"Lord," Isabel said out loud as she turned around in her seat. "Let me see your driver's license." And when he didn't produce it, "Come on." She tapped the watch on her wrist. "Times a tickin'."

"You might as well give it to her," I said. "She won't let me get out of the car until you do."

"Fine," he said. He pulled his wallet out of his back pocket and handed Isabel his license. She examined it closely.

"What are you looking for?" Cabot asked after a minute or so. "My age?" Isabel looked up.

"Well, duh," she said.

"Give it to me," I said and grabbed it from her. "1995."

Isabel counted on her fingers.

"I'm twenty-two," he said. "Is that acceptable?"

"I have t-shirts older than you," she said. She looked over to me. "I'll be back in about an hour."

"Where are you going?" Cabot asked.

"I don't know," Isabel said. "Is that not long enough for you to screw her brains out and kill her afterward?

"Isabel!!!" I turned to Cabot. "She's joking."

"I know. You should come in," he said to her. "My friends are inside. You can hang out with them. That way if I try to kill her you'll hear her scream."

Isabel took a deep breath.

"It's a good idea," I said. She sighed then took the car keys out of the ignition.

"Okay."

There were three other guys sitting in what appeared to be a den passing around a huge bong.

"Cabot!" one guy said leaning back in his chair. "You brought specimens!"

Cabot only laughed.

"Can this specimen join you?" Isabel asked.

"Of course, of course," one of the other guys said.

Isabel turned to me. "Take your time," she said. "But if you're gone too long you'll have to drive."

"By then the alcohol will have worn off," I said.

"Exactly," she said. "And I'll be high as a kite."

It was the first time I'd had sex with anyone other than Eric since the previous summer. We had gone on vacation with another couple last July and I ended up having a three-day affair with the guy. Eric knew about it and said he didn't care one way or the other, but I think he only said it because he was fooling around with the guy's wife. Either way, we had both agreed to it, so I never felt guilty about doing it and we never talked about it again.

I thought I would feel guilty the next time I wanted to sleep with someone else, but I didn't. I felt guilty about my feelings for Tristan, but I didn't feel guilty with Cabot. I didn't really feel anything at all. Emotionally I was numb.

Cabot smelled like incense. His thick blonde hair was blunt cut, close to his neck but full on top. It suited him well. He peeled off my clothes slowly, piece by piece, and ran his hands over my body.

"God, you're gorgeous," he said. "How did this happen?"

I giggled. (I really did.) "I don't know."

He traced his finger across the top of my panties and carefully slid them down my legs.

"How exciting," he said like he was unwrapping a present. "You shave everything."

"Yes," I said. "I do."

I realized most women did not shave themselves entirely. Isabel had what I called a landing strip, but I'd been shaving everything down there since I had started my period in seventh grade. My mother never taught me about tampons and until later in high school when a friend did I had only used pads. I detested the way the blood clung to the hair when I was on my period. It made me sick every time I pulled down my pants to pee so one day after I shaved my legs I shaved off every single hair I had. It seemed the logical answer to my problem. So, although men liked to think it was a sexual thing for me, it was purely for sanitary reasons. I wasn't going to tell Cabot that, of course.

It didn't take long. Men his age only have but so much control. Fortunately, I wasn't expecting anything more so after he finished I figured it was over. But it wasn't over, and he wanted to make sure he had pleased me, too.

I wasn't sure I could have an orgasm with him. It was kind of a trust thing with me. I thought about how I could convincingly pretend I'd had one. I didn't want him to feel like he couldn't satisfy me. At the tender age of twenty-two, if he felt he couldn't it might damage him for life.

It took six minutes. I knew this because I looked at the digital clock on the bedside table when he started touching me and again when I collapsed afterward against him. I was in awe he could do that to me. I'd been so wound up thinking about Tristan. Isabel was right. This was what I'd needed.

"I hope you enjoyed that as much as I did," Cabot said.

"Oh yes," I said. "I did."

We both dressed quietly, and I walked out of his bedroom with a huge smile on my face. I must have still been smiling when Cabot and I walked down the stairs and into the den because all the guys stood up and clapped like they were giving a standing ovation.

"We could hear you," Isabel explained.

My face must have turned crimson because she laughed.

"I can tell the difference between a "someone is trying to kill me" scream and a moan of pleasure. I hope to God you feel better."

"I wasn't moaning," I said covering my face. I fell back against Cabot.

He whispered, "You kind of were."

Isabel jumped up.

"Let's go," she said grabbing her purse and keys. She threw the keys at me, but I didn't catch them. I reached down to the floor to pick them up.

"May I call you?" Cabot asked as I stood up. He kissed my cheek.

"Sure," I said but I wondered how he was going to do that.

I had never given him my number.

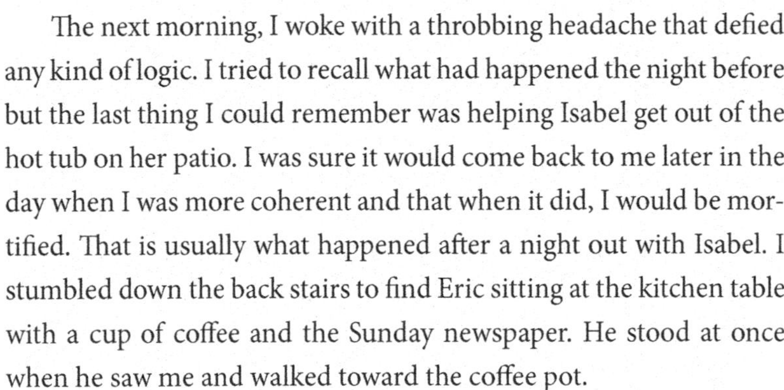

The next morning, I woke with a throbbing headache that defied any kind of logic. I tried to recall what had happened the night before but the last thing I could remember was helping Isabel get out of the hot tub on her patio. I was sure it would come back to me later in the day when I was more coherent and that when it did, I would be mortified. That is usually what happened after a night out with Isabel. I stumbled down the back stairs to find Eric sitting at the kitchen table with a cup of coffee and the Sunday newspaper. He stood at once when he saw me and walked toward the coffee pot.

"I'm thinking you need a cup of coffee and some aspirin?" he asked as he poured me a cup.

"Yes," I said hoarsely. "How did you know?"

I sat down at the kitchen table and he placed the coffee in front of me. He handed me two aspirin from his pants pocket.

"Do I want to know why you have aspirin in your pants pocket?" I asked. He chuckled.

"Because I didn't want to go back upstairs for it when you finally woke up and I knew you would most likely not have the capacity to go get them yourself." He kissed my cheek.

Holy cow, I suddenly thought. I slept with a twenty-two-year-old last night.

"Why are you so good to me?" I asked not hinting at that most recent memory. He was so incredibly good to me. Much better than I deserved.

"Well," he said sitting back down at the table. "For one, you're my wife. For two, I love you. For three, I'm always on your side. Shall I go on?" I smiled.

"No," I said. "Thank you."

"Do you know what happened last night? Or maybe I should ask if you *want* to know what happened last night?" I took a sip of my coffee.

"Do I?" I asked innocently.

"It was a typical Isabel night," he said as he picked up his newspaper again.

"Are you mad?" He laid his hand over mine. I was hoping he didn't know *everything* I had done last night.

"What would be the point?" He asked. "Would it change anything you did?"

"No," I said.

"Would it end your friendship with Isabel?"

"Doubtful," I said.

"Lilah," he said laying the paper back down. "Ever since I met you, you've always tried to get me to stop loving you."

"No, I haven't."

"Yes," he said. "You have. You just had a little too much to drink last night, probably danced with some guy who tried to take advantage of you and then got in Isabel's hot tub naked."

Thank you, Jesus, Lord in Heaven. He didn't know.

"I told you we went to the movies," I said rubbing my temples. He chuckled.

"You did," he said from behind the newspaper. "Did you have a good time?"

I laid my head over on the table. The pain was unbearable. The coffee I was drinking did not want to stay in my stomach. I got up and went to the refrigerator for a bottle of water. Hydrate. I needed hydration. I downed half the bottle and walked out onto the back porch for some fresh air. The sun was high in the sky which meant it wasn't morning anymore. I leaned over the railing and threw up the water I had just drank.

I remembered his name was Cabot. He had on a pair of jeans, an untucked white shirt and a navy blazer. He smelled like incense. He had the brightest blue eyes I'd ever seen with dirty blonde hair that fell across one eye. He was twenty-two and in a moment of intimacy had told me when he graduated college the following year he was going to work with his father in the family business. I didn't ask what kind of business. It hardly mattered. He acted as if he wouldn't really have to work at all. He said he could take care of me and give me anything in the world. His father owned a 75' yacht, he said. We could travel all over the world. Have fine dining every night. Lay on white sand beaches with turquoise waters. Swim with dolphins. I didn't tell him I had done that a few years ago at Disney World.

For whatever reason, none of the things Cabot offered appealed to me. Screwing up what I already had for a white sand beach seemed a little selfish.

I couldn't blame Isabel for using her birthday as an excuse to have a pool party and letting all the kids invite their friends. I *could* blame her for asking me to help chaperone. When I got there she and some of the other parents were sitting in a circle under the trellis at the front of the pool. Everyone had a drink in their hand, whether it was wine or beer or a red cup full of who knows what. Most of them seemed like they were already half way to a nasty hangover. The best aspect of living close to Isabel was that when I got drunk I could walk home.

Isabel had stocked the poolside bar, so it was easy to hop up and make yourself another drink. I walked over and made myself a ***Vodka Tonic*** then plopped down beside Isabel on the wicker sofa. I clinked glasses with her.

"Everyone here knows Lilah?" she asked but before anyone could answer she said, "This is Lilah. Ben, Michael and Vonnie's mom."

"Don't you have little girl?" One mother asked in what seemed like an accusatory tone. Like, what are you doing here when you have a little girl at home?

"Yes, I do," I said. "She's five. Maria. She's with her Daddy tonight."

"Oh," another mother said. "You guys got a divorce, right?"

"No," I said. "We didn't get a divorce."

"Where did you hear that?" Isabel asked.

"I don't remember," the woman replied. "But I'm glad you guys are still together. What, with all the stuff you've been through lately."

I stood up.

"No, no Lilah. Don't leave. It's okay."

I turned around and sat back down but only because it was Isabel. People who listened to rumors and spread gossip were the worst kind of people on earth because they were hypocrites. Do not throw stones when you live in a glass house.

"I would very much appreciate it," I said. "If instead of assuming something is true about me you take the time to ask me before you ask someone else. Thank you." I looked around to the other parents who seemed stunned I'd defended myself. "Is that too much to ask?"

"No, of course not," the woman said.

Her husband's eyes scanned my body and I could tell she didn't like the way he was looking at me. She'd probably been denying him for the last three months and he was hornier than a rabbit on Viagra.

"So, what have you been up to?" he asked me as he leaned forward with his drink in his hand.

"Oh, you know," I said. "Just..."

Before I could say anything else, Isabel had snagged one of the boys' friends as they walked by. I didn't know him, but she held him by his wrist like he was a prisoner.

"Why don't you take Bruce here." She pointed to the man that was talking to me. "And show him the new fish we got for the tank?"

"I don't know anything about the fish you have in your tank," the boy said. I could see her squeezing his wrist tighter. "Take him!"

"Okay, okay," the boy said. "Jeez."

Isabel pointed to the only other man sitting in the circle and said, "You! Go with them."

He didn't question her. Most people didn't question Isabel. If they hadn't experienced her wrath, one of their children had. I downed my vodka tonic and got up to fix myself another one. It surprised me that some of the parents were drinking like fish. I was waiting for one of them to pass out and fall out of their chair. It also surprised me they seemed to be overlooking the fact that their children were drinking, too.

Isabel and I always turned our heads the other way when one of the kids walked by with a beer or a red cup, but no one was going anywhere tonight because Isabel had already used their car keys as an admission "fee." We never bought alcohol for the kids. Sometimes they brought it. Or in some cases, stole it.

It was hot as hell and I pulled off my t-shirt as I got up to get another drink. I had my green bikini underneath. It was provocative but in a parental sort of way. I spotted Tristan in the hot tub and when Isabel looked over I pointed at him as I walked his way. She rolled her eyes. She knew she couldn't prevent from me from doing anything I was set on doing. I wasn't set on doing anything. I didn't have a game plan or any plan, for that matter. Tristan saw me and watched me as I walked toward him. He smiled and lowered his eyes. His eyelashes were so long and dark it looked like he was wearing mascara.

"Get in," he said when I got to the edge of the tub.

"Really?" I asked. I looked around at all the other kids seated inside. It seated eight.

"Yeah," they all said. "Get in."

So, without further ado I stripped off my denim mini-skirt and stepped down into the water.

"Holy shit," I said spilling some of my drink. "Hot…"

"Ease yourself in," Isaac suggested.

There were only two empty spots and one was next to Tristan, which was the reason I had walked over there in the first place. I slowly slid into the seat beside him.

"Oh," I said turning to him. "How are you sitting in here?" He laughed.

"I've been in for a while," he said. "I might be numb."

"I hope not," I said teasingly.

"His wiener is all shriveled up," a boy named Jackson said.

"Dude," Isaac said and pointed to me.

Isaac's girlfriend, Lindsey, leaned over to me and handed me the cigarette she was smoking as if it was a ritualistic thing we did whenever we were together. It wasn't. I had never shared a cigarette with her in my life. When I inhaled was when I realized it was pot.

"I didn't know you smoked," Tristan commented. I handed the cigarette back to Lindsey.

"I don't," I said as I exhaled and coughed.

"You okay?" he asked and laughed.

"Uh-huh."

I felt his hand brush against my leg. I'm not sure what correct terminology to use when someone touches you and it creates a pulsating sensation beneath your skin. I felt his fingers on my hip and I bit my tongue. He slipped his fingers underneath the band of my bikini bottom and pulled me closer to him. It was so unexpected I lost my balance and fell over into his lap. Some of my drink swooshed over the side of my cup.

"Jeez Lilah," Isaac said. "Drink much?"

"Have I not been having happy hour with your mother for the last fifteen years?"

"You could probably drink me under the table," he commented.

"You know I could." He laughed.

Tristan partially stood up and leaned across me to grab another beer out of the cooler behind us. When he did his arm grazed my chest.

"You smell like bubblegum," I said before I could stop it from coming out of my mouth. That is what happens when you've had just enough drinks to lose any inhibitions you might have about *anything.*

"I was chewing bubblegum a little while ago," he explained. "But it doesn't go so well with beer."

"I used to chew the kids' gum when they were little," I said to him – still no inhibitions. "They would give it to me and I didn't have anywhere to put it, so I would put it in my mouth."

Tristan smiled and shook his head a little.

"Gross," Jackson said. "That's disgusting."

Tristan put both of his elbows on the rim and eased himself up a bit, leaning back against the edge of the tub.

"Hot," he said as he looked down at me. "I'm starting to sweat."

I had finished my vodka tonic and I sat the glass on the cement behind me. Tristan handed me his beer.

"You can have it," he said. "It's still cold. I'll get another one."

"Why don't you get her one?" Isaac asked.

"It's fine," I said. "I don't mind."

"She'll chew your gum," Jackson said to Tristan. Tristan looked back to me.

"I'm sure she would."

I looked over to see Isabel running across the patio toward us. She hopped down into the tub.

"Why are you running?" I asked.

"I had to get away from those other parents," she said. "They're talking about the cost of gas and the kind of flea and tick prevention they use on their dogs."

We all looked at her like she had to be lying but I knew from experience she was not. It seemed Isabel and I were the only mothers who knew how to have fun which is why all the other mothers hated us. They acted as if it were our fault they lived a boring life. I could tell them a million ways to have a good time if only they'd ask.

"Tristan, trade spots with me so I can sit by Lilah," Isabel said.

I was going to kill her. Afterward I was going to throw her dead body down an old well and put the top back on. Tristan moved, and she sat next to me. She pinched my leg so hard I was certain it would leave a bruise.

"Ow!" I said. She leaned over to me.

"You need to get a grip," she whispered. "Seriously."

I felt like a child caught with their hand in the proverbial cookie jar. I knew if I tried to get another cookie Isabel would do more than pinch me, but I was hungry. She looked over to Tristan.

"Stop it," she said to him.

"What?" he said holding his arms up in the air. "I haven't done anything."

"You have," Isabel said. "And you know what it is."

I took a swig of my beer. It was Tristan's beer. I took pleasure in that since I knew I couldn't have a cookie.

"Do *I* know what it is?" Ben asked as he walked up behind me. He stepped down into the hot tub.

"Hey man," he said to Tristan and they bumped knuckles.

I had a moment of regret when I thought about how I had been flirting with one of Ben's friends because I knew if Ben even had an inkling of an idea what was going on he would try to kill Tristan and then possibly me. I reassured myself that even if something did happen between Tristan and I, no would ever know. Suddenly it occurred to me that Tristan was staying at Isabel's house that night.

And so was I.

I laid on the chair in Isabel's living room with my head against one arm and my legs over the other. I watched him sleep. It sounds creepy, but it really wasn't. His chest moved up and down as he breathed, and his hand dangled off the edge of the sofa beside me. I wanted to touch him. I moved forward a little, just enough so that my hand hung over his. I thought about what it would be like to entwine our fingers together.

He opened his eyes slowly. My heart beat out of my chest. I wasn't sure what to do. He didn't move or say anything for a minute. He sucked in his breath and stretched his arms over his head. I watched the muscles flex in his arms. He rolled onto his side and looked over to me.

"Can I have you?" He barely whispered.

"Yes," I said breathlessly.

Permission granted.

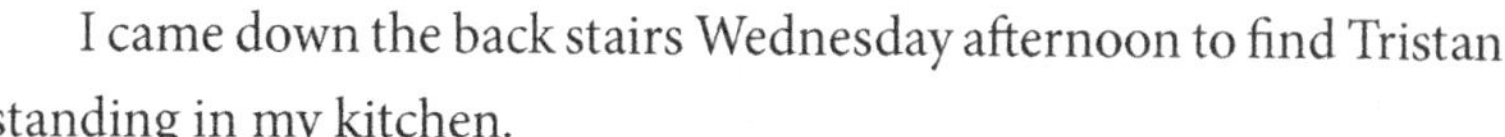

I came down the back stairs Wednesday afternoon to find Tristan standing in my kitchen.

"Oh...hi," I said. "What are you doing here?"

"Sorry," he said motioning over his shoulder toward the door. "I was looking for Ben and the door was open."

"It's one in the afternoon," I said looking at my watch. "He's in school."

This is what we had started to do. We pretended with one another, like what was happening between us wasn't really happening. He leaned against the door jamb in between the kitchen and the den, stuck his hands in the pockets of his jeans.

"Honestly I came to see you."

"Oh? What can I do for you?" I asked as I walked over to the refrigerator. "Would you like something to drink?"

"Sure," he said.

His phone beeped, and he took it out of his pocket and looked at it. He typed something then looked up to me.

"Sorry."

"It's okay."

I took two cans of soda out of the refrigerator and handed one to him. When I opened mine, it spewed all over me and onto the floor. I ran to the sink to try to minimize the mess. Tristan came up behind me, putting his arms around me from behind and reached for the can.

"Here," he said. "Let me help you."

He took the can out of my hand and sat it in the sink. We stood there for a moment with him behind me and his arms around me. I could hear his breath in my ear. He put his hands on my waist and turned me around. I looked up to him.

"Tristan," I managed. "Maybe..."

"Don't say it," he said. He put his fingers across his lips then pressed them over mine.

He leaned down, barely touching his lips to mine then pulled away. It wasn't a kiss and I sucked in my breath. My hands grasped the counter behind me. That wave of anticipation, the way my heart sunk and rose at the same time, how it felt the night he grazed his fingers across my waist, all those things passed through my mind. He put both of his hands on my neck and this time he really kissed me. His lips moved against mine and I closed my eyes.

I thought about Isabel telling me not to touch him. Ever. I thought about Cabot at the club and how he told me he could give me everything. For a moment I felt as if I was watching myself from above, wanting to stop what was happening but not being able to do anything. Frozen in time.

"We can't," I said when he stopped kissing me for a moment.

"Yes. We can," he whispered as he drew me back into him.

I don't remember disagreeing with him. I just remember he had this intoxicating scent that completely overwhelmed me. It wasn't just cookies baking. It was bubblegum, and mint and I don't even know what else, but I breathed it in. When he kissed me again it seemed sweeter but a little less innocent. He pulled away afterward and took my hand in his as he backed away from me, gradually letting my fingers go. He watched me for a moment.

"Don't say it," he said and smiled.

I wanted to say something. Anything. But I couldn't formulate any words. He walked over to the back door and slipped outside onto the porch. I closed my eyes and fell back against the kitchen counter. I bowed my head and covered my face with my hands. I tried to think about what I should do next but as scared as I was of what might happen I was more afraid of how I felt at that moment. I wanted to deny the flutter in my stomach. I wanted to deny I was breathless. Suddenly I realized the alarm on the stove had been going off for a minute and a half and I hadn't even noticed.

Later that afternoon Isabel and I were having wine and cheese on my front porch with a new bottle of Chianti she had gotten that day when she bought groceries. We weren't wine snobs. It didn't matter if the wine came from the grocery store or a winery in Napa. If we liked it, we liked it. If we didn't, we poured it down the sink. (That rarely happened.)

Isabel was amid telling me about her day at school which always involved some form of criminal punishment for one of her students who had disrespected her, another teacher, or the school system in general. Every punishment was a direct response to the offense. Retribution. She was one of those teachers who made the students give her their cell phones when they walked into the classroom and took points off essays when they spelled a word wrong. There were no excuses in Isabel's classes, only consequences and penance.

"I promise you," she said. "If he says that to me one more time I am going to slap him the face."

Usually this kind of admission from Isabel resulted in me telling her how she would lose her job if she followed through with her threat but that day my mind was racing with my own thoughts.

"I have something to tell you," I said.

"I know," she said swirling her wine around in the glass. "I'll be fired."

"Well, yeah, but…" I stopped.

"I don't like that look on your face," she said leaning in closer to me, her elbows on her knees. "What did you do?"

I took a sip of my wine and tucked my hair behind my ear.

"Promise me you won't get mad."

"Did one of my kids talk you into doing something I already refused?"

"No. Nothing like that."

"What? You're scaring me."

"Tristan came by this afternoon," I said as I picked up a thin slice of cheddar and placed it on a water cracker.

"When?"

"Earlier, after lunch."

"Why wasn't he in school?"

"I don't know."

"What happened?" I popped the cracker in my mouth. "Jeez, Lilah. Did you sleep with him?"

"No!" I practically yelled. "Of course not."

"What did you do to him then?" she asked. She took a sip of her wine.

"Why do you assume *I* did something to *him*?"

"Because I know you." I shook my head.

"He kissed me."

"On the lips?" I nodded. "What kind of kiss?"

As if we were both women who had no romantic memories to reflect upon.

"It was a kiss," I said. "I don't know."

"Did you get to run your hands through his hair?" She smiled naughtily.

I must have blushed.

"You kissed him back," she said as she leaned toward me. "Didn't you?" I was quiet. "You did. Didn't you? Damn it, Lilah."

"What?"

"Why did you kiss him back?"

"I don't know!"

"You should have slapped him in the face!"

"I know."

I brought my hands to my face and leaned over onto my lap. Isabel laid her hand on my back.

"What do I do?" I asked.

She took a deep breath but didn't say anything. I don't think she knew what to say. This wasn't just any kiss. This was a kiss with someone I shouldn't have even contemplated kissing in the first place, but it wasn't an affair. It was just a kiss. I pointed this out to her.

"There is not a classification chart for cheating," she said. "Kissing, touching, whatever, it's all the same – at least that's what Tom told me before he left."

I smiled, but sadly.

"I am not talking about what I did. I am talking about who I did it with. Is there a chart for that?"

"I don't think so, hon. I guess you'll have to wait and see what happens." I sat back up in my chair.

"What kind of advice is that?" I asked in disbelief. "You're supposed to help me."

"What do you want me to do?" she asked. "*You* did it."

"I know," I said with a sigh.

"You never listen to me," she said. "You're like one of my children who I repeatedly say no to and then end up giving in when they look at me…" She hesitated. "Like they look at me."

I pulled my legs up into the wicker chair and laid my head on my knees.

"Crap," I said. "I am in so much trouble."

"You're not really in trouble," Isabel pointed out. "Nothing has happened. No one knows."

"Tell me what to do!" I insisted.

"What do you want to do?" She took a sip of wine. "Do you want to pursue this or fifty-eight it?"

"What? What does that even mean?"

"You know," she said. "When you want to get rid of something."

I laughed hysterically, so hard I almost blew wine out of my nose. She laughed with me even though she obviously didn't know why. I loved that about Isabel.

"It's not fifty-eight," I said still laughing. "It's eighty-six."

"See?" She pointed to her head. "Everyone thinks this blonde is fake but it's not."

She picked up the bottle of wine on the table between us and poured herself another glass then offered some to me. I held up my glass for a refill.

"Cheers!" she said clinking her glass with mine. "To romantic relationships with minors."

This thought had not yet crossed my mind. This could not only be morally wrong. It could be illegal.

"Is he a minor?" I asked. She took a sip of her wine.

"Oh, I don't know." She shrugged. "I just said that."

"But what if he is?"

"It was only a little kiss," she rationalized. "Like when I kissed Ben."

"No." I shook my head. "It was not like when you kissed Ben." She rolled her eyes.

“Okay, then don’t do it again. Save yourself the worry. If he tries to kiss you again, slap him.”

“That’s easier said than done when I’ve already let him kiss me once.”

“Well, I don’t know.” She put her feet up on the porch railing. “Keep kissing him then if you want. Make out with him. I don’t care. Just don’t sleep with him.”

She looked over to me and when I didn’t say anything she snapped her fingers.

“Lilah?” I looked up.

“Hmm?”

“Did you hear what I said?”

“Yeah. You said, ‘don’t sleep with him.’”

“You might want to repeat that to yourself a few more times,” she said. “Maybe every night in front of your mirror before you go to bed, like a mantra. Light a candle.”

I cut my eyes at her and she held up her hands.

“I’m just saying.”

The temperature got hotter and hotter. It was so humid outside you could feel a mist beading on your skin as soon as you walked out of your door. The weather forecast included a heat index, but Isabel and I still laid in the sun every day and we both had killer tans. Before that we had killer burns. The only difference between mine and Isabel’s tan was that I always kept on my bathing suit, so I had tan lines. Isabel laid in her back-yard stark naked.

“It’s my yard!” she protested when I told her the neighbors could see her through the fence. Not to mention all the kids.

"Will you go with me to church tonight?"

"What?" she asked. "Me? In church? I'll probably burst into flames when I walk in."

"No," I said. "I don't and look at my life."

"True," she admitted without looking up. "Is your mother after you again?"

"Yeah, but please go with me. I don't want to go by myself."

"You won't be by yourself," she said. "You'll be with your mother."

"Please Isabel," I begged. "I went with you to the club last week." She raised her head and looked over to me.

"Like you didn't want to do that."

"Not at first," I admitted. "But once I got there I had a good time."

"I can't believe you just compared church to a nightclub."

"That wasn't my point. My point was once you get there you'll enjoy it." She narrowed her eyes at me.

"You're only going because you feel guilty about your kiss with Tristan."

"Maybe."

"Well, if you're going to make a confession I guess church is the place to do it." I smiled. "Are you making a confession?"

"I don't think so," I answered. "I can confess at home."

"To who?"

"God. I don't have to go to church to have a conversation with Him."

"You're a nut job."

"Well, at least I'm not Catholic."

"Hey!" She sat up and pointed at me. "I take offense to that!"

"Don't you ever pray?" I asked.

"Lilah, I can't even remember the last time I prayed. It was probably when I was having Isaac because I thought I was going to die and I figured I needed to get right with God before it happened." I shook my head and laughed.

"You're a mess, Isabel." She pointed to her chest.

"I'm a mess?? Have you looked at your life lately? You're kissing teenagers."

"Perfect reason for us to go."

"Good Lord." She pulled on her bathing suit and crossed her chest. "I'm going to church on a Wednesday."

"Lilah," the pastor said as I walked through the door. "Who do I have the privilege of thanking for your presence here tonight?" I looked over my shoulder.

"My mother?"

"Of course," he said. "Thank you, Loretta, for bringing your beautiful daughter with you tonight." My mother smiled and nodded. "Nice to see you Isabel."

"I love being an afterthought," Isabel whispered in my ear as we walked into the sanctuary.

"I told you that you wouldn't burst into flames," I whispered back.

"Not yet," she said.

We found seats in the very front of the church because that is where my mother sat every Sunday. I had no choice but to sit there with her and my father. As the service began I realized that everyone was looking at me shaking their heads like it was a miracle I was there.

"So good to see her," I heard one woman say. "She's always been such a beautiful child," I heard another say.

What they all meant – and they each knew this – was that it was such a shame I had let my life fall to the wayside and no longer came to church every Sunday. The pastor introduced the Bible study leader, Mrs. Beatrice Thompkins.

"Hello everyone," she said opening her study book onto the pulpit. "How is everyone tonight?"

Murmurs from everyone about how they were well.

"Tonight, we are going to talk about Jesus' love for his people," Beatrice continued. "How no matter what happens in our lives we can always depend on Him. Now someone tell me what you think about when you hear the word "permanent." George Holloway raised his hand.

"Seventy-five dollars," he said. His wife looked at him like he had lost his mind.

"Why is that?" Beatrice asked.

"Because every time Myrtle gets a permanent it costs me seventy-five dollars."

I tried holding it in, but I couldn't, and I burst out laughing. Isabel did too. My mother nudged me hard in the ribs.

"Stop it," she said. "It's not funny." My father leaned around my mother.

"It is," he said to me. My mother ignored both of us. Beatrice tried to recover.

"We all know that Jesus' love is permanent," she said. "All of our sins are covered by the blood of Jesus. All we have to do is repent and truly be sincere." She pointed her finger at the congregation. "You cannot repent and then do it again!" She laughed.

Isabel leaned over to me and whispered, "You cannot repent and do it again."

"Let's talk about trust," Beatrice said. "Who do you trust Lilah?"

I looked around. Was she talking to me? My mother and Isabel elbowed me at the same time.

"You," my mother said. "Go." Like I was waiting at a traffic light and it had just turned green.

"Um," I started. "My husband?" Beatrice pointed again. At me this time.

"Excellent answer," she said. "We should all trust our spouses." Reva Alexander raised her hand.

"Yes, Reva?" Beatrice acknowledged.

"I don't trust my husband," she said. Her husband was sitting beside her. He acted like this was the first time he'd heard this. "I don't trust anything that can't be proven."

"God's love can't be proven," Estelle Rawlings said from the back row. "And you believe in that."

I bowed my head to my chest and laughed so hard my shoulders shook. Isabel squeezed my hand.

"Stop it," my mother whispered as she leaned closer to me. "That is not funny. Everyone knows Reva doesn't believe in God. I don't know why Estelle is bringing it up now."

"If she doesn't believe in God," I whispered. "Why does she come to church?"

"I guess because she hasn't given up hope on herself yet."

"Well, apparently, she's given up hope on her husband," Isabel whispered.

I could hear my dad laughing on the other side of my mother. This did not make my mother happy. She gave him what she called, "the evil eye."

"You know you don't have to be perfect to go to church," my mother reminded me as she put her arm around me. "You're still a child of God."

"I know Mom. You've only reminded me of that a dozen times." She pulled me into her.

"Only because it's true."

Isabel leaned back and whispered into my ear again.

"Did you light that candle last night?" I pinched her arm.

The rest of the service went well. Joyce Reynolds asked for prayer for herself because she did not have a car to bring her to Sunday services. Estelle spoke up and offered to pick her up the following Sunday. Refreshments followed the Bible study in the fellowship hall which we were all attending until my cell phone rang. Isabel followed me as I walked out into the hallway. I looked down at the number on the screen and she looked over my shoulder.

Tristan.

Isabel grabbed the phone out of my hand and hit the reject button.

"*Do not* talk to him," she said. "At least, not in here." I looked around.

"There's a fire extinguisher right over there." I pointed to it. "You can put me out if I burst into flames."

"Come on," she said grabbing my arm. "Let's go have a real drink. This punch is giving me a headache."

A little before midnight that same night I was sitting on the back-porch contemplating smoking one of the cigarettes Isabel had left in the console of my car. I was wondering why Tristan would be calling me when he could have simply walked a couple of blocks and talked to me in person like he usually did.

Maybe he had concluded that kissing me was not one of the wisest choices he had ever made. Maybe he regretted it. I didn't think I could call him back when there was a possibility of rejection on the other end. What if he said, 'Lilah, I think the kiss was a bad idea. We should stop before this gets too complicated?'

I thought again about the night he walked past me and ran his fingers across my waist, how he pressed his body against me when we kissed, the smell of his t-shirt, how he tasted like bubblegum. I thought if he told me he didn't want to kiss me anymore I would want to die. Then I thought, what the hell is wrong with me? Am I fifteen?

"Shit," I said disgusted with myself.

I got up and went out to the car to get Isabel's cigarettes. What would she have done? Would she have kissed him? Of course not. She would have slapped him if he looked at her the wrong way. I leaned inside my car, opened the console, and pulled out the cigarettes and the lighter. I lit one as I walked back toward the house and inhaled deeply. No stars tonight. No moon, either. I started to climb the back-porch stairs.

"Lilah." I stopped and looked around.

Tristan stood just beyond the porch, outside the glow of the fairy lights I'd put on the trellis last week. He beckoned me with his finger. I didn't think twice about walking over to him. Because there was no moon I could barely see him. He pulled me around the corner, further into the dark.

"What are you doing here?" I asked looking back toward the porch. "Someone will see us."

"No. I don't think so." He took the cigarette from my fingers and threw it on the ground. He stepped on it and took my hand, pulling me further around the side of the house. "Smoking is bad for you."

"I know but…"

"Shhhh…"

I knew something was about to happen between us. I just didn't know if it would be good or bad. I wasn't sure if I knew the difference anymore. He grasped my wrists and pushed me up against the side of the house, trapping my arms over my head. His mouth came down hard on mine and his lips moved against mine impatiently. I didn't stop him. When he let go of my arms, his hands slid down my body and lifted my long skirt up my legs.

"I can't do this anymore," he said.

I didn't ask him what he couldn't do anymore. I thought somehow, he must be talking about me. He held the bottom of my skirt in his hand and grabbed me by my waist as if he were going to pick me up. I shook my head back and forth. What if one of the kids walked around the corner? What if one of my neighbors saw us together?

"Not here," I pleaded. "Not now."

He knew I didn't mean it.

"Yes," he whispered against my neck and that smell of baking cookies and bubblegum surrounded me.

He pressed himself into me and undid the buttons on his jeans. They popped open easily and slid down his hips. His other hand slipped inside the string of my thong. He raised one of my legs up around his waist and pushed himself inside of me. It all happened so fast I couldn't even think. I clutched the back of his t-shirt in my hands and twisted it into a knot. His hair fell into my eyes and I pushed it back away from his face. I grabbed onto his arms as I struggled to keep my balance. His face went into my shoulder. I could feel the middle of my back scraping against the wood siding of the house. I accidentally bit my lip and tasted blood.

I had never felt what I felt in that moment. I didn't even know it was possible to feel what I felt in that moment. It was an intoxicating blend of excitement and longing, dread, and desire all at once. My heart beat faster, sunk and rose at the same time, like it always did whenever he was around me. I tried to breathe slowly so I wouldn't cry out.

He picked me up and I wrapped my other leg around him. I held my breath and he murmured my name into the crevice of my neck, but it didn't sound like my name. It sounded like an apology. His body shuddered against mine. He pulled away from me as he tried to catch his breath, letting me back down onto the ground easily, as if I were a puppet. He buttoned his jeans quickly and my skirt fell back around my ankles. We looked at each other, our eyes searching for something. Anything that made sense. We had come back down to earth and the realization of what we had done flooded into our minds. There were no words, only a mutual understanding that we had made a huge mistake.

I wrapped my arms around myself and tilted my head back. I looked for the stars, but I couldn't find them, then I remembered there weren't any. Tears sprung from my eyes and rolled down my cheeks. I sobbed as I watched him walk back through the woods behind my house. He turned once to look back at me. He shook his head back and forth as if he were sorry. I tried to compose myself and wiped the tears from my face. Vonnie came around the side of the house.

"Mom?"

I looked up, my heart beating out of my chest.

"Are you okay?" she asked. "What's wrong?"

I calmed myself and took a deep breath, placing my hand over my heart.

"I thought I heard something out here," I said. "It scared me, but it was just a raccoon."

"Oh," she replied. "Okay. Are you coming in?"

"Yeah. I'll be there in a minute."

She turned and went back inside the house. It frightened me that I could so easily lie to my daughter. It terrified me that I would end up lying to the people I loved the most. I realized then that the insides of my legs were wet, so I reached down and grabbed the hem of my skirt to wipe them off. I leaned up against the porch railing and cried. I didn't know if this was the beginning of something or the end.

At the PTA meeting the following Monday night I sat beside Isabel in a panic. Tristan's foster mother, Mrs. Jenkins, sat in front of us. What would she think if she knew what had happened? What would *anyone* think if they knew what had happened? Thoughts and fears raced through my mind. What would happen if someone told my children? Or if someone told Isabel's children? My entire body was shaking.

"What is wrong with you?" Isabel whispered as she grabbed my hand. "Come on."

That was one of Isabel's more commendable qualities. She could always sense when something was wrong even if I didn't tell her. It was if she had this sixth sense when it came to me. I was the one always at the mercy of my emotions. Isabel took her emotions hostage. We balanced each other. If Isabel had been a man I would've already married her. Either that or we'd be having an affair. She pulled me outside the auditorium.

"*What* is going on?" she asked. "Because you have been weird all weekend."

She took a pack of cigarettes out of her bag and handed me one. She always said you couldn't cry and smoke a cigarette at the same time. She was right. I had tried it.

"Here, smoke this."

She lit one for herself and handed me the lighter. My hand shook as I lit mine. Several other mothers walked past us with frowns on their faces. Isabel leaned into me.

"When do you think was the last time any of them had sex and actually enjoyed it?" she asked.

"Probably never," I said. My hand was still shaking as I held the cigarette up to my lips and inhaled.

"You have got to chill out," she said. "I would offer you a Xanax, but I don't have any with me."

"I'm fine."

"You are obviously not fine." She grabbed my arm. "Let's get out of here. They are going to say the same thing in this P.T.A meeting they say in every P.T.A meeting. We won't miss anything."

We walked out into the parking lot and got inside Isabel's SUV. She started it long enough to put the windows down and then we sat there smoking. Neither one of us said a word for a few minutes but tears continually ran down my face. Finally, she looked over to me.

"Lilah," she said. "You're starting to freak me out. Tell me what is going on." I laid my head on the console and she patted my back.

"I had sex with Tristan," I mumbled.

"What?" I sat up.

"I had sex with Tristan."

"When??"

It wasn't an accusation or a judgement. It was a mixture of disbelief with a little bit of compassion on the side. She took my hand in hers.

"Why didn't you tell me before now?"

"I don't know," I cried. "I've been trying to convince myself it didn't happen." Isabel leaned over to look at me.

"But it did happen??" I nodded.

"I think I've been in shock," I said. "The next morning, I woke up and thought I'd dreamed it." I wiped the tears from my cheeks.

"When did it happen?"

"Wednesday night."

"After church!?!" she asked astonished. She saw the shame in my eyes. "Oh honey. I didn't mean it that way. Any night of the week would be troubling."

"Wow. Thanks. Way to make me feel better, Isabel."

"I'm sorry. I'm trying to absorb what you're telling me."

"What if he's underage. What then?"

"Okay," she said starting the car. "Let's not think about that right now. We'll deal with that later if it's even true." I ran my hands over my hair, stopped at the back of my neck.

"Can you take me to your house and fix me a drink?"

"I can fix you multiple drinks." She shifted into reverse. "You'll probably need more than one." I rubbed my hands over my face again.

"I should shoot myself now."

"Stop it. You need a gun for that and you don't have one." I looked over to her.

"Can I borrow yours?"

"No!!"

"I've just screwed up my whole life."

"No," Isabel said as she backed out of the parking space. "You've only made a mistake. Everyone makes mistakes. We wouldn't be human if we didn't make mistakes. Lord knows I've made my share of mine."

"Yeah."

"Are you agreeing I've made my share of mine??" I smiled.

"Yeah."

She stopped at the stop sign before we pulled out into the road. There were several cars coming so she turned to look at me while she waited.

"You didn't repeat the mantra like I told you. Did you?" I smiled again.

"No," I admitted.

"You never listen to me," she said as she pulled out into the road. "Never."

Later that night we were sitting at the poolside bar outside Isabel's house drinking a mixture of champagne, Chambord, and vodka. The fancy bars called them French martinis. We called them ***Death in A Glass*** because that's what you felt like the next day.

The red lights inside the pool clicked on which meant it was ten o'clock. Isabel's ex-husband had installed them a few years ago for a

Halloween party. He was supposed to switch them out for a different color after the party, but he and Isabel could never agree on a color, so he never did. The red lights made the pool look like a murder scene. It was frightening how it somehow comforted me. Maybe it was because that's how I felt – like I had committed a murder. Granted, it wasn't quite that serious, but the guilt and remorse were like a chain pulling me underwater. I rationalized the water had to be red because fire was red and so was hell.

Thankfully, Isabel looked at life through a different color lens than I did. My lens was blue. Sometimes sky blue when I was happy or a turquoise blue when I was having fun. Now it was a gray blue, like despair.

I didn't know what color lens Isabel looked at life through, but I imagined it to be a pink lens. Sometimes hot pink when we were being innocently crazy and pale pink when we were just hanging out solving life's everyday problems. Now I imagined her color was Barbie pink – because Barbie's life was never blue. Barbie's life was Ferris wheels and cotton candy and that is what Isabel was trying to do – take me out of my gray world and give me some cotton candy, maybe a funnel cake if things got worse.

"If you tell me you had sex with Tristan inside your house I am going to beat you over the head with something," she said tilting her champagne glass back to take a drink. "Probably my flip flop because that's all I have access to right now."

"No," I said. "I didn't."

I felt a kind of satisfaction that I could answer no to that question. Trivial things like the fact that Tristan and I had committed our sin outside in the dark instead of broad daylight on the sofa in my living room eased my guilt.

I stood up and turned around, pulling up my shirt to show her where my back had rubbed against the siding of the house. There was a raw scrape up and down my backbone when I'd dressed for bed that night. When I woke up the next morning it had been stuck to my nightgown. Now it was dotted with a thin scab.

"What the hell?" She nearly spat out her drink.

"Up against the house," I said. "Outside. In the dark." She sat her glass down on the bar and rubbed her temples with her fingers.

"I feel like I'm going to throw up," she said.

"Me, too."

"Whose genius idea was that?"

"We didn't really talk about it."

"What *did* you talk about?" She was practically shouting at me.

"Nothing."

She reached under the bar for the bottle of vodka and poured each of us a shot. She slid one toward me and we both downed them. To believe that liquor could solve our personal problems was not a good mentality to share. She looked past me back toward the house to make sure none of our children were anywhere nearby.

"You know something, Lilah?" I knew better than to answer. "I've always wanted to have sex up against a wall. I've always thought it sounded so uninhibited and erotic." She poured two more shots and leaned toward me.

"BUT NOT WITH A FUCKING TEENAGER!"

"I know," I said quietly.

"You know," she repeated. "Have you talked to him since then?" I shook my head.

"No."

"Have you seen him? Because I haven't. He wasn't here at all this past weekend, which when I think about it is kind of weird. He's always here. I get tired of looking at him."

"I saw him," I said. "He was at the house with Ben, but he didn't come inside. I walked down the hill toward the pond to see what they were doing. You know, like I always do." Isabel nodded. "He looked at me as if we had a secret."

"Lilah?" she asked as if I were completely clueless. I looked up to her.

"It *is* a secret and you better hope it *stays* a secret." She pulled a cigarette from her pack.

"Look," she said. "I hate to be the practical one here but did he…" She rolled her hand around in front of her as she inhaled.

"Come?" I offered.

"No," she said disgustedly. "Of course, he did. What guy have you ever been with that didn't?" She blew smoke back out. "I meant, did he use anything?"

I thought about how I'd wiped off the insides of my legs afterward with the bottom of my skirt.

"Protection?" She nodded. "I don't think so."

"Holy shit." Isabel said. "Where the hell are the kids when this is going on? Where the hell was Eric?"

"I don't know," I cried. I put my hands over my face. "Tristan caught me completely off guard." I sniffed, and Isabel handed me a napkin from under the bar. "I didn't even know he was anywhere around much less in my back yard." I dabbed at my eyes.

"And you were a willing participant?" I raised my eyebrows. "I have to ask you this as your friend." She hesitated. "In case you weren't."

Before I could answer I looked over to see Isaac and Tristan coming out of the sliding glass doors onto the patio. The joint sense of dread and desire I felt that night filled me again. Isabel looked over to me as if she were trying to assess whether I was going to hyperventilate or pass out altogether.

"Take a deep breath," she said to me as Tristan walked over to the bar and picked up my drink.

"What is this?" he asked.

"It's a champagne cocktail," Isabel answered for me. Probably because she knew I couldn't answer for myself.

Tristan tilted his head back and drank what was left in my glass.

"Not bad," he said as he looked over to me.

I wanted to ask him what he was thinking, if he had somehow justified what we'd done, or if he still felt dazed and disoriented like I did, but I couldn't tell what he was feeling or if he was feeling anything at all. He sat the glass back on the bar in front of me.

"You okay?" he asked.

I nodded but when I did I lost my balance and nearly fell off my stool. Tristan reached out to steady me. The touch of his hand on my arm sent shivers from my breast bone all the way down to the pit of my stomach.

"Too many cocktails?"

"Maybe," I said.

Isaac reached to pick up his mother's glass.

"No!" Isabel said pointing her finger at him. "Absolutely not."

"Hello Isabel," Tristan said and smiled. "I barely noticed you there."

You know that look your mother used to give you when she knew you had done something wrong even though you wondered how on earth she could know? The one when you knew you were about to suffer the consequences of your stupid decision? That is the look Isabel gave Tristan.

"It is because I'm that unremarkable or because Lilah's beauty overshadows mine?"

He stood with his hands low on his hips. It made me want to wrap my legs around them again. He may have recognized the look from Isabel that demanded remorse, but he gave no sign of it.

"Why don't you guys get in the pool with us?" he asked. "It's really hot out here."

"No. I don't think so," Isabel answered.

"You don't think it's hot or you don't think you'll get in the pool?"

"You know what I mean," she said to him.

"Okay," Isaac said. "You guys enjoy your conversation. I'm swimming." He took off running and dove into the pool behind us.

Tristan leaned against the bar.

"I know you know," he said softly to Isabel. He glanced over to me then back to her again. "I'm not a bad guy. I promise."

"You know what happens if this goes South?" Isabel asked him. He didn't respond. "Do you?"

"Umm…"

"*Do not* make the mistake of thinking you're in control of this situation. Do you know who is in control?" She didn't give him time to answer. "Lilah. Lilah is in control."

"Okay," he said looking over to me.

"Don't forget that," Isabel warned. "Because I swear to you if *one* bad thing happens." She held up her finger. "*One*. I will hunt you down like an eight-legged dog." Tristan chuckled.

"I don't believe I know any eight-legged dogs."

"This isn't funny." Her expression hadn't changed. She still seemed like a mother chastising her child. "So, keep it in your pants."

If there was ever a time something Isabel said mortified me, it was now. My face reddened and I looked away. I shoved my shot glass toward her.

“Another round?” I asked.

She reached under the bar. Tristan pulled his t-shirt over his head and threw it onto a nearby chair.

“Am I dismissed?” he asked. She waved her hand at him and he turned and walked toward the pool.

Across the top of his back from one shoulder blade to another was a tattoo written in script, **Kyrie Eleison.**

“You see?” Isabel asked as she motioned toward it. “This is what you get when you fuck with guys who are barely old enough to spell their own names.”

I took a tentative breath and blew it back out as Tristan dove into the deep end of the pool.

“She must be pretty important if he tattooed her name across his back,” she commented. “Don’t you think?”

I bowed my head, bit my lip to keep the tears from spilling down my cheeks again. My heart sank.

“Maybe,” I said.

When I’d first returned home from “the ward” I’d wanted to concentrate on my children. I wanted to become a better mother. Because the depression began to lift a little I wanted to clean up my house and cook a good dinner every night. It’d been a long time since we’d all sat down at the table on a regular basis and I missed those times. I knew my children did, too. I rationalized that maybe if I became a better mother it would somehow negate my feelings for Tristan.

I was determined on making sure the kids and Eric had a delicious meal every night, so I went out and bought several new cookbooks. Not that I didn't already have enough cookbooks because I had collected close to fifty of them over the years. Half of them I didn't even use anymore but I felt I needed one that made cooking simple and Lord knows, I needed to make things a little simpler in my life.

It was titled *365 Dinners* - a whole year's worth of dinner plans - and if you have ever had hungry children and a husband who want to know what's for dinner as soon as they walk through the front door, you know how much time and frustration this book would save you. Of course, one cookbook was never enough and while I was in the bookstore I contemplated whether this one would be practical. What if some nights the menu was something my family hated? So, I bought three others to be on the safe side. I meandered into the household section and picked out a book that detailed a specific cleaning plan for my house – which had become quite a mess while I was in my depressive funk. Of course, when I was walking to the cash register I had to walk through the fiction section where there was a table of current paperback books – buy two, get one free. So obviously I had to do that.

There was a Pier One right outside the book store, so I went in there and bought new cushions for the porch chairs, a door mat and a summer wreath for the front door. I also bought a set of crackled pink wine glasses for happy hour with Isabel.

Afterward I went into one of my favorite discount stores and bought myself three summer dresses, two pairs of sandals and feeling guilty I hadn't bought the kids anything, decided to buy each of them some new summer clothes. I also bought Vonnie a pair of heels. Depending on what kind of mood she was in when she first saw them would determine whether she'd like them enough to put them on her feet. I came home loaded with bags from my shopping spree. Eric was still at work and Michael was out in the yard playing basketball. He came running over when he saw me trying to lug everything inside.

"Holy cow Mom," he said. "Did you buy the whole store?"

He started digging through all the bags to see if anything was for him. He found the shirt I bought for Ben and grabbed it.

"That is for your brother," I said exasperated. "Put it back."

"But I like it," he said. "And how will Ben ever know it was supposed to be for him?"

Cunning little brat that he was. I didn't have enough energy to argue with him.

"Okay, fine. Take it."

I lugged all my purchases into the house. Vonnie stood on the porch and watched me.

"You could have at least come out to help me," I said.

"Well, I doubt any of it is for me," she said sarcastically as she followed me inside. "So, why do I care?"

"You know," I said dropping the bags on the sofa in the den. "You could care because I am your mother."

"Yeah, whatever." She turned and walked back out into the foyer.

Why I decided to still give her the shoes at that point is beyond me. I should have kept them for myself and not even showed them to her at all, but I dug through the bags to find them anyway.

"Voila!" I said as she started up the stairs. "You're welcome."

I dangled them on my finger as she came running back down the stairs and into the den. She tried to snatch them out of my hand. I held them up into the air.

"Uh-huh," I said. "What do you say?"

"Thank you, thank you," she said as I gave them to her and she kissed me on the cheek. "I love you so much!!"

"Now you do." She kissed her hand and blew it my way.

"Muah!" And up the stairs she went.

Ben came running down as she ran up. She slapped him on the back of his head as he went by.

"What the hell was that for?" he said.

"Because you're an asshole."

"I'm *always* nice to you," he said. "You're such a bitch." Then he noticed I was standing in the den.

"Oh, Mom," he said. "Didn't see you standing there."

"Obviously," I said. "Language??"

"I'm sorry."

"Two dollars in the dirty word jar."

The dirty word jar was Isabel's solution to her boys using bad language. For every bad word she heard them say they had to put a dollar in the jar. It worked so well for her I started using it myself. At the end of the month I usually had enough money to buy a box of chocolate truffles at the bakery in town which I would have never bought for myself otherwise.

"Did you buy me anything?" Ben asked as he rummaged through the bags one by one. He started throwing everything that obviously wasn't his onto the sofa.

"Dress, dress, dress," he said.

"Stop it," I said as I smacked his arm.

"How come you bought all this stuff for Vonnie and nothing for me?"

"Those are for me," I said. "If you must know." He held one up.

"Uh, Mom. Don't you think you're a little too old for this dress??"

It was a super sexy backless sundress. The back of it hung loosely right above my tailbone. I imagined sitting somewhere with Tristan and him putting his hand down the back onto my bare skin. Ben snapped his fingers in front of my face.

"Come back," he said impatiently.

"Oh, sorry."

I dug through the bag to find what I had bought for him. A pair of jeans, a t-shirt – which was for Michael, but Michael had taken the shirt I bought for Ben. I had also bought a pack of Calvin Klein boxers for them to share and Ben grabbed them out of the bag.

"No! No! No!" I said grabbing them out of his hand. "They are for you and your brother to share."

"But there's five pair," he said. "How do you share five pair?"

"I'll keep the other pair and wear them to bed," I said tearing them open. "Daddy will think they're sexy."

"Gross," he said as I handed him two pair. He walked away with his treasures.

"Hey!" I yelled across the room. He stopped. "Do you have something you want to say to me?" He broke out into a huge grin.

"Thanks, Mom."

It made me happy to see my children happy and I thought that with the depressive funk I'd been in lately it was a while since I saw them genuinely happy. I realized then that I was happy too and I'd been happy for some time now. I heard Isabel as she came into the house. The screen door squeaked so you always knew when someone had opened it.

"Hey, hey, hey." She looked at all the bags strewn across the den. "What in the world?"

"I went shopping," I said excitedly

"I can see that."

"I bought some really cool dresses. I'll share them with you if you're nice to me."

"I'm always nice to you," she said, and she came over and gave me a hug.

I started showing her the dresses. When I held up the backless sundress she raised her eyebrows.

"I don't even want to know what you were thinking when you bought that," she said, and she took it out of my hands. She held it up in front of her.

"What?" I said. "It's cute."

"It's, well, it's unique." I stuck out my bottom lip.

"You don't like it."

"I don't dislike it," she said. "But where the hell are you going to wear this? And don't tell me you bought it for a night out with Eric because this is so not his style. You certainly can't wear it to church with your mother." I gave her my puppy eyes.

"Oh no," she said wagging her finger in front of my face. "Don't even think about that."

"What?"

In a world with no accountability Isabel stepped in and made me responsible for my own feelings – at least when it came to Tristan. She sat down holding the dress in her lap.

"Lilah, we have to talk about this."

"About what?" I asked as I started folding up the rest of the clothes.

"You know what." I sat down.

"What do you want me to do Isabel?"

"I want you to think straight for a minute," she said standing up and folding the dress in question. "Grab some wine and two glasses. I'll put all this stuff in your closet before Eric gets home and has a fit. Then we're going to have a serious talk." She started to drag all the bags toward the stairs. "I can't carry all these at once." She sat some of them down on the landing. "Go get the wine."

"I want to stop thinking about him, but I can't."

"You're not trying," she said.

"I am!"

"Who?" Ben asked from the top of the stairs.

"Your Dad," Isabel said before I could answer.

"Why?

"Because he's had a lot going on at work lately and your Mom is worried about him."

"I'm going to your house," he said to Isabel as he came down the stairs. "Do you need help?"

"No," Isabel said. "I'm good. Thanks for asking."

As soon as Ben went flying out the front door Isabel leaned over the railing.

"Wine," she said holding up her hand and spreading her fingers. "Serious talk in five minutes."

At that moment I felt like being with Tristan wasn't *that* big of a deal. It wasn't exactly right either. It didn't occur to me my overall mood had switched from depressive funk to a happy-go-lucky free for all. I thought about the possibility of the rules not applying to me. I thought about how I was going to convince Isabel that the little game Tristan and I were playing was okay. I had a million justifications to present to her. I should have known better.

I grabbed the two pink crackled wine glasses I'd just bought out of the bag. I hadn't washed them yet, but I decided to use them anyway. I opened a bottle of Sauvignon Blanc. It was Isabel's favorite kind of wine. I walked out the back door and down the hill toward the pond and the two Adirondack chairs. It would be a good place for us to talk. Isabel came running down the hill holding her arms out like she was bird. You couldn't help but laugh when she did things like that.

"What are you doing?" I asked. "You look like a lunatic."

She laughed and plopped down in the chair beside me then grabbed the wine off the table between us and poured some into our glasses.

"New glasses?" I nodded. I didn't tell her I hadn't washed them yet.

"Cheers," she said as she handed me mine. "Make a toast."

"You just did," I said.

"No," she said. "Make a toast to christen the talk we're about to have."

"Uh…." I stammered. "To Isabel's lecture."

"Okay," she interrupted. "That wasn't exactly what I had in mind." She leaned toward me. "I had kind of reconciled the kissing thing. Kissing is harmless, and it was consensual, right?"

"No," I said sarcastically. "I pushed him up against the refrigerator and held him at gunpoint until he kissed me." She smiled.

"It's not just a kiss anymore, Lilah."

"It's just a fling," I said pulling my feet up into the chair with me. I took a sip of wine.

"Has something else happened that I'm not aware of?" I shook my head.

"No. Just our usual talks."

"Why are you still talking to him?" she asked surprisingly. "I didn't know you were still talking to him." I shrugged.

"It's just talking." She took a deep breath. "It's not like I'm giving him blow jobs in the pantry." She put her hand to her forehead.

"Lilah, this is not a normal…"

"Fling?"

"No. It's not a normal fling," she concluded.

"Is there such a thing? As a normal fling?" I paused. "I'm a poet!"

"That's not funny," she said. "A normal fling is with a man your age who you have sex with for fun until you don't anymore."

"And then your husband finds out and divorces you," I pointed out.

"True, but Tristan is not like that Cabot guy at the club or any other man, for that matter. He's…"

"He's much sexier than Cabot."

"Lilah!" she yelled. "Stop and listen to me!"

"Okay, okay."

"You have to take this a little more seriously," she said. "How many times have you had sex with him?"

"Just that once," I said in my defense. There was a gnat in my wine. I tried to pull it out with my finger.

"Has it dawned on you yet that he is the same age as your son?"

"Yeah," I said. "It freaks me out a little, but he doesn't look *that* young."

"It doesn't matter," she said. "He *is* that young."

We were quiet for a moment and I poured myself more wine. I'd had to dump out the other glass because I couldn't get out the gnat.

"Okay, listen to me. There are a lot of reasons teachers - and adults in general - should not have relationships with students... kids," she said. "The school administration makes the teachers listen to this at the beginning of every school year. One, they aren't mature enough to handle the complications of that kind of relationship. Two, it's a conflict of interest – educationally speaking and three, do you know what three is?"

"No."

"Because it could be illegal," she said. "You could go to jail for having sex with Tristan if he's under eighteen."

"It's not like I raped him. He practically raped me."

"It doesn't matter," she said. "What do I have to do to convince you of this?" I looked over to her and shook my head back and forth.

"Why are you looking at me like that?" she asked.

"Like what?"

"Like I'm stupid."

"Because," I said. "No one knows. I'm not telling anyone. You're not telling anyone. I don't think Tristan would tell anyone."

"Hello?" Isabel waved her hand in front of my face.

"So, is that what this lecture is about? Me going to jail if he's underage? Am I going to jail?"

"I doubt it but if the wrong person found out and reported it to Social Services you could. He's a foster kid, Lilah. They take that pretty seriously. Do you want to live with that possibility?"

"Who would do that?" I looked over to her. She shrugged and laid her hand on my knee.

"I'm not trying to scare you," she said. "And it has nothing to do with whether I think this is right or wrong. I realize it's consensual. You know, as your best friend, I am going to be here for you no matter what."

"Should I end it?" I asked.

"You should definitely find out if he's eighteen. You should talk to Tristan about it. You guys haven't talked about your relationship at all. Have you?"

"No. Although it seems like we talk about everything else.

"So, just talk to him. It can't be that hard. Then go from there."

"Okay," I said throwing back the rest of the wine in my glass. "That's a good idea. I'll talk to him."

She reached over and squeezed my hand. It was something she did when she was worried about me. I didn't think she should be worried. At least not yet. If Tristan wasn't eighteen that would be when she needed to start worrying. And if he wasn't eighteen I needed to end our relationship. Immediately.

I thought about when I would have an opportunity to talk with him in private. This wasn't a conversation we could have in my kitchen. I wondered again about what would happen if after I talked to him he didn't want to "fling" with me anymore. And unless he wasn't eighteen I still wanted to fling. With a guy like Tristan, who wouldn't?

Suddenly, I had an amazing idea. I knew what I was going to do. I was going to invite Tristan out to dinner. We could go into Richmond and no one would know or even see us there at all. We could talk… and I could wear my backless sundress.

"Oh, and by the way," Isabel said. "That tattoo Tristan has across his back?"

"What about it?"

"It's not a girl. I looked it up on the internet. You know how not knowing things like that drive me crazy."

I couldn't believe I hadn't thought of that myself.

"And? What is it? Another name for the devil?"

"It's Greek."

"For what?"

"Lord, have mercy." I brought my hand to my chest.

"Upon my soul," I said.

"No. I'm serious. Kyrie Eleison. That's what it means. Lord, have mercy."

"Well, then maybe I'm not going to hell," I said. "Maybe he's an angel."

"Like an angel would have an affair with a married woman twice his age."

"They walk among us." She pointed at me.

"You *are* going to hell," she said taking a sip of her wine.

You only live once, I thought.

Isabel

I felt a little better after I had a talk with Lilah about all the complications of having a relationship with Tristan. I want to emphasize "a little" because I didn't think she was taking it seriously. Regardless, I had done the responsible thing which for me was rare. In all honesty I didn't care whether Lilah continued her relationship with Tristan *if* he were of age. I mean, you only live once.

I walked into the house and went directly to the thermostat. I could feel the cold air from my knees down and the stifling heat hovering above it. I needed to get one of those plastic boxes with a key. Matt came walking down the hall toward me. I pointed to the thermostat.

"Do you see this?" I asked.

"What?"

"What does it say the thermostat is set on?"

"It says 64."

"Uh-huh. Does it feel like it's 64?"

"It feels like it's 104," he commented. I pressed the button to view the actual temperature.

"What does it say the temperature is in here?"

"It says 84."

"Do you know why?"

"Because it's broken?" I slapped him with the mail I was holding in my hand.

"No. Because you guys keep moving it and leaving the doors open." He looked toward the kitchen doors.

"Oh, sorry."

"Have you seen your brother?"

"No," he said as he walked back down the hallway toward his room. "I didn't know I was babysitting."

My children were such joys since they'd hit puberty. I walked into the kitchen and poured myself another glass of wine. I grabbed the novel I was reading off the counter and walked out to the pool. It was quiet which was odd. I looked around then noticed a bikini top laying on the edge of the pool. No bottom. Just the top. I looked around again. No one in sight. I went back inside and looked up and down the hallway. I knocked on Abe's door because it was locked.

"Abe," I said. "Open up."

After a moment he opened the door. Abe was the only one of my children whose room I could burst into and take over without starting World War III. I looked behind the curtains of his patio doors.

"Is there anybody else in here?" I asked him.

"No," he said. "Why?"

"Because there is…." I started to tell him what I found by the pool but then thought better of it.

"Do you know where your brother is?"

"Which one?"

"Isaac."

"Uh, I think he's in his room."

"Okay, thanks."

"You're so weird," he said as I walked out his bedroom door.

Before I got to the end of the hallway and Isaac's room I could smell the pot smoke coming out from under the door. Surprisingly enough the door was unlocked, and I flung it open. Isaac was sitting on his bed with a joint in his hand. He blew out smoke as I walked across the room. I grabbed it between my fingers and took it away from him.

"Where did you get this?" I asked. He motioned across the room where Tristan was sitting in the beanbag chair on the floor.

"This is yours?" I said to Tristan holding up the joint.

"Not that one," he said as he brought the one he held between his fingers up to his mouth and inhaled.

Before I could even think about what I was doing I walked over to him and yanked the cigarette out of his mouth. I sat them both down in an ashtray on the table. Tristan started to say something but before he could get it out I reached down and slapped him in the face.

"Ow," he said rubbing his cheek. "What was that for?"

"Mom!" Isaac called across the room. "Jeez."

"Because I felt like it," I said to Tristan. But it was really because Lilah should have already done it.

"Chill out, Is." I leaned down in front of his face.

"Do not call me Is," I said. "Remember what I told you at the pool that night when Lilah and I were sitting at the bar?"

"Yeah."

"Well, this is considered a bad thing."

Just then two girls fresh from the shower walked out of Isaac's bathroom. They were naked except for the towels wrapped around them. Immediately I recognized Tristan's sister, Tiffany, which probably meant she was sleeping with my son.

"Oh shit," she said. "Isabel."

I looked over to Tristan again and asked him to tell me the other girl's name.

"I don't know her name," he said. He leaned around me. "What's your name?"

"Lindsey," she said quietly.

"Mom," Isaac said. "You know Lindsey." I ignored him and turned back to Tristan.

"You're sleeping with a girl and you don't even know her name?"

"I'm not sleeping with her," he said. "Isaac is."

"Wow," Isaac said. "Thanks, man."

I didn't care about Isaac. Well, I did but I had supplied all my boys with an economy size box of condoms when they turned twelve. I was more worried about whether Tristan was screwing everything with a skirt on and Lilah was just an accessory. I pointed to Lindsey.

"So, if you are sleeping with Isaac, who is my son – you know that, right?

"Yes, ma'am." Isaac hung his head.

I pointed to Tiffany.

"Who are you sleeping with?"

"That's a personal question," she said. I was beginning to lose my temper.

"Answer it anyway!" I yelled. She looked over to Isaac.

"Isaac?" she said hesitantly.

"Thanks Tiff," he said. "You could've lied and helped me out a little bit." She mouthed the word, 'sorry' to him. I turned back to Lindsay.

"And you're okay with this?" I asked her.

"Sure."

I stood there for a moment letting everything I had just learned sink in. My son, who I already knew wasn't an angel was having sex with two girls at once and Tristan was possibly a drug dealer.

"You, you and you," I said to Tristan and the girls as I pointed at each one. "Get out."

The girls walked back inside the bathroom to dress. I grabbed Tristan by the arm as he walked past me.

"Do you want me to leave or what?" he asked.

"We…you and me…," I explained. "Are going to have a serious talk later."

"Okay," he said. "Anytime. Call me."

"I'll find you," I assured him. He grinned.

"Like an eight-legged dog?"

"Get out!" I said more forcefully this time.

"Okay, okay…"

The two cigarettes were still laying in the ashtray on the table, so I went over and picked one up.

"Lighter," I said to Isaac as I held out my hand. He handed me one without question.

I lit the joint and inhaled deeply, holding it in my lungs for a while then blowing it back out slowly.

"Mom," Isaac said carefully. "Are you okay?"

"Are you really sleeping with both of those girls?"

"Yeah," he said. "Are you mad?"

"I'm not happy. Is Tristan sleeping with anyone?"

"Well, Tiffany is his sister," he said, his eyes widening.

"I know that, Nutbag," I said. "I meant Lindsey."

"No," Isaac said.

"You're not both sharing her?" I took another hit.

"Jeez, Mom. No. What do you think I am?" I ignored his question because he didn't want to hear the answer.

"Tristan isn't sleeping with someone else?"

"How would I know?" he asked. "Guys don't talk about that stuff. Why are you asking me this?"

"I don't know," I said. "Just curious."

"Why?" Isaac asked.

"Who cares? I just am."

"I think he's seeing someone," Isaac offered. "But I don't know who it is."

"Well, don't ask him who it is," I said quickly and handed him the joint.

"I thought you wanted to know."

"Don't ask him," I repeated a little louder this time.

"Okay," he said. "What is it with you today? You are so weird. And you just handed me a lit joint."

"Well, that's twice today I've been called weird," I said. "And we've had the drug talk about fifty times. I've always told you before if it comes from the ground it's probably okay." He chuckled.

"Right."

I walked out his doorway and into the hall. I had a second thought, so I peeked my head back inside his room. "And stop sleeping with more than one girl at a time. You're going to get a bad reputation." He laughed.

"I already have a bad reputation," he said as he exhaled.

Lilah

I can't remember the last time I'd called a guy and asked him on out on a date – and that is exactly what it felt like to call Tristan and ask him if he'd go to dinner with me.

When I was in high school my mother always told me if I wanted to go out with a guy to ask him and quit waiting for him to ask me. If he said yes, awesome. If he didn't, I'd lost nothing because I didn't have him in the first place. I did it several times and not once did a guy ever say no. I don't think it had anything to do with me personally. I think it had to do with them thinking there was a good possibility I'd sleep with them or in the least they'd get a good blow job. Sometimes they were right. Other times I just needed someone to pay for a movie.

I shouldn't have been as nervous as I was when I called Tristan. I was a grown woman for God's sake, but we'd never talked on the phone. He'd called me the night I was at church with Isabel, but I hadn't answered. What if now he didn't answer *me*? It rang four or five times and I wondered if he was looking at the screen trying to decide whether he wanted to talk to me or not.

"Hello."

"Hi Tristan," I said. I felt like I was in ninth grade. "It's Lilah."

"Hi," he said.

"I know you called me before and I didn't answer." Good Lord, I thought. Why did I even say that? "I'm sorry."

"It's okay."

"What are you doing?"

"Uh, currently I'm watching a tennis match."

"Oh, do you play?"

"Not very well," he answered.

"Oh…"

"What are *you* doing?" he asked. "I'm thinking your life is a little crazier than mine."

You see, here's the thing with me and Tristan. We talked about everything except our relationship. Politics, the occult, whether apples were in season, if I'd ever had a cat.

"Kind of," I said. "Just a lot of commotion."

"Where are you?"

"I'm at home. Well, actually I'm on the front porch."

"Happy hour?"

"Not yet," I said and laughed. "But soon."

"You've never invited me over for happy hour."

"How about I invite you to dinner?"

"At your house?"

"No," I said. "At a restaurant. Just me and you." He seemed taken aback.

"Really?"

"Yes. Will you go?"

"Yeah, sure."

"I'm just going to say what I want to say not what I should say."

"Okay."

"Or maybe I should say what I should say first."

"What?"

"Isabel wants to know if you're eighteen."

"Why?" He laughed. "Is she filling out a census?"

"No. She's worried about me I think."

He was silent. I waited for a minute to see if he was going to say anything. He didn't.

"Well?"

"I wouldn't do that to you, Lilah."

I don't know why but tears formed in the corners of my eyes. I tried to hold them in. I sucked in my breath.

"What's wrong?" he asked. I could never hide anything from Tristan. "Was that not the right answer?"

"No. I just wanted you to say the wrong thing and you never do."

"You want me to be under eighteen?"

"No, no."

"I thought maybe you were going to tell me we couldn't see each other anymore."

"No," I said. "I wish I could, but I can't. I mean…"

"I know what you mean."

"Is this crazy?"

"What? Us?"

"Yeah."

"Maybe. Probably."

"It will only be dinner."

"Was there something else?"

"No," I said. "I mean it will only be dinner. Nothing, you know…"

"X-rated?"

"I think I've already given you a little X-rated," I joked.

"I'm sorry about that night, Lilah. That's not who I am."

"I know."

"So, dinner?"

"Yes. Dinner. Tuesday?"

"Okay," he said. "But just a warning."

"What?"

"I might not say the wrong thing again." I smiled, a small laugh.

"Mm…" I knew he was smiling, too.

"Good-bye Lilah."

"Good-bye Tristan."

I clicked off my phone and laid down on the wicker sofa, putting my feet up on the arm of it. I laid my phone on my chest and covered my face with my hands then rubbed my eyes. Vonnie walked up onto the porch and stood at the end of the sofa.

"What are you doing?" she asked. "You look like a crazy person. And I can see your underwear." I laughed.

"What color is it?" I asked.

"Ugh," she said as she walked through the front door.

I was thinking Tuesday would be a quiet night downtown, but I was wrong. There were people everywhere. I met Tristan outside

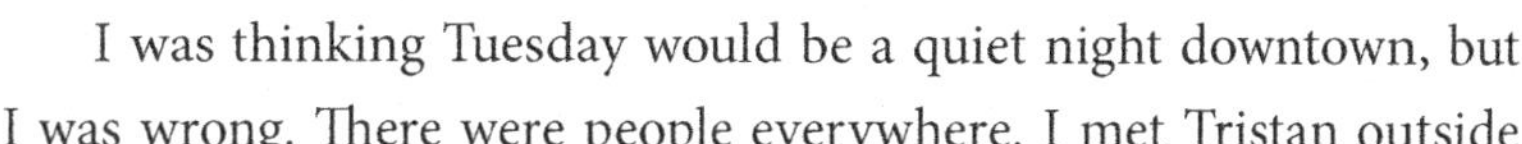

the restaurant. He had on a pair of faded jeans with a hole above one knee and a pale pink polo shirt. He had pulled the front of his hair back away from his face. He smelled like heaven. Eric would have said he was underdressed but there was nothing underdressed about Tristan. He could have been wearing shorts and a ratty t-shirt and still looked good. He slipped his arm around my waist, pulling me into him and I felt his hand against my bare back – because I had worn *that* dress. He kissed my cheek.

"Hi," he said, and my heart beat double time.

"Hi."

We looked down the cobblestoned street.

"What is going on?"

"I have no idea," I said. "But it looks like a party."

I thought given his age he would want to investigate that kind of thing. I know mine and Isabel's boys would have been all over it. Forget dinner. Let's party.

"So, are we dining?" he asked as he escorted me up the stone stairs to the restaurant.

"We are," I said surprised.

Every woman in the restaurant looked up when Tristan walked through the door. Not some women. *Every single one.* He didn't seem to notice.

"Wow," he said as we sat down at a table overlooking the atrium. "This is amazing. How can I not know about this place?" I shrugged.

He picked up the leather covered menu and opened it.

"I hope you're paying," he said once he looked at it.

"Do you think I would invite you to dinner and not pay for it?"

"You never know with women these days."

He smiled, and I shook my head in amusement. After all I had Eric's credit card. Well, it had my name on it, but it was Eric's money. I should have felt guilty about that, but I didn't.

"Wine?"

"Sure," I said picking up the wine list. "Do you want me to pick something?" He reached across the table for it.

"No," he said. "Let me. If you don't mind, I mean."

"Do you know anything about wine?" I asked as I leaned toward him, my hands on the table.

"Maybe. Red or white?"

"Red," I answered.

When the waiter appeared a few minutes later Tristan did, indeed, order a very nice Bordeaux. Maybe he knew what I knew. You could never go wrong with a French wine. Although I couldn't imagine how he would know what I knew.

"I thought he was going to card you," I said after the waiter left.

"Who's going to card me when I order a $85 bottle of wine?" he asked. "I've never been carded in my life."

"Why do you think that is? It can't merely be your good looks." He pointed at me.

"You'd be surprised."

I briefly thought about how I needed to talk to him about the complications of our relationship and how we were going to handle it all, but it didn't happen. We had the freedom to do whatever we wanted without anyone passing judgement on us and I was too selfish to give it up. Plus, I rationalized, he wasn't a minor.

We went downstairs to the bar after dinner and once again Tristan ordered our drinks without getting carded. As we left the restaurant he grabbed my hand and instead of parting ways we walked down the cobblestone street and discovered other bars and clubs, people spilling out of them, singing, and laughing. Most of them drunk.

We, ourselves, had drank a little too much and so when someone told us about a secret, hidden club, it intrigued us. The guy said he was a member then gave us two invitations, pointing us down a dark alley. It was devoid of other people except for a few stragglers, like ourselves. In the distance we could see the entrance to the club bathed in a violet light. Stone walls rose around us with small doors and alleyways that led to, well, we didn't know where. Laughing and full of wine and cocktails I opened one of the doors and pulled Tristan inside with me.

Although we could hear the partygoers around the block laughing and carrying on it was quiet and dark inside the doorway. Another very narrow path lined with stepping stones led straight ahead of us, a small stone terrace to our right. A half wall with an iron gate and what appeared to be small trees, flowers and shrubbery surrounded us. This was someone's private garden and we were completely alone inside of it. A clock tower in the distance chimed and as Tristan slipped his arms around me and lowered his face to my neck we counted each strike.

He whispered into my ear, "It's midnight, Cinderella," and he brought his lips to mine.

I felt his hands on the small of my back against my bare skin and I shivered. He opened the garden gate and picked me up against him. I wrapped my legs around his waist and he laid me down on a small patch of grass on the other side of the shrubs. He lifted the thin material of my dress up over my hips and laid his hands there for a moment while he kissed me.

"Before this happens…"

"Again," I said. He smiled. I started to speak but he put his fingers over my lips.

"I want to make sure this is okay with you." I nodded. "Are you sure?"

"Yes."

"We can't undo this."

"I know."

I felt his fingers fumbling with the buttons of his jeans against my stomach. I started to twist my body to accommodate him. There was no reason to rush like the first time. It wasn't rough. He was gentle with me and when he kissed me his lips grazed mine softly. He had done this before, many times.

"I can't stop myself when I'm with you," he said into my neck. "I want to Lilah, but I can't."

"I know," I said because I felt the same way.

"I'm sorry."

I wrapped my arms around him, pulled him into me and savored the scent of peppermint emanating from his skin. No bubblegum tonight. I pressed my face against his cheek as he moved against me.

"Tris…"

"Yeah?"

"Stay with me."

"I am…I…"

He lost his breath. The world as we knew it paused for a moment. At least the City of Richmond paused for a moment.

"Are you okay?" I asked afterward.

"Mm-hmm."

My body pulsed with what felt like an electrical current. Tristan laid beside me and ran his fingers up and down the inside of my arm which only made the current stronger. He pulled me over on top of him.

"I am going to make you so happy," he said leaning up to kiss me again. "Do you know that?"

I nodded because I believed him, but I wondered as I did, how is that possible? Maybe if I hadn't been so captivated by him I would have asked. Rules are not made to be broken. Rules are made for a reason and it is usually to keep someone or something safe. I should have known Isabel was right. This wasn't a normal fling. This was playing with fire.

Isabel

I met Tristan at a restaurant in Richmond on Sunday to have brunch because I didn't want to take the chance of someone seeing us together in Woodlawn. Mainly, I didn't want to lose my job for socializing with a male student. I told him to meet me at a little café tucked into the corner of Hanover and Robinson Street. I didn't think how about he may not have a way to get there but he'd agreed to meet me, so he must have figured out something. When I walked inside I didn't see him anywhere and I was late. I described him to the hostess and asked if she'd seen him.

"Dark hair, about to his shoulders?" She seemed perplexed.

"Younger," I explained.

"Oh," she said. "The Aladdin guy?"

"Who?" I asked.

"The really tan guy with the long hair?"

I nodded, and she looked over her shoulder at another waitress standing by the bar.

"We were calling him Aladdin." She looked back to me. "He looks like Aladdin, right?"

"Umm…I never really thought about him that way." Lilah had. Obviously. "Where is he?"

"Oh sorry," she said, and she pointed back out the front door. "He's sitting on the patio out front. Can I bring you a drink?"

"Sure," I said. "White wine. Thank you."

I turned around and walked back out the front door. Tristan was sitting at a table in the far corner. The place was packed.

"Wow," I said as I sat down. "I had no idea it would be this crowded."

"You picked it," he reminded me.

He was wearing cream colored linen pants, a tan t-shirt with a tan linen jacket and loafers. If it weren't for Lilah I would have done him in the bathroom. He leaned toward me.

"So, I'm guessing you want to talk to me about Lilah."

"And your drug habit."

The waitress brought my wine and I thanked her.

"Can I have another?" he asked.

"Sure," she said. "Anything else?"

"No," he said. "Thank you."

"You are very welcome. Any time." She pressed her lips together as if she were going to blow him a kiss and he smiled. I bowed my head.

"Thank you," I said to her. "That's all."

"Does Lilah know you're here?" Tristan asked.

"No," I said. "This is between me and you."

"Okay."

"I think there are some things that need to be said."

He crossed his legs with one ankle on the opposite knee and leaned back in his chair. The waitress returned with a platter of calamari and his drink.

"Are you drinking alcohol?" I asked him when she walked away.

"Mint Julep," he confirmed and smiled. "It's a Southern thing. Ya know?"

"I know what a Mint Julep is," I said annoyed.

"Would you like to taste it?"

"No," I said. "But thank you." He nodded, and I motioned toward the calamari.

"Did you order this appetizer? Or is the waitress trying to get in your pants?" He laughed.

"Probably, but yes. I ordered it and I'll take care of the check."

"I'm not worried about paying for it," I said. "It's just nice. Thank you."

"Sure. I'm trying to get back into your good graces after you slapped me in the face."

"Are you sleeping with Lindsey?"

"What?" He seemed taken aback. "I thought you said this was about my drug habit. That, I am prepared to discuss."

"I want to know if you've slept with Lindsey." He scratched the back of his neck.

"First, I don't have to tell you my sexual history or any history, for that matter. Secondly, I would never sleep with Lindsey. She's not my type. I don't sleep around. I'm not like that."

"You look like you're like that," I said.

"Don't judge a book by its cover."

"Right."

"Look, Isabel. You apparently find this hard to believe but I care about Lilah."

"Do you? Do you know what the complications of having a relationship with her are?"

"Well, call me Mr. Obvious but the first thing that pops into my mind is she's married."

"Lilah is infatuated with you. She's not thinking straight."

"I'm pretty much infatuated with her," he said.

I looked down to the floor and then back up at him.

"You know there is an enormous difference between infatuation and love? Right?"

"Of course."

"I doubt it," I said irritatingly. "You aren't old enough to know the difference between the two. I doubt you've experienced either of them."

"You know nothing about me," he replied solemnly. "Don't pretend you do."

"Let's move on," I said looking at my watch. "Because I have somewhere I need to be."

I didn't but there was no way I was explaining the difference between love and lust to him. I didn't even want to talk about it with my own kids. Although given Isaac was sleeping with two girls at once, maybe I should.

"Sure," he said.

"What's with the pot?"

"What do you mean?"

"Where did you get it?" He chuckled.

"I have a guy." He looked at me from under his dark lashes. "Do you want his number?"

Even though I had no desire to buy weed or any other drug I leaned in a little closer to him. That's what happened when Tristan lowered his eyes to you. I tried to regain my leverage.

"Look, Tristan. I know this whole thing with you and Lilah is like a game to you and none of my business. Not really. But she's a little off right now."

"What do you mean she's "off" right now?"

"She's on this new medicine," I said.

"From when she was in the hospital?"

"Yes, and I'm not sure it's working the way it should. I need you to be aware of that."

"Okay." He seemed concerned. "What do you need me to do?"

"I don't need you to *do* anything. Just be careful with her. She's fragile."

"I get the feeling you think this is just a fling," he said. He shook some of the ice out of his glass and into his mouth.

"Is it?"

"No."

"Well, what is it?"

"It's more."

"How much more?" I asked as I leaned back in my chair.

"Can I be honest?"

"I would hope you would be."

"I don't know what it is." I leaned back toward him and put my elbows on the table.

"Are you falling in love with her?" He rubbed the back of his neck.

"Maybe," he said and smiled. "What is love?"

"Good Lord, Tristan." I shook my head. "Stop it. Okay?" He looked down to his lap.

"I don't know if I can."

The waitress came back to our table and stood in front of Tristan as if she were awaiting a command.

"No," I said before she could say anything. "He's taken." She looked over to me, surprised.

"Not by her," Tristan pointed out. "I would never do that."

I narrowed my eyes at him and flipped him the bird. He laughed. I guess you could've said Tristan and I were on the same page at that point but unlike him, I had already read the book. Many times.

I should have recognized Tristan saving Lilah's life would have eventually led to him falling for her. Why? Because that's the way teenage boys operate. I know this because I have three of them. I don't have a vendetta out against Tristan. Not at all. I only think his relationship with Lilah is bound to end in heartache. He said it himself. Lilah was married. Somehow, even though marriage had never seemed to matter to Lilah or me in the past, it mattered with Tristan. Because I knew it wasn't only going to end in heartache, it was going to end in chaos.

Eventually Mrs. Jensen would figure it out and talk to Mr. Jensen, who would take it upon himself to have a talk with Eric. I am not predicting this is what will happen, but I did know Mr. Jensen and it seemed like something he would do.

I honestly thought going out to the club in the city would help get Lilah's mind off Tristan. Maybe it did for that one night. Maybe it made it worse. Maybe when she was having sex with Cabot she was pretending she was with Tristan. That would be exactly like something Lilah would do. So, my plan had backfired. Instead of helping Lilah get over Tristan, being with Cabot made her want him more.

If it had been anyone other than Lilah I would've been like, fuck it. I give up. But it was Lilah and you don't give up on your best friend. Ever. If I didn't take care of her, who would? Certainly not Eric and recruiting Eric now was unthinkable anyhow. I mean, what would I say? Oh, by the way Eric, your wife is obsessed with a teenager. She also had sex with him outside, up against your house while you were inside watching Game of Thrones.

Who did I recruit? Not any of the children. That's for sure. Not any of my other friends. Did I have other friends? Not Lilah's mother. Lilah would kill me if I told her mother. And obviously not Tristan's "mother." In all honesty, if Tom and I were still married I could have told him. I know I cheated on him but that was, admittedly, the worst mistake I'd ever made. Tom was still a good man and I trusted him. He, obviously, no longer trusted *me* but that was my own fault.

I figured the best strategy at this point was not to recruit anyone to help me. There was no way I, or anyone else, could keep Lilah and Tristan from seeing each other. I couldn't change Lilah's mind and trying to convince a teenage guy not to have sex – with anyone - was like herding cats. There was only one thing left I could do.

Protect them.

Lilah

In the Spring I enrolled Maria in a day school at the Baptist church my mother went to every Sunday. A lot of mothers did it and used that precious part of their day to get groceries or clean or even do laundry without interruption. A little sliver of peace in an otherwise tumultuous day. I didn't do it for any of those reasons. I did it so I could be with Tristan.

We spent as much time together as we could manage. We went to parks and movie matinees. We made out in the back seat of my car behind vacant buildings. I always wrote notes to excuse him from class, so he wouldn't have unexcused absences. We played checkers on the picnic table in my backyard. He always won. We took the little boat out into the pond and almost tipped it over. He helped me paint the living room and I introduced him to the wonders of ***Frozen Tequila***.

We took long showers in the marble shower in my bedroom. We made love in my bed, on the oriental carpet in my living room, the dining room table, in the field behind my house. We watched old movies and fed each other popcorn. One day he made love to me in a kitchen chair inside the pantry. It was one of the most erotic moments of my life because it was the first time someone told me what was going to happen before it did. Afterward he tipped the chair backward and it hit up against the shelves behind him. He held it there with his foot while I buttoned my shirt.

"You're going to turn us over," I said and laughed. He rocked the chair back and forth on its back legs.

"Ya think?"

"Tristan. Stop it." He wrapped one of his arms around me and kissed me full on the lips, pointing to a shelf high above us.

"Which one of us is going up there to get that economy size box of tissues? Because I think we might need them." I smiled and shook my head.

"You're so silly sometimes," I said as I pulled my hair out of the back of my shirt. He stood up and I grabbed him around the neck as he hoisted me against him. "Tristan!!"

I wrapped my legs around him and his jeans fell to his ankles as we collapsed into the wall behind me. I reached for a shelf to steady us and a huge plastic container of pretzels tumbled to the floor and burst open. He held me against the wall.

"Tristan! I mean it!"

"Me, too." He nuzzled his face into my neck. "Let's do it again."

"Tristan! Seriously." He loosened his grip as I took my legs from around him. He let me down easily and I stood in front of him.

"Turn around," he said.

I turned around without question and he took my hands in his and placed them on the wall in front of me. I looked to the floor. He ran his fingers down my arms and rested his hands on my waist. He leaned in close to my ear.

"You're under arrest," he said. I laughed.

"For what?"

"You know," he whispered.

Early on a Tuesday morning the following week he walked through my back door into the kitchen like he lived there. He had on ragged jeans and a dark red t-shirt. It took me a few minutes to read it. It said, 'I love how in scary movies the person yells out "Hello?" As if the killer is going to be like, "Yeah, I'm in the kitchen, want a sandwich?"' I laughed out loud.

"Where did you get that?" He smiled.

"Tiffany. She gave it to me for Christmas last year because she knows I hate horror movies. She thinks it's funny, so I wear it to amuse her."

"Why?"

"Why does it amuse her?"

"No. Why do you hate horror movies? Do they scare you?" He smiled and looked at me resignedly.

"Seriously?" Do I look like the kind of person who would be scared of a horror movie?" I raised my eyebrows at him.

"You never know."

"Hmm."

"What are you doing today? I asked leaning up against the sink. "Don't you ever go to school?"

"Sometimes."

He walked over to me, placed his hands on my neck and touched his lips to mine. It wasn't what most people called a peck because his lips were always open. Consequently, so were mine. It made me dizzy. He knew exactly how to elicit the kind of response in me he wanted, whenever he wanted it.

"I want to spend a night with you," he whispered. I pulled away from him.

"That's not possible," I said. He stood back and put his hands on his hips as if it shocked him I'd said no.

"Why not?"

"Because," I said. "It's not possible. How am I supposed to make that happen?"

"Don't you have anyone who can cover for you?" he asked. "Like maybe Isabel? She seems like she'd be a good liar."

"Funny," I said. He shrugged.

I stood there looking at him. The dark eyes, the long lashes surrounding them, the silver cross that always hung around his neck. Spending a night with him seemed like a luxury but a luxury I couldn't afford.

"Um," I managed. "Maybe." He grabbed the belt loops of my jean shorts and pulled me into him.

"Lilah," he said. "I'm sure it will not come as a surprise to you when I tell you I can barely control myself when I'm around you. It takes every ounce of energy I have not to pick you up right now and take you upstairs to bed."

"I don't recall you having a bed upstairs to take me to," I said as he picked me up by my waist and twirled me around.

"You are correct," he said as he put me down. He motioned to the kitchen table, gave me that sultry look he knew drove me crazy. I laughed.

"No! Are you nuts?"

Today, he had a scent that reminded me of the teaberry gum my mother used to buy me when I was little. I didn't think they made it anymore, but it was sweet and minty and smelled like the woods in winter. He looked at his watch.

"I need to go."

He leaned into me, his lips barely touching my ear.

"I have a test in world studies in ten minutes," he whispered as if it were a secret.

"Did you study?" I asked.

"It's an essay," he explained as he backed away. He stuck his hands into his front pockets. "I got this."

And just like that, he slipped through the back door and was gone.

I took a deep breath and wondered if it was a daydream or if Tristan had truly been in my kitchen, picking me up, twirling me around, making me crazy. Fifteen minutes later I was still leaning back against the kitchen sink mesmerized when Eric walked into the room.

"What are you doing here?" I asked in awe. My heart beat faster.

"Wow," he said walking toward me. He sat his briefcase down in the kitchen chair. "What a nice welcome." He placed his hand on my waist and kissed my cheek.

"I thought I'd come home and have lunch with my incredible and amazing wife." He chuckled. "Am I allowed to do that?"

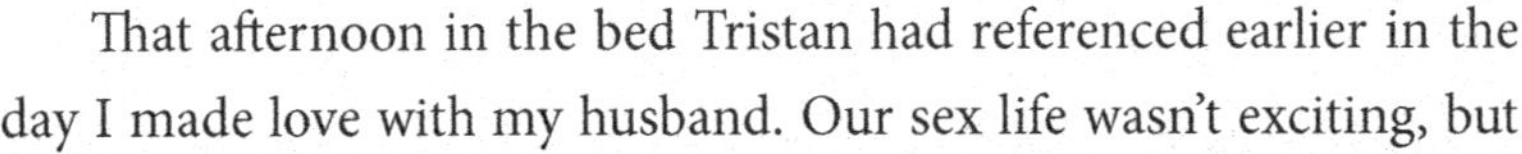

That afternoon in the bed Tristan had referenced earlier in the day I made love with my husband. Our sex life wasn't exciting, but it had always been tender and comforting. After all these years it seemed Eric still had a passion for me I would never understand.

As a little girl when I'd thought about the man of my dreams I had always thought about someone like Eric. I thought college would be where I'd meet him – the man in my dreams - but it never happened. Maybe I didn't give love a chance. Maybe I was hung up on my idea of perfection. I wasn't willing to negotiate anything, and I never thought about the possibility there might not be anyone out there to meet my idea of perfection. Once I concluded sleeping with everyone on campus wasn't the right way to find him I moved through school like I was on auto-pilot. Every day was a chore, a monotonous routine that replayed itself over every morning. I woke up, went to class, came back to my dorm, studied, and went to bed. I knew there had to be something wrong with me if the only reason boys wanted to be with me was because I was "a good time." I relied on that routine to make the rest of my life tolerable. I ended up only adhering to that routine on Mondays and Tuesdays because one Wednesday night I discovered there was a reprieve: college night at the local bar.

You didn't have to be of age to drink at Illusions. Everyone drank at Illusions and everyone knew everyone drank at Illusions. So, it began with Wednesday nights. Soon it was Wednesday and Thursday nights then Friday and Saturday nights because they were party nights for everyone. I partied and passed out in various locations. During the week I hoped I'd wake up in time for class the next day. Sometimes I did. Most times, I did not.

When I met McCain, I was working in a dingy dive bar called Leslie's, serving free drinks to the men who, in return, satisfied my need to feel loved. It was a confirmation I wouldn't go home alone. Sometimes I went home. Most nights, I did not. McCain offered to save me when I was expelled from my dorm because I never met curfew. We'd been sleeping together for about a week when I moved in with him. We drank all day, every day. I went to school drunk. I went to work drunk. I was never not drunk. And then there were the drugs.

Eventually it caught up with me. I sometimes got to class on time. I sometimes showed up for quizzes and tests. I sometimes called my friends who wanted to know where I was and if I was okay. I was my own worst enemy. I had wanted friends who cared where I was and what I was doing but then when they called to check on me I never returned their calls. Even when they called over and over I'd ignore them – because I had McCain.

McCain took care of me when I was sick, satisfied my drug addiction and left me breathless every time he touched me. I craved his body against mine. I never got tired of being twisted around him at night. His breaths were my breaths. We breathed together. This, I thought, was love.

But some mornings I would wake up and he'd be gone. He would always leave me a note telling me how much he loved me and how he'd be back soon. There was always a fresh pot of coffee on those mornings and every now and then doughnuts from the shop on the corner. He never told me where he was going. Sometimes I saw him the next day. Sometimes I didn't see him again for a week and then he'd show up one night at Leslie's while I was working. I always thought he looked like he had just stepped off the cover of *The Outsiders* with his hair slicked back, wearing ripped jeans and his black leather jacket. He would walk toward me with an intent in his eyes everyone else took for disdain, but it always made me smile. I knew from experience when he looked at other people that way it meant they should be figuring out whether they needed to buy him a drink or leave the bar altogether.

McCain was like an insurance policy and being McCain's girl meant something. To me it meant my every need was anticipated and fulfilled before I even knew I needed it – whatever it was – and it was usually some of kind of drug that left me wanting more. It seemed no matter what went wrong in my life he could fix it. If he couldn't fix it, he and his "boys" made sure someone did. No one questioned McCain's authority. He was like Tristan in one way because when McCain talked, people listened.

One night after McCain was gone for several days I sat down to have a drink with Leslie before my shift began. It had become a habit with us and I felt a kind of respect for Leslie. I talked. He mostly listened. He treated McCain and I like we were his children, always protective in a way only a father could be. He didn't ask unnecessary questions because he already knew the answers. I was a little taken aback that night when he did ask a question. He asked me if I had looked in the mirror lately. I shrugged him off, but I knew it meant he knew what I knew: too much, too long, nearly too late.

I stood in front of mirrors every night before I went out on the floor, but I hadn't been seeing what everyone else saw. I saw what I wanted to see. Later that night, in the bright lights of the back room I looked at myself and I didn't like what I saw.

I wasn't the Lilah with the bouncy hair and the enchanting green eyes. I wasn't the Lilah who had a year-round tan and a perfectly shaped figure. I was pale and anorexic. I had dark circles under my eyes. I realized none of my clothes fit me anymore and I always felt a little bit nauseated. I couldn't remember the last time I had painted my nails or worn mascara. I couldn't even remember the last time I had taken a shower.

That night as I stared into the mirror in front of me and wondered where McCain might be, I made a promise to myself. I wasn't going to do it anymore. I called Isabel because she was the only person who wouldn't ask me a million questions. I didn't tell McCain good-bye. Whether he would come after me, I didn't know. I knew if he did he would most certainly find me, no matter where I was.

Isabel showed up three hours later during one of the worst rainstorms I had ever seen. We later discovered it was a hurricane. She's never let me forget that. She took me in, fed me, watched me suffer through withdrawal, gave me a reason to live. I lost many nights of sleep wondering when McCain would show up, but he never did. About six weeks later I found out I was pregnant.

When Eric walked into my life several years later I suddenly felt alive again. My mother did not like the fact that he was ten years older than me or that he smoked cigarettes. I'm still not sure which one she disapproves of most.

Eric was the man you saw on the street who always dressed like he'd just walked out of a meeting that finalized a transatlantic deal. I don't think I'd ever seen him without either a tie or a jacket. He rarely wore jeans unless we were going to be outside for an extended period. He was the one who taught me it was always better to be over-dressed than to wonder whether you could meet the dress code. Hence, why our boys never wore shirts without a collar when we went to dinner.

He exuded confidence and wisdom. He never complained about how I ran the household and gave me a piece of fine jewelry for every special occasion – birthdays, anniversaries, holidays, even the birth of our children. One day he came home with a garnet necklace. Ben's birthstone. I cried on and off for days. When he found out our favorite jewelry store was going out of business he went in without my knowledge and bought me diamond earrings, a diamond necklace

– which was my birthstone - and a gold bangle bracelet. The gold bangle bracelet I never took off. Ever.

Our children looked up to him, respected him, never questioned his authority. When I threatened them with the typical "wait until your father gets home," they knew they better get their act together or else face a stern reprimand that would make the Pope feel guilty. Eric wasn't a hands-on parent. Those stern talks worked fine for him because the kids knew there would be consequences for bad choices and most often they were in accordance with the offense.

After Vonnie was born I went into a deep post-partum depression. No amount of medicine or care seemed to help. Although Isabel would say Eric did nothing to help, he did. He just got tired of doing it. That was when my doctor suggested I take a break from "real" life and go to a treatment center for a little while. Her and Eric both agreed I needed some breathing room. People say once you go to jail you are never the same person again. I think that must be true of mental institutions as well because once you go there you are never the same person again either. They take something from you. A part of your soul is missing afterward.

Once I returned home Eric suggested we move back to Woodlawn to be closer to my parents. His mother lived halfway across the country and I think he felt my mother was the only other person he could count on to take care of the children if I lost my mind altogether. At the time it did not seem entirely out of the question I may not be able to handle the care of three children under the age of eight.

To compensate for us leaving the home we both loved Eric let me pick an old farmhouse in my hometown. Owning an old house had always been a fantasy of mine and it just so happened one of the houses I'd loved for years was up for sale at the same time we were looking to buy. Eric must have seen the look on my face as we walked across the property under huge old oak trees and down a sloping hill to a small pond complete with four white geese. I could remember fishing in that pond as a child. As we stood there at the bottom of the hill and looked back up toward the house he took my hand and looked over to me.

"This is what you want," he said. "Isn't it?" I smiled.

"Yes. Can we afford it?

"Not really, but if it will make you better it will be worth it to me."

"Oh Eric, I don't want you to do that. You like the brick rancher over on Estes Street."

"And you hate it." We started walking back up the hill.

"It's dark and gloomy," I explained.

"This one is full of old house smell and dust."

"I know," I said ruefully.

All three kids came running down the hill toward us, my mother following them.

"This house is not what Lilah needs, Eric. It's too big. She'll never be able to keep it clean."

"She's in love with it," he said.

"I'm in love with her father but that doesn't mean I want to live with him all the time."

"Mom!"

"It's too late anyhow," Eric said. "I already signed the papers."

"You did?!" I exclaimed. Eric had sacrificed a lot for me over the years. My problem was that I rarely appreciated it.

The medicine my doctor put me on while I was in the hospital ended up being exactly what I needed, and I was able to be a good mother to our children. They grew up in a house where we sat around the dinner table every night and discussed our day. Everyone had a turn and it sparked some interesting conversations. Eric and I were not strict parents, but we did have rules that were not negotiable.

Our children knew you never spoke to an adult unless they spoke to you first. They were all taught which fork was the oyster fork and how it was proper to turn your utensils upside down when you finished eating so the waiter knew it was okay to take your plate. (My mother.) They all knew to order their steak medium rare. (Eric.) They knew to answer the phone with 'Trenton Residence' and that 'Yes Ma'am', 'No Sir', 'Please' and 'Thank you' were not optional but expected. They all knew they had to sit at the top of the stairs Christmas morning until Eric and I had a cup of coffee. (That was me because I am the devil until I get a little caffeine in my system.)

Their friends knew I stocked the freezer with chicken nuggets and mini-bagels covered in cheese. It didn't matter who you were or where you were from, you were always welcome in our home. (That was me, also. I loved a house full of activity.) Everyone was familiar with the electric glitch that set off the house alarm when the lights blinked and how to disarm it. Everyone knew which boards in the foyer creaked when you stepped on them in the middle of the night and that the clean kid's plates were in the bottom drawer of the dishwasher. They all knew we didn't use paper plates or cups indoors because it was trashy. (My mother.)

One summer, I think Ben and Michael were around ten and twelve, they saw a commercial on television for a pool. Because I loved to give the children what they wanted, I ask Eric about it when he got home from work that night.

"No," he said. "They are too expensive and too much work. We'll have it for one summer and then the kids will never use it again."

I complained to my mother the next day hoping to get a little sympathy. Maybe her and Daddy would want to put one in for the grandchildren.

"Are you crazy?" she asked me. "No. Absolutely not."

"Well, what about we get a little above ground pool for them?"

My mother looked at me like I'd lost my mind.

"Did I not teach you anything? Above ground pools are tacky. You live in a beautiful, historic home, not a trailer. Plus, it would devalue the house. Inground pools turn houses into estates. Above ground pools make you look like you shop at Walmart."

"Mom, that is crazy."

"Mm…"

Still, no pool. You can imagine how excited the children were when Tom and Isabel bought an entire house built around a pool.

"See?" Eric said. "Problem solved. Now the kids have a pool and Tom can clean it."

One night, Eric came home with a huge bird cage covered in a white muslin cover. The children followed him into the kitchen like he was the pied piper. I turned around from the stove, a pot holder in my hand, just as Eric pulled off the cover.

"Cool!" Ben said. "A bird!!"

"Yay!" Vonnie said. "A bird!!"

Michael stared at it. It was jet black with a yellow beak.

"What is that?" I asked.

"It's a crow," he replied.

"What? Are you nuts? That thing could have fleas, lice, who knows what else."

"Like I could chase down a crow and put it in a cage." Michael laughed. "It's not a crow. It's a Myna bird."

"What is a Myna bird? I've never heard of one."

"They are indigenous to southern Asia, mainly India."

"Do I want to know where it came from?"

"Funny story."

I sat down at the kitchen table. The kids all lurked around the bird and it stared back with its beady eyes.

"You know I talk to people all over the world, every day."

"Uh-huh."

"Indivar came into town today and this is what he brought me. He said it was a gift for my children."

"Are you kidding?"

"No, and I'm sure you are just as surprised as I was, but he is a pretty cool bird. I think we should keep him."

"Look!" Vonnie said. "He's pooping."

"Eric? I am going to kill you. You know good and well I will be cleaning up after this bird by myself."

"I'll help," Ben said. "What's his name? Does he have one?"

"Indivar told me his name is Rufaat, but he prefers Ru." I put my hand my forehead. "Oh, my Lord."

"He talks," Eric offered as if that were a consolation. "Tell him hello, Veronica."

"Hello," she said as she walked closer to his cage.

"Hello, hello, hello," the bird sang.

"Cool," said Michael. "Does he say other things?"

"I'm not sure," Eric said. "But Indivar said they are like mocking birds. They repeat everything they hear."

"Perfect," I said.

"Perfect, perfect, perfect."

I took a deep breath. The "perfect" place for Ru ended up being in the breakfast nook because there were windows on three sides.

He didn't repeat everything he heard, only one word at a time. Prior to Ru I had a horrible bad language habit but once he took over the kitchen saying bad words became less of a routine because whatever you said, Ru repeated three times.

The next day Isabel came through the front door. Not with her typical, hey, hey, hey but just, hey. Of course, Ru repeated it as she walked into the kitchen.

"What the hell is that?"

So, I had to explain the whole story to her.

"I would take that damn thing to the pound." I poured her a cup of coffee.

"You can't take birds to the pound, Isabel. That's only dogs and cats."

"Damn."

"Damn, damn, damn."

"He only repeats one word at a time," I explained.

"Have the kids started teaching him dirty words yet?" She laughed.

"I don't think you can actually teach him anything. He only imitates words. And sounds," I added. "Watch this."

I opened the back door, reached outside, and rang the doorbell. Predictably Ru repeated the doorbell sound three times.

"Holy shit," Isabel said. "I have to admit he's pretty cool and obviously smart. Will he live forever like most birds?"

"Probably. That would be just my luck."

Over the years, once Eric brought Ru home we had every pet you can imagine from a hamster to a corn snake and everything in between. When one died we'd get something else, but Ru lived on.

I was the only person in the house he continually tried to bite. He'd even jump on Isabel's hand. I hated that bird. I still hate him.

As mine and Isabel's children grew older they began to spend time down at the pond with their friends. On Mondays I'd go down and collect all the cups, beer cans and sometimes panties, even jeans. How do you leave without your pants? I washed all the clothes and stacked them on the dryer. Their friends expected to hear: "look on the dryer to see if any of your clothes are there." Eric hated it but followed up the sex talk with the boys with a box of condoms.

When the boy's friends got old enough to appreciate women they started talking about how they thought Isabel and I were the "hot moms." They only said it to Ben once. Afterward they knew if they even looked at either of us sideways Ben would beat them with a baseball bat. Isabel and I discouraged them as well because we didn't want Ben to go to jail.

There was always music. All kinds of music, from country to jazz to hard rock. The hard rock was an interesting stage for Vonnie simply because she had learned how to play the drums in middle school and then, wonderful grandmother that she is, my mother gave her a drum set for Christmas. She was fourteen. Eric told her she could play it anywhere except inside our house, so she conned Ben into helping her set them up in the garden shed. Next thing you knew, Michael took his guitar out there, some other kid brought over his keyboard and voila! We had a band.

"See?" I told my mother one evening when she came over to visit. "See what you've done?"

"Oh honey," she said. "They're having the time of their lives. Enjoy it."

"My neighbors aren't enjoying it."

"Oh, stop it. Mrs. Rawlings told me the other night at prayer meeting she liked it."

Ben came flying into the kitchen and went straight for the refrigerator.

"Oh, hi Grandma." He walked over and gave my mother a hug.

"Hi honey," she said patting the back of his head. He was about a foot taller than her. He went flying out the back door.

"You know he's my favorite," my mother said.

"I know. It's because for the first year of his life you felt sorry for him."

"I did not feel sorry for him," she said as she sipped her wine. I looked up to her.

"You did."

"Eric has been a good father to him."

I warned her with my eyes because we didn't say those things out loud. Ben wasn't old enough to remember when I met and married Eric. Eric adopted him, and I changed his name at once. He still didn't know Eric wasn't his biological father, but I knew without a doubt it was better that way. I never wanted Ben to have a reason to look up McCain.

I'm not sure why Eric put up with all my shenanigans over the years. He said he loved me and I knew he did, but it was very seldom I felt lovable. I was impulsive, and my impulsivity almost always trumped my judgement – if I had any judgement at all.

Knowing myself the way I did I should have given drinking so much alcohol a little more thought but that went over my head like most things that made sense. Isabel once told me if she sat a pot of my gold at my feet I'd step over it to get to the bar on the other side. The one-night stand with Cabot was typical of my wayward behavior. I would never blame my "sins" on Isabel but she sure as hell didn't help curb my appetite - for men or booze. The problem with me and Isabel was we were too much alike. Her one redeeming quality was she wasn't bi-polar.

I'm not saying what happened between Tristan and I was because of my mental health but, like Isabel, it didn't help. I'd like to think I would have thought twice about sleeping with a teenager if I wasn't half crazy but still, whenever I think of him, I lose my breath.

I had never fallen in love with anyone else like I had with McCain until I met Tristan. I was always able to remain distant with men. Sex was fun. It was a distraction, at least for a little while, and that's exactly what Tristan was in the beginning. Fun. I didn't know I would fall in love with him. I didn't plan to fall in love with him. I didn't plan to fall in love at all. When you fall in love with someone, even if you don't want to be in love, it doesn't make it magically go away. It makes your life hell on earth.

I wanted something I knew I shouldn't have but I wanted it so much I couldn't think straight. It made me dizzy when Tristan walked past me in the kitchen or at the pool. The thing is, I had to act like he was just another kid. But he wasn't. He was everything I had always told myself I couldn't have. It wasn't his age. It was his outlook on life. No matter how horrible things got there was always an answer and if there wasn't an answer right away there would be – and it would be fine. It was also his body. I'm not going to lie.

He was famous for saying, "Lilah, relax." He said it when I turned over my glass of wine on the kitchen table, when I dropped the bucket of paint on the living room floor, when we made love and I couldn't let go.

I didn't fall in love with Tristan because of anything he did. I fell in love with him because of who he was on the inside. I kept telling myself I deserved him. Well, it was those little voices that told me I deserved him. And yes, I really had those little voices. They were like a fuzzy radio station playing inside my head and despite there being a little static in the background, I could still hear their song.

So, don't ever tell me you can't blame things on those little voices. You should, however, try to figure out if those voices are coming from a trusted Source or are an invitation for disaster. Because we all know the origin of those disaster voices, and those invitations? They are always written in gold on thick, cream colored stationary.

Isabel

I've kept Lilah's secrets all her life. Truth be told, she's kept all of mine, too. We've always joked with each other and said we could never *not* be friends because there was too much information worthy of blackmail.

When I moved from Florida up to Virginia Lilah was the only girl in our third-grade class who would sit with me for lunch. I was a little overweight as a child and Lilah protected me from the other kid's bad manners and teasing. It was essentially Lilah's mom who protected me because Lilah's mom was the elementary school PTA President. She was not someone the other mothers wanted to tango with, if you know what I mean, and she was the one who arranged our first play date. My mother thought she was a little uptight, but she was grateful Loretta had taken us under her wing and so a friendship developed - between us and them.

I was at Lilah's house most of the time because I had three younger sisters who drove me mad. She had an older brother, but he was never home and pretty much hated everyone. Except Lilah. No one hated Lilah.

Lilah was what people called a "change of life" baby. Her mother was nearly fifty when she was born so when she finally arrived she was treated more like a grandchild than an actual child. Her brother, Vernon, spoiled her rotten. It's a wonder all her teeth didn't rot out because he was always bringing her candy. She never gained a pound. She was as skinny as a stick, but she was strong and could be volatile if she didn't get her way.

I remember once when a boy who lived a few doors down from her parents pissed her off. I can't remember what he did and for that reason I can only assume it was trivial but if Lilah didn't like something all hell broke loose. It was the first time I had ever done anything I thought could harm another person. I found out later it couldn't have harmed him but at the time I was afraid he would die.

Lilah asked her mom to make us some Kool-Aid. It was cherry. Lilah's favorite flavor. We took the entire pitcher behind her garage and peed in it then offered it to Earl. He drank it and asked if Lilah's mom had forgotten to put in the sugar. Lilah shrugged and said, "Probably." I was terrified every morning Earl wouldn't show up for school, but he always did.

"See?" Lilah asked me one day at lunch. "It can't kill him. He's immune to that kind of thing."

"What does that even mean?" I asked.

"I don't know," she said taking a bite of her peanut butter and jelly sandwich. "He's just stupid."

That was Lilah's dark side, but it wasn't who Lilah was at all and about a week later I saw the other side. I walked into her room to find her sitting on her bed balling her eyeballs out.

"What's wrong?" I asked. I couldn't understand a word she was saying. "What? Tell me." She sat up.

"I'm trying to tell you!!"

"Okay." I sat wide-eyed, afraid to move.

"I feel so bad," she said.

At this point I was lost. It had a been a week. A million things had happened that week including my youngest sister cutting off part of her toe.

"About what?"

"Earl."

I thought for a moment.

"Oh, that." She nodded.

"Yeah," I said. "I feel a little bad about it, too. Should we apologize?" Lilah laughed sadly.

"I hardly think it matters now," she said. "What would it accomplish?"

She was right. It would accomplish nothing and make Earl feel horrible. It was the first time in my life I realized sometimes doing the "right" thing isn't the right thing at all.

As Lilah and I grew older we came to depend on one another for everything. We talked on the phone every night. Lilah had a phone in her room and could talk as long as she wanted. I had the hall phone and could talk for thirty minutes. With four girls in my house and all of us having thirty minutes, it tended to take up most of the evening. There were a few nights I was able to convince my Dad that, since one of my other sisters wasn't using her minutes, I should be able to use them in her absence. Every now and then he gave in and said okay.

Boys came and went. We never fought over them, but Lilah and I had an unusual rule. While most girls agreed you shouldn't neglect your friends when you got a new boyfriend, Lilah and I believed the exact opposite. We agreed when you had a boyfriend it wouldn't last forever so you should enjoy it as much as you could before he dumped you, which meant going out with him always came before going out with each other.

We planned to go to the same college and join the same sorority, but most girls know that doesn't usually happen and it didn't happen with us either. Lilah wanted to go to some preppy college down South whose campus I would have never set foot on unless I'd had to go rescue her one night during the biggest rainstorm since the great flood. I, on the other hand, decided to stay close to home and go to a local college, where I met Tom and managed to get myself knocked up before the second semester. Lilah and I both eventually graduated, but neither one of us from the school we had initially intended.

Tom wasn't ready to get married so at the tender age of twenty Lilah and I were sharing an apartment downtown with two babies, two jobs and two class schedules we worked around, so we didn't have to pay a babysitter. It was chaotic. It's funny because neither Ben nor Isaac remember those days and as much as Lilah and I would like to talk about them, we can't. Occasionally we will treat ourselves to a pedicure and dinner and talk about our insane beginnings but only then because the pedicurists are Vietnamese and don't understand half of what we're saying. We have Chinese food afterward for the same reason.

When Lilah met Eric, I'd been "dating" Tom off and on for several years. It would have been a double wedding if Tom's mother hadn't insisted we fly to St. Lucia for the wedding and Tom's mother got her way because Tom is a Mama's boy and God forbid if we disappoint "Mama." She never liked me even though I was the mother of the grandchildren she called her "angels." They did look like angels. We agreed on that. Mixed babies always do.

I married in June (also Tom's mother's idea because that's when you were supposed to have a wedding), and Lilah married the following September. Isaac was two. Ben had just turned one.

I helped Lilah quit smoking and she helped me lose the fifty pounds I gained while I was pregnant with Isaac. Lilah, of course, went back to stick size as soon as Ben popped out. Since then we'd been trying to keep each other sane. I always knew there was something a little off with Lilah. I could never quite put my finger on it, but I was certain something wasn't right when she got back from her honeymoon and told me she'd decided to put Ben up for adoption.

"Have you lost your mind completely?" I asked as she sobbed into her pillow. "What on earth possessed you to even think about that?"

"It's what's best."

"From whose perspective?" I asked. "Have you talked to Eric about this?"

"No," she cried. "From my perspective." I handed her a tissue.

"Explain this to me," I said as I sat down on her bed. "And where is Ben now?"

"He's with my mom."

"Okay." I laid my hand on her shoulder. "Explain it to me then."

"I'm not a good mother," she said as she began to cry again. "He would be so much better off if he weren't with me." This made me angry.

"What are you talking about?" I asked. "You are an amazing mother. Ben adores you."

"He won't remember me if I do it now," she said. "I can't be the kind of mother he deserves." She stood up and walked over to her dresser. I followed her, and she turned around to face me. "I am not the right kind of mom."

"I didn't realize there was a right kind of mom," I said. "Which kind am I?"

"Not like me." She twisted her new wedding band on her finger. "I didn't miss him," she said. "Not even a little bit."

"You're not supposed to miss him on your honeymoon," I said honestly. "He cries all the time. He nearly drove me mad while you were gone. Is there ever a time he stops? Because I've never witnessed it." She smiled.

"Not very often."

"Okay look," I said taking her hands. "If you are going to put Ben up for adoption then I want to adopt him." She pulled away from me, but I saw a slight smile on her face.

"You just told me he drives you mad," she said. "Why the hell would you want to do that?"

"Because you will change your mind," I said seriously. "And when you do I don't want to have to help you find him." She smiled again. "I have rescued you many times before and I'll do it again and again if you need me to, but this is not logical. It makes no sense and you're being retarded." I turned to walk away.

"Where are you going?" she asked.

"I'm going to your mother's house to get Ben," I said. "Then I'm going to the lawyer's office and get the adoption papers done. You should come with me. It'll take less time if you're there to sign them."

She ran over and hugged me tightly.

"I love you Isabel."

"No, you don't."

"I do."

"You don't. If you did you wouldn't let me adopt your devil baby."

"Very funny," she said as she pulled away. She took my hand. "You're an amazing friend. We should have a drink and celebrate our friendship."

"We should," I said.

And that's the day we created ***Happy Hour.***

I've always loved Lilah's children like I did my own. Sometimes more because when the boys were little I thought I was going to lose my mind at least once a day. At one point I had three boys under the age of five which should be an understandable reason all by itself.

Soon after Tom and I married I discovered I was pregnant again. It wasn't necessarily a happy time. I didn't want to be pregnant. I can't remember whether I cried more because it was a boy or because I was pregnant in general. Either way, I cried a lot.

I know postpartum depression exists because of Lilah but is there such a thing as pre-partum depression? Because if there is, I had it. And if there's not, there should be. I can't possibly be the only person who was depressed their entire pregnancy. I kept telling Tom not to worry because I was sure I would love it as soon as I saw it. He shook his head and reminded me I was calling our baby an "it."

I would never in a million years tell any of this to Matt. He has turned out to be a wonderful child and now I am happy he came when he did. As it turns out, once he was born I *did* love him. I fell *in* love with him. I think in the beginning I was afraid he would turn out like Ben and cry incessantly day in and out, but he barely cried at all. Just when I thought things were getting easier I found out I was pregnant again. I told Tom if he didn't get a vasectomy we would never have sex again. How many people do you know who've gotten pregnant three times in a row using a condom while on birth control?

I know Lilah would have helped me if she'd been nearby but while Tom and I had chosen to live in Woodlawn, Eric already had a house one town over, so naturally Lilah moved in with him. Not long after she moved even further away, and I rarely got to see her or her children at all, but we talked on the phone every day. We had a standing phone appointment of ten in the morning. By then we had fed and dressed our children and could sit down and chat without constant interruption. We called it "Barney" time because we sat the kids in front of the television with Barney the dinosaur and dared them to get up. Kool aid and goldfish were the staples of our homes. Once, I decided to vacuum out the sofa and lifted the cushions to find two cups of crushed goldfish. When I say cups, I mean measurement cups. I know this because I poured them out of the vacuum cleaner bin, so I could see how much was in there. I'm weird like that. Knowing answers to trivial questions is a form of amusement to me. Lilah thinks it's because I have a chemistry degree. It's not. It's just because I love math and have OCD.

"How do you know it was two cups?" Tom asked when he got home from work that day.

"Because I poured them out and measured them."

"Do I even want to know what else was in there?"

"No," I assured him. "You do not."

Every now and then Lilah would come for a day visit and bring all the kids. Maria hadn't been born but together we had five boys under the age of eight. And then there was Vonnie. I always felt sorry for Vonnie because she never had anyone to play with her. It's a wonder the boys didn't kill her. I know now why she turned out so tough. She had no choice. It was fight or die. Since she had gotten older she knew, like Lilah and I did, if you give boys an inch they'll take a mile. In *so* many ways.

Late one summer afternoon as Lilah and I sat in my back yard – this was before Tom and I bought the house with the pool – we looked around and noticed Vonnie was missing.

"Where is your sister?" Lilah asked Ben. His mouth was red with Kool-Aid stains.

"I don't know," he said. Lilah grabbed him by his arm.

"You do to," she said. "Tell me."

He pointed to a tree on the side of the yard. Lilah and I turned around to see Vonnie tied to the tree with a jump rope. We both jumped up, knocking over our lawn chairs and ran across the yard. Vonnie was standing there, a grim look on her face but she wasn't crying. Vonnie never cried.

"Oh sweetie," Lilah said. "Mommy is so sorry. What happened? Did the boys do this to you? She nodded.

"Which ones?" I asked as Lilah and I tried to figure out how to get her loose.

Her bangs were too long, and she looked at us from under them with her cool, green eyes.

"They're going to die," she said solemnly. Lilah and I stared at each other.

"Honey," Lilah coaxed. "Tell Mommy what happened."

"They're going to die," she said again.

"Okay," I said hesitantly. "How about we go get some ice cream?" Vonnie nodded.

She skipped off toward the house with Lilah and I following behind.

"That was weird," I said to Lilah

"We should keep a close eye on the boys," she replied. "You know, in case she tries to kill them."

"She's three," I reminded her. "What could she possibly do?"

"She scares me sometimes," Lilah said. We didn't realize Isaac had walked up behind us.

"She scares me, too," he said.

"Oh, don't be silly," I told him tussling his hair.

I think to this day the boys are still afraid of Vonnie. She has that "take no prisoners" attitude. It's proved helpful to her over the course of her life, especially since Maria was born.

Most of Maria's care fell on Vonnie when Lilah's condition worsened. Once Lilah had Maria she was seldom in a motherly frame of mind and after Tristan came into the picture she had a tough time being a mother at all.

Lilah

"I need a favor," I said to Isabel the following week while we were cleaning her bathrooms. Isabel had six bathrooms and it would be a sin against our friendship if I didn't help her clean them once a week.

"You're asking *me* for a favor? Imagine that." She pulled the curtain shut on Isaac's shower.

"I need you to cover for me one weekend soon." She narrowed her eyes at me.

"Why?"

"Because Tristan and I are going to a little cottage in the mountains for the night." She threw her hands up in the air.

"He's legal," I said in defense.

"He's still a teenager!"

"Point taken." I sat down on the toilet.

"This will be bad if you get caught," she said. I laughed. "It's not funny."

"Not that," I said. "You standing there waving that toilet brush around." She ignored me.

"This isn't some random guy no one knows," she continued.

"I know that."

"Which means everyone who matters to you already knows and loves Tristan. Can you imagine the outcome of that?"

"Well, I wouldn't say everyone loves him."

"Most people love him, Lilah."

"You hate him."

"I don't hate him. I just hate the idea of you *and* him and then only because I know what the consequences from all this will be. Get up. I need to clean that toilet."

"I'm a grown woman, Isabel."

"Yeah, but you're not acting like one." She stood with her hands on her hips, the toilet brush dangling from one hand. "I want you to seriously consider all the implications of this." I brought my hands to my face.

"I know." She threw the toilet brush into the sink and squatted in front of me.

"What is it about him? Why?"

"He touches me." Isabel looked to the ceiling.

"Yeah. I'll bet."

"Not like that, you pervert!"

"Well, I'm thinking at this point he must have a fucking magic wand."

"Stop it!" I said but I was laughing.

"I'm trying to figure out why he's so worth it, honey. Why is he worth all this trouble? You could have any man you wanted. Not to mention, you have Eric."

"You say that like you're completely disgusted by Eric."

"Eh…"

"I don't really know why he's worth it."

"What do you mean you don't really know?

"He knows me."

"*I* know you," she said. "Better than anyone."

"He understands my depression. He even knows about the bi-polar thing." She pointed to her chest.

"So, do I."

I only had but so much patience when it came to this kind of thing. I wanted what I wanted and that needed to be the end of it. I shoved Isabel out of the way and stood up.

"Oh my God, Isabel! Stop asking me so many goddamn questions. Are you going to do this for me or not?"

She stood up beside me. The fact I'd pushed her out of the way didn't matter. Our friendship was past the kind of immaturity that reasoned anything other than my impatience.

"Are you going to regret this?" I looked over to her.

"I don't know."

"The thing with you is…you're going to do this no matter what I say."

"Yeah."

She sat down on the edge of the tub and I sat back down on the toilet. We sat in silence for a few minutes, but I could tell she was furious. Not with me but with the fact I wouldn't listen to her, that she couldn't get through to me and now she would have to sit idly by and watch me self-destruct.

"I love him," I finally said.

"What?!"

"I love him."

"No. You don't."

"I do. I promise you. I do."

"Good God, Lilah. I don't even know what to say to that."

"Can you just do this for me?" I asked.

"Are you serious? You really want to do this?"

"I think so."

"I don't like it," she said without even considering my answer.

"Please?" She sighed.

"I'm not sure who I'm going to hate more after this, you or me."

I smiled but it wasn't because I was getting my way. It was because I knew Isabel would have done the same thing. She just didn't want to admit it.

"Can you do me one favor?" she asked.

"What?"

"Take a box of condoms with you."

"Tristan is fine. We already had that discussion." She shook her head. "Sometimes I wonder if he's even been with anyone other than me."

"That's disappointing."

"Why?"

"I just have these dreams at night…I wake up covered in sweat…" She grinned at me evilly. "Him being an inexperienced lover totally screws that up for me." I wasn't amused.

"I'm serious, Isabel. Plus, you know I'm on birth control. I don't need condoms."

"Lilah?"

"Yeah?"

"How did I get pregnant with all three of my children?" I thought about the truth of this question.

"Okay," I said, annoyed. "I get it."

"Thank you."

We stood, and I picked up the toilet brush out of the sink. I turned to her.

"Do you really dream about him at night?" She smiled and nodded.

"Sometimes."

The following week Eric told me he had work "friends" coming over for dinner. I ask him whatever happened to taking people out to restaurants. He said he wanted them to meet our family.

"Is it Vladimir or whatever that man's name is?"

"Who?" he asked thoroughly confused.

"The man who gave us that damn bird because if it is, I want to poison him."

"Oh Lilah," he laughed. "You crack me up sometimes. Do you know that??"

Isabel came over to help me prepare. We were cutting up vegetables and three bottles of wine in when she held up her cucumber.

"Cheap date," she said. "You don't need to take me out to dinner. Just take me to the grocery store and buy me a cucumber." We rolled in laughter.

"You know what I hate?" I said as I cut peppers in half.

"Hmm?"

"I hate it when a man automatically assumes you want to go down on him. I mean, don't get me wrong. I enjoy it as much as any woman."

"Most women don't enjoy that." I pointed my knife at her.

"But you do, right?"

"Well, yeah, but we aren't most women."

"True."

"I look at some of the women at the PTA meetings sometimes and I think about how long it must have been since they had an orgasm. Because you know with that scrunched up look they have on their faces, they can't possibly have done anything enjoyable in the last decade."

"You know," I pointed my knife at her again. "I think a lot of women don't get as much pleasure after they have kids. They look at their sexual organs like production machines."

"Milk will never come out of these nipples," she said pointing her knife at her boobs. I laughed. "If I didn't have a good orgasm every now and then I think I would spontaneously combust."

"I know, right?"

"I guess we're every man's fantasy."

"Well, duh." I motioned to our bodies. "Look at us. How many women do you know who can still get away with wearing a bikini at our age?"

"Can you think of anything sexual a man has wanted you to do over the years you've not done?" she asked thoughtfully.

"Um," I laid down my knife on the counter and pretended to think. "Well, I had this boyfriend one time that had a foot fetish and wanted to come on my feet all the time. It was weird as hell, but I let him do it."

"I think I remember that," she said. "Tom always wanted me wear that black vampire dress. Remember?"

"Remember the time you put in the vampire teeth?" She bent over and held her sides.

"He about had a heart attack when I opened my mouth."

"Well, you were in between his legs," I pointed out.

"Men are so weird," she said. "Where do these fantasies come from?"

"Porn," I said. "Men love porn."

Ben came storming into the kitchen.

"What the fuck, Mom?"

I looked over to Isabel and she shrugged. I looked back to Ben. He threw his backpack on the kitchen table and strode over to me.

"I beg your pardon? What did you say?"

"What the hell is going on with you and Tristan?"

"What are you talking about?"

Dear God, I prayed. Please don't let this be happening.

"There is a rumor going around at school that you and Tristan are sleeping together. Is it true?"

"Of course not." Isabel tried to step between us.

"Okay," she said. "You need to calm down, Ben. Think about what you're saying."

"I know what I'm saying," he said. "I'm not stupid." He looked back over to me. "He's always here, talking to you. You know, I thought, 'What could they possibly be talking about?' But now? It all makes sense. Because you're doing more than just talking. Aren't you?"

"This is crazy," Isabel said. I stood there, immobile, waiting to see if what was happening was truly happening.

"You're lying," Ben said. "Both of you are lying. I can see it on your faces."

I shoved Isabel out of the way and grabbed Ben by his arm, twisting it behind his back before he knew what was coming. Most people didn't know what I was capable of, including at that moment, Ben.

"Don't you dare talk to me that way," I spat. I tightened my grip on his arm." And if you ever talk to me that way again the consequences will be a hell of lot worse than this. Do you understand me?" He didn't answer.

"DO YOU UNDERSTAND ME?"

"You're hurting me!"

Isabel had stepped back and was leaning against the counter. If she had thought about doing something she had now changed her mind.

"I am *not* hurting you," I said. "If I wanted to hurt you, you'd be on your knees. Now let me ask you again. DO YOU UNDERSTAND ME??" I was on the verge of tears.

"Yes! Let me go!"

"What?"

"Yes Ma'am."

I released his arm and he jerked away from me, began walking across the room.

"Stop!" I yelled across the kitchen. "I did not dismiss you."

He stopped and turned around.

"Do not *ever* disrespect me like that again." He was silent. He was probably afraid to say anything else. He should have been. "Have I made myself clear?"

"Yes, ma'am."

"You may go."

I took a deep breath. My entire body was shaking. Isabel walked over and put her arm around me.

"Are you okay?" I nodded.

Vonnie walked into the kitchen holding her phone in her hand as if she were getting ready to call someone.

"*What* is going on?" she asked.

"Nothing," I said as I started to chop vegetables again. "Just your brother being your brother." She looked to Isabel.

"What is going on?" she asked again.

"Everything is fine," Isabel reassured her. "Ben is just a little upset."

"A little? It sounded like World War III in here."

"It's fine," I said. "Where's Maria?"

"I'm here!" Maria said peering through Vonnie's legs.

"I'll take Maria for a walk," Isabel said. Then to Maria, "Let's go, honey. Let's walk down to the pond, look for the fish." She glanced over her shoulder to me as she took Maria's hand.

"What is going on?" Vonnie asked for the third time as she sat down at the kitchen table. She pulled her school books out of her backpack. "I have so much homework."

Veronica was my favorite child. I know you're not supposed to have one, but I did. She was my second, my first little girl after a rambunctious boy who nearly drove me crazy. She wasn't a little girl anymore. Where had all the years gone? I sat down at the table with her and tucked a lock of her dark hair behind her ear. It was halfway down her back.

"I'm sorry, honey. Is there anything I can help you with?"

"Yeah. You can take my biology test for me tomorrow." I smiled.

"I don't think that's possible." She looked over to me.

"Maybe Isabel can fix it."

We laughed together because we both knew Isabel would never do that kind of thing – for anyone. This was one of those rare moments when Vonnie's actions proved she still cared about me. And, yes. I did question whether she cared about me sometimes. A lot more often than I wanted to admit. There weren't very many moments when Vonnie showed she still loved me and when she did, it never lasted very long.

"Vonnie," I said. "You know I'll always love you no matter what, right?" She looked over to me.

"Why are you asking me that?" I shrugged.

"I don't know." I laid my head on her shoulder. I reminded myself: This isn't a normal fling. This is playing with fire.

"Does Tristan know about the rumors?" she asked as if she could read my mind. Sometimes I honestly thought she could.

"What?"

"The rumor about you guys at school. Does he know?"

"I don't know if he knows," I admitted. "I imagine he does. Why?" She turned to me.

"Mom, come on. You can tell me."

"Tell you what, honey?"

She jumped up and grabbed her books, shoved her chair under the table. Typical Vonnie. Her moods changed from one minute to the next. Now she wasn't my sweet, little Vonnie. Now she was a mercurial nightmare.

"Fine. Don't tell me, but I see the way you look at Tristan and so does everyone else." She held her books close to her chest. "There's nothing respectful about any of this. If anything, you should be embarrassed to be a part of it."

"What the hell are you talking about?"

"Don't act like you don't know. Tristan's reputation precedes him. You think word doesn't get around from school to school? He's using you and you're letting him."

"What??"

"It doesn't work with me," she said. "I'm not that dumb. I won't get caught."

I stood up from the table as she ran up the back staircase.

"Veronica Lauren!" I called as I walked to the foot of the stairs. "Come back here."

She ignored me, and I should have gone after her, but I didn't. I wasn't mentally prepared for the kind of argument that would ensue between us. Isabel and Maria came through the screen door as I turned around to walk back over to the table. Vonnie's bedroom door slammed so hard it shook the house.

"Well," Isabel said. "I see Vonnie is being Vonnie."

"And Ben is being Ben."

She opened the refrigerator and pulled out the Kool-Aid, poured a glass for Maria.

"Kool-Aid?" she asked as she held up the pitcher.

"Sure," I said. "Why not?" She smiled.

"I can put vodka in it."

"Even better."

The next morning after everyone had left for school and Eric had gone to work, Tristan popped through the back door. I was sitting at the kitchen table with a cup of coffee wondering how to justify my relationship with him to Ben and Vonnie or if I should even try. After all, they were my kids. I didn't need their permission to do anything, much less have a love affair.

"Hi," he said as he sat down at the end of the table. He reached over for my hand. "You look like you're in another world."

"I am. Kind of."

"What's wrong?" I took a sip of my coffee.

"Ben."

"What about Ben?"

"He confronted me about us yesterday."

"What did you say?"

"I denied it, of course." Tristan looked relieved. "Then I showed him how I can still take him down if I need to." I laughed nervously.

"Wait a minute," he said. "What?"

"I man-handled him," I said. Tristan looked at me suspiciously.

"What does that mean?" he asked.

"It means I put him in a position where he couldn't get away from me without hurting himself. At least not until he said what I wanted him to say."

"Lilah," he said. "You're starting to scare me."

"Oh, ha ha. Like I could hurt Ben."

"I'm only wondering what you could have possibly done to put him in that position."

"It's an old technique," I bragged. "I've been doing it for years."

"With who?" he asked surprised.

"Anyone who doesn't agree with me." He raised his eyebrows.

"I'm kidding," I said. "You have to be aggressive with boys. It's the only thing they respect."

"Hmm…"

"Anyhow, it's fine."

The longer I talked to Tristan the better I felt. I could talk my way out of anything – to someone else, to myself. It was a like a verbal power point presentation. Everything I said was one point closer to the ending I wanted.

"So, I shouldn't be worried?"

"No. I don't think so. I'm not sure where Ben is getting his information, though."

"What could he possibly have heard? Or seen?"

"I don't know. Maybe we've taken some chances we shouldn't have taken but I can't imagine anyone having seen us when we're together that way."

"What's *that* way?"

"I don't think we should worry at this point. Are you going to school today?"

"You ask me that like I have a choice."

"Don't you?"

"Not really," he said. "I've missed too many days. I've got to get my act together."

"Uh-oh," I said chidingly. He stood up from the table then reached down with his hand and took my chin in his fingers. I looked up to him.

"I want you to know this means something to me," he said. "This isn't just fun and games for me."

“I kind of like being fun and games, “I teased.

“I didn’t plan it this way,” he said as he leaned back against the counter behind him. “It’s making my life way too complicated.”

“It?”

“You, I mean.”

“Wow. Thanks.” He shook his head, looked down and smiled.

“I’m wondering,” he said. “Do you think we should still take our trip? I mean, where do we go from here?” I sat back in my chair.

“Are you joking?”

“No,” he said. “Why would I be?”

“Please don’t do that to me.” He laughed and walked over to me.

“I didn’t know you were that into me.”

I raised his t-shirt and kissed his stomach, unbuttoned the first button of his jeans.

“I am.”

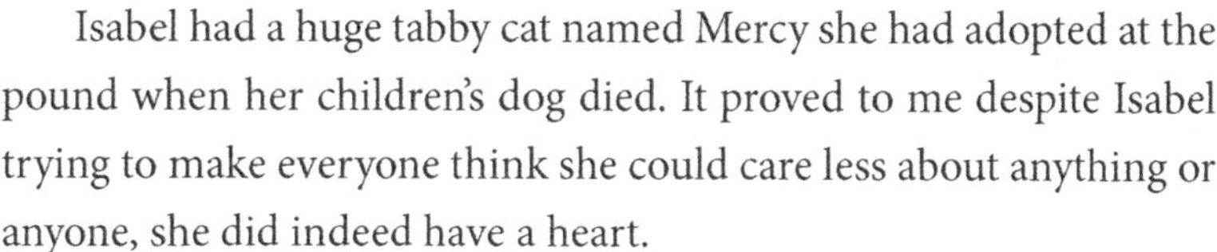

Isabel had a huge tabby cat named Mercy she had adopted at the pound when her children’s dog died. It proved to me despite Isabel trying to make everyone think she could care less about anything or anyone, she did indeed have a heart.

“Wait a minute,” she said picking up Mercy and flopping back down on the sofa with him. She had made a huge cheese tray and sat it on the table between us.

“Tristan asked you what to do?”

“He asked me where we should go from here.”

“Oh,” she sighed. “Why did he ask you that?”

"Ben, I guess." I popped open a bottle of wine for our daily happy hour. "I guess he is worried Ben will find out we have a…."

"Thing?"

"Good word. Thing."

"So, why don't you wait and see what happens? Ben has no solid ground to stand on. It's all hearsay right now and your "thing" with Tristan is just that, a thing."

"Ah…. The story of my life. Wait and see what happens. Wait and see if you're going to make it to class today. Wait and see if you have to work tomorrow night. Wait and see if McCain will show up. Wait and see if he will give me more drugs or if I have to appease him before I can get more. Wait and see if he looks for me. Wait and see if I'm pregnant. Wait and see if I can get another job and support a baby by myself. Wait and see if Eric loves me enough to marry me. Wait and see if he will STILL love me when I screw up repeatedly."

"Wow," she said. "Have you been practicing that? Because that was good." I rolled my eyes.

"And this is not just a thing." Now, she rolled her eyes at me.

"Look Lilah, all I keep thinking is, he's a boy…I'm sorry, but he is. This is just a phase he's going though. He'll get over it."

"He'll get over me?" I poured her a glass of wine.

"You'll get over him."

"You think *I'll* get over *him*?"

"Yes," she said as she took the wine from me. "I know you think it's love but it's not. You ought to know that by now."

"Well, then what is it? Because it feels like love." She rolled her eyes again.

"Do I really have to explain this to you? We don't fall in love. Remember?" I nodded.

"That's what you keep telling me." Isabel sat her wine glass down on the table with a thud and a little sloshed over the side.

"Oh, my Lord," she said leaning toward me. "You haven't told him you love him, have you?"

"Of course not. I'm not *that* stupid."

"Has he said he loves you?"

"No," I said.

"Well, that's good. That I take a little comfort in." She held out her glass for a toast and I clinked my glass with hers. "To a moment in time."

"A moment in time," I repeated. I thought for a minute. "Do you think Tristan is a bad guy?"

"Why would you ask me that?" I shrugged. "Morally twisted, maybe. I mean, he is having an affair with a married woman who is old enough to be his mother." I ignored her comment to prevent another lecture.

"So, do you think he's bad?"

"If you mean in an evil sort of way, no."

"He told me yesterday it wasn't fun and games anymore, that I meant something to him." I thought of Vonnie and about what she'd said. About him using me. "Do you think he has an ulterior motive?"

"Like what?" she asked. "He's already gotten into your pants."

"A multitude of times," I said taking a bite of my cheese and cracker.

Neither one of us laughed, resigned to the fact that I was most likely ruining my life. Mercy jumped down and walked over to me, figure-eighting around my legs. I reached down to pat the top of his head. I wasn't really a cat person.

"He deserved a second chance," Isabel said. I shrugged and nodded.

Someone knocked on the front door and I got up to pour myself more wine.

"Come in," Isabel yelled.

Tristan walked into the living room as I sat back down in my chair. He still always appeared when you least expected him. Isabel looked over to me, widening her eyes. He came over and sat on the arm of my chair.

"Hi," he said squeezing my knee.

"Hi," I said. He looked over to Isabel.

"What are you doing here?" she asked.

"Um, I was in the neighborhood. Is it happy hour?"

"It is," I said. "Would you like a glass of wine?"

"May I have a glass of wine?" He looked over to Isabel.

"Under normal circumstances," Isabel said. "I would say no."

"No, you wouldn't," I commented.

"But this is obviously…" Tristan interjected. He leaned over and kissed me deeply, lingering on my lips for a moment. It was the first time he'd kissed me in front of Isabel. "Not normal circumstances."

"No," Isabel said as she took another bite of her cheese and cracker. "This is twisted."

Mercy jumped up into my lap. He never jumped up into my lap because cats know when you're not a cat person. I don't know how they know. They just know. Maybe he knew I had a huge bird in my kitchen. I leaned back in my chair as he walked over to Tristan. Tristan rubbed his head and he purred loudly. I moved further out of the way and Mercy put his two front feet on Tristan's leg, continuing to rub his head against Tristan's hand.

"Do you have catnip in your pocket?" Isabel asked. Tristan smiled and shook his head.

"No," he said, and he looked down at Mercy. "I think he just likes me."

"They say animals can tell," I said.

"Tell what?" Isabel asked as she handed Tristan a glass of wine.

"A person's character." Isabel snickered.

"He's a cat, not a fortune teller."

"I take exception to that," said Tristan.

"He's a traitor," Isabel said of Mercy. "He does that to Tom every time he comes to pick up the kids, too. It means nothing."

"It means Tom is a good man," I said. Isabel rolled her eyes at me. She'd been doing a lot of that lately.

Mercy was still rubbing up against Tristan. He sat his wine glass down on the table and picked him up. He looked into Mercy's big, green eyes.

"You're just a cat. Aren't you?"

Mercy purred loudly, swished his tail back and forth slowly. I looked over to Isabel and gave her a knowing smile. She opened her mouth and stuck her finger inside like she wanted to throw up. We both knew Tristan wasn't a bad guy. Whatever Vonnie knew was only a rumor she'd heard at school. It was ridiculous I'd even considered it at all. Later, after Tristan had left, we were standing in Isabel's kitchen and she surprised me.

"There's something about him," she said. "He seems like a good guy but then every time I'm around him I get this weird feeling. I can't put my finger on it."

"You're overthinking this and so am I. Stop it."

"Tell me what Vonnie said again."

"She said he was using me and there were rumors at school."

"Do you know what those rumors are? Besides you and him, I mean." I shook my head. "Have you thought about trying to find out?"

"You're the teacher there. You find out."

"Like the kids tell me anything." She took another sip of wine. "Didn't Vonnie say something about not being caught?" I nodded. "Caught doing what?"

"I have no idea."

"I don't understand you, Lilah. If one of my kids told me that I'd tie them in a chair until they explained themselves."

"You know how Vonnie is. She hates me."

"Jeez, Lilah. She does not hate you." I poured myself another glass of wine. "You nearly broke Ben's arm the other day and you can't ask Vonnie a simple question?"

"It's not any of my business."

"You're her damn mother. Everything is your business!"

"She'll just lie."

"So, what you're telling me is you don't want to hear what she might have to say because you want Tristan to be perfect." I looked to the ceiling. "Lilah! Look at me!"

"I don't know!" I screamed. I threw my glass of wine into the sink and cracks spread over it. It didn't break, though. "I wish everyone would chill out. It's not a big deal. So, what? I'm sleeping with someone other than my husband. I've been doing it for years. What's new? I am so sick of this shit."

"You did it," she said crossing her arms over her chest. "This is what you get when you play too close to home."

"Go to hell, Isabel," I said as I pulled on the sliding glass door.

She stood there watching me, took a sip of her wine and let me go.

I was standing at the kitchen sink the next morning loading the dishwasher when Tristan walked up behind me and kissed my neck. He had slipped through the front door without me even hearing him. Isabel and I still hadn't made up.

"Hi."

Somehow coming out of his mouth, 'Hi,' seemed extremely erotic.

"Hi," I said leaning back into him. His hands went to my waist and I felt his calm bleed into me.

"What are you doing?"

I didn't turn around, but I looked at my watch.

"You should go to calculus."

"I should," he agreed. He kissed my neck again.

"Are you okay? You seem upset."

"Why do you think I'm upset?" He leaned up against me and pushed me into the edge of the sink.

"Because I can feel it." I knew he had that playful smile on his lips. He rubbed my shoulders.

"Mm…" I laid my head back against his chest.

"Don't let this all stuff with the rumors bother you," he said quietly. "It's high school. That's what they do." He tickled my sides.

"Stop!" I said but he had made me laugh.

"Do you feel better now? Because that's my goal in life; to make you feel good." He tickled me again.

"Stop it!" I said laughing. I tried to pry his hands off me.

"Why do I always want you?"

It isn't love, I thought. At least that's what Isabel said.

"Because you're infatuated with me."

"Is that what it is?" I bowed my head.

"Yes." He patted his hands on my waist and backed up.

"Okay," he said. "I'm going." I turned around.

"Where?"

I had already forgotten I'd told him to go to school. That's what he did to me. He shrugged.

"Uh, I don't know. Maybe school? That would be good, right?" I smiled. "I'll see you in a little bit," he said. "Have on something sexy when I get back because after calculus, I have…"

I shook my head in amusement as he waited for me to finish his sentence.

"Study hall," I said. He pointed at me.

"Yep."

Definitely not love. Nope.

Isabel

I think Lilah would agree with me when I say I am her children's second mother. I've been around since the beginning. I would do anything I could to help Lilah's children. I always have, and I always will but lying to them was not normally in my bag of tricks. I realized now, however, with the situation at hand I may very well need to lie to them. I guess in a way I was already lying to them – and everyone else – because Lilah's secret was also my secret. It wasn't a matter of saying it out loud. Would I deny it if one of the children asked me? I don't know. Would it be better to protect Lilah or them?

I knew the answer to that question under any other circumstances would be to protect Lilah and in a way maybe the kids *not* knowing was the kind of protection they needed. Maybe I needed to shield them from this situation. While Lilah and I had never agreed on putting our children in a bubble, this might qualify for an exception. It was with great surprise when I discovered I wouldn't need to talk to Lilah's children about it one way or the other. Isaac already had.

If there was one thing I could say about Isaac it was that he was logical and level-headed. He never jumped to conclusions, and although he may not tell me something voluntarily, if I ask him he would always tell me the truth. To find out he and Ben were talking about Tristan and Lilah should not have come as a surprise to me. I was grading end of the week quizzes on the chaise lounge in my bedroom when Isaac walked in with a cup of tea for me. Immediately I knew there was an issue.

"Tea?" I asked. He sat the cup and saucer down beside me.

"It restores the soul," he said with a grin. He sat down at my feet on the end of the chaise lounge.

"What is going on?" I asked as I laid my papers on my lap and picked up my tea. He didn't answer me right away but looked at me as if I should already know. "Well?"

"Mom," he said. "You know."

I must admit I honestly did not know. I mean, I did but I was still hoping Isaac knew nothing about Lilah and Tristan at all. It wasn't probable, but it was possible.

"Is something going on with one of your brothers?"

"No," he said. "Ben." I took a cautious sip of my tea.

"What about Ben?" He took a deep breath.

"Mom," he said. "Do we really have to do this? Because I know you know. You know you know and I really don't want to have to draw a diagram about it."

"You have such a way with words."

"It's true. Isn't it?" I sighed.

"I don't know what to say," I admitted. "You know Lilah is my best friend. I won't defend her actions, but I will protect her."

"Well, Ben is my best friend," he replied. "And I feel the same way." And I was thinking I still had a little boy. I didn't.

"Honey, I get that. I really do, but I can't talk to you about it."

"Then tell me what to say to Ben."

"What do you want to say to Ben?"

"Not to worry? But it's more than that, Mom. It's Ben's reputation."

"It's not," I said. "It's not about Ben."

"Well, try telling that to the student body of our school. Because everyone is talking about it."

"What about Vonnie and Michael?" I asked.

"I have no idea. I don't talk to Michael about those kinds of things and I'm scared of Vonnie." He smiled.

"Right."

"He's questioning it, Mom. He's still trying to figure it out. His biggest problem is he likes Tristan a lot." I nodded. "He doesn't want to accuse Tristan of something he's not guilty of, but at the same time he wants to protect his mother, defend her. How does he do all of those things?"

"That's a very good question," I said.

"Can you just nod or shake your head or something and tell me whether it's true or not?"

"What exactly are we talking about?" I took another sip of my tea.

"Are Lilah and Tristan sleeping together?"

I pressed my lips together. Dear Lord, please help me. Should Isaac know this? Here's the thing with me and God: I was raised by parents who took me to church every Sunday. My sisters and I used to fight over who got to wear Mom's earrings and shoes and a million other things. Much to my mother's dismay, I had stopped going to church years ago and I rarely prayed but this was one of those times when I needed to pray. And I knew beyond any doubt God would answer me, even if I hadn't talked to Him in months – or years. He always answered me, but not usually in the way I wanted or even expected, which was one of the reasons I was sometimes afraid to ask. I rationalized it was a yes or no question so there would be no unexpected outcome.

"Isaac," I said. "Before I answer you, would you tell me how *you* feel about this?"

"About Lilah and Tristan?"

"Or the possibility of them having a relationship."

"I don't know," he said. "If it's consensual, I guess it's okay. Who I am to judge? You can be with anyone you want…I guess."

I thought about the reason Tom had left me. No, you really couldn't. Wow, thanks God. I reminded Him it was supposed to be a yes or no question. He laughed.

"Well, you have to be willing to accept the consequences," I said.

"Yeah," he agreed. "But are they?" I nodded. "Wow," he said sitting back on his hands. "Do I even want to know how that happened?"

"It would take a while," I said. "And I'm not at liberty to discuss it with you, anyhow."

"Right." He thought for a moment and sat back up "So now that I know, what do I say?"

"To Ben?"

"Yeah. Do I tell him it's true or let him find out on his own?"

"That's a decision you must make," I said. "But keep in mind you have no way to prove it. Not that you need to, or would want to, but you know what I mean."

"Right," he said again. "I think he should know the truth. If for no other reason than to defend himself…or his mother's reputation, if there's anything left of it."

"You know Lilah," I said. "You've known Lilah your entire life."

"Yes."

"So, tell Ben what you *do* know."

"What do you mean?"

"Tell him what kind of person you know Lilah is and how what other people think of her doesn't matter. Tell him everyone makes mistakes, how his mother is a good person and has a good heart - to not to let other people change the way he sees her. Do you believe Lilah is a good person?"

"Of course," he said. "I don't have to always agree with what she does to love her."

"Don't you think Ben should feel that way, too?"

"Oh, I know he loves her," he said. "That's not in question."

"That's not what I meant." I laid my hand over Isaac's. "You always defend the people you love to the outside world. No matter what they do. I realize Ben is embarrassed by his mother's behavior, but it hasn't changed who she is on the inside and, quite honestly, it's no one else's business."

"I don't think you should encourage Lilah's behavior." I smiled.

"How old are you again?" He laughed. "You couldn't even imagine some of the talks I've had with Lilah about this and they are far from encouragement. You scold in private. You protect in public."

"So, what you're telling me is Ben should protect Lilah??"

"He should still respect her. Not what she does, just as his mother."

"He's furious."

He was more than furious. I had seen it myself.

"I imagine he is. He has every right to be." Isaac leaned over and kissed my cheek.

"You're an amazing mom," he said. He got up and walked toward my bedroom door.

"Remember that the next time you think you hate me."

"Right. Hey," he said turning around.

"Yeah?"

"Would you talk to Ben for me? With me?"

I took in a deep breath and exhaled slowly. God was doing this to me. I knew He was. If He was trying to prove a point, He was winning.

"Let me sleep on that," I said. "Is that fair?"

"Yeah, that's fair."

Dear God, I prayed one more time. Please tell me what to do. I don't want to have to figure it out. Just tell me.

Don't let anyone ever tell you God doesn't answer you if He hasn't heard from you in a long time - or that He doesn't have a sense of humor.

"Isabel," He said. "You already know the answer."

"No! I don't!" I insisted. He laughed again.

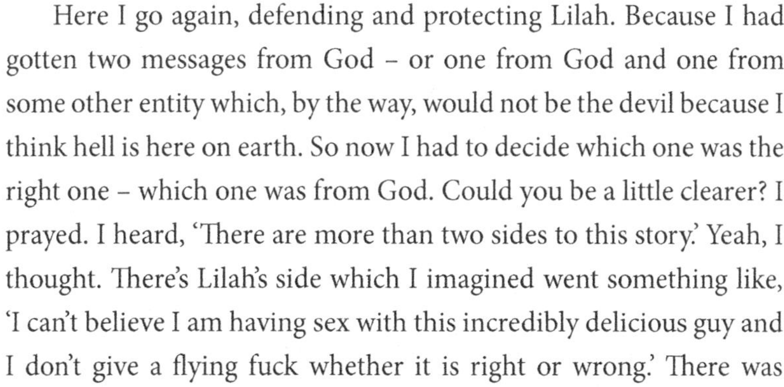

Here I go again, defending and protecting Lilah. Because I had gotten two messages from God – or one from God and one from some other entity which, by the way, would not be the devil because I think hell is here on earth. So now I had to decide which one was the right one – which one was from God. Could you be a little clearer? I prayed. I heard, 'There are more than two sides to this story.' Yeah, I thought. There's Lilah's side which I imagined went something like, 'I can't believe I am having sex with this incredibly delicious guy and I don't give a flying fuck whether it is right or wrong.' There was

Tristan's side, which was completely unknown. There was my side, which is 'I can't believe I'm letting this happen and why didn't I think of it first?' And now there was Ben's side, which probably went something like, 'if Tristan is sleeping with my mom, I'm going to wrap his head around a steel pole.'

I guess my first decision was to decide whether Ben should know – from me. Should I be the one to tell him? There was no way I could do this without involving Lilah. Or could I? Would it be better to discuss it with her first or counsel Ben first? I already knew if I discussed it with Lilah first she would go into a headlong spiral, back into the depths of despair and possibly have another nervous breakdown. If she knew how this was affecting Ben, she would want to die or, so I thought. Lately though it seemed like Lilah didn't have much of conscience. So maybe I was wrong.

If I discussed it (and I rationalized it would be a discussion) with Ben, 'Let me tell you the truth about your mother and one of your best friends,' he would have a meltdown. Trust me when I say Ben's meltdowns are scary. I once thought he had a demon inside of him. He didn't but that's the kind of meltdowns Ben has when he's angry.

When Ben was a baby he used to hold his breath if he didn't get his way. Call it selfishness or stubbornness or a multitude of other things but what it boiled down to was anger. He was angry Lilah wouldn't give him what he wanted so he would hold his breath thinking she would give in. In Ben's defense, I don't think a two-year-old could be that cunning but, nonetheless, that is what he did. It scared Lilah to death so she asked the pediatrician what to do.

"One day he will do it and pass out," the pediatrician said to her surprise and dismay. "It will scare the bejesus out of him and he'll never do it again."

He was right. Not too long afterward we watched Ben scream and cry (a normal everyday occurrence because he was a devil child) and then hold his breath. When Lilah ignored him, and he started to turn blue she looked to me and asked, 'What now?' But within minutes Ben had passed out, hit the floor, and continued screaming at one decibel higher than a dog whistle. He also never did it again.

Ben's temper hadn't changed much over the years. The only difference now was he had learned how to control it a little better, but it didn't mean it had gone away. He could be volatile if provoked (like his mother) but that rarely happened. It was, however, the reason I wondered if telling him would create a fury and cause imminent danger to anyone who happened to be close by. It was either Lilah having a nervous breakdown or Ben losing his temper – Ben's temper would subside. Who knew what would happen if Lilah had another nervous breakdown. Therefore, I had my answer. Talk to Ben.

"God," I prayed. "If this isn't the answer, now would be a good time to intervene."

I waited.

Holy shit, I suddenly thought. I did not sign up for this when I become Ben's godmother. But I had. It was wrong to leave this entirely to Isaac. I had to step in and, if nothing else, referee.

It had taken me all night to come to this conclusion and now, at six in the morning, I had to get the children up and get us all to school - but not without a little fortification first. I walked into the living room instead of the kitchen and poured myself a shot of whiskey instead of a cup of coffee. A shot of whiskey in challenging times never hurt anyone, I told myself. No matter what time of day it is.

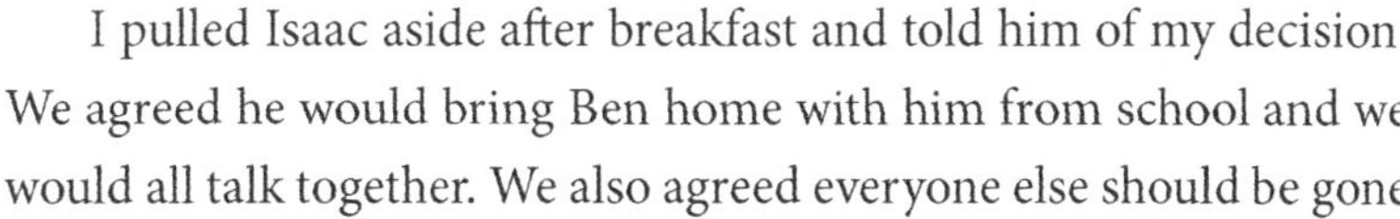

I pulled Isaac aside after breakfast and told him of my decision. We agreed he would bring Ben home with him from school and we would all talk together. We also agreed everyone else should be gone so I planned with Lilah for Matt and Abe to hang out at her house. I rarely lied to Lilah and it had to be for her benefit if I did. This was one of those times. I told her the exterminator was coming and I wanted all the kids out of the house. It was the only thing I could think of at the time that made any sense. She didn't ask where Isaac or I would be. I knew she wouldn't. She did, however, ask what I was trying get rid of.

"Fleas," I said because it was the first thing that came to mind. "The cat. I mean, I want to get rid of the fleas. Not the cat. The cat has fleas."

"Oh," she said. "Poor kitty."

Ben came in with Isaac around quarter after four. I was a nervous wreck. Not because I had to tell Ben this information but because I didn't know what his reaction would be. It might be like Isaac's reaction, non-judgmental and logical but I doubted it. It was Ben. There was a distinct possibility he would want to beat Tristan with a tire iron.

Let me preface my next action with my belief that if my or Lilah's kids were drinking at my house and I was in control of their transportation I didn't think there was anything wrong with them partaking in a little alcohol. So as soon as Ben walked into the kitchen I asked him if he wanted a beer.

"Uh, yeah."

Of course, if Ben had one I had to let Isaac have one, too. I normally did not let the kids drink during the week. It would not be good if a teacher's son showed up drunk for his SAT's. Ben picked up on it at once.

"What is going on?" he asked as I poured some vodka into my glass of lemonade - because this was not a wine situation. This was a hard liquor situation. Tom used to call it ***Electric Lemonade.*** Today, I called it relief.

"Sit down," I said, and I gestured to the kitchen table. He looked over to Isaac.

"Are you kidding me? What the hell, Isaac? Your mom?"

"We're not talking about Mom in a mom capacity," Isaac said calmly. "We're talking about my mom being your mom's best friend."

Ben understood this, so he sat down at the table.

"I hope you're going to tell me I can beat Tristan's ass," he said to me.

"I'm afraid not," I said.

"Well, I'm going to do it anyway…if I think what you're about to tell me is what I already know."

"Ben," Isaac said. "Will you listen to Mom for a minute?"

Ben took a swig of his beer.

"I'm not here to tattletale on your Mom," I said. "I'm here to help you understand it."

"What is there to understand other than one of my best friends is sleeping with my mother?"

"I think Tristan truly cares about your Mom," I said. "It doesn't make it right, but I think he does."

"The hell he does. He just wants to get in her pants." Isaac shrugged.

"Most of your friends do," he said.

I looked over to Isaac and raised my eyebrows. Really? I mouthed.

"Shit," Ben said and took another swig of his beer. "Has anyone taken Dad into consideration here?" He looked over to me. "It's not like Mom is single and can sleep with whoever she wants like you do. No offense."

"None taken," I said.

"Jeez," Isaac said. "Thanks for the visual."

"The visual?" Ben stood up. "You think I don't have a visual?"

"Ben, sit down," I said. He did.

"Is that what you think?" he asked me. "Do you think it shouldn't matter to me that Tristan is sleeping with my Mom? That she's cheating on my Dad? That everyone at school is talking about it?"

I had to give it to him. He really put everything in a nutshell there. He slid back in his chair and looked over to Isaac.

"Isn't it a felony? To sleep with someone under eighteen? Can she go to jail?"

"I think that's directed at you, Mom," Isaac said.

"He's eighteen," I explained. "So, no. I don't think she can go to jail."

"Oh, that makes it SO much better."

Isaac and I looked at each other. There was still no telling how this would end.

"So, let me get this straight," Ben said. "Mom is sleeping with one of my best friends and embarrassing the hell out of me at school and this is okay with you?"

"It's not okay with me," I said. "But your Mom is an adult. I can't keep her from doing anything she wants to do."

"You could at least tell her she's being an idiot," he said.

"Don't talk about your mother like that. It's not necessary and, yes, I have talked to her and I've reminded her of all the things you've said." He wiped the back of his hand across his mouth.

"And she's still hell bent on doing it?" I nodded. He shook his head back and forth. "You can't stop her, can you?"

"No."

Ben looked to Isaac, but Isaac said nothing.

"I'm going to beat Tristan's ass," Ben said. "I'm going to grab him by the neck and beat him in the face until he's a bloody pulp." He slammed his hand against the table and kicked his chair back. It fell onto the floor. Isaac stood up.

"That's not going to solve anything," Isaac said.

"Your mother cares about him" I added. "I think you should take that into consideration."

"So, what? Now you're defending Tristan?"

"I'm not defending anyone," I said. "I'm only trying to help you understand what's going on before you do something you'll regret."

He threw his half empty beer bottle against the wall and it crashed to the floor, beer spattering everywhere.

"Fuck both of you. I don't care what you think." He headed for the sliding glass doors but turned back before he opened them. "There won't be much left of Tristan when I'm done with him, then we'll see what Mom thinks. There might not be *anything* left of Tristan."

"Ben," I said. "That is not a good idea. You should calm down and think about all this. I'm telling you right now, if you do something like that, you will regret it."

"Oh no," he countered. "Tristan will be the one with the regrets."

The door came off the track as he pulled on it and when he slammed it shut the glass inside shattered. The tinkling of glass hitting the stone floor reminded me of the time he'd broken out one of the windows at school trying to get to a guy who'd catcalled Vonnie. He'd told Ben he thought Vonnie was hot and how he'd love to get her alone, so he could 'teach her a few things.' Ben had tried to control his anger that day, so instead of punching the guy in the face, he'd punched his fist through the science lab window.

Currently, it did not appear Ben was trying to control his anger. It dawned on me then that Ben was not only intent on hurting Tristan, but that he could possibly kill him. Isaac looked to me.

"That went well."

"Fuck," I said bringing my hand to my forehead. "Holy shit."

Lilah

Tristan wasn't shy. As soon as I sat down my bag inside the cottage doorway he walked over and pulled me into him. His hand immediately went underneath my shirt to my waist. Despite the balmy temperature outside his hands were freezing cold. I sucked in my breath.

"Sorry," he said between kisses. "I'm a little impatient."

Patience means two entirely different things to a woman my age and someone Tristan's age, but Tristan didn't *seem* that young. Was I looking through the same lens as everyone else or was I off kilter somehow? I couldn't help but wonder what Isabel saw when she looked at him. Did she see Tristan the same way I did?

Deep inside, I guess I was expecting or hoping Isabel would somehow save me from myself. She had tried. I just wanted it too much to listen. Isabel did what Isabel thought I wanted her to do. Sometimes that is the definition of a best friend, but not always.

"It's okay," I breathed because my patience was being tested, too.

Whenever Tristan's hands moved over my skin they did so hesitantly, as if it were the first time he'd ever touched a woman that way.

Sometimes he seemed so experienced. Like that first night when he'd picked me up so easily and sat me down again so gently. I remembered wrapping my hands around his biceps and feeling them flex against my weight. We had made love many times since then and I went back and forth between thinking he'd been with a million different women to thinking I was the only one, but I couldn't have been the only one. Could I?

"You are so beautiful," he said tucking my hair behind my ear.

He maneuvered me backward to the bed. I sat down, and he moved over me, his hands on either side my head. He leaned down to kiss me.

"Wait," I said placing my hands on his chest.

He backed away and stood up, running his hands through his hair. I knew how much he wanted me, but he never tried to convince me of anything. There wasn't one time we'd been together he'd forced himself on me. Not even the first night when I'd gotten the scar on my back did he ever take anything that wasn't already his. Permission granted.

"What?" he asked trying to catch his breath.

"I want to go slow," I said. "We have all night." He looked down to me.

"Lilah," he said shoving his hands down inside his jeans pockets. "I hate to be the one to tell you this but I'm not going to last all night. I don't even know if I'm capable of an hour at this point."

I laughed and took his hand in mine. He sat on the bed beside me. We turned, facing each other. He put his hand on my face gently and kissed me.

"But I will try."

"We can do it more than once," I said and smiled. He looked at me as if he'd just won a huge stuffed animal at the fair.

"Oh good," he said sarcastically. "I *know* I can do that."

I rubbed my fingers over his lips. They were a little chapped, probably from kissing me so much. We'd driven two hours and not been able to keep our hands off each other the entire time. I craved him. I needed him. And I had convinced him to have sex with me in a convenience store bathroom. It wasn't difficult.

"Your lips are chapped," I commented. He pressed them together then reached into his jeans pocket.

"Lip balm," he said taking off the cap. He put some on his lips and offered it to me. "Please tell me we can spend the day together tomorrow."

"We can," I said after I'd coated my lips. I leaned back on my arms. "Isabel is covering for me."

"What are you supposed to be doing?" he asked as I handed the lip balm back to him.

"I don't know," I said. "Whatever she comes up with. She's good at that."

"Shocking."

He shoved his lip balm back into his pocket. I reached down and tugged on the first button of his jeans and the rest of the buttons popped open easily. There is something to be said for worn in button-fly jeans: easy access. He pulled me closer and I slid my hands inside the back of them. He murmured into my ear.

"What?" I whispered.

"I want you to know I've been with other women."

"Okay."

"I mean," he hesitated. "I do know what I'm doing, kind of." I smiled and kissed his cheek.

"I know," I said. "We've done this before. A lot."

"I just…I don't want you to be disappointed."

"Why would I be disappointed?"

"I don't know," he said. "I've never done this whole night thing. I've never had the opportunity to take my time."

I took a deep breath and blew it back out. What guy this age even thought of these things? He was so serious it scared me a little bit, but his intensity was one of the things that had drawn me to him in the beginning.

Isabel once told me affairs are supposed to be fun and if they aren't fun to end them. Immediately. You weren't supposed to have to think about affairs. They were supposed to be an escape, a diversion, a Shangri-La in the middle of the hell you called your life. So, I tried to lighten the mood a bit. I slipped my hand over the fly of his boxers and he drew in his breath.

"I already know what's in here," I whispered as I leaned in and kissed his neck.

He shifted on the bed to allow me to slip my hand further into his jeans. He unbuttoned my shirt and his fingers slipped underneath the front of my bra. The clasp snapped open easily.

"I want this to be the best night of your life," he said.

I didn't answer him. I just kissed him softly and we laid back on the bed. Whether it was the best night of my life wasn't important to me, but I had no doubt he might be capable of it. You see, when you're as high strung and craving something as much I was craving Tristan, it wouldn't take much to make it the best night of my life. His abilities were hardly even a thought at that point. I only wanted to, as he'd put it, "have a whole night thing." And maybe the whole night wouldn't be long enough. I thought I could stay in bed with him for days. Naked, making love, worshipping each other.

Possibly with a pizza. Because that kind of energy needed sustenance.

Somehow, I talked him into getting into the jacuzzi with me. It was a beautiful ceramic tub, surrounded by huge candles on candle stands and fresh white towels. A gas fireplace separated it from the bedroom and even though it was eighty-five degrees outside, Tristan flipped the switch and it lit instantaneously.

"Ambiance," he said and smiled.

After we'd drank a bottle of champagne and I'd teased him into a state slightly south of rapture, I suggested we dry off and get into bed. It was close to midnight. We slipped under the sheets and I turned off the light. We still hadn't made love.

"Please let me have you," he said grabbing me around the waist.

I nestled against him and he rested his hand on my hip. When he moved over me he did it slowly, running his fingers up and down my side. I shivered. His lips moved against mine and I opened my mouth.

"Lilah," he said into it as he pushed inside of me.

I gasped because I wasn't expecting it so soon. We moved together slowly at first, our bodies in sync with one another. Being with him that way always seemed instinctual.

"This is amazing," he breathed.

"Mm-hmm."

He held himself up on his arms as he kissed me. His mouth moved against mine like liquid silk, his lips encompassing mine completely. He tasted like cherry lip balm. He slipped out of me and moved down my body. I shifted my hips toward him, wanting more. He looked up to me in response.

"You said go slow," he explained kissing my stomach. "This is the only way that's going to happen."

His lips moved down my stomach and he grasp my wrists in his hands. My entire body shook. I couldn't remember the last time I had wanted something so much. I wasn't sure where we were going with this. He kissed my belly button then trailed his tongue across my hipbone. I may have lost consciousness at that point. I know I lost track of time. When he moved back up my body his lips grazed my breastbone and settled next to my ear. His hair fell into my face and I arched my back against the bed, toward him.

"Please let me have you," I said breathlessly.

"Oh yeah?" he said and smiled. "Now who's impatient?"

He slipped back inside of me effortlessly. Once he started moving against me we fell back into that natural rhythm.

"Lilah…I…"

"It's okay," I said as I brought my legs up and wrapped them around his waist.

"I can't do this much longer."

"I know," I said, and I thought of all those times he had told me to relax, to just let it happen. "Relax. It's okay."

I reached up and ran my hands over his hair, stopped at the back of his neck and held onto him. His arms shook. The bed hit up against the wall and I let go of him and grabbed the headboard behind me. There is a fine line between pleasure and pain and Tristan found it. It no longer mattered whether it was right or wrong. A wave of pleasure coursed through me and I gave in to the release my body so desperately needed. I leaned up and kissed his lips and he sucked in his breath.

"I don't want it to end," he whispered but his body tensed, and I felt his muscles flex against me. As we both struggled to catch our breath, he kissed my forehead then my lips.

"I love you," he said against them.

I wasn't expecting to hear those words from him. I wasn't expecting anything even close to those words. I expected our night together to be about anything except his feelings for me. Anything but love.

"What?" I asked because I thought I had misheard him.

"Tell me you love me," he said as he looked into my eyes.

"Tristan…I…"

The worst part about this was that I did love him, and I knew eventually my heart was going to be broken, but I couldn't do that to him. I couldn't break his heart, too. I shook my head back and forth.

"I can't, baby," I said tucking his hair behind his ear. "You can't fall in love with me. You just can't."

He laid his head down on my chest and I felt his body tremble against mine. I'm not sure if it was hurt or disappointment or something I would never understand. I wrapped my arms around him.

"I need you," he said into my neck. "You have no idea how much I need you."

Up until then I had no clue I meant so much to him. I had no doubt he cared about me, but I didn't know he had fallen in love with me. What did Isabel say? 'He'll get over it.' Would he? Would I?

"You're going to be okay," I said running my hand over his hair. "I promise."

"Not without you," he said as he raised up and looked at me. "I can't do this without you."

"Do what?" I asked.

"Just life," he said quickly. Almost too quickly. "Whatever comes next."

What was I supposed to say to that? What did he expect me to say to that? I guess the best question was, what did I want to say to that? And then without giving it any more thought, I defied my own rules. Never. Never, ever tell a man you are sleeping with that you love him, even if you do. With sirens going off inside my head and that little voice telling me not to do it, I did it.

I said, "I love you, too."

He relaxed against me, kissed my temple.

"I know," he said.

The next morning, I awoke to Tristan standing in the doorway between the bedroom and the bathroom fresh from the shower with a white towel wrapped around his waist. It made his skin seem even darker.

"Hi," he said. His typical greeting, no matter what time of day.

He came over and sat down on the bed beside me, laid his arm across my hip.

"Did you sleep good?" he asked. I stretched.

"I think so. You?"

"I can't remember the last time I slept that good." He leaned over and kissed my cheek. "I brought you some muffins and coffee." I sat up in bed and propped myself up on the pillow behind me.

"When?"

"This morning after my run. There's a little restaurant over there…" He motioned over his shoulder. "Down by the entrance."

"I didn't know you ran," I said.

"There are a lot of things you don't know about me." He stood up and went over to the table, brought over a basket of muffins and a cup of coffee.

"Wow, it's been a long time since someone brought me breakfast in bed." He smiled.

He unwrapped the towel from around him and threw it onto the bed, walked over to his duffle bag. I almost spit out my coffee. *That* couldn't possibly be mine.

"I want to go hiking today," he finally said.

"Hiking?" I asked. "Seriously? Why?"

"Because supposedly there is a huge waterfall at the top of the mountain and I want to see it." He looked through his bag. "The lady at the restaurant said she could pack us a picnic lunch." He hesitated and looked up to me. "With some wine."

"Mm...how steep is this mountain?"

"I don't know. I'm sure it's not that bad. Apparently, people do it all the time."

"What kind of people?" He laughed and pulled a t-shirt over his head.

"You can do it," he said smiling. "I have faith in you."

"Can I get in your backpack?" He laughed again.

"No."

I barely did it. It was the hardest I'd worked my body in years. My workout plan was doing yoga with Isabel whenever we got drunk and remembered we needed to exercise. I was not ready for that kind of exertion. Later that day and after only God knows how many miles (I later found out it was four), we got to the top of the mountain.

"See I told you, you could do it." I leaned over with my hands on my knees. I could barely catch my breath.

"I haven't worked that hard in a very long time," I admitted.

I looked over to him. He hadn't even broken a sweat. I stood up and walked over to him. We watched the waterfall. There was a crystal-clear lagoon beneath it.

"It's beautiful," I said. He grabbed my hand.

"Come on. Let's go down."

"What? We just got up here!" I exclaimed.

"I know." He laughed and pointed down the cliff. "See that flat rock?"

"Yes," I said hesitantly.

"It's the perfect place to have lunch."

There was a path, but it was steep and rocky.

"Tristan," I said. "I don't know if I can get down there."

"Come on," he said. "Step where I step."

"I feel like I'm on a field trip with one of my kids. This is like something they'd make me do." He laughed again.

"It's fun. You underestimate yourself."

"If you say so."

When we got to the bottom he sat everything down on the rock and we took off our shoes, dangled our feet over the edge. There was a huge weeping willow tree above us and I could feel the spray from the waterfall. It was cold, but refreshing, and it felt good. He took out the wine and I realized we didn't have a corkscrew.

"It's a screw top," he said when I told him of our dilemma.

"Screw top wine? Yuck."

"Don't be such a prima donna," he said.

"I'm surprised you know what that means."

"I have a sister," he replied screwing off the top. "She's a pain in the ass but she's all I have so I love her anyway."

He began to tell me more about his parents and the car accident. He said he and Tiffany were eleven. He told me how they had lived with his aunt and uncle for a while. I would have never guessed he was lying to me, but he'd probably told the story a million times. I told him I was sorry and asked if there was anything I could do. He shook his head. Even though I knew he was lying, I also knew he would never try to deliberately deceive me. He had lost his parents. It didn't matter how.

After we ate lunch we laid back on the rock in the sun for a while. It was hot. Tristan took off his t-shirt and I stripped down to my bikini. I laid my hand on his chest after a while and he turned to me.

"Thank you," I said.

"What for?"

"For reminding me what it's like to be in love." As soon as I said it, I thought to myself, 'what the hell is wrong with you?' He leaned over and kissed me. We sat up.

"I'm sorry about last night," he said.

"Why are you sorry?"

"Maybe I don't know what love is yet," he said. He leaned over with his elbows on his knees. "But that's what I feel when I look at you. I think about you all the time. I can't *stop* thinking about you."

"What do you think about when you think of me? Like, me naked in a pile of pillows, feathers drifting down over me?" He shook his head back and forth, amused.

"That's a vision." I took his hand in mine. "I think about how beautiful you are, and I think about how screwed up I am to be falling in love with a woman who's married to someone else."

"You're not screwed up. It happens."

"I have reservations at the restaurant tonight," he said suddenly. He stood up. "We should get back and shower."

"Okay." I stood up beside him.

We packed our leftovers and the empty wine bottle into his backpack and stood looking out over the water. The waterfall must have been at least fifty to sixty feet high. The water cascaded into a pool not far beneath us. It was surrounded by mossy rocks and the biggest weeping willow trees I had ever seen. He took my hand and swung it back and forth between us.

"Can you swim?" he asked. I looked over to him.

"What do you mean, 'Can I swim?' Of course, I can swim. Even cats can swim." He laughed.

"Was that sarcasm?" I shrugged.

"Maybe." He squeezed my hand.

"How good can you swim? Could you, like, save me if I was drowning?"

"I doubt it," I said.

"Wow."

"Not because I didn't want to," I explained and laughed. "I just don't think I'm that strong."

"But you can swim?"

"Yes! Why??"

And before I knew it, he had picked me up and thrown me over the edge. He dove in behind me. I surfaced, blowing air out of my nose. He swam over to me. The water felt like ice.

"Oh my God," I said as I rubbed my hands over my face. "I am going to kill you."

He leaned in and kissed me quickly.

"No, you're not."

He swam off and left me treading water. I looked around, but he had gone under and I couldn't find him. I waited for him to surface. Suddenly he came up behind me. He grabbed me by the waist.

"Breathe," he said. "And open your eyes."

I don't know how I knew that meant he was taking me back under with him, but I did. I took in a deep breath as he pulled me under the water. He wrapped his arms around me from behind and I opened my eyes. In front of me were the roots of the weeping willow tree above us, glittered with tiny incandescent fish. It was one of the most beautiful things I have ever seen.

When I got back home from that weekend the reality of my life settled over me. I wasn't a woman who had the freedom to do whatever she pleased with whomever she pleased whenever she pleased. I wanted to be that woman, but I had a husband and four children to take care of.

I didn't normally feel guilty. It just didn't happen. Possibly because the men I were with prior to Tristan had never mattered to me. There were never tears or any kind of remorse. Most often I didn't think about it at all. But this time it was different because I was in love with Tristan and I knew he was in love with me. I didn't think about how that simple fact would affect the rest of my life. I only thought about what my life would be like without him.

"I'm feeling guilty," I said to Isabel the following week at happy hour.

"You?? Oh, ha ha." She handed me a martini glass. "Here, try this." I took a sip.

"Oh…gross. What the hell is this?"

"Fairy Nectar. I thought we needed to try something a little different, so when I went to the liquor store yesterday I bought some absinthe."

"Am I going to start seeing green fairies in a minute?" She laughed.

"Maybe. Only time will tell." She took a sip of hers. "Look, you know that feeling guilty serves no purpose." I shrugged. "You've already done it now. It's not like you can un-do it."

"Well, yeah, but I have an issue."

"What kind of issue?"

Isabel and I rarely had issues. It was never that complicated. If there was an issue, we ended it. We had enough drama in our regular lives.

"Are you pregnant?" I sighed, a little aggravated.

"Well, if I was I wouldn't know it yet. Now, would I?"

"Did you…"

"Stop," I said holding up my hand. "What is wrong with you?"

"I feel like it's inevitable."

"What are you? Psychic??" She shrugged. "I'm not like you, Isabel. I don't get pregnant when a man looks at me."

"Ha," she said unenthusiastically. "Is that what you and Tristan did all night? Look at each other?"

"Listen to me!"

"I'm listening!" I got up and walked around the bar. I had downed my Fairy Nectar and needed another.

"You might not want to drink those so fast."

"Well, I am," I said as strained another into my glass.

When I sat back down Isabel said, "Lilah, you're keeping me in suspense on purpose. What is going on? What is your issue?"

"First, thank you for this weekend."

"Uh-huh."

"We had a good time."

"I'll bet you did. Looking at each other." She waited. "Well?"

I put my hand to my mouth and closed my eyes. I tried to keep the tears from coming but they slid down my cheeks anyhow. Isabel hopped up and came over to me.

"Oh honey," she said as she sat beside me. "What's wrong? Tell me what's going on." Once I started crying it was hard for me to stop. Isabel knew this. "Okay," she said. "Take a deep breath."

"It was supposed to just be fun. It was supposed to be anything except what it was."

"What happened?" she asked leaning over to look in my face. "Did he hurt you?" I looked up quickly.

"No." I said. "No. Nothing like that."

She sighed, and I searched for the words.

"He just…"

I began to cry again but Isabel didn't say anything because that is what Isabel does whenever I'm upset: she listens. It was several minutes before I could calm myself enough to talk.

"He told me he loves me," I finally said. Isabel playfully hit me on my leg and jumped up.

"Oh, he does not," she said as she walked back across her living room. "He just had really good sex with you and *thinks* he loves you."

I wiped the tears from my eyes. Sometimes I thought the insensitive things Isabel said weren't truly meant to be insensitive. I was fairly certain they were intended to make me feel better. It worked occasionally, but not this time.

"Wow," I said. "Thanks."

"Jeez, Lilah. He's eighteen. He doesn't even know what love is."

"I think he does," I said thoughtfully. "I don't think he's ever had anyone show it to him, though. I'm going to break his heart."

"That might be true," she said. "If he means it."

"He said he couldn't do it without me."

"Couldn't do what without you?"

"I don't know. He was crying." Isabel was still standing the middle of her living room. She turned around to face me and put her hands on her hips.

"He was crying??" she affirmed as if she didn't hear me the first time. I nodded.

Abe walked into the room with a huge sandwich in his hand, dropping crumbs everywhere.

"Who is crying?" he asked.

"You," Isabel said. "If you don't take that sandwich back into the kitchen where it belongs. Go away."

"You are so rude sometimes," he said. Isabel pointed toward the kitchen and came over and sat on the floor in front of me.

"Why?" she asked quietly. "Why was he crying?"

"I'm not sure."

"He didn't tell you?"

"I didn't ask."

"Let me get this straight," she said. "You have sex with this boy." She must have noticed the look on my face. "Sorry, but he is still a boy."

"Okay."

"And he cries afterward, or was it before?"

"After."

"You didn't think it was important to ask him why?"

"I thought if he wanted me to know he would tell me."

"I swear, I wish sometimes I could get inside your head and figure out what the hell you are thinking. Or, in this case, not thinking."

"I think it was about me loving him."

My glass was empty. I got up and sidestepped her toward the bar. I loved that about Isabel's house. There were multiple bars.

"What? You loving him? He wants you to love him?"

"Yes. I think so."

I went through the cabinets again and rinsed out my glass in the bar sink. Isabel stood on the other side of the bar. She looked under the glasses hanging above me.

"Please tell me you have not fallen in love with him," she said. "Please, I beg of you. I mean, I know you say you love him, but you haven't fallen *in love* with him. Have you?"

"What's the difference?"

"Seriously, Lilah?" I pulled a bottle of rum out of the cabinet and started to read the label.

"That is 151 Rum," she said. "It will knock your ass on the ground." I opened it.

"I know what 151 Rum is, Isabel." I poured some into my glass.

"Have you?" she asked.

"Have I what?"

"Fallen in love with him?"

"That's ridiculous." I threw back the rum.

There was no way on earth I was going to admit to Isabel that, yes, I had fallen in love with Tristan. I didn't even want to admit it to myself. I was definitely not telling her I'd said, 'I love you' to him.

"Holy shit, that's strong."

"Lilah?"

"I have not fallen in love with him, Isabel," I said adamantly. I sat my glass down on the counter a little harder than I'd intended. "I swear to you."

She looked at me, knowing it was a lie. Best friends are like that.

"You're lying," she said. I poured myself another shot of rum.

"I am."

"Yoo-hoo, Lilah!"

My mother. She always said that as she came through my front door. Tristan and I were laid back on the old loveseat that had somehow landed in the breakfast nook with the bird instead of going to Goodwill. I jumped up out of his lap. It wasn't easy.

"Yeah?" I called back. "I'm in the kitchen." Tristan laughed and shook his finger at me in reprimand.

"We really need to start locking the door." I turned back to him.

"What?"

"Lock," he said as he twisted a key in an imaginary lock.

"Lock, lock, lock," Ru said. Tristan rubbed his hand over his eyes and sunk down further into the cushions.

"Oh," my mother said as she walked in from the living room. "I don't believe I know you."

You could hear the disapproval in her voice. Tristan stood, trying to compose himself. Because he'd been to a college interview that morning, he had on khaki pants and a white oxford shirt with a cool, mint green tie. The tiny navy-blue stripes in it somehow accentuated his sable eyes. He'd loosened the tie and rolled up his shirt sleeves. His hair hung past his collar in dark waves. I knew it was a little longer than my mother thought decent. He tucked some of it behind his ear and extended his hand.

"I'm Tristan." She only looked at him.

"Mom!" I said. "He's trying to be nice." She still didn't extend her hand.

"Well, who is he?" she asked looking him up and down.

Not even my mother could deny Tristan's good looks or ignore the intoxicating scent that followed him wherever he went. Or maybe the scent thing was just me. The fact he was impeccably dressed did not prevent her from looking at him like he was something unknown she'd found in her refrigerator.

"I'm Lilah's lover," he said. "We have to meet in the middle of the day, you know, because of Eric and the children."

OH MY GOD, I thought. I am going to kill him. My mother sucked in her breath, her hand going to the pearls at her neck.

"Mom," I said touching her arm. "He's kidding."

"Oh," she said as she studied him. "And who are you really?"

"He's a friend of Ben's," I interrupted. "He's waiting for Ben to get home."

"At two-thirty?" She looked at her watch. "Isn't he a little early?"

"They have early release today." That wasn't a lie. They did.

And just like that she snapped out of it and pretended he wasn't there. My mom regularly did that. If she didn't like something she put her head in the sand like an ostrich.

"Oh honey," she said handing me a shopping bag on her arm. "I bought you this..."

Tristan sat back down on the loveseat and picked up his beer. I shook my head at him and he sat it back down. I took the bag from her.

"What is it?" Inside were a pair of tights – black with orange cats. "Um...these are for me?"

"Halloween!" she said. "Don't you have to dress up for the school thing with the kids?"

"That's not for months," I said. "But what would I wear with this and what would I be?" Tristan laughed out loud, but my mother completely ignored him.

"I don't know, honey. Don't you have a little black dress or something?" She opened the wine refrigerator in the corner. "Why don't you have any wine chilled and where is Maria?"

"There's red," I said pointing to the rack on the counter. "And Maria is upstairs taking a nap." Tristan jumped up.

"I'll get it." He grabbed a bottle of wine and the corkscrew, instantaneously popping out the cork and pouring my mother a glass. He handed it to her.

"Who is he again?" she asked me. She couldn't deny he was there if he was handing her a glass of wine.

"Grandma!!"

Michael and Vonnie bolted through the door and over to my mother. By the way they were acting, you'd think they hadn't seen her in years. Ben saw Tristan on the couch and immediately dropped his backpack. He jumped over the back of the chair sitting slightly out from under the kitchen table and grabbed Tristan by the collar of his shirt, shoving him backward into the sofa. He did it with such force the loveseat fell backward, and Tristan slammed up against the wall behind it.

"What the hell, man?" Tristan said as he struggled to get up.

Ben stepped over the overturned sofa and punched Tristan in the face before he could get to his feet. Blood trickled from Tristan's lips. Ben hit him again and I could see the fury on Tristan's face. As he rose, Tristan stepped onto the back of the sofa with one foot and flipped it back up into the proper position with his other foot. He grabbed Ben by the neck, lifting him off the floor. He shoved him backward and when he let go, Ben fell onto the kitchen table behind him. Papers, drinks, and a potted plant all went tumbling onto the floor.

Michael jumped out of the way and fell up against the sink. Vonnie was videotaping, probably live on Facebook. My mother had backed up into the living room but now she came into the kitchen in full force. She yelled at the top of her lungs.

"STOP IT! THIS INSTANT! NOW!"

Everyone stopped. Silence - because it was my mother. She snatched Vonnie's phone out of her hand before Vonnie even realized she'd taken it.

"You!" she said to Tristan. "Leave! Now! Everyone else, in your rooms." Ben didn't move. "Ben," she said. "NOW! Upstairs."

I looked over to Tristan. His lip was busted, and a small drop of blood had landed on the front of his white shirt.

"I'm sorry," I mouthed to him but I'm not sure if he saw me. The back door slammed as he went out of it.

My mother leaned against the counter – still holding her glass of wine – and said, "Lilah Anne, explain to me what is going on, so I can help you."

No real emotion that I could tell. She only wanted an explanation, or a confession. Maybe both. I wasn't ready to give her either one.

"Help me?" I asked, disgusted with the whole situation. "Why would you think I need your help?" She sat her glass of wine down on the table and held up her hands, looking around the room at the disaster.

"Are you kidding me?" she asked. "But, I must admit, you've taught him well."

"What are you talking about?"

"Tristan," she said. "That's his name, right?"

"Yes," I said looking at the floor.

"I've always stressed to you how important it is to tell the truth," she said. "And you know the reason why. Why?"

"Because no one will believe it," I said quietly.

"When I asked Tristan who he was he told me the truth. Didn't he?" I didn't say anything, but I looked down to the floor again.

"Mom, I really need to clean this up." She walked over to me and put her hands on my upper arms.

"Tell me what is really going on between you and this boy because obviously he was not waiting for Ben."

"I don't know."

"You don't know, or you don't want to tell me?" My eyes watered as I tried to stop the tears. I had to bite my tongue to keep my composure.

"Tell me this instant, Lilah, and don't lie to me. I am your mother and if you lie I am going to know."

"I think you already know," I managed.

"Have you had sex with him?" she asked, lowering her voice.

"That's the first question?" I asked, astonished.

"That's the most important question," she replied. I nodded, and she looked up to the ceiling, probably in a silent prayer for God to intervene.

"What were you thinking? How old is he?" I shook my head in disbelief. I could not believe I was having this conversation with my mother.

"Tell me," she demanded.

"Eighteen," I whispered, almost to myself. My mother stepped back and fingered her wedding ring then held it up for me to see.

"You have one of these, too," she said. "Does it mean anything? Because I know in the past there have been times when you've apparently forgotten about it." I covered my face with my hands and began to cry. She took my upper arms in her hands again.

"I am not judging you, sweetheart. I'm only trying to understand."

"I don't know what to say."

"Do you have feelings for him or is he just a fling?" I swallowed and brought my hands to my face again, sobbing this time. My mother took me into her arms.

"It's okay," she said rubbing her hand over my hair. "We're going to fix this. You must not see him anymore." I pulled away.

"Mom, I can't."

"You can, and you will," she commanded.

"But it will devastate him."

"He's eighteen. He'll get over it."

"He said he loves me."

"Oh, good grief," she said turning around and picking up her glass of wine. "He doesn't even know what love is."

"Where is your mother?" I heard Eric ask one of the children later that night while I was in the bathtub. It wasn't a bathtub like Isabel's bathtub, but it was the bathtub I had asked for when we'd first moved into the farmhouse.

Knowing my love of baths, Eric had re-done the master bathroom as a surprise for me. A deep clawfoot tub up against the window so I could sit candles on the ledge with a curtain to pull around it for privacy. Above it hung a crystal chandelier with soft, pink lights.

When the children were a little too much for me to handle Eric handed me a big, fluffy towel and pointed toward our master suite. I always filled the tub with the hottest water I could stand and my lavender bubble bath. I lit the candles and sunk down into the water. On most occasions, Eric brought me a glass of wine. He hadn't brought me a glass of wine that night, though, because I had taken an entire bottle into the bathroom with me.

"Are you drunk?" he said as he opened the door. It wasn't in an accusatory way. Maybe even a little playful.

"Not yet," I answered. He smiled and came over to sit on the edge of the tub with me.

"I know you're upset," he said. "I can see it in your eyes. Tell me what's going on." I decided to be as honest as I could without being completely honest.

"Did you hear about the fight this afternoon?"

"No," he said.

"None of the kids told you? I thought Vonnie would be chewing your ear off by now."

"Nope. Everyone's quiet tonight. What happened?"

"My mother was here earlier," I began.

"Did you two get into a spat?"

"No," I said. "But Tristan came by. He has early release from school, you know."

"No, I didn't know."

"Well, anyhow, he came by to wait for Ben. Apparently, they had some plans or something." (Lie #1)

"Okay."

"But I think Ben asked him to come over here, so he could attack him." (Lie #2)

"What? Why would he do that?"

"Ben thinks, for some odd reason, Tristan has a thing for me. It makes him madder than a wet hen." (Half of a lie, but still #3)

"Makes sense," Eric said smiling. "He's upset one of his friends thinks you're hot."

"Yes."

"I can't blame the guy. You are hot."

"Funny." Eric chuckled.

"Anyhow, so when Ben gets home from school he throws his backpack on the floor and goes for Tristan. He jumped over the kitchen table to get to him. Tristan was sitting on the sofa and Ben hit him so hard the sofa flew backward."

"Oh, my."

Eric was the only man I'd ever known that said, 'oh, my.' It was his response to anything that would shock the hell out of most people. No real response at all.

"Ben punched him in the face. Tristan shoved Ben backward onto the kitchen table – things went flying everywhere…"

"Gosh," Eric said. "That's not good." Another one of his nonchalant responses. "Do you want me to talk to him?" I panicked.

"Who? Tristan? No."

"I meant Ben. His response to a suspicion should not be physical violence. That never solves anything."

"I know but you know how Ben is. You talking to him will only make him madder." And he will tell you truth, I thought.

"You're right. Do you think Tristan likes you?"

"I don't know. Maybe." (Lie #4) Eric laid his hand on my knee that was protruding out of the water.

"What does Isabel think?"

"You don't want to know what Isabel thinks."

"Actually, I do. She's around teenagers every day at school. I'm sure she has some interaction with Tristan."

"Not really. He doesn't have any classes with her."

"She must see him at school, though. She must witness his personality, you know?"

"She says he flirts with me." (Another half of a lie but #5.)

"Ah, and does he?"

"Sometimes."

"How do you respond?"

"I try to discourage it." (Lie #6)

"Look," Eric said as he rubbed his thumb over my kneecap. "Given how Ben feels about the situation, it seems you need sit down with Tristan and have an honest conversation with him."

"That would be awkward." (Lie #7)

"I don't think so," he said. "He's nearly a grown man. He has to understand on some level where you're coming from even if it doesn't change the way he feels."

"He already knows how Ben feels. That should be discouragement enough." Eric stood up and wiped his hand on the towel hanging beside the tub.

"You do what you feel is best," he said. "But I think a talk with Tristan would be beneficial to you and him. It can't possibly make the situation any worse." I shrugged. "Take him out to dinner."

"What??"

"Take him to dinner," he said. "You can be away from everyone else, so no one overhears your conversation. Go into the city."

"Eric, that's crazy."

A date with Tristan in the city, away from my mother, with my husband's approval. Could it get any better?

"You need to get everything out in the open. No one has ever solved anything by hoping it will go away. You concur?" I nodded. "I know this little restaurant over by Regency. It's quiet, darker."

"Oh great," I said. "A romantic restaurant. Exactly what I want to do with Tristan." (Lie #8.) He laughed.

"It will be discreet, solve your issues and thrill him all at once." I stood up and grabbed my towel, wrapping it around myself.

"I really don't think this is a good idea, Eric." (Lie #9)

"Trust me," he said as he opened the bathroom door. "It is."

I had almost made it to ten.

"Eric wants me to go out to dinner with Tristan," I told Isabel the next day at happy hour. I had already told her about the fight between him and Ben. She didn't seem surprised. Now, she snorted.

"You never cease to amaze me, Lilah. How did you manage that?" She raised her arms over her head and shook the shaker full of some new pink cocktail she'd created to use the banana liqueur she'd found in the bottom of her bar cabinet. Isabel never wasted alcohol.

"I told him about the fight and how that, more than likely, Tristan has a crush on me." She burst out laughing.

"A crush?"

"It's not funny, Isabel. What do I do now?"

"What do you mean, what do you do now?" She strained the concoction into two martini glasses. "What do you want to do now?"

"You really have to ask that question?" She walked around the bar and handed me my drink.

"***Bubblegum***," she explained. "Don't go to the restaurant you went to with him last time. We know too many people there."

"You assume I'm going," I said. I took a sip of my drink. "This martini smells like Tristan."

"Hmm…"

"I shouldn't be going."

"But you will." Sometimes Isabel knew me better than I knew myself.

"Eric gave me the name of some little restaurant over near Regency. He said it would be discreet."

"You're kidding," she said. She took a sip of her martini. "Woo, this is good." I took another sip of mine.

"It's definitely bubble-gummy."

"Do you want to know what I would do?"

"I don't know. Do I?"

"Keep in mind I am talking about me with some other man, not a teenager, because I cannot condone that."

"Oh, stop it, Isabel."

"I would go. I would take advantage of the situation. When have you ever had Eric tell you to go out to dinner with one of your lovers?"

"That sounds so wrong."

"That's because it is wrong. What's the name of it?"

"What?"

"The restaurant, goofball."

"Oh. Umm…The Vineyard."

"Oh, my."

"That's the exact response Eric had when I told him about the fight." She chuckled. "You know The Vineyard?"

"I've been there a few times. It's somewhat expensive. You should wear something nice."

"What? Are you serious?"

"Yeah, white tablecloths, real china and crystal. I can't believe you and Eric haven't been there together."

"It's probably because that's where he takes everyone else." Isabel huffed.

"I love it that you say, 'everyone else.' I ignored her.

"I can't take Tristan somewhere like that."

"Why not?"

"He won't know how to behave."

"I think you should give him a little more credit," she said. "He seems to be pretty adept in social situations."

"This is making me nervous just thinking about it."

"You've been to a million restaurants like that," she pointed out.

"*With Eric.*"

"Just do it. I'll help you pick out something to wear. Come over here and get dressed. Otherwise, your kids will ask where you're going. The less lies you have to tell the better off you'll be."

"How will we get there?"

"Tell Tristan to borrow Mrs. Jenkins' Mercedes. Tell him to meet you at the grocery store right outside town. I'll take you over there." I brought my hand to my forehead.

"It's like you're a master of deception." She smiled.

"I can be."

"Good Lord, Isabel," I said. "We're both going to hell. You know that, right?"

She downed the rest of her martini. I had already finished mine. She walked over to me and took my empty glass.

"At least we'll be together," she said.

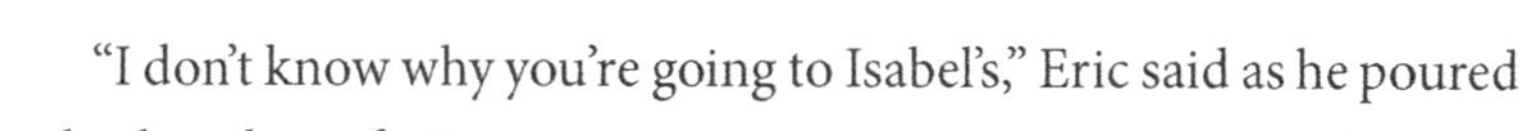

"I don't know why you're going to Isabel's," Eric said as he poured us both a glass of wine.

"I don't want the kids asking questions," I said. "And if I'm dressing up and going somewhere without you, they will."

"True," he said. "How is Tristan doing with all this?"

"What do you mean?" I took a sip of my wine.

"You did ask him? You're not tricking him into it?"

"No," I said and laughed. "I had to tell him I was taking him out to dinner. Otherwise, it would be kidnapping."

"I've always loved your dry sense of humor."

"I wasn't joking." He smiled.

"Does he know *why* you're taking him out to dinner?"

"No. If I tell him I'm going to lecture him, he won't go."

"True," he said. "This wine is good. Don't you think?"

"Yes."

"You know I got this when I went to Napa to meet with that client?"

"Oh yeah," I said picking up the bottle. "I forgot about that." He pulled me over to him.

"Lilah, I'm sorry you're having so many issues with Ben right now. He should know you better than that." He kissed my cheek.

"Maybe," I said. "Which is another good reason to be going to Isabel's house."

"You've made a point. Do you have a speech?"

"No. You know I've always been a spur-of-the-moment kind of girl." He laughed.

"Oh, yes." He took my wine glass from me.

"I love you very much," he said. "Don't overthink this." I laid my head on his shoulder because that's what he expected me to do. He lifted my chin.

"This isn't a big deal. Do it and be done with it. After that, you must let it go. Ben will come to his own conclusions. He'll figure it out. I'm sure Tristan will talk to him."

"Doubtful," I said. "But okay."

"You can't dictate what people are thinking or second guess what they might do, Lilah."

"I know."

"So, don't assume you know how Tristan is going to react tonight."

"Okay."

"Give him the benefit of the doubt. He seems like he would be a level-headed young man."

"Hmm..." He handed my glass of wine back to me and clinked his glass to mine.

"To doing what's right," he said and when I said nothing, "Because I know you will."

I wore a black lace sheath dress. I'd had it forever, but it was one of those dresses that never went out of style. I'd paired it with diamond solitaire earrings and black leather sling-back pumps. If I'd been with Eric I would have worn stockings, but Isabel told me people didn't wear stockings anymore. They did. She just wasn't in a position where she had to wear them. I'd put a black silk slip underneath. No panties. Isabel reminded me to be careful crossing my legs to avoid a Basic Instinct moment. As I got out of her car, she blew me a kiss good-bye.

"Don't do anything I wouldn't do," she called. I waved my hand at her.

Mrs. Jenkins' Mercedes was a dark shade of green with tan leather interior. It smelled like a cedar closet.

"Hi," I said as I got in and shut the door.

Tristan was wearing a black shirt and tie with a gray suit. He had the sleeves of the jacket and shirt pushed up. I'm not sure if it was intentional or if he was just hot. He looked like he'd just stepped off an Armani runway. I felt strangely underdressed.

"Hi," he said as he leaned over to kiss me. Barely. I touched my finger to his lip. It was still cracked and bruised, but the swelling had gone down.

"It looks a little better."

"It hurts like hell," he said. "Do you think I should send Ben a thank you note?" I smiled.

"What is it with you and thank you notes?"

"I was being facetious," he said. "But, proper etiquette."

And I'd thought Tristan would have been furious, but I guess being a foster kid taught you there were some things in life not worthy of bitterness. Holding a grudge toward someone never solved anything, apart from making *you* feel miserable. I kissed him again.

"At least he didn't break your nose." He brought his hand to his lips.

"Ah," he said. "Careful."

"Sorry," I said. "I'll try to avoid that area."

"Not what I meant," he said as he lowered his eyes. He leaned over closer to me. "But I can't do any soul kissing tonight." He leaned over even closer. I could feel his breath on my neck. "Only vanilla," he whispered.

"Okay."

I wish there was an app for smell because I cannot describe the way Tristan smelled that night. One of these days – and I hope it's me, although it won't be because I'm technologically challenged – someone is going to figure out how to put smells into a computer. Who wouldn't want that?? You could type in mint, or citrus or even "cookies baking" and voila! Add in a little patchouli and bubblegum– maybe the scent of a deep, red rose. That is what Tristan smelled like that night – all those things together in one. There should be a name for that scent because I can guarantee you it would sell out at Macy's in about fifteen seconds. If I could pour Tristan into a bottle, I'd be rich.

"Where are we going?"

"The Vineyard."

"You look nice," he said as he backed out of the parking space. "Very sophisticated."

"Thanks."

His hand went to my knee. I didn't like that he was only driving with one hand. He was left handed though, so I reassured myself it wasn't necessarily a bad thing. This is where my motherly instincts kicked in and totally ruined any other feeling I might have had earlier. I wanted to protect him and make love to him at the same time. There was something wrong with me.

"You realize this is supposed to be about your strange obsession with me?" He smiled as he pulled up to a traffic light, moved his hand a little further up my thigh.

"Yeah, I know," he said. "You can lecture me now if you want."

"I can't believe Mrs. Jenkins is letting you drive this car."

"I'm like the son she never had."

"Funny."

"Have you been to this restaurant?"

"No," I said. "We don't have to go if you don't want." He glanced over to me.

"Why wouldn't I want to go?"

"I don't know. It doesn't seem like your kind of place." He chuckled.

"You have so much to learn about me." He rubbed his thumb on the outside of my leg.

"Do you know how to drive in the dark?" He looked over to me again.

"Would you relax?" I took a deep breath. "What is going on with you tonight?"

"Eric."

"What about him?"

"He told me earlier today he knew I'd do the right thing." Tristan looked over to me.

"What's the right thing?"

"You tell me."

"Look Lilah, I know you feel guilty about this relationship."

"Not really." He squeezed my kneecap.

"Don't lie." I turned in my seat toward him.

"I don't normally feel guilty."

"You've done this before?" he asked, surprised.

"Yes."

"Wow. And I thought I was so special."

"Not like this," I said. "Not with anyone like you." He turned left toward the interstate.

"Like me? Hmm…you're starting to give me a complex."

"Younger," I explained. "And I've never felt like this with anyone else."

"I'm almost afraid to ask what *that* means." I took his hand in mine, looked down at our fingers entwined together.

"I've never fallen in love when I was, well, you know." He looked over to me. "In the past it has always been for fun."

"If it makes you feel any better, I've never done this at all."

"Does it make you feel guilty?" I asked. He squeezed my hand and smiled.

"Your mother makes me feel guilty."

"My mother makes everyone feel guilty. Especially, me."

"Why?" I gestured toward him.

"Uh...you."

"She knows?"

"She's my mother. Of course, she knows."

"What did she say?"

"Take this exit," I said pointing at it. "She asked what she could do to help me and when I asked why, her next response was, 'Have you had sex with him yet?'"

"Please tell me you didn't tell her." He pulled up to the light at the end of the exit ramp. "Which way?"

"Left. Not voluntarily. No."

"What did she do?" he asked. "Pull a gun on you?" I laughed.

"She didn't have to do that. She knew just by looking at me."

"So, what does that mean? Your mom knowing, I mean."

"It means I'm not supposed to be seeing you anymore. She said I *must* stop seeing you." He pulled into the mall entrance.

"Where?"

"Anywhere."

"No, I mean where is the restaurant?"

"Oh, over there." I pointed to a lighted entry on the right.

"Valet?" he asked pulling into the parking lot. "Seriously?"

"Eric," I replied simply.

"Of course."

We pulled up in front of the restaurant and the valet opened my door to usher me out of the car. Tristan gave him the keys and he asked for a last name.

"Collins."

"Enjoy your dinner, Mrs. Collins," he said to me as he opened the restaurant door.

Being called Mrs. Collins shocked me so much my clutch slipped out of my hand and fell onto the sidewalk. Tristan reached down to pick it up and handed it back to me. He escorted me inside. He put his arm around me, his hand resting on my hip. He pulled me into him and kissed my temple. He spoke softly into my ear.

"Mrs. Collins."

It shocked and surprised me how easily Tristan adapted to every situation he encountered. Isabel was right when she said he seemed "socially adept." I guess given his history, I didn't expect him to be fancy restaurant savvy. Come to think of it, I also didn't expect him to know how to save my life.

It made me wonder about the time he'd spent in the foster care system. What was it like to leave one home for another and another and another? Did he remember his life with his biological parents or had he purposefully shut the door to his past completely? Was he able to conjure those memories at will or did they haunt him every day? I guess I would never know.

All I knew was what Isabel had told me from his school records – which neither of us should have known – and what Tristan had told me from the beginning. They didn't quite coincide with one another. What if none of it was true? How would I even know?

I'd been a sort of chameleon all my life, but it wasn't a personality trait. It was how my parents had raised me. My mom and dad were very social people so there weren't very many social situations I hadn't been in over the years. It was the part of me Eric said he loved – the chameleon who was comfortable anywhere but in all honesty, nothing could be further from the truth. I was only a good imposter. It puzzled me about Tristan though. Adapting to a social situation was one thing, knowing the things Tristan knew was another.

I don't know how many times my mother had read Letitia Baldridge's book on etiquette and she'd ingrained all of it on my brain as I grew up. I remember her sitting down with me and teaching me about the proper places for silverware and the purpose of each one. She not only taught me. There was a test.

Tristan knew all these things too - which fork was for which course, which stemware was for the water and which ones were for the red and white wines. It seemed it came so easily for him, like he'd been doing it his whole life. Had his mother taught him like my mother taught me? Had there been a test?

That night at The Vineyard he ordered my dinner for me but only after asking my preferences. He chose a bottle of wine from the wine list and ordered it as easily as Eric did. No one asked for his identification. No one questioned his age at all and they assumed I was either his wife or in the least, a woman he wanted to impress. Our table sat back in the corner of the restaurant, a place where certainly no one other than a couple who wanted privacy would sit. We didn't even have a reservation, which was my fault because Eric had told me to make one, but Tristan had asked for a quiet table and he'd received one.

I didn't want to question Tristan on who he was, where he had come from, anything about his past at all. What if it was horrible?

What if he and Tiffany were abused? Did I dare ask him about something he didn't want to remember?

No, I couldn't ask him those questions, but I *could* talk to Isabel about it. Certainly, she would have some insight on the issue. She had an insight on every issue. We had never discussed Tristan's behavior at school, but then I'd never asked. She may have never even thought about it. I was the one having the affair with him. If anyone knew him, it should have been me.

Isabel

I never sleep. I have never been able to sleep my entire life – unless I drug myself. I honestly believe I could stay up for days before I would pass out from exhaustion. So many things go through my mind every night when I lay down to sleep. Silly things, like whether I turned on the dishwasher or if I put the clothes in the dryer.

Sometimes it was more important things, like when Abe got chickenpox and some of the bumps got infected. That night I worried about whether he would live because I thought it might not be chickenpox. What if it was leprosy? I know now this was ridiculous but at the time I didn't have any idea what happened when a kid got chickenpox. Isaac nor Matt ever had it so why did Abe get it? Was he undernourished? Should I make him drink more water? Play sports? (How playing sports would have prevented chickenpox, I don't know.) And on and on these thoughts would go, until I finally got up and made coffee. I knew Lilah had these nights, too. Some of the time our nights would coincide with one another and we'd end up talking on the phone at four o-clock in the morning like no two sane people ever do.

That night I was stressing over whether Lilah was dead in a ditch somewhere. I was the only one who worried about these things. Her mother would have worried if she'd known what Lilah was doing but that was something Lilah would never tell her mother voluntarily. We all know Eric wasn't worried.

It was three in the morning and I hadn't heard from Lilah at all. She'd told me there was a chance her and Tristan might go to a club after dinner, but I wasn't expecting that to happen. Maybe it did. Or maybe a million other things happened. Maybe they were holed up in a hotel screwing each other's brains out. I hoped so because I hadn't had sex since I'd met "Justin" in a restaurant two months ago and we'd done it in bathroom while his girlfriend ate dessert. I know. Wrong. So wrong.

Despite this, and because lately I'd somehow developed a conscience, I'd expressed to Lilah quite a few times how I felt about her relationship with Tristan. Hell, I had even told *him* how I felt about their relationship. Lilah heard what I said, but had she listened? It was becoming harder and harder for me to fathom how this relationship outweighed the consequences. If Lilah simply wanted a lover, it wouldn't be hard for her to get one. She was a beautiful woman. In the least I knew she could find someone who was old enough to go to the liquor store by themselves. He was barely old enough to buy cigarettes.

I had to admit the main reason I hadn't put my foot down completely with their relationship was because I liked Tristan. Not that I could've stopped Lilah, but I could have refused to cover for her when she wanted to be alone with him. In my defense, I *did* think it was only a harmless fling in the beginning. Now it was so much more complicated. I wanted to pull Lilah back from her life and say, 'Look at this. Is this what you want??'

As far as I knew, Tristan was a good guy. He was good-looking, funny, thoughtful, a little mysterious. Everything you want in a man. Well, he didn't have any money so that could be an issue, but you get the jest of it. For someone with Tristan's qualities, I might be willing to overlook the lack of funds.

Oh, my Lord, I suddenly thought. What was I thinking? You see, now, where I go with things when I overthink them. In this case, I had started to subconsciously convince myself the relationship Lilah had with Tristan was okay and it was not.

"It is not okay, Isabel," I said out loud to myself. Mercy heard me and jumped up onto my bed. "It's not okay. Is it, boy?"

He meowed loudly. He always "talked" to me. He was a good listener, too - unlike other men who only appeared to be listening while in their head all they were thinking about was the possibility of you having on a red lace thong and that, *if they listened,* they could get you out of it.

I held out my hand and Mercy meandered toward me. He laid on the pillow beside my head. Damn cat. I hated it that I loved him so much. I also hated it that I worried about Lilah so much. I worried more about her than I did myself, but Lilah needed me. I was her rock and after everything we'd gone through together I would always be there for her. Especially now, when what she was doing ranked right up there with me letting a man take naked pictures of myself. I wanted to be so mad at her for putting herself in this position.

Whether you called it intuition or ESP or a sixth sense, I knew something bad was going to happen. That kind of feeling doesn't usually develop out of thin air, yet it had. There was a reason I had that sixth sense. I just wish I'd figured it out sooner. At least then one of us would have been prepared.

"What in the hell are you wearing?" I asked as Lilah walked out of the sliding glass doors the next day onto the patio of the pool.

I can only describe it as a black and white feather print cover up with an attached boa. I hoped to hell she had not walked from her house down the sidewalk to my house wearing only that thing. But these last few months I wouldn't have put it past her. She walked over and pulled it off.

"And it gets worse," I said when I saw her bathing suit. She laughed and sat down in the lounge chair beside me.

"I found this today when I was digging through some boxes under my bed."

"Both?"

"Yeah."

She reached over to the table between us where I had already set out wine glasses and poured herself some of the ***Sangria*** I'd made from the pitcher on the table.

"Maybe you should consider putting them back in there."

"What is wrong with this bathing suit?" she asked. "It's a one piece. We said we were going to be less provocative and wear one pieces."

"We did?" I asked. "When did we say this and..." I reached over to stick my finger underneath the strings of her shoulder strap. "How is this not provocative?"

"You honestly don't remember this bathing suit?"

"Uh, no. I think that is something I would remember. Are you sure it wasn't a Halloween costume?"

"Oh, ha ha," she said.

Lilah's bathing suit was a basic black bikini with a white and black one-piece netting over it. It was atrocious. The netting appeared to be cotton strings and were somehow woven into diamonds. It hurt my eyes. A tan with this bathing suit would have looked like a scored ham. Lilah laid back in her chair and threw her legs up in front of her. She stuck her finger under her butt and tugged at the bottom.

"It's going up my crack," she said and laughed. I couldn't help but laugh, too. She settled back down into her chair and turned to me. "Do you know anything about Tristan I don't know?"

"What? Why are you asking me this?"

"I feel weird about him."

"Weird?" I asked. "You're having sex with him. If you feel weird about him, you should stop. Come to think of it, you should stop anyway."

"Oh, please," she said. "How is he at school?"

"What do you mean?"

"Have you seen him with other kids?"

"We see him with other kids almost every day. Here." I pointed out.

"It's different," she said. "School is a very different atmosphere."

"True."

"Does he hang out with the same people at school?"

"I guess. Honestly, Lilah, I don't watch him that closely."

"Okay." She seemed disappointed.

"What did you want me to tell you? Do you have a specific question you need answered?"

"Not really."

"Well, you haven't told me about your date yet. I texted you around two-thirty this morning and you didn't answer me. I'm glad to see you're still alive." I took a sip of my Sangria.

"You are turning into my mother."

"I was worried."

"I'm sorry," she said. "I'm on edge."

"Why?"

"I have this feeling something weird is going on with Tristan."

"Why? What happened?"

"Nothing really happened. It's just we went to the restaurant... we went to The Vineyard, you know." I nodded. "Tristan acted like he'd been to places like that a million times."

"Like Eric?" I asked sarcastically.

"Yes," she said. "Like Eric." She drank some of her Sangria. "I honestly was worried about how he would act. You know?"

"I know. You mentioned that earlier."

"I had no idea what he was accustomed to," she continued. "What if the fanciest place he'd ever been was Ruby Tuesday?" I laughed.

"I like Ruby Tuesday."

"Eric. We're talking about Eric."

"True. So, what happened?'

"He ordered my dinner after asking my preferences. He read the wine list and ordered a Beaujolais. I'd never even heard of it. I mean, who does that? Besides Eric?" I shrugged. "He knew every utensil, every glass, everything. He even turned his fork upside down when he finished eating."

"No one does that but you Lilah," I said. "You and your mother."

"I know! Who else knows to do that??"

"I don't know," I said. "Maybe one his foster parents taught him those things."

"That doesn't seem like something you'd learn in foster care. Anyhow, do you have any cheese and crackers?" I looked at her sideways.

"You know I always have cheese and crackers." She jumped up and ran toward the kitchen.

"I'll be right back."

So, Lilah was beginning to have that sixth sense, too. I thought about the time Tristan had met Lilah at the pond. What had he been doing behind her house in the dark that morning? And what about the night they had sex up against her house? What was he doing in the woods behind her house *that* night? He wasn't a stalker. I did know that much. He didn't need to be, anyway. Lately Lilah would have shown her boobs to the Mayor if he'd asked.

I needed to do a little detective work. I needed to pay more attention to Tristan at school. You would be amazed at what you can figure out about kids if you give them an opportunity to show it to you. Obviously, I had to teach my classes, but I could stand outside my door between them. Occasionally I had seen incidents that needed attention. Not often but every now and then.

Most people in our town found it hard to assimilate my strict school persona with my lenient regular life. I was hard on the kids at school and if I knew they could do better I always made sure they did. Most of the them hated me but to me that meant I was doing a decent job. All the kids who came to my house *after* school knew I wasn't quite that strict at home. Okay, not strict at all. Lilah always said I was business in the front and party in the back. That wasn't one of her metaphors. It was a song, although currently, I couldn't remember the name of it. She came out with a wooden cheese board, about five kinds of cheese, crackers, and grapes.

"Are you hungry?" I asked.

"A little."

She sat down and started spreading goat cheese on a Wheat Thin. I picked up a piece of smoked gouda.

"Did you eat today?" She looked over to me.

"Do coffee and doughnuts count?"

"Lilah, seriously. You have to eat with the medications you're taking."

"I eat. Just not every day. Plus, last night I ate enough to feed an elephant. And here's another thing…" She stopped to chew her cracker. "Tristan paid."

"For everything?" She nodded. "How? Where did he get the money?"

"I don't know." She laid back in her chair.

"Didn't you ask him?"

"No," she said. "That would've been rude. Don't you think?"

"Not really," I said. "You kind of have an intimate relationship with him already."

"Well, I didn't." I sat up straighter in my chair.

"So, you don't ask him why he cries after making love with you or how he manages to pay for a two-hundred-dollar dinner when he's student in high school without a job?"

"I admit it's a little weird," she said.

"A little? Where in the world would Tristan get that kind of money?" She shrugged.

"I'm sure the Jenkins give him money for everyday expenses."

"That's not exactly an everyday expense, do you think?" She wiped a cracker crumb from the side of her mouth. "Jeez, Lilah. What if he's doing something illegal?"

"Like what?" she asked.

"He could be selling drugs, he could be stealing stuff and selling it. Who knows?"

"Good grief," she said. "He's not doing any of those things."

"And you know this how?"

"I don't."

"What about the weird thing you were talking about earlier?"

"I told you, Isabel. It's just a feeling. It doesn't mean he's a drug dealer."

"Well, what if I told you I had a feeling, too?" She turned to me.

"Really? Or are you telling me that to make me feel better? Or worse?"

"Why would I just be telling you that?"

"I don't know." I reached over and touched her arm. She looked down at it like I'd lost my mind.

"*Really*," I said. "I really have a feeling. A bad feeling."

"Then I guess we're up shit creek without a paddle."

"I have a paddle!" I exclaimed.

"Relax," she said. "The water's not that deep." I crossed my arms over my chest and she grinned at me, like she'd made a very important point. "You don't need a paddle yet. Just stand up." I took in a deep breath to appease my impatience.

"I used to think your metaphors were funny," I said. She laughed and took a sip of her Sangria. "I'm not even sure that was a metaphor."

"They're not funny anymore?"

"No," I said. "They're not."

That night after dinner I cornered Isaac in the kitchen.

"Wait," I said when he put his plate in the sink. He turned around.

"Yeah?"

"I need to talk to you."

"What about?"

"Can we go outside?" I asked wiping my hands on a dishtowel. "I don't want anyone else to hear."

"Okay," he said. "But let me get my pipe."

"Pipe?" I asked. He laughed.

"Not that kind of pipe, Mom." I put my hand on my hip.

"When did you start smoking a pipe?" He smiled.

"Yesterday?"

I shook my head in amusement and looked around the kitchen. It was a disaster, but I would load the dishwasher later. This seemed more important. A few minutes later, Isaac came out onto the patio from the kitchen. I had already made myself a ***Lemon Drop Martini*** from the bar.

"Cheers," I said when he walked over to me.

"Cheers!" Smoke rolled out of his pipe.

"That smells so good," I said. "What is it?"

"Cherry."

"Sit down." I patted the chair beside me.

"I know what this is about," he said as he sat down. "It's about Tristan and Lilah."

"How do you know that?" He looked up.

"Mom? Seriously?"

"I have this weird feeling. Something weird is going on."

"Like what?" Smoke puffed out of his pipe and he leaned over on his knees.

"I don't know," I said. "I can't put my finger on it, but you know they went on a date last night, right?"

"A date?" He raised his eyebrows.

"We're talking about Lilah," I reminded him.

"Okay, whatever."

"She said Tristan knew everything, the place settings, the utensils. Apparently, he ordered wine – not just any wine, a good wine."

"So, he looked it up online."

"He paid for it."

"Dinner?"

"Uh-huh."

"How much was it? Where did they go?"

"They went to The Vineyard. It was close to two-hundred dollars."

"Holy shit," he said as he re-lit his pipe. "Where did he get that kind of money?"

"I don't know. You tell me."

"How would I know?"

"You're one of his best friends," I said.

"I'm *one* of his friends," he corrected me. "I'm not his best friend."

"Who is?" He took a deep breath.

"I don't think he has one."

"A girl?"

"Not that I know of. I've never seen him with a girl." I pressed my lips together.

"I'm worried about Lilah," I said trying to reassure myself. "Maybe it's just my overactive imagination."

"Ben's apparently gotten over it. I mean, he hasn't tried to kill Tristan lately and they see each other all the time."

"How did that happen?" He shrugged.

"I have no idea. Maybe Tristan talked to him. He's good at that, you know."

"Ben wanted to kill him."

"I know but Tristan is a peace maker."

"Hmm…"

"Yeah, anyhow, I think you should leave well enough alone."

"They're still sleeping together."

"I figured." He pondered this fact for a moment. "Probably not a wise decision on Lilah's part. Not that it's any of my business."

"Coming from you? The boy who is sleeping with two girls at once?"

"I can't keep them off me." He grinned and pointed to his eyes. "It's the blue eyes."

"Yeah. Uh-huh."

"It's your fault," he said smiling.

"You think I should leave well enough alone? That's your advice?"

"I know you're going to hate this," he said. "But what would Dad say?" I rolled my eyes.

"He'd say leave well enough alone." Isaac reached over and patted my arm.

"Yep."

I couldn't justify spending a hundred dollars to color my hair when I could do it myself, so I bought a box of blonde hair dye at Rite Aid to brighten up what I already had. My hair was now bleach blonde. That is not what I intended but I left it on too long while I watched a re-run of Dynasty and that's what I got. Afterward when I looked at myself in the mirror, it scared me a little bit. Then I thought, who cares? It's just a thing. I think Lilah's attitude was starting to wear off on me.

"Wow," Matt said as he walked into the kitchen for breakfast. "When did you do that? Because I'm pretty sure when I went to bed last night you had…" He whirled his hand around over his head… "less blonde."

"I did it late last night," I said, a little aggravated. "I didn't want it to be this blonde. Does it look bad?"

"Uh, no." He sat down at the counter bar. "It looks good with your tan." I knew he was lying to make me feel better.

"Great," I said. Abe flew around the corner in his socks, skidding to a stop by grabbing the counter.

"Holy cow, Mom. What did you do?"

"Shut up dude," Matt said. "She's already upset."

"I'm not upset." I sat two cereal boxes in front of him. "Lucky Charms or Blueberry Morning. That's all I have left." He opened the Lucky Charms and poured some into his bowl.

"There are no marshmallows!" He shouted as he looked over to Matt. He dug through the box. "Seriously, this is not cool."

"Get over it," Matt said. "It's called life."

"Where is your brother?" I asked them.

"Don't know," was their unison answer.

I walked around the bar and down the hall to Isaac's bedroom. He was still in bed. I shook his shoulder.

"Wake up," I said. "It's Tuesday." He rolled over.

"Is there something significant about Tuesday?" he asked yawning.

"No. Just that it's not Saturday or Sunday and you have to get up and go to school." I walked back down the hall to the kitchen.

"Are you guys about ready?"

"I'd like to finish my cereal," Abe said. I looked at my watch.

"Okay, but get a move on."

All the boys usually rode with me to school until Isaac got his license and at that point I decided to let him drive to school by himself. I really had no choice after Tom bought him a truck. Thank you, Tom.

Matt and Abe pestered me to death about letting them ride with him but so far, I had refused. None of Isaac's friends could ride with him either. All their friends said I was the "cool" Mom but I was hard on my boys. I made them do chores. Apparently, no other child *ever* on the face of the earth had to do chores.

I despised a lack of respect and laziness. I did not allow my boys to be lazy. If they complained they were bored, I gave them more chores. If they sat in front of the TV too long, I gave them more chores, and Lord forbid if they sat staring at their phones. Lilah told me when she took Vonnie's phone away she had to stick it down the front of her pants so Vonnie wouldn't grab it back out of her hand. No child of mine would ever grab anything out of *my* hand. But then I didn't have girls.

This morning I was in a bad mood, not only because of my hair but because I was tired. I had barely slept the night before and despite Isaac telling me to leave well enough alone, I could not shake the feeling that something wasn't right. Maybe it had nothing to do with Tristan and Lilah. Maybe it was my typical ADD. I thought I should sit down and make a list of all the facts, not assumptions, I had about Tristan. I had a lot of assumptions but when I thought about it, not very many facts.

As if my day couldn't get any more aggravating, my car refused to start so I had to ride to school with Isaac - which meant I had to go back into the house and drag him out of bed and into a pair of jeans, so I wouldn't be late.

Because Isaac had one of those trucks with half of a backseat, all of us riding together was like the side show at the circus when all the clowns kept coming out of the Volkswagen Bug. Once we got there, I realized I hadn't packed Abe a lunch and he hated buying the food in the cafeteria. I gave him ten dollars and told him to walk across the street to the diner and get a cheeseburger. He wasn't happy.

This day had already proven to be "one of those days." It would be a day when I would have to sneak around the corner of the building and smoke a quick cigarette to keep my sanity. I tried not to smoke at school. It was hard to discourage the children from smoking when you did it yourself. Isaac and his pipe or his occasional pot smoking didn't bother me as much. They were only passing fancies not lifelong addictions.

When I was finally able to get away from my classroom mid-morning, I walked around the corner of the building with my hidden cigarette in the pocket of my dress. I was looking forward to enjoying a few moments of solitude, but I wasn't the only one around the corner of the building.

There, directly in front of me, were Vonnie and Tristan.

I didn't dare say a word about Tristan and Vonnie to Lilah at happy hour. It killed me, but I couldn't tell her until I had more information. It's not like they were kissing or doing anything illegal – that I could tell, anyway. They were simply talking and as soon as I walked around the corner, they stopped.

After dinner that night I took hold of Isaac's arm as he was leaving the kitchen.

"Grab your pipe," I said. He stood there for a moment.

"I should start charging you for this," he said. "It's beginning to eat into my "me" time."

"You're hilarious," I replied. "Give me a minute. I'm going to put on my bathing suit and get in the hot tub."

"Seriously. I should open a side business. I could call it, 'Therapy with Isaac' or 'Time to think with Isaac Lund.' Kind of sounds like a talk show, doesn't it?" I smiled.

"Shut up and go get your pipe. Can't you see how stressed I am? You are the only voice of reason I have."

"I thought Lilah was your voice of reason." I laughed.

"When has Lilah ever had a voice of reason??"

"Very true. Be right back."

I slipped into my swimsuit and padded through the sliding glass doors of my bedroom onto the patio. The hot tub wasn't on, but it was so hot outside I'd decided to leave it off. I could just sit in the water, cool off and relax. I made myself a ***Manhattan*** and sunk down into the water. I took a sip. It was a little more like straight whiskey with a hint of cherry. Perfect.

Isaac came out his sliding glass doors on the other side of the house and walked around the pool. I had never known another teenager who wore a Speedo, but he'd been wearing one ever since he was four when his Dad bought him one as a joke. He refused to take them off the entire summer. Tom and I only laughed and shook our heads. Little did we know when he outgrew it he would want another one and another one. I finally gave up and gave in, buying him a new Speedo until he was old enough to buy his own. The only fortunate thing about it now was I didn't have to go with him to the store.

"Hey," he said as he slunk down into the water beside me. He reached over and plucked the cherry out of my drink, popped it into his mouth. "What's up?"

"I'm going to cut to the chase and tell you what I witnessed today."

"Oh good," he said. "Because I have a conference call in fifteen minutes."

Isaac could always make me laugh with his dry sense of humor. His outlook was always positive no matter what the situation. Some people always looked for the worst outcome. Isaac always looked for the best. He didn't get it from me.

"I went around the side of B building today to smoke a cigarette." Isaac took his pipe out of his mouth, raised his eyebrows.

"I thought you had a rule about smoking at school." He grinned at me. "Were you having a rough day?"

"Did you drive me to school this morning? Have you taken the time to look at my bleach blonde Playboy bunny hair? I'm stressed about this whole situation with Lilah and Tristan. You tell me." He chuckled.

"Mom," he said. "You've got to stop stressing over Lilah all the time. It's like the story of your life." He pointed at his chest. "I love her, too, but she's going to do what she's going to do. It's out of your control."

"I know that," I said, frustrated. "But I can't help but worry."

"Worry about something worth worrying about - like where Abe's frog is."

"Why? Is he not in his cage?" Isaac held up his arm and looked at his watch.

"As of fifteen minutes ago, no." I rolled my eyes. "It's fine, Mom. Chill. It's a frog. It'll show up."

"Yeah," I said. "Probably in my toilet." He smiled.

"You said you witnessed something today. What was it?"

"When I walked around the corner to smoke my cigarette this morning, Vonnie and Tristan were back there." He sat up a little straighter.

"Doing what?" I shrugged.

"They appeared to just be talking."

"About?"

"I have no idea," I said taking a sip of my drink. "They stopped talking when they saw me."

"What did they say to you?"

"Nothing really. Vonnie said, "Oh hey, Isabel" and Tristan nodded at me and walked away.

"And you have no idea what they were doing?"

"None. Do you know anything?"

"Not really. I mean, I know Vonnie and Tiffany have become good friends. Vonnie is over at Tristan's house all the time with her. Maybe her and Tristan are just friends, too. Ever think of that?"

"They have to be friends around the corner of the building?"

"Well, ask Vonnie if you want to know."

"You do it."

"No," Isaac said, chuckling again. "You want to know, not me. You always told me growing up if I wanted to know the answer to something I had to ask the right questions."

"Did I say that?"

"Yeah." He nodded. "Take you own advice."

He got up and stepped out of the hot tub onto the patio, grabbing a towel from the chair behind him. He wrapped it around his waist.

"You can do it, Mom. I have faith in you. My conference call is getting ready to start."

"Well, you have been no help whatsoever," I called after him.

I downed the rest of my Manhattan as he walked back around the pool and into his room. He closed the sliding doors and pulled the curtain across. I could talk to Vonnie. Of course, I could talk to Vonnie but Vonnie wasn't exactly the kind of person who was approachable in these situations. I knew this and so did Isaac. Despite being like a second mom to her, she was likely to say something like, 'That's none of your business,' or 'Why do you need to know that? Are you writing my life story?' Anything I said after her curt response would fall on deaf ears. Getting an answer out of Vonnie over anything, other than what she wanted you to know, was like feeding spaghetti to a toddler. Frustrating and tedious.

Vonnie could have been confronting Tristan about his relationship with her mother. It would certainly be possible because Vonnie didn't take crap off anyone. If she wanted to know the answer to something she wasn't afraid to ask the right questions. I only had myself to thank for that though, because I'm sure at some point I was the one who taught her how to do it.

Later that night when I was getting ready for bed my phone rang. It was nearly ten. I looked down at the display. It was Vonnie.

"Hi, honey. Is everything okay?"

"Yeah," she said.

"You never call me anymore." She laughed.

"I know. I'm sorry."

"What's up?"

"Can I set up my drum kit at your house?"

She caught me totally off guard. This was the last thing I expected to come out of Vonnie's mouth. She hadn't played her drums in over a year. She didn't even have them set up anywhere anymore.

"Uh, maybe. Why?

"Well, you know Daddy won't let me play in the house."

"Yes, which I think is ridiculous."

"Yeah, I know but it is what it is."

Was I talking to Vonnie Trenton?? Yes. Because she wanted something.

"Where are you planning on doing this? Setting up the drums, I mean."

"In your living room??" And before I could answer, "You never use that room, Isabel."

"Well, the piano is in there."

"There's room. I already measured it."

I should have known. Vonnie was like that, always ahead of your next thought.

"Okay," I said. "I guess."

"When was the last time you played your piano?" she asked.

"Vonnie, you know I don't play anymore."

"How come? You used to play all the time."

This was something most people didn't know about me. Most people didn't know I had a piano at all because I kept the living room closed off from the rest of the house.

"I don't know, honey. I don't have as much time as I used to have, you know, with teaching school and all."

"Will you play with me?"

"Sure," I said. "You know I will."

"You can do all those sounds and stuff, right?"

"The synthesizer?"

"Yeah."

"Yes. Why?"

"Oh, I don't know. I was thinking about how you used to play all those cool songs and you don't anymore."

"Way to make me feel bad, Vonnie."

"Oh, I didn't mean it that way. Sorry, Isabel."

"It's okay. You're right. I should play more."

"Yeah. Okay. Thanks, Isabel. You're the best."

"Sure, honey."

This wasn't exactly what I'd had in mind when I'd made the decision to talk to Vonnie, but then God always worked in mysterious ways. There was no way I was going to ask Him what the call meant though, because I knew if I did, He would answer.

A couple of nights later I came home and heard Vonnie playing before I even got out of the car. I started to seriously reconsider my decision while thinking Eric wasn't being entirely unreasonable.

Of course, it only got louder when I walked through the front door. As usual, the sliding doors on the other side of the kitchen were sitting slam open. I sat down my bag and walked straight through the kitchen to the patio. All three boys were in the pool – a rare occurrence.

"Hey guys," I said as I sat down on a stool at the bar. Vonnie's drums were just as loud on the patio as they were inside. "What's up?"

"I couldn't hear myself think," Matt said. "I still can't hear myself think."

"Is she in there by herself?" I asked.

"Yeah," Isaac said. "But she has on her earphones."

"Oh."

"It probably wouldn't sound as merciless if you could hear the whole song," Matt added. I laughed.

"Maybe."

"I have to give it to her, though," Isaac said. "She's good."

"Yeah," I said thoughtfully. "She always has been."

Matt threw the beach ball in his hands hard and it slammed Isaac in the head. Isaac took off toward him and Matt hopped up onto the side of the pool.

"You better run," Isaac yelled.

"Why did she stop playing?" Abe asked me.

"I'm not sure," I replied. "But Eric wouldn't let her play over there."

"How come?" I motioned outward with my hand.

"Can you hear this?" He laughed.

I walked into the kitchen and down the hallway to the living room. Vonnie looked up at me but didn't stop playing. I waved to her as I walked into the room and she nodded her head. I walked over to the stereo and pulled out the cord for her headphones. The music of Phil Collin's "*Easy Lover*" filled the room.

"Better," I yelled.

She smiled and nodded.

"Much better," she yelled back.

When we were seniors in high school Lilah and I were addicted to clubbing even though we weren't old enough to go. We had some remarkable fake ID's and if one club discovered we weren't of age we started going to another one across town. When it got to the point where we stopped having hangovers we decided we needed to cut back a little on our drinking habit.

It's easy to do that, you know. Drink every night and then suddenly realize while you don't need to drink all day every day, you no longer get drunk when you do. You should get drunk when you've had fourteen ***Margaritas.*** You should get drunk when you have *three* margaritas.

Once we had the boys our clubbing days were over and for a while we hardly drank at all. We didn't stop for ourselves. I think we would've slowly and unknowingly drank ourselves to death if we hadn't had children. We might not have cared about our own well-being but having the boys changed our perceptions on a lot of things. If asked, we'd both admit we had a glass of wine every now and then while we were pregnant, but Lilah quit altogether once she started nursing Ben.

I knew I should have breastfed Isaac, but I couldn't separate the difference between the sex side of nipples and the motherly side of nipples. Lilah tried to explain it to me once – about how it created a bond between you and your baby, but it freaked me out to think my baby was going to be sucking on something that when sucked on by a man gave me immense sexual pleasure. Lilah is one human being level higher than me.

I spoiled my children as they grew up, but they were nowhere near as spoiled as Lilah's children. I used to think it was because she loved her children more than I loved mine, but then I realized she just loved hers in a different way. She showed love by giving material things. That was her love language. Gifts. My love language was Knowledge. I wanted my kids to know everything. I never wanted them to be in a situation without me when they didn't know what to do. I didn't believe I should shield my boys from anything they were going to encounter in real life. I wanted to prepare them for leaving my nest, not have them call me every fifteen minutes after they left it to ask me what to do.

Lilah and I agreed there were three things every kid needed to know how to do: shoot a gun; drive stick-shift and make homemade spaghetti sauce. Homemade spaghetti sauce goes with everything and always impresses people when you make it. Even if you don't like spaghetti sauce, it's still impressive.

We usually told our kids the truth about most things if they asked, and one day after a few too many cocktails, we confessed to Ben and Isaac the reason we'd created a daily happy hour in the first place was because we'd had them. It wasn't the smartest answer we'd ever given but they looked at each other like it was the answer they'd expected. We should have emphasized we meant the stress they put us under, not the fact that they existed. They had never stopped putting us under stress. Therefore, we still had happy hour.

The next afternoon, despite it feeling like it was a hundred and twenty degrees, Lilah had somehow convinced me to sit outside at the bar while she sunbathed. She had this thing now about having a natural tan. No tan lines -which I totally understood because I laid in my yard topless most of the time. All our children knew to check to see if I had on my top before they brought their friends out onto the patio. Most of their friends had seen me buck naked at least once – but it was *my* pool, so I didn't feel but so bad about it.

Now Lilah had come up with this thing about how we should stop using sunless tanning lotions for touch-ups because it rubbed off on the bed sheets. I knew this was true but only if you moved around a lot; or became tangled up in them with another person who I knew wasn't Eric. I had mostly given up on lecturing Lilah about Tristan. I had concluded it was a waste of my time and breath. I hadn't changed my mind about it and I hadn't stopped worrying about it. I had just stopped talking about it.

While I sat in the shade of the bar, Lilah began telling me about the new guy Vonnie had brought home. She said he had spoken a total of three words to her during what she deemed a conversation. I told her it wasn't a conversation unless both people were talking. She said he looked Russian, so I told her there was a possibility he didn't understand English.

"He understands his mouth on Vonnie's," she said. "He can't keep his hands off her. It's driving me crazy."

"That's disrespectful in so many ways," I agreed. "Did you say anything to him about it?"

"Yeah," she said as she rolled over onto her stomach. "I told him to get the hell off my daughter. Can you undo my strap, please?"

I was sweating like a pore-less pig, but we were drinking ***Cherry Kool-Aid with Vodka*** over copious amounts of ice. Lilah didn't know that, though. She probably thought it was some exotic drink I'd made up. I unhooked the strap of her bikini top.

"You didn't say that."

"Okay. No. I said, 'Would you *please* get the hell off my daughter?' He moved away from her after that. Then I told him he had to leave because I was sick of looking at him. He rubs me the wrong way."

"Did he?"

"What?"

"Leave?"

She raised her head and looked over to me.

"Yes. Vonnie asked me why I was being so mean."

"It's hard for me to really grasp this," I said. "I only have boys. I can't imagine what it would be like to have a teenage girl."

"If she gets pregnant I'm going to kill her."

"Um...I hate to be the one to point this out, but isn't that what happened to you?" She picked an ice cube out of her drink and threw it at me.

"Shut up, Isabel." I got up and started walking toward the pool.

"Oh, I meant to tell you," I said as I turned around. "Vonnie set up her drums in my living room." Lilah raised her head.

"Why? She hasn't played her drums in forever. They're packed away."

"They're not anymore. They're in my living room. She was just over here the other day playing them. Matt said he couldn't hear himself think."

"Hmm... What is she up to?" I shook my head.

"I have no idea, but she asked me if I'd play the piano with her."

"I thought you'd forgotten how to do that," Lilah said smartly. "Don't ya lose it if ya don't use it?" I shook my head.

"No," I said. "I can still play. Thank you very much."

"Oh good, because my mom asked me if you could play at church Sunday. Apparently, their pianist is on vacation. I told her you would." I panicked. That is exactly like something Lilah would do to me.

"Are you serious?" She grinned.

"No. I'm kidding." She laid her head back down on her chair. "I love you, Isabel."

"You will pay for that later."

"Mm…"

I walked over to the pool and dove into the deep end to cool off. I never stayed in the pool very long. I swam to the shallow end and walked up the steps onto the patio, grabbing my towel as I headed back to the bar. I leaned over Lilah and wrung out my hair.

"Isabel!!!" She yelled jumping up when the icy water hit her back.

I'd forgotten I'd unhooked her bikini top earlier, so when she jumped up it didn't go with her. The devil was the only one who could have orchestrated Tristan walking through the sliding doors of the kitchen at the same time.

"Nice," he said and smiled. Ben and Isaac walked out behind him.

"Mom!!" Ben yelled.

"Mother of God," Isaac said.

I threw Lilah my towel as a peace offering which she quickly wrapped around herself. Behind Isaac and Ben were Michael, Abe, and Matt. Tiffany, Vonnie and Vonnie's new boyfriend brought up the back end.

Vonnie's boyfriend, whose name I did not know at the time, had black hair with blonde tips. The sides were shaven so close to his head I could see his scalp. He may have had on eyeliner. The scowl on his face indicated to me he was not happy to be a part of this group. While everyone else had on their swimsuits he had on jeans and a dark blue t-shirt with a fire graphic that read, "Come and Get Me." It could have been a line in a bad death metal song or a jingle from a car dealership commercial. It should've have been the slogan for the S.P.C.A.

"Here to swim?" I addressed all of them at once.

Tristan sat down at the bar in royal blue swim trunks but no shirt. It was a little distracting. The rest of them were like my children. They could have been stark naked, and I wouldn't have noticed. All the boys except Tristan and Bret dove into the pool. Tiffany and Vonnie arranged chairs around Lilah and covered them with towels. Vonnie's boyfriend stood at the end of the bar in what seemed to be a daze.

"What is he doing?" I heard Tiffany ask Vonnie.

"I don't know," she said. "Bret, what are you doing?" He walked over to her.

"What do you want me to do, babe?"

He had a bold and arrogant way about him that made me want to hit him in the head with a 2 x 4 and he hadn't even said anything to me yet. He sat down on the end of Vonnie's chair and laid his hand on the back of her thigh, his fingers moving back and forth between them. I tied the back of Lilah's bathing suit.

"Bret," she said. "I swear to you, if you don't get your hands off my daughter I am going to chop your arm off and shove it down your throat."

No response. Only a blank stare.

"Mom!" Vonnie called. "Stop it! Okay?"

"Tristan," I said standing up and turning his way. "Can we talk for a moment?" Lilah looked at me like I was crazy, warning me with her eyes but I led Tristan away from the bar over to the hot tub area.

"Who is he?" I demanded.

"The Bret guy?"

"Who else would I be talking about?"

"I don't know," he said. "He doesn't go to our school."

"Where did he come from?"

"I don't know."

"What do you know?" I asked, aggravated with him. "I'm worried about Vonnie."

"Why are you worried about Vonnie?"

"Have you looked at him??"

"I can research him if you'd like," he offered.

"Research him? What does that even mean?" He shrugged.

"It means I can research him."

"I keep asking myself why I like you so much."

"I'm offering to help you," he said. "You knew I'd offer to help you or you wouldn't have asked me. That's why." He hesitated. "I'm also fascinating, mysterious, crazy good in bed…" I held up my hand.

"Stop." I took a deep breath and he raised his arms over his head and stretched.

"I'll take care of it," he finally said.

"How?"

"I don't know but I'll figure it out. Just don't ask me how I figure it out."

"Tristan, you freak me out when you say shit like that." He laughed.

"Jeez, Isabel. I'm not a serial killer. I'm just going to talk to him."

"Well, I hope you'll have better luck than Lilah. What are you going to say?"

"I don't know yet. I'm one of those people who can just come up with something at the last minute." I narrowed my eyes at him.

"Okay," he said looking down at me. "I'll admit I do know one thing."

"What?" I asked impatiently.

"He's not a very nice guy."

"I think that's kind of obvious." Tristan looked at me as if he were trying to tell me something without saying anything. "How do you know this?"

"I just do, okay? Don't you trust me?"

"No."

I turned and walked away. He ran up behind me and picked me up. I thought he was going to throw me in the deep end of the pool, but he put me down just as we got to the edge. He held on to my forearm, dangling me off the rim. I had nowhere to go but down.

"Tristan!!" I screamed. "Don't do it!"

He laughed and pulled me toward him but let go before I could regain my balance. I started to fall backward. I prepared myself to plummet to the bottom but within seconds he had grabbed me by my waist and pulled me back up on the side of the pool with him. There must have been less than a centimeter of space between us.

"Do you trust me now?" he asked.

I slapped him in the face and pointed my finger at him.

"Don't you ever touch me like that again!"

For some reason Lilah thought this was hilarious, but she was the one who wanted to be that close to him, not me.

He did kind of smell like chocolate chip cookies, though.

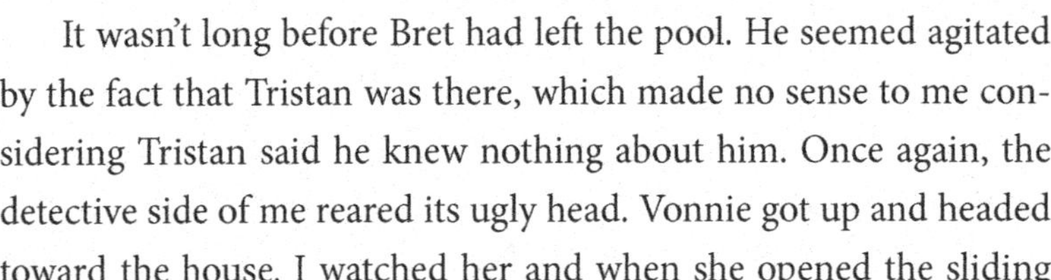

It wasn't long before Bret had left the pool. He seemed agitated by the fact that Tristan was there, which made no sense to me considering Tristan said he knew nothing about him. Once again, the detective side of me reared its ugly head. Vonnie got up and headed toward the house. I watched her and when she opened the sliding doors to my room, I yelled after her.

"Where are you going?"

"To the bathroom?" she asked sarcastically. "Is that okay with you or would you rather me use one of the boy's bathrooms and catch some viral strain of chlamydia?"

"Vonnie!" Lilah scolded.

"I resent that," Isaac called. She turned to him and blew him a kiss.

"Muah!"

"Alright," I told her.

I thought I should be nice to her now if I wanted to get anything out of her later. Tristan had jumped into the pool as soon as he 'saved' me and was now in the hot tub. Given I'd seen him and Vonnie around the corner at school, I shouldn't have been surprised when she came back out of my room and got into the hot tub with him, but I was a little taken aback she did it so openly. Her bikini was about two sizes too small, but I think that was on purpose.

She stepped down into the water slowly, but she lost her balance and I sucked in my breath. Tristan caught her by the tops of her legs and steadied her. She stood in front of him and leaned over, whispered something to him. As she did her hair fell into his face and he reached up and tucked it behind her ear. She sat down beside him and put her arm across the back of his shoulders. They talked for a moment and she laughed, kissed his cheek. When she stood she used his shoulder as a brace to step on the seat of the tub and up onto the patio. I briefly wondered if Lilah had seen them, but she was facing the other direction.

When Vonnie came back from the hot tub she laid down on her stomach beside her mother. I'd seen the tattoo on the bottom of her back a million times, but now that I was closer I saw what I'd thought was a design were letters written in script. They read 'Chattel.' That meant a belonging, a personal possession, property. Of who?

As if worrying about Lilah wasn't enough, now I started worrying about Vonnie. I worried about the kids – hers and mine. I even worried myself over some of my students. Tom used to tell me if I worried any more I'd spontaneously combust. I worried about the people I loved – and yes, I did love some of my students. You just do when you're with them every day.

I momentarily wondered if it was possible to love too many people. I asked myself this because I had even started worrying about Tristan. I wouldn't go so far as to say I loved him, but I did care – for Lilah's sake, anyway. Lord knows, if something happened to him, she'd lose her mind completely and never come back from it.

I'd never seen Lilah this preoccupied with any other guy, and I had seen Lilah with a lot of guys over the years. When she looked at Tristan, it wasn't with lust or any other kind of visceral passion. There was a glimmer in her eye and a flushing of color across her cheeks. When he looked back to her and caught her eye, he smiled and quickly looked away. Afterward, I'd noticed he was always lost in thought for a few minutes.

For Lilah, it was love. I wasn't sure what it was for Tristan, but I did know their affair had surpassed the simple fling stage. Tristan had an intention and it wasn't about his feelings for Lilah. Something brewed under his surface, an intangible emotion. I didn't think there was anything sinister about him, but what I did know was that guys like Tristan didn't play games. They did, however, write the rules.

On Thursday all the teachers received a notice informing us there would be a drug search the following day. We rarely got any earlier notice for fear word would get around to the students and they'd have time to prepare. We hadn't had one in quite some time. In fact, the school year was nearly over, and we hadn't had one at all which I found highly unusual. Immediately I thought about Isaac, Ben and Tristan smoking their weed a few weeks ago. Hell, I was smoking weed a few weeks ago. Holy cow. I needed to talk to all of them before the drug search. I didn't think they were stupid enough to take it to school, but you never really knew when it came to teenagers. If anyone knew about how stupid they could be, it would be me. I saw it every day. Right away, I knew I had to tell Lilah. She would flip her damn lid but then she'd been a little distracted lately.

"They're doing a drug search at school," I told her at happy hour that day.

I had finally convinced her it was hot as hell outside and I needed to sit inside before I had a heat stroke. Maria was sitting in the middle of the living room floor in front of us playing with little cars and trucks. They were the only toys I had saved after I threw everything else out of the boys' toy box.

"What's a drug search?" she asked.

"It's when they go to the school and take dogs to sniff for bad things," Lilah said.

"What bad things?"

"Like cigarettes," I said. "No one can have cigarettes at school. They're bad for you."

"But you smoke cigarettes."

This little girl. So smart for her age.

"Well, I know honey," I answered. "But I'm an adult and I can make the decision whether to smoke or not myself."

"Will you die?" Lilah laughed, and Maria looked over to her and frowned.

"No, sweetheart," she reassured Maria. "Isabel is not going to die."

"Well, that's good." She looked back to me. "Because I love you, Isabel." I smiled.

"I love you too, honey."

"Should we warn the boys?" Lilah asked. "Isn't that against the rules?"

"Of course, it's against the rules. But I do things against the rules all the time."

"True. Very true."

"We should warn Tristan, too. Have you seen him lately?" She grinned like a possum who'd just successfully crossed the road without being slammed by an eighteen-wheeler.

"Yesterday."

I got up because I knew there would be a sexy side to this story and I wanted to hear it. When your best friend is having sex with someone like Tristan and you haven't had sex in months, you want to hear it.

"Maria, do you want to go in the den and watch Barney?" She jumped up.

"Yes! Yes! Yes!"

"Be right back," I told Lilah. She took a sip of her wine.

"I'll get more wine."

"Great idea," I said over my shoulder.

When I returned from the den with Maria entranced by Barney, I sat down in my favorite chair and pulled my feet up underneath me. Mercy jumped up and laid beside me and Lilah handed me another full glass of wine. It was a tart Sauvignon Blanc, perfect for a sweltering day, *if* I was sitting inside in the air-conditioning.

"Tristan left me fast asleep in his bed yesterday afternoon."

"What?? Are you nuts?" She continued as if she hadn't heard a word I'd said.

"When I woke up, it took me a few minutes to realize where I was, and then I grabbed my clothes and snuck down the hallway."

"For God's sake, Lilah. Where was Mrs. Jenkins?"

"Not at home," she said and laughed.

"Please don't do that again."

"What? Fall asleep?"

"You know what I mean. Not over there, anyway."

"His door was locked."

"Who cares!?!" I exclaimed. "You're asking for trouble." She waved her arm at me.

"It's fine. Don't worry."

"Um…I…"

"You know how you used to call me to come over when Joe across the road mowed his lawn in the compression shorts?' I couldn't help but smile.

"Yes."

"It's like that," she said. "I'm not kidding."

This wasn't the kind of story I was expecting. I pulled my hair up off the back of my neck, blew out a cleansing breath, and laid my hands on top of my head.

"Oh, Lilah."

"It's fine. You always worry about things that haven't happened yet. Relax. You're worse than my mother.

"If your mother knew this was still going on, she would have shipped you off to another country by now with your passport and a couple thousand bucks."

"Oooh, that sounds like fun. Maybe I should tell her."

I was going to spontaneously combust. All those feelings I had, the questions I didn't have answers to – everything – was going to mutate into some strange molecule and explode inside my head. Tom was right. As long as I was friends with Lilah, I would never sleep again.

"Lilah!!" I screamed into the screen door of her back porch. It was locked. Middle of the day. Of course.

"Lilah!" I banged on it with the palm of my hand. "Come open this door. Right now!"

She came flying around the newel post of the back staircase wrapping a silk robe around herself. Tristan followed, buttoning his jeans.

“Holy shit,” I said as she unhooked the lock. “I would ask why the hell you have the door locked.” I looked over to Tristan. “But now I already know the answer to that question.”

“Does this constitute an emergency?” he asked. “Because we were kind of busy.”

I shoved him out of the way and opened the freezer, took out two shot glasses and the bottle of tequila. I poured Lilah and I both a shot. Tristan raised his hands.

“Uh?? There are three of us.”

“Shut up, Tristan,” I said as I handed the shot to Lilah. “Down it, then I have some not so good news.” I took my shot. I never said, ‘bad news’ to Lilah because it put her into a dead panic.

“What kind of not so good news??” I pointed to her shot and she took it.

“What??” she said as she slammed it back down onto the table. “Tell me!”

“They did the drug search this morning.”

“Which is why I’m not there,” Tristan added.

“Shut up, Tristan,” Lilah said.

“Supposedly, they randomly pick students.” Lilah nodded.

“Okaay…”

“Did Isaac get busted?” Tristan asked. I gave him my death stare.

“No. Not any of the boys.”

“Who then?” Lilah asked. She pulled her robe a little further around her and nervously reached up to touch one of her pearl earrings. She never took off her pearl earrings, but she constantly checked to make sure they were still there. “What? Who?”

“Vonnie,” I said. “They took her in for questioning.”

"Took her where?" Tristan placed his hands on Lilah's shoulders from behind.

"It's fine," he said leaning around her. "They're only questioning her. They won't take her anywhere. Don't worry."

"How do you know?" I asked.

"Because I've been through it before." Lilah turned around to face him.

"When?" we both asked at the same time.

"At other schools," he explained. "I have this little affinity for weed every now and then, you know. They'll ask her where she got it. That's all."

"Where did she get it?" Lilah asked. He shrugged.

"I have no idea."

"Well, where do you get yours?"

"I've had the same guy forever – downtown."

"You honestly don't know where Vonnie gets it?"

"No," he said. I narrowed my eyes at him. "Isabel, I swear. Don't you think I would tell you if I did?"

Later that afternoon I walked through my front door to a quiet house. I sat my bags down in the kitchen and walked toward my living room, opening the French doors. I turned on the lights. Vonnie's drums were there. So was my piano, which for some reason made me sad. I guess it was because I used to play all the time when Tom and I were married. He loved to listen to me play, so maybe once he left I subconsciously decided I wasn't going to play anymore.

I walked over to the piano and turned it on. I sat down at the keyboard and tested a few keys. I tried to think of something I knew by heart because I had no idea where I had put all my songbooks. I'm sure I hid them from myself, so I wouldn't able to play whenever I decided I wanted to do it again.

I laid my hands on the keys. The Christopher Cross song, "*Sailing*," came to mind and I began playing it from memory. It took a few minutes before I remembered how to coordinate all the sounds at once. I had only been playing for a few minutes when Isaac walked into the doorway and leaned up against the frame. He smiled.

"I haven't heard you play in a long time," he said.

"Yeah, well, you have Vonnie to thank for this." I nodded toward her drums.

"I know." Matt came around the corner with Abe.

"What is going on?" he asked looking inside the French doors.

"Mom is playing," Isaac said.

"Well, duh. I can see that."

They all stood and watched me as I played. I don't know why but tears ran down my cheeks. I didn't stop playing though, because I didn't want them to see me cry. The boys had no idea why their father and I had decided to separate. I wasn't sure if they knew it was because I'd been unfaithful.

I knew Vonnie had walked in from the patio because I could smell her perfume. The boys all turned around as she walked into the house toward them. Neither they nor her gave any indication they knew what had happened at school a few short hours ago. She pushed past them, like a typical sister would do, and they let her pass.

She dropped her backpack on the floor and walked over to her drums without saying a word. She sat down and listened to me play. After a moment she picked up her sticks and began playing with me.

She had that ability – to pick up a beat and play by ear. It gave me chills to hear her play her drums again. It had always given me chills because it came so naturally to her.

I thought at that moment these were the times I wouldn't trade for anything in the world. I only wish Lilah could have seen Vonnie playing that afternoon because within minutes she became lost in the music…and so did I.

Lilah

Vonnie's artwork began to look different somewhere between Christmas and Spring Break. She always left her drawing journal on the table in the living room and occasionally I would pick it up and look at what she had drawn. She used to draw flowers and unicorns and hearts - but now all I saw were empty faces. Some with tears, some with scars, all with the weary look of the world on their face.

I flipped through the pages. Why hadn't I noticed this before? Two sections. An imaginary divider between them. I would have labeled the first section "Dreams." The second? Well, I didn't know what I would label the second section. Not anything close to dreams, that's for sure. Three blank pages in between. So somehow, she had known even it was subconsciously, that you couldn't draw fairies and gardens on one page and haunting eyes with black landscapes on the next.

Vonnie had drawn two different worlds. One full of strife and discord, the other with nursery rhymes and unicorns. But where was she right now? Was she even in one of those worlds? Or floating around somewhere on the pages in between? I had to accept the fact as her mother I didn't know. I was in my own world. In Tristan's world. A world I should have never been in at all. Falling in love with Tristan was my downfall. I should have been able keep him at arm's length, far enough away from my heart so I had to think twice before letting his life gradually trickle into mine. It was the one thing in my life I knew needed to fix. Only I didn't know how. Tristan was like a drug to me. Every time I had him, I wanted just a little bit more.

I tried not to think about the fact that Tristan was just a kid, but by the time you are a thirty-seven-year-old woman you've learned to appreciate the difference between what Tristan had and what other women settled for - especially if you were standing up. Isabel is the only one who understands this because she knows me. Good sex is one of the hardest things for me to give up. Ever. Maybe I am selfish. Maybe Tristan and I are both selfish – because I didn't think he wanted to give me up either. Only now it wasn't just about sex. Now, it was about love. Love complicates even the simplest of relationships. So does sex. Both of them should be banned. There should only be like and lust.

I wondered what Tristan thought was going to happen with us? What was he expecting? Did he think I would leave Eric for him? Where were we going with this relationship? I didn't like to think that it would eventually end. It had to end. There was no other way.

I laid Vonnie's sketchbook back on the table and about jumped out of my skin when the phone rang at the same time. Instantly, I knew it wasn't Isabel asking me if her kids were at my house. I knew it wasn't my mother telling me I needed to appreciate Eric more. Neither was it the school calling to tell me one or more of my kids had missed a class at school that day.

It was the beginning of the answer to all my questions about Tristan. And consequences. Because for every action you take, there is a consequence that follows it.

Lilah

As I sat in the lobby of the Social Services Department waiting for my meeting I watched a little girl, about three, play with the toys from the toybox in the children's play area. Her mother had asked the receptionist what forms she needed to fill out to become a foster parent. The receptionist explained there were many requirements other than an approved application including parenting classes and sessions with the department psychologist.

I wondered if I would qualify. What did they think constituted being a good parent? Was it about rules and discipline? How much money you made? Would they allow you to use your better judgement in giving each individual child what they needed? Or did you have to follow the department's rules to a T? I seriously doubted Social Services would approve some of my parenting skills.

"Mrs. Trenton?"

"Yes," I said, standing up.

"Hi," she said reaching out to shake my hand. "I'm Reva Latimer, the Director." I nodded.

"Nice to meet you."

"You can come with me."

She turned quickly, and I followed her down a long white hallway. The last time I remembered feeling so cold and sterile was when I had visited my great uncle in the hospital before he died. I was quite surprised when I followed her into a cozy, plush office with leather arm chairs and a dark green velvet sofa which, coincidentally, also reminded me of my great uncle. There was a silver and glass pitcher full of water and ice on the coffee table along with two short glasses. Ms. Latimer sat down at her desk.

"Have a seat," she said, encouraging me to sit on the sofa. She didn't look up as she shuffled through the paperwork on her desk. "And some water if you'd like."

"Thank you but no. I'm fine."

I wondered if I would be fine after this meeting. Somehow, I felt like I wouldn't be. An inkling of dread crept into my mind. A sense of impending doom. Ms. Latimer folded her hands in front of her on her desk. I sat on the edge of the sofa holding my bag in my lap.

"I understand Tristan Collins is a friend of your son? Ben? Is that correct?"

Not Tristan, I thought. Please.

"Yes," I answered hesitantly.

"And that he spends quite a bit of time at your home?"

"Yes," I said. "He's friends with my other son Michael, as well." She lifted her hands and looked down at the papers on her desk.

"Yes, I see that. Tristan is also friends with Isaac and Matthew Lund? Whose mother is a friend of yours?"

"Yes," I responded. "Isabel is a good friend. Why are you asking me all this? What is this about?" She sat back in her chair.

"Mrs. Trenton," she said. "I don't believe this situation is in Tristan's best interest." My heart thundered in my chest.

"What situation?" I asked.

"I'd like to remind you at this point that Tristan is a ward of the state."

"What?"

"Tristan is a ward of the state. His parents' parental rights were terminated. When that happens with children under the age of eighteen the state is awarded custody and acts on behalf of those children."

"I'm sorry," I said. "But why are you telling me this?" She sat forward and leaned over her desk toward me.

"Mrs. Trenton," she said looking down. "This is not an easy task for me." She looked back up to me again. "I'm going to have to ask you to have no further contact with Tristan. I believe the current relationship you have with him is detrimental to his emotional well-being." I took a deep breath. She couldn't possibly know anything about what kind of relationship I had with Tristan.

"I'm not sure I know what relationship you're referring to."

"Nevertheless, Mrs. Trenton, I must restate my request that you have no further contact with Tristan." I leaned forward with my elbows on my knees. If I hadn't learned how to control it, I would have been hyperventilating.

"You cannot possibly be telling me Tristan can no longer be friends with my children or Isabel's children. They are his best friends. You honestly think taking away his best friends is in his best interest?"

"I am not saying he cannot be friends with your children, Mrs. Trenton. I am simply saying he is no longer allowed to be in your home or have contact with *you*."

"Me?" I asked putting my hand over my heart. "Why?"

"Let's be honest with one another," she said folding her hands in front of her on her desk. She leaned toward me. "I know how you feel about Tristan. I know what you *think* you feel."

"What I *think* I feel?" I asked incredulously. "You don't know me. You don't know anything about me and how I feel."

"I'm sorry, Mrs. Trenton."

"Have you told Tristan this?" I asked. "Does he know he's no longer allowed to have contact with me?"

"No," she said. "But that will be a conversation I have with him later today."

I looked around the room. The sofa. The coffee table. The floor. I felt like I had lost something. I felt both of my ears to see if my earrings were still there.

"You can't take away his friends and the people he loves," I said. "It will devastate him."

"I understand your perspective," she said calmly. "But it does not change my decision."

"Your decision?" I asked as I stood up. "Why is it your decision? Does anyone who knows Tristan ever get to make a decision?" I walked toward her desk and thrust my finger down onto her papers.

"You don't make decisions based on real people," I said adamantly. "You make decisions based on the paperwork other people give you. You have no idea what is best for Tristan." She stood up to face me.

"Mrs. Trenton," she said. "I understand you care about Tristan. There is no doubt in my mind about that, but it is my job to protect him. I do not believe the relationship he has with you is healthy."

Tears trickled down my cheeks and I tried to wipe them away quickly with the back of my hand. "You have no idea what you're talking about."

"I think I do," she said.

"But..."

"I have to remind you once again," she said. "Tristan is a ward of the state. If you do not abide by the directions of this department the state will press charges against you. I am trying to do you a favor."

"A favor?" I yelled. I was completely losing it. "How the hell is this a favor?" She walked around her desk and took my arm. I jerked away from her.

"I have to ask you to leave now," she said. "I'm sorry."

"I'm not finished talking to you," I pointed out. My hands shook.

"You are," she said. "Please don't make me call security." I turned around and grabbed my bag off the sofa. I looked back to her.

"You will soon find out how "detrimental" this is to Tristan. Let me know how your little talk this afternoon goes with him. Let me know how much better he is after you tell him all of this." I started to walk out of her office, but I turned before opening the door.

"I don't know what you think you know," I said more calmly. "Or why you think you know it, but I would never do anything to hurt Tristan. He talks to me and I listen. He trusts me. I am the *only* person he trusts. You can't change that no matter what you do."

She stayed silent, but I saw the compassion in her eyes. I half walked, half ran down the hallway, my heels clicking on the linoleum floor. The little girl who was in the lobby playing with the toys was gone.

When I got to my car I unlocked it and got inside. I fumbled with the keys and finally managed to get them in the ignition. My body shook with fear, frustration, and anger. I brought my hands to my face and tried to breathe. What had happened to my motherly instincts? How had I allowed myself to go this far? Where did I go from here? Did all the children know? I knew Ben and Vonnie *thought* they knew. But did they really? Did Isabel's children know? Did Eric? My mind raced with endless possibilities and, of course, consequences.

It was only after I had thought through every question anyone could ask, and rationalized every single answer I would give, that I leaned over the steering wheel and allowed myself to cry.

An hour later I was sitting at the bar in Isabel's kitchen.

"It's not like you won't see him at all, "she said as she opened the fridge and pulled out a container of juice. She took a swig then looked at the bottle. "This should have alcohol in it."

"But I can't be around him," I said. "At all." Isabel leaned up against the counter. "Like they can see inside my house." She shrugged. "He's here all the time."

"She said the state could press charges against me."

"Oh fuck, Lilah. Nobody is pressing charges against you."

"That's what she said. That's what *you* said."

"That's what she wants you to think, and I only said that because, well, I don't know why I said that. I mean, it was possible. It is possible…but they'd have to have proof and that is near *impossible.*" She laughed. "I would know, right?"

"Are you drunk?" I asked.

"Sort of," she admitted.

I put my head in my hands. My whole life had turned upside down in a matter of hours. I'd wanted to be friends with Tristan, but everything had spiraled out of control so quickly. My feelings had escalated and the next thing I knew we were kissing in my kitchen. What the hell had happened to me? How had I crossed that line so easily? I didn't want to cry anymore but my shoulders shook, and I laid my head over on the bar. Isabel came over and put her hand on my back.

"Oh, come on Lilah," she said. "You know how Tristan feels about you. That's not going to change. Everything will be fine." I looked up to her, tears streaming down my face.

"Everything will *not* be fine," I said. "Nothing about this is fine."

Isabel reached for her pack of cigarettes and lighter on the end of the bar. She never smoked inside her house, but she pulled out one and lit it, inhaling deeply.

"Here," she said as she put it between my fingers. "Smoke this."

Mrs. Jenkins lived in a stately brick home several streets over from mine where all the old grand homes of the Victorian era sat on a tree lined street that lead into town. Consequently, I had to drive past her house every time I went to the post office or to get groceries. Sometimes she was out working in her famous rose garden, sometimes sitting on her porch drinking what I imagined to be a cold glass of sweet tea or lemonade.

Ever since the meeting with Social Services I imagined Mrs. Jenkins had a lot of things she'd like to say to me, but she never would. Why? Because she was Mrs. Jenkins and Mrs. Jenkins was a docile woman. Her husband was a hardworking man, their home the jewel in their crown. I also imagined them lovingly doting on two abandoned teenagers who needed them as much as they needed each other.

Where in this twisted world did someone like me come from? My mother hadn't raised me this way. While it was true she was high maintenance and a little self-centered, I had never lacked for anything. As long as I could remember, she had always protected me like a hen on her egg. She'd fight for me. She wasn't like Mrs. Jenkins, which is why I called her.

"Hi Mom," I said when she answered the phone.

"What is wrong?" she asked immediately.

"Why? Can I not call you just to say hi?"

"Lilah, you have never called me just to say hi. You call me when the world is getting ready to collapse or you need money. Which is it?"

"I don't need any money," I said wearily.

"So, the world is getting ready to collapse? Or maybe I should say *your* world."

"Pretty much."

"I'm coming over." Click.

"Mom? Mom!"

I hated it when she did that. Whenever she believed you needed her guidance, talking on the phone just wasn't good enough. She had to see you face to face. Fifteen minutes later she walked through my front door.

"Grandma!" Maria exclaimed as she ran to hug my mother's legs.

"Hi, honey." She kissed Maria on the top of her head. "Someone had a shampoo today. Didn't they?"

"Vonnie did it!" Maria exclaimed.

"I figured as much." She looked over to me. "Lilah."

"Hi, Mom."

"Maria, honey, why don't you run upstairs and check on Vonnie?"

"She's sleeping. She'll get really mad if I wake her up."

"Well, then go check on Michael."

"Okay," Maria said contentedly, and she skipped off to the staircase. I led my Mom into the kitchen.

"Wine?" she asked. I pointed to the open bottle of red on the counter. "I don't understand why you never have a chilled white wine in your refrigerator. Didn't I teach you better than that?"

"Isabel has all the white wine," I said dryly. She turned to look at me.

"Does this have something to do with that boy?" I wasn't sure how my mom knew these things, but she always did. I nodded.

"Good God, Lilah." She pulled a wine glass off the wine rack and filled it with what was in the bottle on the counter. She lowered her voice to a whisper. "Does Eric know?"

"I don't think so," I said. "Not yet."

"What do you mean 'not yet?" She took a sip of her wine. "Are you planning on telling him? Because I highly discourage that train of thought." I shook my head.

"Mom," I said as I sat down in one of the kitchen chairs. "Social Services called me and told me I couldn't have any more contact with Tristan." She sat down beside me.

"Social Services? Are they pressing charges against you?"

"Not yet." She brought her hand to her forehead.

"Oh, my Lord. I am so glad you are the only daughter I have because I don't think I could take two of you." I sniffed.

"Thanks."

"What is happening?" she asked. "What do you need me to do?"

"Nothing," I said quietly. "I just wanted to talk to you." I hesitated. "On the phone. I wanted to talk to you *on the phone*. But here you are." She snapped her fingers.

"It's like magic. Here I am."

I lowered my face into my hands and began to quietly cry. The tears rolled down my cheeks and my mother reached across the table for a napkin. She handed it to me.

"Honey," she said. "You have to let him go. I told you to let him go, but you didn't listen. So, now someone else is telling you to let him go. Please let him go." I leaned over into her lap and sobbed. She put her arms around me.

"Okay," she said. "Okay. It's okay." She rubbed her hand over my hair.

"I don't know what to do," I cried. "Tell me what to do."

"I did," she said softly. "Let him go." I cried harder.

"I can't. I just can't. I love him so much." She pulled me up to a sitting position and wiped the tears away from my eyes with her thumb.

"I love him, Mama. I do."

"You love your family more," she said. "I know you do."

"But I can't. I can't just leave him." She took my upper arms in her hands, soft but firm at the same time.

"You're not leaving anyone," she said. "He has a home and people who care about him. Let him go."

"He doesn't really." Her grip tightened.

"Lilah Anne, you listen to me. This is one of those times when I tell you what to do, not ask you to do it. Do you understand?" I nodded. "Find a way to see him if you must but be very careful. Tell him goodbye. Tell him you love him, if you want. Tell him whatever you need him to know. Walk away."

"I wish it were that easy," I said.

"Sweetheart, I know this is heart wrenching, but it is necessary." I wiped my nose with the napkin.

"Do you know what the last thing he said to me was?" She shook her head. "He told me no matter where I went I was always the most beautiful girl in the room." Mom smiled.

"You are," she said. Tears rolled down my cheeks again.

"How do I let him go?"

"One day at a time," she said.

"You think it would be okay for me to see him one last time? That's what you said, right?" She nodded.

"But be very careful. Apparently, there are people watching, Lilah. I don't think I have to tell you this."

"Okay." She stood up and took me by the arm.

"Come on," she said. "I'm putting you to bed."

"What?" I asked. "It's five-thirty and I have to fix dinner."

"No, you don't," she said. "I'll take care of it."

"Mom, I can't go to bed for no reason."

"You have a reason. If this isn't a reason, I don't know what is." She led me to the back staircase. "You need time to think. Quiet time. Alone time. Let me take care of everyone tonight. You know I love to do it." I took a deep breath. I wanted to give in, give up, so I did.

"Okay. If you insist."

We walked up the stairs and into my bedroom. I sat down on the bed - the one I shared with Eric but had made love with Tristan in many times. Day before yesterday. I could still smell his cologne on the sheets. I didn't tell that to my mother. She helped me get undressed and into my nightgown. A mother hen guarding her egg. She reached into the pocket of her well-tailored jacket.

"Here," she said handing me a small white pill. "Take this."

"What is it?" She sat down beside me.

"Trust me."

"I am not taking a pill if I don't know what it is."

"Damn it, Lilah. Don't argue with me. Just do it." She handed me the glass of water sitting on the bedside table. "When have I ever lead you down the wrong path? When?"

"Never," I said quietly.

"Never," she repeated. "And you know why?" I was silent. "Because you are the love of my life." I smiled.

"Your Daddy thinks it's him." I smiled again.

"Ever since the day you were born, you've been the love of my life - because you were a miracle. I know this is hard." I pressed my lips together and tried to stop the tears. She lifted my face to hers.

"I know you love him. Don't think I don't know that." I brought my hand to my face. My body shook with grief.

"Heartbreak is never easy," she said. "It doesn't matter how old you are." I looked up.

"You just said it was easy."

"No, I said doing the right thing was *necessary*. There's a significant difference. Now, lie down. Take a little nap and when you wake up I'll be here, and we can talk some more. Okay?"

"Okay." I leaned back against my pillows. "What are you going to tell them?"

"Who?" she asked as she stood up.

"The kids. Eric. Why I'm in here."

"I'm going to tell them you're not feeling well."

"Vonnie will be so mad. She's always saying I spend my whole life in bed."

"Well, Vonnie doesn't understand right now. She will one day."

"One day," I said frustrated. "When is 'one day?' Shouldn't someone by now have defined how long 'one day' is?" My mom stopped at the threshold, her hand on the doorknob.

"'One day' for Vonnie will be the day she falls in love. When it happens, she'll think back to this summer. She'll think about Tristan. And you. And she'll have an 'aha' moment."

"Right," I said. "Sure, she will."

"Vonnie is a lot smarter than you think she is," she said. "She's just like you."

"No. She's not."

"She is. I raised you. I should know. She's doing stupid things right now."

"How do you know that?"

"Because I'm her Grandma, that's how – now rest, think about Tristan, go to sleep."

"I can't rest and think about Tristan at the same time." She opened the door and immediately pushed it closed again.

"Think about all the good things – think about the sex, hell, I don't care." She shrugged. "Get him out of your system. Cry. Ruminate. Masturbate. Whatever."

"Mom!!" She winked at me. Only my mother.

"There are good things with every bad thing, Lilah," she said. "You just have to figure out what they are."

A couple of hours later, my mom came to the door of my room and knocked softly.

"Come in." She had the house phone in her hand.

"Here," she said. "It's Tristan." I reached for it.

"What?"

She rolled her arm in my direction. Her signal to just do it. Like the way she told me to "go" when I needed to say something but didn't know what it was yet. She stepped back outside into the hallway and closed my door.

"Hello?"

"Hi," he said.

"Hi."

"I can't talk to you but a minute."

"I know."

"No, you don't know," he said impatiently.

"What is going on?" I asked.

"Vonnie is going to be arrested."

"What? Why? When?"

"Possession with intent to distribute." My heart pounded.

"Oh my God," I said.

"Get down to the police station. Don't tell Eric or anyone else. Bring money for bail."

"What? How much money?"

"I don't know," he said. "I have to go."

"Tristan, wait!"

But he hung up the phone.

I threw back the covers of my bed and grabbed my clothes off the chair. As I pulled my shirt over my head, my mother came back through my bedroom door. She had the decency to leave me alone while I talked to Tristan on the phone but not enough willpower to walk away from the door.

"What is going on?" she asked.

"Vonnie's been arrested."

"What??" She shut the door behind her. "Are you kidding me?"

"I wish."

"What is it with the two of you lately?" I turned to her.

"The two of us?" She sat down on the ottoman in front of my reading chair.

"What did she get arrested for?" I zipped my jeans.

"Possession with intent to distribute."

"This is what Tristan called to tell you?"

"Apparently."

"How does he know this?"

"I don't know," I said, searching around the room for my flip flops. I could only find one. "He told me not to tell anyone." She leaned down and picked up my missing flip flop from under the edge of the ottoman and handed it to me. "What number did he call from?"

"It wasn't a number." I looked over to her.

"What do you mean it wasn't a number?"

"It said restricted."

"What? Why?"

"I don't know. It's not important. Do you want me to go with you?"

"No," I said as I fell into the chair trying to put on my shoe. "I'm not supposed to tell anyone. Which means I have to go by myself."

"Lilah." She grabbed me by the arm as she stood up. "I don't like this. I don't like it at all." I pulled my purse off the back of the closet door.

"Well, I don't know what to tell you," I said as I grabbed my cars keys from the dresser. "I have to go."

"What do you want me to tell Eric when he gets home?" she asked, calling after me. I stopped and turned around.

"What? He's not home yet?"

"No," she said. "He called earlier and said his meeting was running late."

"Ah, of course."

"You really have no room to talk," my mother said. "If I were you I wouldn't be pointing fingers right now." I ran down the back stairs and she followed me.

"Right." I agreed with her. "But, I gotta go. Tell Eric whatever you want. I don't care but don't tell him the truth."

"I love it when you do that to me," she said as she stopped on the landing. Now, I'm an accomplice." I stopped at the newel post and turned to her.

"I'll call you." She put her hands on her hips.

"Okay," she said, exasperated. "I'll be here."

There were many times I had slapped Vonnie in the face for her disrespect toward me. I never planned it, but every now and then, she said something to me that hit a cord and incited an anger I couldn't explain. I rationalized she deserved it because she'd said some pretty nasty things to me over the years. The first time I slapped her came after she told me she knew I was sleeping around with other men. She told me I was nothing but a whore and I should consider making a profession out of it.

Isabel told me she was glad she'd had all boys but there were plenty of times she'd wished the opposite. She'd cried at Vonnie's ballet recitals, taken pictures of her at all her school dances and even gone with her to doctor's appointments when I couldn't get out of bed to do it myself. Vonnie had fire in her and while I was rarely able to come up with something to match her cynicism, Isabel could always put her in her place. She was sitting on her front steps when I pulled into her driveway.

"Get in the car," I yelled out of my car window. She took a drag off her cigarette.

"What? Why?" She stood up and walked toward me.

"Just get in the damn car," I said. She threw down her cigarette at once and stepped on it then turned around and ran back to her front door.

"Okay, okay, let me get my purse," she called over her shoulder. She ran back out and jumped in the passenger side. Abe came to the front door.

"Where are you going?" he called.

"I won't be gone long," she yelled back to him. He shrugged and shut the door.

"Vonnie got arrested," I said before she could ask what was wrong.

"For what?" she asked nonchalantly. I looked over to her, surprised she wasn't hysterical like me.

"Drugs."

"Awesome," she said. "What kind?"

"Seriously? That's your response?"

"I'm just curious."

"I don't know what kind, but I guess I'm about to find out."

"Did the police call you? What did Eric say?"

"Eric isn't home, and Tristan called me."

"What did *he* call you for? I thought you couldn't have any contact with one another. Oh wait, I'm talking to my friend Lilah, who never listens to anyone." I ignored her comment.

"He called to tell me about Vonnie."

"The police didn't call you?"

"No one has called me," I said. "Except Tristan."

I pulled into the police station a few minutes later and slammed on the brakes at the front door.

"You can't park here," Roy said as he walked down the sidewalk in front of me. He pointed to the parking lot behind us. "You need to park over there."

I handed Isabel the keys and jumped out.

"I'm looking for Vonnie," I said as I followed him inside.

"Who?"

"Vonnie." He said nothing. "Veronica? My daughter? She just got arrested, I think." He didn't seem surprised.

"For?" He walked around the front counter to face me.

"I'm not sure," I said, not wanting to give him any details. He typed into the computer and stared at the screen then looked up to me.

"Are you Mrs. Trenton?"

"Roy," I said. "You know who I am."

"I just gotta ask the questions. You are her mother, correct?"

"Roy," I said impatiently.

"She hasn't been brought in yet," he said.

"What do you mean?"

"I mean she's not here yet."

"Why not? Where is she?"

"What's going on?" Isabel said as she walked up behind me.

"She's not here," I said.

"Why isn't she here?" Isabel asked Roy.

"I just told Lilah. She hasn't been brought in yet." Isabel and I looked at each other.

"Okay," Isabel said, laying my keys down on the counter. "Where is she now? I think that's the question."

"En route," he said. He said it like root instead of route. "There's no official charges yet. How do you know about this, I might ask? Did your daughter call you?" Isabel and I looked at each other again.

"Yes," Isabel said. "Yes. She called me." I punched her in her side. "I mean, she called Lilah."

"Okay," Roy said. "You two have a seat over there in the lobby. I'll let you know when she gets here."

Isabel and I walked over and sat down in two hard back metal chairs, one on either side of a huge, fake palm tree. Isabel moved it out of the way and pulled her chair closer to mine. My cell phone rang at once.

"Hello?"

"Mom?"

"Yes?" I said, trying keep my composure. I didn't want her to know I was beside myself with worry.

"I think I'm about to get arrested."

"For?"

"Why are you so fucking calm?? I just told you I'm getting arrested!" Isabel jerked the phone out of my hand.

"You know what, Vonnie? Your mom and I are just sitting here, wasting away our Wednesday night at the police station, waiting for you to get here. Nothing else better to do except bail your ass out of jail. You're on speaker phone, so watch your words." She wasn't on speaker phone. I grabbed the phone out of Isabel's hand.

"I'm here," I said. "Tell me what is going on." I could tell she'd been crying.

"Nothing was going on," she said. "Bret and I were here watching TV and…"

"Where?"

"At his apartment. They knocked on the front door. They had a search warrant." She broke into tears. "Mama, I'm so sorry."

"It's okay, baby," I said. "Why would they have a search warrant? For what?"

"I don't know. They just got here."

Evidently, Isabel could still hear her because she whispered, "Probably because Bret has a dead body hidden in there somewhere."

I shushed her and mouthed the words, "Stop it."

"Where are you, honey?"

"I'm in the bedroom."

"Where are the cops?"

Click. I held the phone out from my ear and looked at it.

"What?" Isabel said, taking it from me. She put it up to her ear. "What did she say?"

"She said she didn't know."

"Didn't know what?"

"Didn't know why the cops were there."

"Didn't Tristan say drugs?"

"Yes."

"Does Vonnie not know that? Or is she lying?"

"I don't know." Isabel punched the code into my phone to unlock it. She scrolled through my received calls.

"What are you doing?"

"I'm looking for Tristan's phone number. I'm going to call him back and ask him what the hell is going on."

"No!" I said, grabbing the phone from her. "He said not to tell anyone. Plus, he called the house phone." Isabel looked over to me.

"Why? Why didn't he call your cell phone? Doesn't he have your cell phone number?"

"Yes," I said.

"Then why did he call your house phone?"

"I don't know."

"What number did he call from?"

"It said restricted."

"What? Why?"

"I don't know!!" I yelled. I laid over in my lap and hugged my knees. Isabel put her hand on my back.

"I feel like I'm in the twilight zone," she said. "Do you?" I sat up.

"I was humiliated and threatened this morning by Social Services, cried my eyes out this afternoon, told by my mother to masturbate while I think about Tristan, only to find out my daughter has been arrested for possession of some unknown drug, or whatever she's being arrested for. Yeah, I'd say the twilight zone is accurate." Isabel scrunched up her face.

"Your mother told you to masturbate??"

"Yeah."

"Did you?" I slapped her on the arm. "I'm trying to cheer you up!"

"Oh my God, what is wrong with you??"

"Vonnie is going to be fine," she said more seriously. "No matter what it is - it's a first offense." I suddenly had an 'aha' moment.

"Tristan said she was *going to be* arrested," I said thoughtfully. "Not that she'd *been* arrested."

"How would he know that?" Isabel asked.

"And he called me over an hour ago. Vonnie said they just got there."

"Again, how would he know that?" I shook my head back and forth.

"He wouldn't."

"Unless he's dealing drugs himself," Isabel said. "Which I told you I suspected before, but you told me I was being ridiculous. That would explain a lot of things, Lilah."

"Oh no." I turned to her. "The money. That's where the money came from."

"Uh-huh. That's what I said. You never listen to me."

"How?" I said, bringing my hand to my mouth. "How could I be this stupid? How could he do this to me?" I leaned into her.

"I don't know, honey," Isabel consoled as she put her arm around me. "But he's gonna wish he'd never met *me*. That's for sure."

The next morning Vonnie came downstairs wearing a denim miniskirt up to her ass with a white tank top just short enough for me to see the pearl belly button ring I didn't know she had. She had so much product in her hair it looked like she'd been on the beach for about three days without a shower. She walked around the corner of the kitchen table in black ankle boots and picked up her phone charging on the counter. She smelled like smoke with a light frosting of pine tree. I didn't say anything. Ben looked at me like he wanted to hit something. He had no idea what we'd been through the night before.

"Are you going for the homeless hooker look today?" he asked her.

"Shut up," she said to him as she opened the refrigerator.

"Hey," I said. "Both of you. Stop it."

"She's dressed like a hooker," Ben said. "She needs to change." She turned to him.

"Like I care what you think."

She flopped down at the table with a can of Mountain Dew and grabbed a bagel off the plate in front of her. Isaac walked in through the back door. He had finally convinced Isabel to let Ben ride with him to school. He raised his sunglasses when he saw Vonnie and looked over to me. I shrugged. Michael came down the back stairs and slapped Vonnie on the arm.

"What the hell??" she asked.

"Language!!" I warned.

"She's wearing my cologne," Michael said. I knew I recognized it. I just didn't know from where.

"Why are you wearing your brother's cologne?" I asked her. "Don't you have enough perfume of your own?" She cut her eyes at me. I was biding my time. Maria ran in and hopped up in Vonnie's lap.

"Hi, sweet girl," Vonnie said and kissed her cheek.

"You smell good," Maria said.

"She smells like a whore," Ben said as he got up from the table.

"Well," Isaac said. "Good morning, everyone." I motioned to Isaac to get a move on.

"Take Michael," I said. I took Maria's pop tart out of the toaster and sat it on the table. "Here, honey." I reached over and took the cup of milk Michael hadn't drank and gave it to her. She willingly accepted it.

"Vonnie," I said. "On the porch."

She got up and sat Maria back down in her chair, grabbed her backpack off the floor. I held open the screen door and followed her outside. I gestured toward her outfit.

"Anything you need to say before I go off the deep end?" I asked. She rolled her eyes at me.

"What's wrong with it?"

"It's not your usual style," I said cautiously. "Not quite, anyway. When did you get the belly button ring?"

"When did you get yours?" she asked.

"I've had mine for quite some time. Thanks for asking." I crossed my arms over my chest. "Was last night not enough?"

"What?"

"Isabel had to do a lot of fancy footwork to get you released last night with no charges. Thank you, Isabel." She frowned at me. "Are you trying to make me crazy? Because you're doing an excellent job."

"You're already crazy," she said.

"Look, I'm not going to pretend I know what's going on with you because I don't, but would you please think about what you're doing right now? Because you are about to make some really big mistakes."

"Like what?" she asked smartly. "Being with Bret?"

"I didn't say anything about Bret."

"You might as well," she said as she leaned against the porch railing. "You hate him."

"I don't hate him, honey. I just think you're worth more than that."

"That?? Like he's not even a person?" I took a deep breath.

"That is not what I meant."

"It is what you meant," she said. "You know good and well it's what you meant." She stepped forward, closer to me. "You think you know everything."

"I don't think that at all."

"Maybe *you* should be a little more careful about making," she put her fingers up in the air to symbolize quotation marks. "Some really big mistakes." I narrowed my eyes at her.

"I've seen you with Tristan, Mom. I'm not stupid. I don't need a rumor to tell me what I already know."

"Vonnie..."

"No! Listen to me! You don't know him like you think you do. I don't give a rat's ass who you fuck. It's not like you've ever been a real mother to me anyhow. I hate you." She turned and ran down the porch stairs.

"Vonnie!! Come back here." She stopped and turned around.

"Tristan tries to make everyone think he's Mr. Wonderful. Well, guess what? He's not." I walked down the steps toward her. "No! Stop!" she screamed and held up her hand. "Don't touch me." She was crying now, her mascara running black down her cheeks. I stood at the bottom of the stairs as she took staccato breaths. "You should be nicer to Bret," she said, calmer now. "You're going to need him when you're tired of fucking Tristan." I said nothing, but I brought my hands to my face and closed my eyes. "Because you *will* get tired of him," she said. "Just like you do everyone else."

I wanted to cry out to her. I wanted to tell her how much I loved and adored her and how she had my attention now. Tears rolled down my cheeks. I wanted to tell her I was sorry I didn't go to the mother-daughter luncheon for Mother's Day when she was in sixth grade or the ninth grade formal when she had the beautiful blue dress, but I couldn't. The words wouldn't come so instead, I just watched her walk away.

Despite everything I knew, I half expected to hear from Tristan that day. He always came over to my house unannounced and I didn't think the Social Services warning would mean anything to him. Seeing him was never a planned occasion, although Isabel always called it a tryst. I kept telling her I never knew when he would show up and she always said, 'yeah, right.' But it was true, I never *did* know when he was going to show up.

I liked to think Tristan checked to see if Eric's car was in the driveway before he came through the back-fence gate. Sometimes, I would be upstairs cleaning the girl's rooms or making beds and he would come up behind me and scare the living daylights out of me. On those days, he brought me flowers from the field behind my house, a Slurpee (which I hadn't had since I was sixteen) and every now and then, a pack of bubblegum. I think the bubblegum was a joke.

I didn't normally take Maria to day school on Wednesdays but that day I did because Eric was coming home for lunch, so we could talk about Vonnie. We knew we wouldn't be able to talk about it once he got home from work because all the kids would be there. He offered to take me out to lunch but I didn't feel like going anywhere. I almost felt like if one more tiny thing happened I was going to lose my mind. I thought if I could only talk to Tristan everything would be okay because he would be able to explain everything to me.

I made Eric's favorite chicken salad for lunch and some deviled eggs. The eggs were mainly for the kids. They all loved deviled eggs so much I made two dozen at a time. They were still all gone the next day. I don't know how in the world they ate all those eggs in two days. Sometimes I thought they must be giving them away to their friends because it seemed everyone knew about Lilah's deviled eggs. I heard the front door swing open.

"Honey?"

"Yeah," I called. "I'm in the kitchen." Eric walked in and kissed me on the cheek.

"I am so sorry you are going through all of this with Veronica. I feel like I've been such a horrible father. I never talk to her anymore." Eric insisted everyone call Vonnie by her given name - Veronica Lauren - but no one ever did.

"Sit," I said. I went to get our lunch out of the refrigerator. "You're not a horrible father. She's just at that age."

"Ben texted me and told me the two of you got into in an argument this morning before school."

"Well, yeah. She was dressed a little provocatively. Ben called her a homeless hooker."

"Oh, that's brotherly love."

"It wasn't inaccurate." He laughed.

"I guess I shouldn't be laughing."

"We'd die from the stress overload if we didn't."

I sat down at the table with him. He was always so composed and quiet. He never raised his voice to me or the children. He seemed unruffled by their behavior. He laid his hand over mine.

"It'll all be okay. I think we should sit down and talk to Veronica tonight, though."

"Probably," I hesitated. "But I don't want to."

"I can do all the talking if you'd like." He picked up a deviled egg with his fork.

"I would like," I said. "Because no matter what comes out of my mouth lately, it seems like it's wrong."

"Do you think she was guilty?"

"If you'd listened to Isabel at the police station, you'd say no. But in all honesty, I wonder." I gave him a roll and some chicken salad.

"Who is this new guy she's dating? Bret? Is that his name?"

"Yes."

"Have you met him?"

"I tried to have a conversation with him."

"Tried?"

"He's not very talkative." I took a sip of my tea.

"I see. Should we bring him up tonight or leave him out?"

"Given she told me this morning she *knows* I hate him, we should probably leave him out."

"Hmm... that may or may not be possible because I'm going to ask her some questions she doesn't want to answer."

"Such as?"

"I'm not like you, Lilah. You know that." I nodded. "I will ask her direct questions and get direct answers." I took a bite of my chicken salad.

"Good luck with the direct answers."

The screen door opened slowly behind Eric and I sucked in my breath. Tristan.

I put my hands over my eyes, leaned my head down into them. Eric turned around to see who was behind him. Tristan walked through the doorway. His presence took up the entire room. His scent and the outdoors flooded the kitchen. Eric stood up. Tristan ran his hand through his dark hair, pushing it away from his face, and extended his hand. He didn't seem bothered at all by Eric or the fact he was at home.

"Tristan," Eric said and took his hand. "Good to see you."

"You, too, Sir."

I was still sitting at the table. I wanted to get up, but my legs wouldn't move. I couldn't even speak. I didn't realize one of my hands was covering my mouth until Eric sat back down.

"I'm sorry to be interrupting your lunch and I didn't know you were here, Sir." My heart thundered through my chest.

"It's fine," Eric said and motioned to the table. "Sit down. Have some lunch." Tristan walked around the table and sat across from me. "I take it you know my wife rather well." Eric chuckled. "You must, since you assumed I wasn't here." I pressed my lips together.

"Yes Sir," Tristan said. "I came to talk to her about Vonnie."

"What a coincidence," Eric said. "That's what we were talking about." Tristan nodded. "Did you come to enlighten her?"

"I'm sorry. What?" Tristan asked.

"You must have some pertinent information regarding Veronica's current situation?"

"Who?"

"Vonnie," I spoke up. "Veronica is her birth name."

"Oh," he said. "I didn't know that." I nodded.

"So, you are friends with Veronica?" Eric asked.

"Well, we go to school together. I think I am."

"You are," I assured him.

At least you were, I thought. Before Vonnie figured out we were sleeping together. He laid his arms on the table. A silver ring on his thumb and another on his middle finger. The white V-neck t-shirt he had on stretched across his chest. I had never seen him with his hair up, but it was up today, pulled into a knot at the nape of his neck. His lips looked like he'd just finished eating a cherry popsicle. I closed my eyes again.

"This is probably none of my business," he said looking to me. "But I thought you might want to know a few things about this Bret guy she's dating. Isabel asked me to look into it."

"Isabel?" Eric asked. Tristan nodded. I didn't know this either. Thank you, Isabel.

"Yes Sir."

"And might I ask how you got this information?" Tristan looked down.

"Actually, no Sir." Eric seemed taken aback. No one said no to Eric.

"I see." Eric hesitated. "Go on."

"Bret doesn't go to our school, as you know." He looked over to me and I nodded. "He has an apartment on the East side. Not a good area. At least, as far as I'm concerned."

"Is this where Veronica was arrested? This apartment?"

"Yeah, I mean, Yes Sir." He looked down at the table.

I rubbed my temples with my fingers. My heart felt like it was going to burst out of my chest. Tristan looked up to me, gave me a slight smile, as if to reassure me everything would be okay.

"And?" Eric asked.

"Uh, he hangs with some pretty messed up guys. Bret, I mean."

I was going to jail. I knew it. We wouldn't need the money to bail Vonnie out of jail. We'd need the money for my lawyer. Tristan's cell phone beeped, and he pulled it out of his back pocket. He glanced at it.

"Yeah?" he answered. He pushed away from the table and stood up, listening to whoever was on the other end.

"Hold on." He covered the speaker with his other hand.

"I'm really sorry, Sir. Miss. Lilah."

Miss. Lilah?

"I have to go. I apologize." He held up his phone to his ear again. "Yeah?" Eric stood.

"Don't worry about it," he said, and Tristan nodded to him. "Thank you for stopping by."

Tristan placed his hand briefly on my back as he walked around the table. I wondered if Eric had noticed. He turned slightly as he went out the back door and mouthed, "I'll be back."

Usually, that meant later in the day. Or even the next day at the latest, but I didn't see or hear from Tristan again until a month later, when he showed up at the beach.

I didn't usually call Isabel on the phone during the day because she was at school, but I called her that afternoon once Eric had left. I'd thought about what kind of ammunition I needed for my conversation with Vonnie that night and I knew Isabel would be able to help me. Not because she was any cleverer than I, but because I knew she could get the information I wanted.

She didn't answer, but she texted me back at once and said, "What's wrong?"

I texted back, "Everything is fine. Just call when you can."

She texted, "Can it wait until happy hour?"

I texted back simply, "No." Fifteen minutes later she called.

"What is going on?" she asked. "I know it's not Vonnie because I literally just saw her."

"It's *about* Vonnie," I said. "And this isn't something we can talk about at happy hour."

"What? Hurry up, my students are coming in."

"Can you find out what Bret was arrested for?"

"Maybe," she said. "Why?"

"Because Eric and I are having a talk with Vonnie tonight and I want to have the correct information."

"Just the charges? Because if I talk to my uncle, he'll only tell me the charges but if I tell Roy I'll give him a blow job, he'll fax me the entire report."

"Funny," I said.

"True. I gotta go. See you at four."

"I don't think Vonnie is taking this seriously," I said to Eric before we called her down for our talk later that night.

We were having a glass of his favorite whiskey on the rocks. Not something I would normally drink but something he loved, and I partook in occasionally to make him happy. Honestly, whiskey wasn't one of my favorite liquors. I only drank it when Isabel slipped it into a cocktail or when I felt sick, because my grandmother always told me whiskey could kill anything. She meant germs.

"She should take it very seriously," Eric said. "Life is not a game."

"Just so you know, Bret was arrested for possession. They couldn't prove intent. They found pot…" I listed them on my fingers, starting with my pinky…" a small bag of cocaine, ecstasy, Xanax and prescription pain killers, which of course, weren't prescriptions. He resisted arrest, so things got kind of ugly."

"How do you know all of this?"

"I have my sources."

"So, Isabel?" I nodded. He turned and directed his voice up the stairs.

"Veronica Lauren! Downstairs. Now!"

She came down the stairs at once. If I'd been the one to call her I would've gotten the 'What?' yelled from upstairs, but not with her Daddy. Not only did she respect him, she was a Daddy's girl.

"Yes, Daddy?" Oh my, I thought. The devil in sheep's clothing.

"Come down here, sweetheart. I think we need to talk."

Is there an emoji for rolling your eyes? Because I'm technologically challenged but there must be. She came into the living room and sat on the opposite end of the sofa from me. I had a favorite chair, but Eric always sat in it when he was home.

"Your mother already enlightened me about what happened last night, but do you want to give me your version?" As if he had to decide between my story and hers. She picked at the polish on her fingernails.

"I don't know," she said as she tucked her feet up underneath of her. "Bret's apartment got raided."

"There must be a reason why this happened. What is it?"

Direct questions.

"I don't know."

Not so direct answers.

"You must know, Veronica. No one gets their apartment searched for no reason. Tell me what the reason is."

"I don't know, Daddy," she pleaded with him. "I don't."

"Okay," he said. "You don't know. What do you *think* it was for?"

"I don't know."

"Veronica Lauren," he said. "Please tell me you are smart enough to ask yourself these questions and come up with a logical answer." She pouted and gave me the evil eye, like it was my fault Eric caught her in her little white lie.

"I guess drugs," she said.

"Drugs?" he asked. "What kind of drugs?"

"I don't know."

"You do," he insisted. "Tell me what they are."

"Daddy…I…"

"Stop," Eric said. "I'm going to ask you again and give you a chance to tell me the truth this time. What kind of drugs are in Bret's apartment?" She took a deep breath.

"Um…pot…" She looked to me. "Obviously."

Why did she look at me? Isabel was the one who smoked it.

"And?"

"Why 'and?'"

"Veronica," he warned.

"I don't know, coke, ecstasy…I don't know, Daddy."

"But you know for certain, marijuana?"

"Yes," she said.

"Are you smoking marijuana? Tell me the truth because I already know the answer."

He didn't. Neither did I.

"Sometimes," she said.

"Thank you," Eric acknowledged. "Do you realize the predicament you've put yourself in?"

"Yes Sir."

"What are you planning on doing about it?"

"What do you mean?" she asked, blue fingernail polish flaking off her fingers onto the sofa.

"How are you going to fix this?"

"You mean, break up with Bret? Because that isn't happening."

Ah, the real Veronica rears its ugly head.

"I never said you had to break up with Bret," Eric said. "But I think you should seriously consider how being with him will advance your educational objectives. We've talked about this. We've agreed on your goals. You need to decide whether Bret helps you achieve your goals or prevents you from achieving them." She blew out a frustrated breath.

"Yes Sir."

"Now look," he said leaning toward her, elbows on his knees. "There is nothing wrong with smoking a little pot every now and then." He looked over to me. "I'm sure your mother has had that talk with you. Haven't you, Lilah?"

"Yes."

"Vonnie." (A rare occurrence with Eric, where he calls our daughter by the name everyone else does.) "You already know the answer to this dilemma. Do you not?"

She nodded, and a tear spilled onto her cheek. It seemed genuine, but I can guarantee you it wasn't because she didn't think she had done anything wrong. It was only because she knew she had disappointed her Daddy.

"That's what I thought, because I know how smart you are." Eric looked over to me. "Like your mother."

Ha.

"Come here," he said. "Give Daddy a hug."

Vonnie rose off the sofa and went to Eric. He patted his leg and she sat on his knee. She laid her arm around his shoulders and he wiped the tear off her cheek.

"I know growing up is hard," he said. "Your mom and I, we've all had these issues." He patted her back. "But we always come to the right conclusions. That's who we are, Veronica. Don't pretend you don't already know the answers."

"Okay," she said quietly.

"So, tell me," he said. "What are you going to do tomorrow to make your life better?"

"I'm not sure what you mean," she said.

"What are you going to do to prevent what happened last night from happening again?"

"Um…"

"You're going to stop going to Bret's apartment. Yes?"

"But…"

"That does not mean you can't see him. You can have him here anytime you like, as long as your Mom or I are home."

She can???

"But I think it is in your best interest not go to his apartment anymore. You agree?"

Like she had a choice.

"Yes Sir."

"You know I will know if you do," he said.

She looked at him as if she wondered how and he gazed back at her, eyes low. Vonnie didn't question her Daddy's authority. She might not understand what the hell he was talking about… half the time, I didn't understand what the hell he was talking about… but she knew not to question him.

"Yes Sir."

"Time for bed," he said as he pulled her close to him. He kissed her cheek. "Now tell your mother how much you love her."

Ha, again.

"I love you, Mom," she said in monotone.

"Veronica Lauren," Eric warned. "That was not acceptable. Go give your mother a hug."

Vonnie got up and came over to me. She leaned down, and I put my arms around her shoulders. She smelled like my coconut shampoo. She had stolen it out of my shower again.

"I love you, Mommy."

That, I knew, was heartfelt.

"I love you too, honey."

"Go get ready for bed," Eric instructed. "Mommy will be up to say prayers with you in just a bit."

I always said prayers with the girls before bed. I used to say prayers with the boys every night, but they outgrew it as they got older. Girls never outgrow Mommy and prayers at bedtime, no matter what their age. They'll act like they do, but they don't. Ever. If your daughter ever tells you she doesn't want you to tuck her in, in some capacity, she's lying. Do it anyway. She'll act like she hates it, but she doesn't. Trust me on this one.

There is no way in hell Tristan didn't know what was going on. He must have because obviously he knew much more than Eric and me, or even Isabel. He had this 'information,' as Eric called it that he wouldn't or couldn't divulge to us and I couldn't see him or talk to him – unless I wanted to be arrested. Maybe Vonnie and I could share a cell, or maybe Eric could put both of us in 'The Ward' and get a discount.

I was determined to talk to Tristan one way or another. I chalked this up to being a mother and needing an answer when fifty percent of it was wanting to unbutton his jeans one more time. I loved the way they popped loose with one swift pull. I should have been ashamed of myself. The fact I wasn't verified I was temporarily insane.

I couldn't call him on the phone or go to his house. He knew he couldn't come to my house and he rarely showed up at Isabel's house since the Social Services meeting. The one day he did I wasn't there. Isabel sent me a text.

"Tristan is here."

"Eric is *here,*" I texted back.

"Want me to take a picture??"

"You're hilarious."

"I know. It will be okay. Love you."

I broke down and cried. I missed him. There had to be a way for me to get in touch with him with anyone knowing about it.

The next afternoon Tiffany was at Isabel's pool with Vonnie. I tore a piece of paper out of Isabel's day planner and wrote:

Meet me at the clock tower. Tuesday, seven o'clock.

Lilah

I slipped it into Tiffany's hand and ask her to give it to him. She nodded and smiled. She knew.

Don't ever put something illicit on paper. Just don't.

And if you do, don't sign your name.

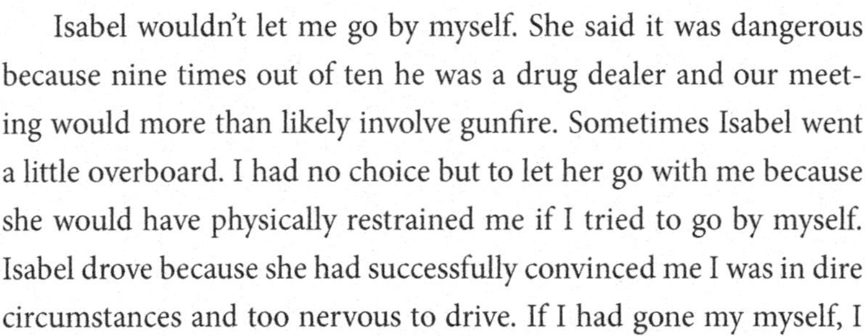

Isabel wouldn't let me go by myself. She said it was dangerous because nine times out of ten he was a drug dealer and our meeting would more than likely involve gunfire. Sometimes Isabel went a little overboard. I had no choice but to let her go with me because she would have physically restrained me if I tried to go by myself. Isabel drove because she had successfully convinced me I was in dire circumstances and too nervous to drive. If I had gone my myself, I would have been fine but then I could've been shot and laid in a gutter for two days before anyone found me. At least that's what Isabel said.

There was nowhere to park except the street, so we had to stop and switch seats because of Isabel's inability to successfully parallel park without hitting another car. Cars blared their horns behind us. Isabel flipped them the bird. We parked in a place where we could see the clock tower and sat in the car. It was six-thirty.

"What are we going to do for thirty minutes?" I asked Isabel.

"People watch." She pulled a bag of popcorn out of her bag. "Want some?"

"Are you kidding me?" She slid down into her seat.

"No. Why? Oh wait," she said, and I watched her pull two wine coolers out of the same bag. She twisted off the top and handed one to me. "Classic lime margarita."

"Isabel! We have to drive!"

"Are you being serious?" She twisted the cap off hers. "We drink three or four glasses of wine every day, martinis and everything else and *one* wine cooler is going to get us drunk?"

"Okay. Fine." I took a sip. "Mm, these are good." Isabel nodded.

"Popcorn?" She handed me the bag and I took a handful.

We sat for what seemed an eternity. At ten after seven, Tristan had not shown up.

"This is not like Tristan," I said. "He's never late."

"I thought you told me all of your love scenes were unplanned?" I shook my head and she continued. "Maybe he's sitting in Mrs. Jenkins' Mercedes somewhere watching for you and thinking the same thing." I took a deep breath.

"I guess I should walk over there then, huh?"

"Couldn't hurt." I flipped the visor down and looked at myself in the mirror.

"Lip gloss," I said as I held out my hand.

She reached inside her bra and pulled out her tube of lip gloss. She always kept it there, under her bra between her boobs. She said she did it was in case there was an emergency. I'd never ask her what kind of emergency. She handed it to me. It had a small penlight on the end.

"Seriously?" I said as I turned it on. "What is this for?"

"Have you never had to figure out how to put on your lip gloss in the dark?" I narrowed my eyes at her.

"Why would I be putting on lip gloss in the dark?" She widened her eyes and turned her head slightly.

"Holy cow, Isabel." I dabbed some on my lips, handed it back to her and opened the car door.

"I'll get in the driver's seat in case we have to make a fast getaway." I rolled my eyes.

"Right."

"You never know. I always tell my kids to be prepared for the worst."

"That is horrible advice," I said standing with my hand on the top of the car door. "You should tell them to always expect the best."

"And then they are not prepared when the worst happens. I deal with facts. You deal with emotions." She got out and walked around the car.

"I'll be back," I said as I walked off toward the clock tower.

"Tell Tristan I said, 'fuck you.'" I stopped and turned around.

"Isabel! That's not very nice."

"When have I ever been nice?" I nodded my head in agreement.

"I'm sure there is a logical explanation for all of this," I offered.

"Right." I prepared myself for the worst.

At eight, there was still no Tristan. Isabel walked over and sat on the bench beside me underneath the clock tower. She didn't say anything. Not I told you so or 'you should you light him on fire the next time you see him.' Nothing. But she did take my hand in hers. We sat there in silence for a few minutes.

"Honey," she said squeezing my hand. "I'm sorry."

All I could do was nod my head. Tears trickled down my cheeks, but I wasn't going to cry over him because he didn't deserve it.

Isabel said, "You can cry if you need to. I get it. I understand. He's a jerk but I get it." I turned to her.

"What if he's not a jerk?" I said. "What if there is something keeping him from being here even though he wants to be?"

"Is that your 'expect the best?'" Fresh tears spilled out onto my cheeks and she squeezed my hand again.

"Yeah," I said.

"Okay. Let's expect the best."

We sat there a few more minutes.

Then finally she said, "I'm sorry, Lilah. I'm trying."

"Trying what?"

"To think the best."

"Good Lord, Isabel. I thought you were going to say something poetic." She smiled.

"Love isn't logical, you know. I will admit that." I looked down to the sidewalk beneath me. "You don't get to pick who you fall in love with…" She hesitated. "Usually, it's someone you least expect – like a teenager – who also happens to be a drug dealer." She waved her hand in front of us. "But that's beside the point." I shook my head in amusement. "The point is that when it comes to love, you can't have expectations." She shrugged. "I learned that the hard way. You have to take it as it comes, leave it to the stars…which is nonsense and totally unscientific, not to mention ludicrous." I laughed and shook my head again.

"What?" she asked and laughed too. "It's true."

"So, you say."

"That's what you do, Lilah." She put her arm around my shoulders. "There are never any guarantees when it comes to love. Sometimes the gates of heaven open and you get a beautiful cloudless blue sky and sometimes the earth cracks open and you fall into the pits of hell." I looked over to her.

"You should do metaphors more often," I said. "That was good."

"There is hope for me yet." She pulled me into her and I laid my head on her shoulder.

"Thank you, Isabel. I love you."

"Oh," she said reaching for her bag on the other side of her. She pulled out her gun and handed it to me.

"Isabel!!!" I stuffed it between my legs. "What the hell?"

"You never know!" she said as she continued to dig around in her bag and pulled out a black t-shirt.

"Here," she said handing it to me.

"What is it?" I asked taking it from her.

"Smell it," she said.

"What?!"

"Just do it." I brought the shirt up to my face and inhaled. I turned to her.

"He left it on a pool chair," she explained. "I know you have this thing about his smell." I brought it to my face again.

"It's not chocolate chip cookies," she said. "But it's close. It's kind like vanilla with maybe cedar, patchouli." I turned to her again.

"Seriously?"

"I slept with it last night," she said teasingly. I hit her with it.

"You are so retarded," I said laughing.

"To only ten more days of school!" Isabel said as she held up her martini glass. She threw it back like it was a shot.

"If you were a stay-at-home mom like I am, you would not be toasting. You would be writing your own eulogy." I laid back in my lounge chair and she sat her empty glass on the umbrella table beside me, then tugged on her bikini top.

"I have to make sure my boobs aren't going to fall out before I dive in."

"I don't know why. Everyone has already seen your boobs. For the most part, involuntarily."

She flipped me the bird and walked over to edge of the pool. Ben sneaked up behind her and stood quietly. He motioned with his fingers for me not to say anything. I watched in amusement. When Isabel realized someone was that close to her, she let out a scream and fell over the edge of the pool into the deep end. She surfaced blowing water out of her nose and pushing her hair back.

"You little shit!" she yelled to Ben.

"I didn't even touch you!!" He said and laughed. She swam to the shallow end and came up the stairs to the patio. Ben jumped in before she could get to him.

Not one person had asked about Tristan or why he hadn't shown up at the pool for the last week and I was afraid to ask any of our kids if they knew anything. Isabel said he'd been on the absentee list every day at school, but the absentee list didn't give reasons.

I could have called Mrs. Jenkins if I'd wanted to cut to the chase, but I'd need some other reason to cover my true inquiry and I already knew what Mrs. Jenkins thought of me. Tiffany had also mysteriously gone off the radar. Isabel walked over and sat down on the end of my chair, towel-drying her hair.

"One of these days," she said of Ben.

"It's a love-hate relationship."

"You're exactly right," she said. "I loved him when he was little. Now, not so much." But she was smiling. "You should have drowned him at birth."

"Well, I tried to give him away, but you wouldn't let me."

"Ha," she said.

I was desperate for information. Call it a fixation, an addiction, insanity. Isabel would have called it an obsession. Maybe they were all the same thing.

"Has anyone said *anything* to you at school about Tristan?" She shook her head.

"No. Nothing. Don't you think I would've told you if they had?"

"What are the teachers saying?"

"Nobody is saying anything. Kids are sometimes out for weeks at a time if they have the flu or are in an accident. It happens all the time."

"Isn't there, what do they call it? The person who goes to check on kids who skip school?"

"A truant officer?"

"Yeah."

"I don't think they have those anymore. Lack of funding."

"What?"

"That was a joke. Never mind. The principal usually calls to check on kids who miss a lot of time, but that information is private." I looked over to her.

"No," she said. "It's not in his file. I already checked. I'm sure Mr. Miles has called about Tiffany and Tristan. I'm sure they aren't missing or dead somewhere. I think if they were, we'd know about it by now."

"Have any of your kids said anything?"

"No." I shook my head, brought my hands to my face. Isabel grabbed my foot and shook it.

"Stop it," she said. "It's out of your control. You're putting yourself in an early grave."

"What's the possibility he is involved with Bret somehow?"

"Fifty-fifty. If he's dealing drugs, more." She got up and walked over to the bar.

"Do you think he is?"

"Who knows," she said. "Maybe you should ask Vonnie. She probably knows more than anyone. Have you thought about that?"

My mind went back to the morning we'd argued. What had she said? That Tristan tried to make everyone think he was Mr. Wonderful, but he wasn't? That I was going to need Bret? What would I need Bret for?

"You know that morning I had the fight with Vonnie?"

"Yes," she said as she filled our glasses with ice from under the bar.

"Did I tell you she said I was going to need Bret?"

"What? Why would you need Bret?"

"I don't know."

"In what context did she say it?" I thought for a moment, felt the heat rising from my neck to my face.

"She said I was going to need him when I got tired of..." I mouthed the word... "Tristan." Isabel poured grenadine down the sides of the glasses.

"Did you tell Vonnie you and Tristan were sleeping together??"

"No. Of course not. She just thinks she knows. She knows the rumor."

"It's not a rumor," Isabel reminded me.

"Yeah, well." She handed me my glass. It was orange with red streaks in it.

"What is this?" I asked as she handed me the glass. I took a sip.

"Southern Sunset."

"Hmm.... cool. Does it have alcohol in it?" She scrunched her face up at me. "Well, it doesn't taste like it."

"Coconut Rum."

"Ah, well, there's my answer."

"If Tristan is somehow involved with Bret," she said. "Then it would make sense how he knew Bret's apartment was going to be raided."

"But why would he come to the house and offer Eric and I information on Bret? Wouldn't that be a conflict of interest?"

"He didn't really offer any information. He said he had it, but he never gave it to you." I nodded in agreement. "Other than saying Bret lived in a rough neighborhood, what did he tell you that you didn't already know?"

"Nothing."

"Nothing," she affirmed. She took a sip of her drink. "How convenient he got called away right before he was going to give you whatever information he had."

"I don't think that was his plan," I said. "Why would he show up at my house like that and offer information he didn't want me to have? That makes no sense."

"That's a good question."

"I think someone told him not to tell me. That was the phone call he got. Someone telling him not to tell me!" I jumped up. "That's it! I know that's it!"

"Okay, okay," Isabel said walking over and taking my drink from me. "You're spilling this everywhere. Chill out."

"I'm right. Aren't I?" She sat both of our drinks on the bar top.

"I have no idea," she said plopping down on a stool. "Maybe. Or maybe he has some infectious disease and they've quarantined him in some remote location."

"Stop it."

"Maybe he's an alien and he got called back 'home.'"

"Isabel!"

"You know nothing," she said. "These are all hypothesis'. What if this? And what if that? What matters are facts, not assumptions. Do you have any facts?" I sat back down on the lounge chair. The sun had gone behind a cloud.

"No. But I had started to feel better."

"Well, I hate to tell you this but nothing about that is factual. So, you're living in fantasy land." She pointed downward. "And you live here. On Earth."

"What if I'm right?" I said smartly. "I'm not stupid, you know."

"I never said you were stupid. I said you needed facts. And maybe you are right. But you can't go around jumping to conclusions and getting yourself into trouble. Are you following me?"

"Yes."

"Because you know what will happen. You will get too involved in this and before I know it I'll be rescuing you from the East side like I rescued you from..."

"Don't..."

"...everything I've rescued you from. Mainly yourself." She offered my drink back to me.

"I know."

"What's our motto?"

"Don't do anything I wouldn't do," I said. "Which covers everything and nothing at the same time."

"Yep," she said. "You got it."

Why don't I ever listen to my inner judgement? Why do I always think, 'Oh, it's okay. Everything will be fine, Lilah.' Why? Because I have inner judgment. I do. Those voices inside my head are not always telling me terrible things. Sometimes they tell me good things too. Warn me, for instance.

"Mom!!"

It was Michael, screaming his head off from the bottom of the staircase instead of walking up it, like I've always told him to do. I picked up the laundry basket full of Ben and Vonnie's dirty clothes and walked around the corner to the newel post.

"What?? Stop yelling." He was holding the phone in his hand.

"Phone call."

"Who is it?" He shrugged.

"I dunno."

"I'll get it up here. Listen for me to answer then hang up."

"Okay."

"And make sure you hang up," I yelled.

I walked into my bedroom and shut the door. I sat the basket of clothes on my bed and picked up the receiver on my nightstand.

"Hello?"

"Mrs. Trenton?"

"Yes? Hang up, Michael."

"Excuse me?"

"My son. I'm sorry. He was holding the line downstairs."

"I see. Mrs. Trenton, this is Reva Latimer with the Department of Social Services."

"Yes?" I sat down on the bed with the basket.

"Did you misunderstand our meeting?"

"I'm sorry. What?"

"Tristan's foster mother, Lucy Jenkins, found a note from you to Tristan on his bedside table. Are you aware you wrote this note?"

"What kind of question is that?"

"Did you write it? Asking him to meet you? I couldn't lie. It was a direct question.

"Yes," I said resignedly.

"This is my final warning to you. If you see Tristan again, in any capacity – whether it is your idea or his – we will take legal action. There will be no more phone calls or meetings with me. There will be police at your door with an arrest warrant. Do we understand one another?"

"Yes."

"Good day, Mrs. Trenton."

I took a deep breath. I pulled air in through my nostrils and held it for a few seconds before blowing it back out through my mouth. I got up, walked over to my dresser, and looked at myself in the mirror. I picked up a ponytail holder and secured my hair with it then redid my mascara. I thought about doing barbecue chicken for dinner. I could make potato salad or coleslaw. I thought I remembered seeing a cabbage in the fridge, but it could have been a head of lettuce. My toenails needed painting and Maria needed a bath. I picked up the laundry basket and walked out into the hallway. Ben was standing on the landing and turned around when he saw me.

"Hey," he said. "Can I borrow the Jeep tonight?"

"As long as it's okay with your father. Why?"

"Vonnie invited me to a party. Well, she asked me for a ride. I think Bret's car is in the shop."

"Where?" I asked.

"Where's the party?"

"Yes."

"I don't know. Some warehouse downtown."

I loved this about Ben. If I asked for the truth, he gave it to me.

"A warehouse downtown?" I asked. "That sounds a little sketchy."

"Since when did you start using the word 'sketchy?'"

"Since I just said it." He started off down the stairs again.

"Hey!" He stopped.

"What?"

"When you find out where this random warehouse is, I want to know."

"Mom, it's fine. I promise it's nothing 'sketchy.'"

"Will Tristan be there?"

It popped out before I could stop it. If I was going to ask any of my children about Tristan, my last choice should have been Ben. He pressed his tongue against his teeth and scratched his nose, shook his watch – which needed a link taken out – on his arm.

"I honestly don't know, Mom."

"Have you seen him?"

"Not in a while. No."

He came back up a few stairs to the landing, maybe so he could see my facial expression or maybe because he didn't want anyone else to hear him. I'm not sure.

"Look, Mom, I know you care about Tristan. Everyone does." He watched me. "He's a good guy for the most part but he's got something going on right now."

"What is it?"

"I don't know. I wish I knew because people keep asking me and it's starting to get annoying."

"I'm sorry." He shrugged.

"I know you're freaked out over him disappearing like this."

"A little."

"Dad asked me about him the other day."

"Oh? What did he ask you?"

"He asked me if you and Tristan ever hung out together alone."

"And what did you tell him?"

"I told him I didn't think so, but I really didn't know."

A wash of relief flood over me.

"I don't *really* know," he said. "I only know what I've heard, which is very contradictory…" I started to say something, but he held up his hand.

"Don't," he said. "I don't want to know. I only wanted to give you a heads up. I'm sure he's talked to Vonnie and Michael, too." I nodded. "I'm sorry, Mom."

"It's fine," I said. "I'm fine. Don't worry about it."

"Are you sure?"

"Absolutely." And before he could walk away I asked, "If I do barbeque chicken for dinner tonight, can you light the grill for me?"

"Sure," he said as he turned to go back down the stairs.

"Thank you." He turned around briefly.

"I love you, Mom."

I stood, shocked. Ben hadn't told me he loved me in years. The last time he'd told me he loved me was when he'd written it on a note. I kept it in my bedside table drawer to remind myself that, yes, Ben does love me. He'd been in fifth grade.

You know how people say terrible things happen in three's? I don't think people consider it if only one terrible thing happens. But what if two terrible things happen back to back? Then you start to wonder what the third one will be. You know it's coming so you're always holding your breath, waiting. After a while when nothing substantial happens you forget about it. But then a month or so passes by and another catastrophe befalls you. That's when you know, without a doubt, its number three.

Of course, number one was the meeting with Social Services. The original meeting when Reva chastised me for my relationship with Tristan but followed it up by saying she knew I 'cared' about him. Like that wasn't a slap in the face. Number two, of course, was when Tristan disappeared without a trace.

Most people in my situation would think the drugs with my daughter and her drug dealing boyfriend would be number three. Under normal circumstances that would've been true but what most people didn't understand was I knew Tristan's disappearance and Vonnie's troubles were related. I didn't know how they were related, but I would figure it out.

I saw Vonnie every day and even if she told me to leave her alone, I still said prayers with her every night. I might have worried about her, but she was still living under my roof so, for the most part, I knew she was okay. I didn't know if Tristan was okay. I didn't know anything at all.

Consequently, number three would have been when Eric asked me out to dinner at The Vineyard only to tell me he thought we should separate for the rest of the summer. According to him, we needed time to 'get our ducks in a row.' He said he knew I needed a break. That is, I needed some quiet time to organize my thoughts and 'deal with Tristan.' As my mother so eloquently put it, I needed time to think about how my family was more important than a love affair with a teenage boy. She said life can deal you hard blows and sometimes you had to choose between someone you loved and someone you loved more. It was never an easy task, she'd said. She assured me I already knew the answer.

The concept of *how* to have a family was never a question for me. You just married the man you loved and had one. But what if something happened to change the dynamic of that family? No one ever expects to lose a family member – a mother, a father, a brother, a sister, a husband - like Isabel did when she lost Tom. Isabel never thought 'oh, I think I'll take these naked photos with Chris today, so my husband will leave me.'

No one ever thinks, you know what? I'm gonna get married today and then I'm going to have three kids with a white picket fence and a golden retriever. We're going to church on Wednesday nights and to the lake on the weekends. We'll have friends over every Sunday night for canasta and drink wine on Tuesdays with our next-door neighbors. Oh, and after seventeen years, we're going to experience something catastrophic, or not so catastrophic, and our marriage is going to end.

Now my dilemma was not how to save my marriage but how to save my family. I poured myself a glass of wine and went out onto the back porch. I leaned over the railing and stared into the darkness.

I knew my marriage would most likely end. It's hard to save a marriage when you love someone else. When that 'something catastrophic' happens to you is when realize the importance of the word "family." It is also when you realize you'd do pretty much anything to keep them close to you. I wasn't going to take a chance on losing my family – ever, which meant I had to consider the possibility that I *would* lose Tristan. I looked upward to the stars, toward where I thought God must be, somewhere in the heavens.

"Are you there?" I whispered. "Tell me what to do. Please."

A tear rolled down my cheek and I reached up to wipe it away, but there was no answer. There were also no stars, so I sat down on the porch stairs and cried.

Tristan

"Hey," Tiffany said as she walked up behind me. "Nana wants to see you."

I turned from the window where I'd been watching the rain pour down in sheets. There was nothing comforting about the sea today.

"Okay."

I followed Tiffany through the house and up the grand staircase – the one with the red carpet, the one with the curving banister I could remember sliding down with my cousins when I was a child. I could hear Nana's voice coming from the kitchen. 'You boys stop that this instant!'

I walked down the hallway through the arched entryway that led to the back stairs and the bedrooms that were what Nana called the 'family quarters.' I could smell her Opium perfume drifting down the hallway, like it always had.

Inside my Nana's room was the rest of the family, but she'd already told them to leave. They all looked up as I walked in and shuffled out into the hall. Not one of them could look me in the eyes.

"Hi Nana," I said as I leaned down to kiss her cheek. She took my hand in hers.

"You know what I told your mother when you and Tiffany were born?" she asked.

"No," I said. I sat on the edge of her bed underneath the pink canopy she insisted not be taken off because no one knew how to put it back on the right way after they washed it.

"I told her you were going to turn out to be something special." I smiled.

"Me?"

"Yes. She told me I was crazy and that you and Tiffany were a curse."

"That sounds about right."

"She never meant it."

"Oh yeah?"

"Nope. She was a tortured woman. She never healed."

"I know." She rubbed my hand.

"I tried," she said. "Lord knows I tried."

"I know," I reassured her. "I remember."

"Your daddy didn't help." I nodded in agreement.

"No, he didn't." She wiped a tear from her cheek and I squeezed her fingers. "It wasn't your fault, Nana." She smiled, put her other hand around mine.

"Let's talk about something happy." She raised my hand and looked at it.

"No ring?" She seemed disappointed.

"No," I told her. "Do you think I'd get married and not tell you?"

"You better not even consider getting married without telling me." I laughed. "Do you at least have a girlfriend?"

"Kind of."

"What is that supposed to mean?" she asked. "Either you do, or you don't."

"She's kinda, well, she's not mine."

"Well, make her yours. Do you need a song? I can write one." I chuckled and shook my head.

"I think I already screwed it up. It may need more than a song." She reached up and tucked my hair behind my ear.

"It's probably because you need a haircut." I laughed again, and she motioned toward her piano in the corner.

"Will you play for me?"

"It's been a while."

"Oh, you can shoot those guns, but you can't play the piano for your Nana?" I laughed again.

"Okay," I said as I got up. I walked over to the piano and lifted the cover off the keys.

"It's probably out of tune," she said. I played a few chords.

"Yep."

"Sit down," she insisted. "You can't play standing up."

"Okay." I sat on the bench and laid my hands on the keys.

"You know the song," she said and when I didn't start playing instantly, "Amazing Grace."

"Give me a minute," I said. "Jeez, Nana."

I began playing, hesitantly at first, but it became easier as my fingers loosened, and I let the music flow through me. She began singing along with me. It wasn't the voice she once had but it wasn't difficult to hear the talent, the devotion she'd had to her music. Tiffany opened the door when she heard me playing and walked back inside the room.

"Wow," she said to Nana and motioned to me. "How did you manage that?"

"He loves me," Nana said mid-song.

"He does," Tiffany affirmed.

I squeezed my eyes together and took a deep breath, held it for a moment. Tears rolled down my cheeks anyhow. I couldn't wipe them away, so I let them fall onto the sleeves of my shirt. Tiffany walked up behind me and laid her hand on my shoulder. I stopped playing for a moment and took another deep breath. She leaned down close to my ear.

"You can do it," she whispered, and I began playing again even though I could no longer see the keys very well.

"Sing, Tiffy," Nana said so Tiffany began singing with her.

You don't forget the hymns you used to play every day. They knew all the words by heart. I knew the music.

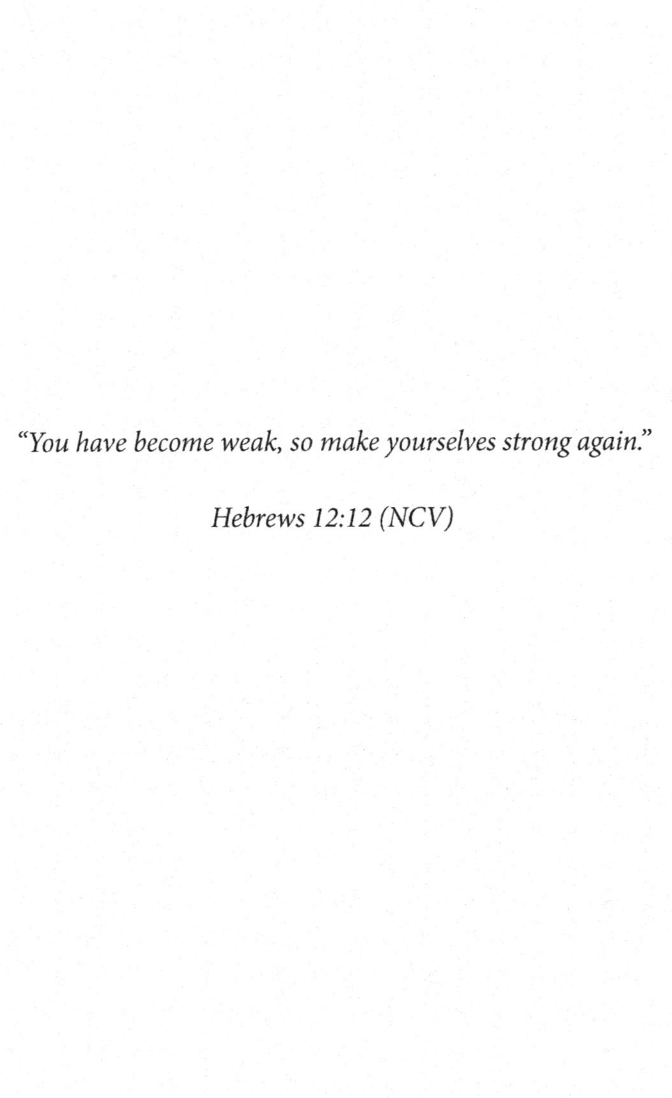

"You have become weak, so make yourselves strong again."

Hebrews 12:12 (NCV)

Lilah

What I really needed that day at happy hour was one of those Death in a Glass martinis because I knew it would obliterate all the madness going on inside my head, but Isabel had already picked out a cocktail for the day. Today the cocktail was: ***Mountain Dew Me.***

"You know the cocktail book you gave me last year for Christmas?" she asked as I watched her pour the ingredients over ice. She topped them off with a splash of Sprite.

"Yes," I said. "And I hate to be critical here but isn't that supposed to be Mountain Dew?"

"Yeah, but I don't have any."

"***Sprite Me*** doesn't sound as appealing."

"You're hilarious." She handed me the drink. "You should be proud of me. I've been using that book. I used to make this shit up in my head."

"And this is what I get? A Sprite Me?"

"I thought you needed a good laugh."

"I don't even know if I'm capable of laughing at this point. In fact, I'm pretty sure I'll never laugh again."

"You will," she assured me.

"When?" I took a sip of my drink.

"When one of our kids plays one of their off-the-wall totally inappropriate jokes on another one of our kids. Something so inappropriate that, as mothers, we should not be laughing."

"I can't imagine what's left."

"*Our* kids, Lilah.

"Do you know what Eric said to me?" I asked changing the subject. Isabel adjusted the beach towel on the back of her chair and settled down into it.

"Tell me."

"He said flings and affairs are different than marriage in that they mean nothing. They are only for fun. You can have a fling with anyone, but you should be a little pickier about who you marry."

"See? I told you!" Isabel said excitedly. "For once, Eric and I agree on something." I held up my finger.

"*But* the chance you take when you have an affair, or a fling is the possibility of falling in love and that is when you get into trouble."

"I have never 'fallen in love,'" she said. I pointed to myself.

"Me. He's talking about me."

"I know."

"He said there's no way you can love two men at once."

"Well, Tristan isn't a man."

"That's not funny."

"I'm not trying to be funny. And you can too love two men at once. Just not in the same way."

"I think he means the 'in love' part."

"No one stays 'in love' forever," she said. "At least I think the way you're in love changes over time. You're never going to have that first time feeling after you've been married for ten years. You just aren't... but that doesn't mean you love each other any less."

"It's not as exciting."

"Exactly. But you settle into a way of life. There's not as much hanging in the balance. You develop a routine. I guess for some people that routine gets boring after a while. I only wish Tom had seen it that way."

"In what way?" I asked. "That you settle?"

"Not so much settling as realizing love changes. Just because I slept with other men for excitement didn't mean I didn't love him anymore."

"Do you know how fucked up that sounds?" She shook the ice in her glass.

"It doesn't make it any less true."

"I guess Tom didn't want to take the chance of losing you, of you falling in love with someone else, like Eric said."

"So, what then? He doesn't want to lose me, so he divorces me instead?" I shrugged. "People make no damn sense. Why can't you have your cake and eat it, too? Why?"

"Because we're only supposed to look at the cake," I said.

"That's pure agony!"

"That's marriage."

"Tom was my best friend, you know. I thought I was his."

"You were, Isabel. He just didn't want to share you with anyone else."

"You know," she said with an impish grin on her face. "I don't understand why we can't all play together like good boys and girls and stop taking sides. Let's all just love each other together."

"I don't think most people look at it that way. People want commitment."

"Screw commitment," she said. "It's not about commitment. It's not about anything except agreeing you'll always have each other's back. Like us. You don't get jealous when I go have lunch with another woman." I stared at her.

"Do you?" I shook my head.

"No, but I'm not having sex with you."

"True." She paused. "I think sex is the root of all evil."

"It might be," I agreed. "That woman from Social Services called me again."

"What? Why?"

"Why do you think?"

"Tristan is not even around for you to be with," she said. "That woman is nuts."

"She found out about the note."

"What note?"

"The note I wrote Tristan about asking him to meet me downtown?"

"How did she find out?"

"She said Mrs. Jenkins found it on Tristan's bedside table."

"Jeez," Isabel said. "Holy cow. Did you tell her Tristan didn't show up for the meeting? That you never saw him?"

"No."

"Why not? You should have."

"Because I wouldn't be telling her anything she doesn't already know."

"You should have asked her where the hell he is."

"Like she would have told me." I pushed my hair back off my face. "My life is going to hell."

"No, it's not."

"It is," I cried. "Everything. You know how all the kids now are saying FML?"

"Yeah. Fuck my life."

"That's how I feel."

"I think they're kidding," she said.

"I hope so. But I'm not kidding." Isabel leaned over toward me and took my hand.

"We are in this together," she said. "We always have been. We always will be. Stop worrying so much. Everything will work out. Give it a little bit of time."

"I'm running out of time!!"

"No, you're not. Running out of time is when you turn fifty."

"Fifty is not that far away," I reminded her.

"Okay, sixty then."

"That's better."

"You know school ends next week. Wednesday is the last day."

"Yay for you."

"Let's go somewhere."

"What? Where would we go?"

"Duh…your parent's beach cottage?"

"My mother will not let you and I go to the beach cottage without her. You know how she is."

"She will after I talk to her."

"Well, I hope you can come up with something better than all the things I've tried over the years."

"I already know what I'm going to say." I turned to her.

"What?" I asked suspiciously.

"I'm going to tell her you're having a nervous breakdown."

"I AM HAVING A NERVOUS BREAKDOWN!!"

"Oh! Good!" She slapped her hand on my leg. "Now I won't have to lie about it."

The following Wednesday night (the last day of school), Isabel threw a surprise dinner for me at her house with all our kids. She got me there by telling me she needed my help in getting a dead snake out of the pool filter. Bring Maria, she said. I didn't question her because snakes terrify both of us – dead or alive. I didn't think she had an ulterior motive.

While it was difficult to convince Maria to walk anywhere it was not difficult to convince her to walk to Isabel's when I reminded her we would walk past Mrs. Brightwell's house. Mrs. Brightwell once told Maria she didn't like anyone picking her flowers, but that Maria was an exception and she could pick them any time she wanted. Maria was thrilled. Oh, to be five again when having permission to pick flowers was the highlight of your day.

When I walked out of the sliding glass doors onto the patio of the pool everyone jumped out from behind the pool furniture and yelled, "Surprise!" They waited for me to respond but I was confused. Maria looked up to me.

"Is it your birthday?" she asked. "Did I forget?"

"No, honey," I said. "I don't think so." I turned to Isabel because I thought with everything else going on in my life there was a good possibility I had lost track of time.

"Did I forget my own birthday?" She walked over and put her arm around my shoulders.

"No, Hon. You're good."

Each one of our children came over and handed me a card then put a lei around my neck. Isaac was last.

"What is going on?" I asked him.

Smoke drifted out of his pipe. When did he start smoking a pipe?? How had I not noticed this?

"Mom said you were depressed and we needed to cheer you up." He swung his arm out wide. "So, here we all are, and the leis were not my idea."

I narrowed my eyes at Isabel and she smiled in return. Isaac turned back to me.

"Don't let all this stuff with Tristan get to you. He's an asshole."

"Why?" I asked.

"Because he's not worth it."

"No. Why is he an asshole?"

"Do you know where he is?" he asked, his eyes widening.

"No, do you?" He shrugged and took another puff off his pipe.

"No clue. That's why he's an asshole. I mean, come on, he could have at least said goodbye to you."

"Yeah."

"And one more thing," he said before he turned to walk away. "I cancelled a date I had tonight with a really hot girl, so I could be here for you."

"I know that was a sacrifice for you." He put his pipe in his mouth and mimicked having big boobs.

"Hot," he mouthed and smiled.

I smiled, too. It wasn't a laugh, but it was progress.

Later that night in bed while Maria slept beside me I pulled out the cards the kids had given me. I didn't know until I opened them they were all handwritten letters on Isabel's stationary. She must have made everyone sit down at her house before I got there and write a note to me. Isabel knew I loved handwritten notes, that I treasured and kept every single one I'd ever gotten. It was exactly what I needed.

From Isaac: "Don't worry. Life is full of potheads…I mean holes. Ha, ha! Now, I lost track of what I was writing…Mom is telling me to hurry up…so thanks for being a second Mom to me. I love you!

From Ben: "Mom, you are an amazing Mom. I love you." (Short and sweet – that was Ben.)

From Matt: "Remember the time I got my shoe lace hung in the escalator and Mom was going to leave me there? Thanks for not leaving me. You probably saved my life. You're the best."

From Abe: "Jack is still missing. I've looked everywhere, and I thought maybe I brought him to your house one day? Okay. Just let me know. Love you."

From Michael: "Mom, you rock. One day, when I'm famous, everyone is going to look back to my childhood and realize you were my inspiration. Every song I write, I write for you. XOXO."

From Vonnie: "Mama, I know I am a bitch to you sometimes. I'm sorry. I get mad and say things I shouldn't and then I can't take them back. I wish I could take some of them back. I almost lost you

– the night you took your bath at Isabel's – and I remember thinking, what would I do without her? I don't act like it most of the time, but you are everything to me. Always and forever, Veronica."

And finally, one from Maria, which was a bunch of squiggly lines with Isabel's handwriting underneath:

"Mommy, you're beautiful. Love, Maria."

Tears sprang to my cheeks. I had vowed to myself I wouldn't cry but I should have known it was an impossibility. I looked over to Maria sleeping peacefully on my pillow, her long blonde hair curled around her face. I watched her tiny chest move up and down as she breathed. I touched her little hand with my finger and, just like when she was a baby, she wrapped her fingers instinctively around mine. But she felt safe. Didn't she?

I hadn't felt truly safe since I was a little girl living at home with my parents, but I hoped Maria would feel safe her entire life - safe and treasured not only by whoever she shared her life but content with what she'd become one day. I hoped if I couldn't be there for her someone else would be, someone who would love her as much as I did. I slid down in the bed next to her and pulled her closer to me.

There is nothing that can describe a mother's love. There is no way to explain the feeling you get when the doctor places your newborn baby in your arms for the first time, when you realize that not only is that baby a part of you, but that it belongs to you.

I could see a little of myself in every one of my children. Ben had my temper. Vonnie had so much of me in her it scared me. I swear that girl gets more like me every day - looks, actions, attitude. Mostly attitude. My mother wasn't kidding when she said one day I would pay for everything I did to her when I had my own daughter. Why are mothers always right? It was one of the more frustrating parts of my life – admitting that yes, Mom. You were right. Michael had my love of the arts and Maria? She was my little angel, so full of love and compassion. There was a quiet knock on the bedroom door. Eric. I could never figure out why he knocked on his own bedroom door.

"Is she out?" he asked as he motioned to Maria. He walked around the end of the bed and sat down. I nodded.

"She was tired." He laid his arm across my legs.

"I've found an apartment downtown on the river."

"Oh, I didn't know you were looking."

"Well, I have to go somewhere when I leave here."

"Yes."

"I can move in at the first of the month. It's a nice apartment. You can come look at it if you'd like. I'll probably need some decorating advice." I smiled.

"I might."

"You'll be okay here by yourself? I know we agreed on all this, but it doesn't mean I feel good about leaving you here alone."

"I won't be alone. The kids will be here."

"I know," he said. "But it's not the same."

"I'll be okay."

"I'm going to have to trust you on that for now," he said getting up. "I guess I really don't have a choice." He kissed the top of my head.

"Good night, Lilah."

"Good night." He stopped before he closed the door, leaned back around the casing.

"I hope you find happiness," he said. "I want you to be happy."

"I know."

"I know it's going to sound crazy..." He hesitated. "But I think if Tristan were still around I wouldn't worry about you as much. I mean, leaving you here."

Tears popped out onto my cheeks and I wiped them away quickly.

"It's fine. I'll be fine." He nodded.

"Okay, then."

He closed the door. He'd been sleeping in the guest room for the past few days – however long it'd been since we'd decided to separate. I wasn't sure if the kids had noticed. No one had said anything about it at all. Eric and I were going to have to sit down and talk to them. No details. Only that we'd decided to be apart for the summer. A break. A reprieve. Did you get one of those when you were married?? Should I consider myself still married?

Isabel informed me a few hours earlier she'd somehow convinced my mother I was having *another* nervous breakdown. I asked her why she had to point out it was another one.

Once I'd gotten home, true to form, my mother rang my phone every fifteen minutes until I finally sent her a text and told her to stop it. I was fine. She texted back, 'Okay. Love you.'

I knew it was a relief to her she didn't have to worry about me anymore tonight and that I was still alive. She was probably thinking more about the dinners she'd have to cook Daddy when Isabel and I went to the beach than she was about whether I was hanging from the kid's swing set in the back yard. Mom never let me down. She was always there when I needed her but most of the time she wasn't that thrilled about it.

So, I guess that meant Isabel and I were going to the beach. By ourselves, without the children - which meant I would have to tell Eric we were going to the beach, by ourselves, without the children. Under normal circumstances, Eric would've given me a lecture on how going on vacation with my best friend and leaving our children behind wasn't a responsible thing to do. He would've told me how other mothers would wonder why on earth we didn't take our children with us. Why would we want to go on a vacation without our children?

When my children were younger I'd chased them up and down the beach and worried they'd drown if they went in the ocean further than their ankles. Now, I worried where they were when they said they were going to the beach but never showed up. Now, it wasn't physical exertion. It was mental anguish.

My mind concocted crazy assumptions. I worried Ben had gotten into a fight over something trivial, like who caught the biggest fish, or that Vonnie was doing some random guy in the public bathroom. Hopefully, Michael was still sitting in the dunes playing his guitar and hadn't been kidnapped by a pedophile who'd been watching him for the last three days. So, yes, I would cut off my big toe to take a vacation without my children.

I started thinking. Me and Isabel. At the beach. Alone. I'm not sure we'd ever taken a vacation together alone. What would we do in a 3000-square foot beach house alone with a private beach?

"Kids!"

Even though I constantly yelled at the children about yelling I stood at the bottom of the stairs doing just that - yelling. I had asked them several times to help bring down my luggage. So far in the last hour my toiletry bag was the only thing that'd made it down the steps and I'd brought that myself.

"Stop yelling," Eric said from the living room. "They'll come soon enough."

This was one of my problems with Eric. He had too much patience and not enough emotion. I didn't want the kids to come soon enough. I wanted them to come now. I told him this. He laid down the newspaper and looked at his watch.

"What time are you leaving?"

"I told Isabel I'd pick her up at ten."

"Which means you'll be there by eleven."

"You know me so well." He shrugged and smiled.

I saw Vonnie walk past the baluster.

"Veronica Lauren!" She stopped.

"Yes?" I took a deep breath.

"Are you guys going to bring my luggage down for me or do I have to come get it myself?"

"Oh," she said. "I forgot. Yeah. We'll bring it down." And off she went.

Ten minutes later, after I had loaded the breakfast dishes into the dishwasher, there was still no luggage. Eric walked over the bottom of the stairs.

"Ben?" He called quietly.

I never understood how I could yell and no one heard me, but Eric could quietly say their names, as if he didn't want to wake them, and they'd hear him two stories above. Instantly Ben was at the top of the stairs.

"Yes Sir?"

"Your mother's bags?"

"Oh, right."

Immediately Ben and everyone else descended the stairs with my luggage. Maria had my favorite round pillow in her arms. When she got to the bottom she handed it to me.

"Here, Mommy. I thought you'd want your favorite pillow." I squatted down and kissed her cheek.

"Why thank you, sweet pea." She beamed.

I'd made plans for my mother to keep Maria while I was gone. It wasn't because I didn't trust Eric, but he tended to focus on things other than the children, like where he'd put his 9-iron or if Ben had cut the grass too short. He told me he was going to cut back his work hours. He was going to leave later in the morning and come home earlier in the afternoon, which I knew he entirely intended but which would never happen. So, even though Eric thought he was in charge, he really wasn't. My mother was in charge. And she could do it. Even from across town.

The fact of the matter was my children never knew when Grandma might show up, so the house would stay clean like I left it. Plus, there would be a lot less trouble between them. No one was afraid of me. *Everyone* was afraid of my mother. I never understood why. She was 5'1" and weighed less than a hundred pounds.

I arrived at Isabel's at five to eleven. Her house was in complete disarray.

"Hello?" I called as I walked through the foyer into the kitchen. I closed the sliding glass doors out onto the patio.

"I'm back here."

I heard Isabel's voice, so I followed it down the hallway to her room. As I went I stepped over a half-rolled roll of toilet paper; two dog chewy toys – Abe had gotten an Irish Setter puppy for his birthday, which in some crazy way was supposed to make up for the dead frog they found in the pool filter; a bright yellow, plastic lemon juicer, which I'm sure the puppy was also using as a chew toy given it had teeth indentions in it; and a wet beach towel (on the parquet floor) which I picked up and carried with me into Isabel's room.

"Holy shit, Isabel. What is going on?" She turned around. It looked like every single piece of clothing she owned was stretched across the chaise lounge behind her.

"Did you hear?" she asked. "We got a puppy!"

"I told you," I said. "I told you. I told you. I told you."

"Shut up," she said turning back to her clothes. "Abe is happier than a bird with a French fry." I wanted to laugh but my heart wouldn't let me.

"And your house looks like you just a had a fraternity party." She pointed her finger at me.

"Don't start with me." She sunk down onto the chaise lounge. "I am so tired and it's not even noon."

"Where are the boys?"

"They're with Tom."

"And the puppy?"

"With Tom." She laughed hysterically. "He buys Isaac a truck. I buy Abe a puppy."

"But you have to live with the puppy," I pointed out.

"It's worth it just so I can hear about the havoc it creates at Tom's house on the weekends."

"You are sick," I said. She raised her eyebrows and smiled. "Are you almost ready?" She waved her arm around her room like Vanna White showcasing a new car.

"Do I look like I'm ready?"

"I'm nearly an hour late! It'll be midnight by the time we get to the cottage at this rate."

"Not if I'm driving."

"You're not driving," I said as I sat down on her bed. "The jeep is stick-shift."

"Do you know me? Plus, you hate to drive." I shrugged, and she got up off the chaise lounge. She walked over to the bed where I was sitting.

"Lift your feet."

I did, and she pulled out her two suitcases from underneath. She began to throw everything on her chaise lounge into the bigger one. She opened her lingerie drawer, yanked it off the track, and dumped everything inside of it into the smaller one.

"Isabel, you don't need all that lingerie."

"How do you know? I might be with a different man every night."

"If you're with a different man every night you can wear the same thing over and over and no one will know the difference." She thought about that for a moment.

"True."

"Plus, I imagine you'll be in your bathing suit most of the time."

"Oh wow," she said. She sat her lingerie drawer on top of her dresser. "Bathing suits." She ran to the other side of the room and opened a small trunk up against the wall. She pulled out about sixteen different bathing suits.

"Are you serious?" I asked. "You were going to forget your bathing suits?" She stood up.

"Do you have a puppy?"

"I have Eric."

"You *had* Eric." She threw all her bathing suits into the suitcase with the lingerie, closed the lid and zipped it. "Let's go."

It took us about an hour to load the jeep because I'd forgotten the bungee cords we needed to strap down all our luggage, not to mention all the other stuff we decided we'd need - Ben and Isaac's fishing poles so we could fish, although we wouldn't and we both knew this; twelve beach towels - despite my mother having a state of the art washing machine which I had no idea how to operate; a lantern (Isabel's idea) and a cooler full of wine coolers both of us could drink without ever getting a buzz. We drove three and a half hours, stopped for an early dinner, and rolled into the Outer Banks about half past six.

It wasn't hard for Isabel to talk me into letting her drive the Jeep because she was right. I hated to drive. Although I had to drive the final hour because she was too drunk from the six margaritas she'd had at dinner. That was okay because it meant I got to drive across the bridge from Nags Head to Hatteras. There aren't many places more awe inspiring than the Oregon Inlet at dusk. Halfway across I concluded Isabel's drunken insistence we take the top off the Jeep in the restaurant parking lot was actually a good idea.

When we pulled into the oyster shell lined driveway I punched her in the arm because she was almost asleep. Fortunately, she had not been able to convince me to take off the doors. Otherwise, she would have been laying in the middle of Route 158.

"Hey," I said, and she jumped. "Listen."

The ocean. The sound of waves rolling in onto the beach. The smell of the salt air. The thought of putting my feet in the sand. The sunset I knew we were getting ready to witness. I gazed distractedly at the grass blowing in the wind on the dunes in front of us.

"I miss Tristan."

Isabel pulled the Sunny Days guide she had picked up at the restaurant out of the glove compartment and hit me over the head with it.

"Ow."

"I swear to God, Lilah. Don't start."

She narrowed her eyes at me and I bit my lip. In that instant she knew. She unhooked her seatbelt then fell back against her seat when I didn't move. Her eyes softened.

Best friends are like that. They know what you want to say but can't. They know what you feel even if they've never felt it before themselves because they know the truth of who you are. Even when everyone else in the world passes judgement on you, best friends know your heart.

It didn't make the relationship I'd had with Tristan any less wrong. It only made me realize I didn't have to be perfect. For myself. For anyone else. Not my children. And, according to my mother, not even God. I had made a mistake, but Isabel wasn't about to crucify me for it. She wasn't going to tell me it was a great decision either, but she wouldn't let me go through it alone. She reached over and squeezed my hand.

"He's gone, Lilah," she said. "You realize that, right?" Tears rolled down my cheeks and I reached up to wipe them away.

"I know."

"I know you loved him." She hesitated. "But you have to let him go."

I sniffed and brought my hand to my mouth. I tried to hold in the heartbreak, but I couldn't. It hurt so bad it made me sick. I leaned over the side of the Jeep and threw up my entire dinner into the driveway. Isabel reached into her bag for some tissues.

"You can't wash puke off oyster shells," she said as she handed them to me. I wiped my mouth and blew my nose.

"The birds will eat it."

"Gross!" She shouted and brought her hands to her face. She rubbed them up over her forehead. "That is the most disgusting thing I've ever heard in my life and I live with three boys! Ugh…" I laughed and wiped my nose again.

Best friends did that, too. They brought out the coarsest part of you – because I would have never said 'the birds will eat it' in front of anyone except Isabel. Oddly enough at the same time she'd made me realize my heart was still beating. In my state of mind there was no one else in the world, besides Isabel, who could have made me laugh at that moment.

I was running on two short, but glorious hours of an alcohol induced sleep and my head was pounding like a bass drum. Once Isabel and I had opened the cottage, we'd taken two bottles of my mother's chilled white wine out onto the beach and drank them both before returning to the back deck to follow them up with two shots Isabel called ***Blood Clots***. Who else, except my mother, would have 151 Rum and fresh cream in their refrigerator? But then again Isabel could make a drink out of the rarest of ingredients. She said it was one of her gifts in life. Not very many people in our town would take pride in being an expert in libations, but Isabel did.

I could hear the lull of the ocean waves outside of the living room window which supposedly cured anything that ailed you, but they weren't doing much to help my hangover at all. In typical Isabel fashion, she was walking around the beach cottage completely naked looking behind pillows, under sofa cushions, in kitchen drawers.

"Where is my red bikini top?" she yelled to me as I walked toward her.

"I doubt it's in a kitchen drawer."

I poured myself a cup of coffee hoping it would help sober me up a bit and sat down at the kitchen table. I was already regretting leaving the children with Eric. I hadn't even explained to them the real reason I'd left. They thought Isabel and I were going away for a girl's weekend together. They didn't know I was on the brink of losing my mind.

"Where did you last see it?" I asked somberly.

"Oh, come on Lilah," Isabel said with her hands on her hips. "Don't start this pity party with me again. We had so much fun on the beach last night. Didn't you have fun?" I took a deep breath.

I wanted to give in to the wave of self-pity coursing through me because when I thought about where Tristan might be my heart felt like it was going to burst out of my chest. When it did it would inevitably land somewhere on the other side of the room and then I would be heart-less, which wouldn't make me feel any differently than I did now. If I gave in to those feelings and let the despair have its way with me Isabel would hit me over the head with something again and this time it would be bigger than the Sunny Days guide. Despite this, I laid my head down on the table. I didn't cry but I wanted to cry. I briefly wondered if tears were like windshield washer fluid. Did you eventually run out? Isabel wrapped a towel around herself and came over to sit beside me at the table. She laid her hand on my back.

"What if he is in trouble? What if he needs me?"

"He's fine," she said.

Sometimes it seemed heartfelt when Isabel tried to comfort me. Other times I wanted to slap her because she wasn't as upset as me. This was one of those times because I wasn't only sad, I was angry – at everyone except Tristan - who was the only one who truly deserved it.

"You know Tristan. You know he's okay."

"I don't know anything," I sobbed. "Nothing." Isabel grabbed me by my arms and sat me up in the chair. She held onto my shoulders.

"Look at me," she said and when I didn't, "Look at me!! Are you looking at me?" I looked up and wiped the tears from my cheeks. I hadn't run out yet.

"Yes."

"Do you honestly think, after everything Tristan has been through in his life, whether his parents are dead or in jail or wherever the hell they are, he can't handle this?"

"What's *this*?" I asked. She took an impatient breath.

"I don't know," she said. "Whatever." I sniffed and rubbed my forehead.

"Do you?" she asked.

"I don't know."

"You do know. Now, stop it." She reached for her pack of cigarettes and lighter laying on the end of the table.

"Here," she said picking up my hand and putting one between my fingers.

"I don't want a cigarette."

"And I don't want to watch you cry any longer. Tristan is a grown man…"

"What?" I asked. "He's what???" She looked to the ceiling and threw up her hands.

"Lilah."

"No, no. Tell me what he is." She sighed.

"I'm not going to say it again," she said as she took the cigarette away from me and lit it for herself. "I am so mad at him right now." She blew out smoke. "Aren't you mad?"

"Yes," I said quietly as I wiped my eyes. "I just wish I understood. I wish I knew why." Isabel was silent. "Why??" She shook her head.

"I don't know, honey."

"Give me that," I said taking the cigarette out of her mouth. She smiled.

"I have a whole carton upstairs in my room. I can keep giving you one right after another if you want…" I blew smoke into her face and she waved it away. "If we run out though, you'll have to go to the store on the corner and buy more."

"I can do that," I said.

She pulled another cigarette out of her pack and lit it.

"How 'bout a cocktail?" she asked standing up. "Hair of the dog." I looked at my watch.

"It's not even noon," I answered. She shrugged, her cigarette hanging between her lips.

"So?"

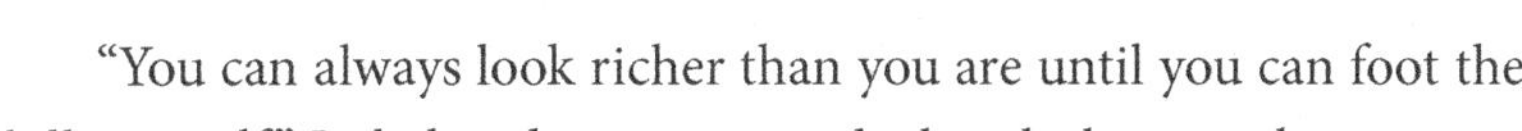

"You can always look richer than you are until you can foot the bill yourself," Isabel said as we sat on the beach the next day.

She was filing her fingernails and looking at a magazine she'd picked up at the corner store when we went to get more cigarettes. She flipped the page.

"Or you can find someone else to foot the bill for you." She looked over to me.

I wasn't sure if she was talking about me or herself. I laid my head back against my chair and closed my eyes.

"You mean Eric?"

"Well, I doubt this article is talking specifically about Eric but, yes, a man in general."

"Is that what the article is telling you?" I asked without lifting my head off my chair. "I thought you were more liberal than that. You know, women's rights and all. God forbid ever having a man support you. That means you're the weaker sex."

"I always thought I wanted to be independent." She flipped a page. "But then Tom and I started having kids and, well, I changed my mind after *that*."

"Changed your mind about being independent?"

"Yeah, I mean, sort of. Didn't you? You're coming home from work every day exhausted, you've got kids who need to be fed – one's on the boob, the other one will only eat Froot Loops. Your husband wants to know where dinner is, or even if you're having dinner and your house looks like a tornado has been through it."

"You didn't nurse your babies so don't pretend like you did."

"I was talking about you, smart ass. Do you not remember when all Ben would eat was Froot Loops?"

"Oh, yeah. Fun times. But your house was worse than mine. It still is." The sun felt good on my face.

"My house isn't that bad."

"You had toilet paper rolls laying in the hallway, Isabel."

"Eh…"

"And a dog tooth dented lemon juicer." She turned to me.

"See? You've made my point. Now I'm working again, and my house looks like shit. But didn't you ever think back then: 'Wow, if I didn't have to work, my house would be spotless? My kids would have eaten? I would've worn underwear today?'" I laughed.

"You wash the kid's clothes first," she explained. "Then if you have time – while you're working a full-time job – you wash yours."

"Maybe you should have hired a maid."

"And that was going to make me feel like a better mother how?" She flopped back against her chair again. "Anyway, we couldn't afford a maid."

"I remember those days," I said. "When Eric told me, we were spending more in daycare than I was making. Then I ended up staying at home with your kids *and* mine."

"That's probably why you lost your mind." I gave her the look she called a warning. "So, I quit." I turned to her.

"Because of me?"

"No. Because Tom said I needed to focus on being a mother."

"Oh, right. So, you started focusing on other men."

"Not right away!" She said and laughed. "It was a few years."

"Uh-huh."

"I got bored!"

"Are you listening to yourself??"

"I would mention your little flings over the years, but I won't give your current situation. Plus, I don't want to hear your whining anymore. I swear if I hear his name come out of your mouth one more time I'm going to shoot myself."

I reached into my beach bag for the flyswatter I'd brought to swat the mayflies and slammed it down on Isabel's thigh. She flew up to a sitting position and rubbed her leg.

"Ow!!! Oh, my God."

"There was a huge fly on you."

There wasn't.

"Jeez, you could have warned me first."

"There wasn't time," I explained and snickered. "He would've gotten away."

"You suck," she said as she got up off her chair.

She threw her magazine at me and I caught it before the wind could blow it away. I loved that about the Outer Banks. It could be hot as hell but there was always a cool breeze blowing in off the ocean. Except in August.

"I'm going for a swim," she yelled as she walked toward the water.

I noticed every man within a half-mile radius turned to watch her walk across the beach. A dark tan, a neon pink bikini – she couldn't find the red top - and bleach blonde hair. Men were so predictable. Well, at least most men. Not Tristan. Because if he had been I'd known where he'd gone.

I opened the cooler behind me and pulled out the flask, a chilled martini glass and the shaker full of ice. We both thought it was a sin to drink coolers or beer seaside. If you were going to drink on the beach, you needed to do it right.

A little spiced rum. A little coconut rum and some pineapple juice.

A Jaded Woman.

Perfect.

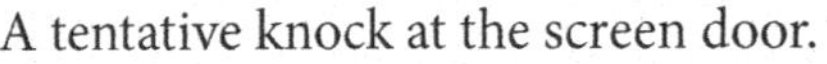

A tentative knock at the screen door.

I got up off the sofa and walked around the bar into the kitchen. For a moment, I thought I may have been hallucinating. It wasn't like it hadn't happened before and my stress level over the last month had been at an all-time high. Maybe I'd finally gone over the edge, but then that scent floated through the screen door. The one I wanted to put in a bottle and sell at Macy's.

"Oh, my God," I said. My heart plummeted to the bottom of my chest. I knew this because I could feel it beating there. "What are you doing here?" He shrugged.

"I'm not sure." I brought my hand to my heart.

"How did you know I was here?"

"Your mother," he said simply.

"My mother?" I asked astonished. "What did you do? Hold her hostage?"

"She called me."

"How? Did she have your number?"

She better not have his number. If she did I was going to move to another country because that is what she told me was her biggest fear – that one day I would leave her.

"She called Mrs. Jenkins."

"What? Why?" I grabbed hold of the counter because I thought I might faint.

"To find me, I guess. Are you going to let me in?" I motioned for him to come in and he pointed down at the latch. "It's locked."

"Oh."

I'd forgotten I'd locked the screen door once it had gotten dark outside, so I had to let go of the counter. I cautiously walked over to the door and flipped the latch. As soon as I did he opened the door and enveloped me in his arms. I buried my face in his shirt and cried.

"Shhh," he said rubbing his hand over my hair. "It's okay." I cried harder and his arms tightened around me. "Lilah." He kissed my temple. "Stop. It's okay."

Isabel came through the living room archway into the kitchen holding a martini glass full of some lavender drink she had concocted with vanilla vodka and only God knows what else.

"Holy shit," she said as she sat her drink on the counter. "What the hell are you doing here?"

"Good to see you too, Isabel."

"Seriously, what are you doing here?"

"I'm not sure."

"You're not sure?" she asked. "I should slap you. Do you even have any clue what Lilah has been through this past month?"

"I think I have a pretty good idea."

"Good idea?"

"Isabel," I interrupted as I held onto Tristan's waist. "It's okay."

"It is absolutely not okay. What? He shows up out of nowhere and now everything is honkey-dorey?" Tristan chuckled. "You think it's funny?"

"Isabel," I said. She turned to me.

"Is it funny to you, too?"

"Let's just get past the fact that I'm here," Tristan said. "I'm here."

Isabel gave him her death stare and turned around. She walked toward the living room, but she had forgotten her martini, so she turned around again and walked back into the kitchen. She picked up her martini off the counter.

"Fuck you," she said to Tristan. "Fuck both of you." I let go of Tristan.

"Isabel!" I called as she walked away again. She waved her arm behind her.

"Nope. Not doing this."

"I'm sorry," I said to Tristan.

"It's fine. I get it."

"She'll be okay. She has to process you being here." He blew out a deep breath.

"She's undoubtedly gone upstairs to plot my murder." I smiled.

"No. She'll get over it." I hesitated. "Eventually."

He stood back, rolled up the sleeves on his shirt. He was wearing navy blue shorts with an untucked lavender oxford. It takes a real man to wear lavender. Somehow, I didn't think Tristan was one of those guys who thought color defined you.

"It's hot as hell in here." He motioned over his shoulder. "Should I get my bag? I don't want to piss off Isabel any more than I already have."

"Your bag?"

"My clothes? A toothbrush?"

"Are you staying?" I asked in disbelief.

"I just drove nine hours. I hope so."

"You're staying here??" I pointed to the floor.

"I was thinking about it," he said. "But I don't have to."

I walked to the screen door and opened it, peeked outside.

"What are you driving?"

"Uh…" He followed me out the door and down the deck steps. "It's a rental." I walked around it.

"It's a…what is it?"

"It's a Stingray."

"What is a Stingray?"

"A corvette."

"No one on God's green earth would let a guy your age rent this kind of car," I said looking back to him.

"Yeah, I know."

"Well, then how did you rent it?"

"It's not a rental. It's my car…look…Lilah…" He ran his hand through his hair. "I came down here because we need to talk about some things."

"I thought you came down here because of my mother."

"Well, yeah but…" I interrupted him.

"What things?" He took a deep breath, blew it back out, shook his head back and forth.

"I wasn't planning on it going this way." He reached into his back pocket for his wallet. "But, okay."

He opened it, pulled out a business card and handed it to me. I had to step under the porch light to read it. It had the State Police emblem engraved across the top. Underneath it read:

Special Agent

Adrian C. Bennett

Drug Enforcement Section

Division One

"What is this for?" I asked him. "Is something going on with Vonnie? Is that why you're here?" I started to panic. "Should I call this guy?

He was silent.

"What?! Tell me!!" I screamed.

"You don't have to call him," he said quietly. He paused for a moment as if he were trying to figure out how to explain it to me. "He's standing right in front of you."

I stood in confusion for a second and then it dawned on me what he was trying to tell me. He must have noticed right away what was getting ready to happen because he grabbed my arms before my knees buckled beneath me.

"I couldn't tell you Lilah," he said as we sat on the beach a little while later. "I wanted to, so bad."

The waves rolled in. The surf was rough. Big crashes followed by the drawing sound of water returning to the ocean. I still couldn't formulate any words.

"Say something. Please."

"Just keep talking," I murmured. "Tell me what you want me to know." He leaned over, his elbows on his knees, his head down.

"Well, maybe the first thing I should tell you is I'm in deep shit over you." I turned to him.

"What do you mean?" He looked over to me.

"I mean you weren't supposed to happen. It's why I was so upset at the cottage that night."

"What cottage?"

"When we went to the mountains?" I shook my head in disbelief.

"I knew I was falling in love with you," he said. "I was so mad at myself for letting it happen. Then you told me I *couldn't* fall in love with you and I thought, 'What the hell do I do now?' I had this beautiful, amazing woman in my life…in my arms…and I couldn't even get her to tell me she loved me." He looked over to me when I didn't say anything.

"Maybe it's a good thing it happened that way because I was on the verge of telling you everything that night, and if you think I'm in trouble now, I would have really been in trouble then. I would have lost my job."

"I told you I loved you that night," I said without looking up.

"Yeah, but not right away." He paused. "I had time to come to my senses and remember what I was supposed to be doing and, no offense, but it wasn't you." He waited for me to respond but I said nothing.

"I have one focus when I do this," he continued. He put his palms together. "At least I'm supposed to have one focus. Everything in my life is discarded. I am not Adrian anymore. I am Tristan. I am everything Tristan is. Whatever story I'm told I have to live it."

Tears sprang to my cheeks and I wiped them away quickly. He turned to me and took my hand in both of his.

"Everything I know about you is wrong," I said. I felt nothing at all. Void. Blankness.

"Not everything," he said. "I'm still me. What I believe in, who I am inside – how much I care about you and everyone else – none of that has changed."

"Everyone else?" He hung his head.

"You know what I mean."

"You mean all the people you lied to…" I said getting up. *Now* I was angry. "And you 'care' about me? If you cared about me, you'd have told me the truth from the beginning."

"Lilah…"

"And what were you planning on doing when this little mission you're on ended, huh? Were you thinking all along I was only an occupational hazard? Something you didn't really have to deal with because when you were gone I would be, too?"

"Lilah…"

"No," I said.

He stood up, wiped the sand from his hands on his shorts and reached for me. I jerked away, turned away from him and put my hands over my face.

"How could I be so stupid?" I sobbed. "How could I let this happen?" I wasn't talking to him, but he answered me anyway as he came up behind me. I let him put his hands on my waist but only because I was numb.

"Lilah."

He turned me around and suddenly, déjà vu. The day at the sink in my kitchen. The first time he kissed me. What had he been thinking? Had he been thinking what I was thinking? 'Holy shit. I am *so* in trouble now.' Yes, come to think of it, he probably was thinking the same thing I was thinking. Just from a totally different perspective. I refused to look at him.

"Lilah," he said as he lifted my chin with his fingers. "Look at me."

"I can't," I said coldly. He let go of me and walked away.

"Fuck!"

I had never heard him say that word. Ever. He ran both of his hands through his hair but stopped on top of his head and turned around.

"Do you think this is easy for me? He asked. "Like it's been a game or some shit?" He put his hands low on his hips and leaned toward me. "Do you think I'm lying to you right now?"

"Well, you have the card," I said smartly.

"What card?" He looked at me, confused.

"The business card."

"Are you serious??" He ran his hands through his hair again. "Fuck, Lilah. I could've had that card made at Office Max two hours ago. I meant, do you think I'm lying about how I feel about you? Do you think I would have driven nine hours to come down here if you didn't mean something to me?"

"Something," I muttered. "Nine hours? Where the hell were you?"

"Long Island. My grandmother died."

"I'm sorry." He walked over and stood in front of me.

"Lilah, I *love* you. Do you even know what that means? Love, I mean?"

"What do you mean? Do I know what love means? Of course, I know what love means. It means you don't keep secrets from one another."

"Lilah, I had no choice."

"You had a choice," I said. I started to walk away, and he grabbed my arm. I yanked it away from him.

"Lilah, please. I know how much you love me." And when I said nothing, "Vonnie told me how much you love me."

"Vonnie?" I asked incredulously. "My daughter, Vonnie?"

"Do you know another Vonnie?"

I slapped him in the face. I wasn't planning to do it. My hand just came out of nowhere and smacked him. He brought his hand up to his face and rubbed his cheek.

"Okay," he said. "I deserved that."

"I should have smacked you a long time ago," I said. "But I didn't think you deserved it. Isabel did. I should have listened to her."

"You should've, because we both know that Isabel is always right." He backed away. "You know what, Lilah? Let's forget it, okay? I'm sorry I bothered you. Go back to your girl's getaway with Isabel."

I watched him turn and jog off down the dark beach. I didn't want to forget it.

"Tristan!" I yelled as I ran after him. "Tristan!" Finally, he stopped.

"What?" he asked. "What this time? More insults about what a horrible person I am? How you can't believe what I've done to you??"

I stopped short of him to catch my breath. I leaned down with my hands on my knees.

"I…"

"This wasn't a well thought out plan," he said. "In fact, I'm just sitting in a hotel room watching Family Feud and I think, 'I should really tell Lilah the truth. Then, like a sign from God - or an omen, I'm not sure which, your mother called."

"Family Feud?"

"What would you be doing in a hotel room in the middle of nowhere without room service or a bar?"

"I don't know but I doubt I would be watching Family Feud." He ignored my sarcasm.

"Lilah, do you know how hard it is when telling the truth is against the rules? When you want to tell someone something or in my line of work warn them, but you can't? How you know if you do you'll nine times out of ten lose your job and everything you've worked for?"

"Maybe you should consider another line of work," I said flatly.

"Maybe."

"So, what now?" I asked. "Your 'mission' is over so you can tell the truth?"

"No. Can we sit down?"

"Here?"

"Yes. Here." He sat down in the sand, brought his legs up and leaned onto his knees. He looked up to me. "Would you please sit down?"

I heard this voice inside my head telling me not to do it, but I sat down beside him anyway. Those voices were little liars. Half the problems in my life came from those voices. It seemed I could never turn them off. I felt so deceived, so manipulated. By the voices and by Tristan. Adrian. Whatever the hell his name was.

"My mission, as you call it, is not done."

"Well, what is it?" I turned to him. "If it's not a mission?"

"An investigation?" he asked as he looked at me sideways.

"Oh, right."

"Do you realize I'm taking a huge risk right now? You could go back home and totally blow my cover. Everything I've done…" He snapped his fingers. "… gone down the drain in a matter of minutes." He looked over at me. "If you decide to do that. *You* have that power…" He motioned to his chest. "Over *me*…right now."

"And my mother." I rubbed my temples with my fingertips.

"Well, yeah, but I'm not really worried about Loretta right now."

I gasped. I audibly gasped.

"What? You're on a first name basis with my mother?"

"Kind of. Yeah. I guess I am." I was going to kill my mother. Afterward, I was going to throw her into the same well as I did Isabel.

We sat in silence for the next few minutes, nothing but the crash of waves in the distance. He reached over for my hand and I let him take it. He caressed my fingers with his own, looked at them as if he were inspecting them to see if they were blemished somehow.

"You have beautiful hands."

"Sure."

"Look, I know you're mad right now," he said. "I don't blame you. You should be mad. You should be pissed." I turned to him.

"That night you called me around the corner of the house?"

"That night," he repeated and then as if a lightbulb went off, "*The* night?" He rubbed my fingers with his.

"Yeah."

"I was sort of high," he admitted. "Not that being high is an excuse."

"High?" I asked. "I thought you were drunk."

"Well, it's true I'd had a few too many beers at the house with Leon..." He hesitated.

"Leon?"

"Mr. Jenkins."

"Mr. Jenkins knows?"

"They both know. I'd probably have blown my brains out by now if they didn't know."

"I would have never imagined that about Mr. and Mrs. Jenkins."

"It wasn't easy for them. They're used to having normal foster kids. That's one of the reasons its worked so far."

"Because no one would ever expect Mr. and Mrs. Jenkins to be in on something like that," I reasoned.

"Yep. They take no chances, you know."

"Who?"

"The Department."

"Are you going back?"

"To Woodlawn?

"Yes."

"I'm supposed to, but we'll see. They're so pissed at me right now over you. I might be put on desk duty."

"Seriously?"

"Yes. Seriously."

"What about Tiffany?"

"Tiffany." He smiled. "She actually is my sister, you know."

"Why is she here?" I asked. "Is she undercover too?" He laughed.

"Have you met my sister?"

"Yes," I said, amused.

"She's a marine biologist."

"That's even more unbelievable." He nodded.

"Kind of like Isabel teaching physics." And when I didn't say anything, "No offense."

"None taken."

"Tiffany is on sabbatical right now waiting to see if the rest of her grant comes through. I needed some help, a diversion, and we really didn't have any one else in the field who wanted to deal with it. Apparently, I'm difficult to work with."

"Why?" I asked.

"Why did I need extra help or why am I difficult to work with?"

"I can imagine why you're difficult."

"Because they're expecting it," he said caressing my fingers again. "They know someone is here, well, there. So, coming in with mine and Tiffany's story was much more believable. If I had showed up by myself, it would've been a dead giveaway. I'm under high suspicion now as it is. She's good company for the Jenkins and she's quite enjoying herself. She told me the other day she felt like she was on vacation." I chuckled.

"I'll bet. She's sleeping with Isaac."

"She is? I thought he was kidding."

"I don't think so, but maybe."

"Tiff knows how to push my last button."

"Is that why you left Woodlawn? Because you're under high suspicion?"

"Partly. That and you." He squeezed my hand. "You truly are an occupational hazard."

"Oh, right."

"Did Social Services tell you there were placing me with a different family?"

"They didn't tell me anything," I said. "They only told me they could press charges against me."

"They were supposed to tell you that," he said. "I asked them to tell you they were placing me with another family, so you wouldn't worry about me." I shook my head.

"They didn't." He looked over to me.

"I'm sorry, Lilah. They used our affair to get me out of there. There is always a precautionary measure, a back-up story. Sometimes they tell me what it is, but not always. Jenny said this was what I got for not keeping it in my pants."

"Who is Jenny?"

"She's my boss. She was kidding. Sort of."

"Weird sense of humor."

"I know."

"Who knows about all this?"

"Uh, the Social Services stuff?"

"Yes."

"School administration, mainly, but they would tell anyone who asked about me, I guess. I mean, that's the story."

"So, the school didn't know who you really were?"

"No one knows that…except Tiffany and The Jenkins."

"So, everyone thinks I'm a pedophile. That's awesome. My mother, for God's sake."

"Your mother knows you're not a pedophile, Lilah." He hung his head. "I couldn't leave town indefinitely without any kind of explanation to anyone."

"Well, it was a bad explanation. I thought I was going to jail."

"Would you have had a better idea?"

"How about 'my grandmother died?'"

"Anything other than what was said to you at the time," he rationalized. "And somehow you would have convinced Isabel you needed to find me…and knowing Isabel she would have helped you."

"You're right," I agreed.

"Which would have put you and Isabel in a dangerous place." I sighed because what he said made sense and I didn't want it to make sense. I only wanted to be mad.

"I had nothing to do with the connection the Department made with Social Services," he explained. "They concocted that entire story by themselves. I had no choice but to go along with it."

"Because our relationship was detrimental to your emotional well-being."

"Is that what she said?"

"Yeah."

"I'm sorry." I shrugged. "Can I shed a little light on everything for you?"

"There's more?" He took a deep breath.

"Something big was getting ready to happen in Woodlawn. I can't tell you what and I wish I could, but I can't. Do you get that?"

"Yeah," I said reluctantly. "I don't like it, but I get it."

"When I found out my grandmother was sick, and they were calling in the family, well, it just so happened to coincide with everything going on in Woodlawn. I was going to tell you about her – because I thought I was only going to be gone for a few days – and I needed to be out of Woodlawn *for a few days.* That's why I came to your house the day you and Eric were having lunch.

"To tell me where you were going?" He nodded.

"Yes." I laid my head on his shoulder.

"Oh, Tristan."

"We'd been playing everything by ear, but something happened – and again, I can't tell you what – but when my team found out about it they went ballistic. They pulled me out immediately. That's the phone call I got that day. When they say leave immediately, they mean immediately."

"But you said you'd be back."

"I meant eventually…because I didn't know when I'd be back."

"I thought you meant later that day."

"I know. I'm sorry."

"You couldn't have sent me a text?"

"All communications cut off…" He snapped his fingers. "Just like that."

"On your personal phone?"

"There is no such thing as a personal phone when you do what I do," he explained. "I have…*had*…" he emphasized. "…All these leads and all I can think about is you… my friend's mother – which, despite my actual age, still seemed extraordinarily wrong." I squeezed his hand.

"Does that happen often?" I asked with a slight grin. "Falling in love with married women?"

"No," he said shaking his head. He pulled his hand away, pushed his fingers back, cracked his knuckles. "It has *never* happened. You have no idea how much it…it's screwed up and I know that but… well, I'm not good at self-deprivation. I mean, I should be, given my profession."

"Maybe."

"Nothing changed the fact that I thought you were the most beautiful woman I had ever seen. I kept trying to convince myself I was wrong."

"Please tell me it wasn't easy." He reached for my hand again.

"Are we sitting here right now?" I smiled.

"I saw you walk out onto your back porch that night in that gauzy skirt. I could see right through it – all the way through it."

"And you were trashed."

"Maybe…" I looked over to him. "Okay."

"I didn't know that. That you could see through it, I mean." He nodded.

"You can." I shrugged.

"Good to know."

"I'm not any less sorry about that night now than I was then. I didn't plan it, if it makes you feel any better."

"You don't have to apologize," I said. "It takes two to tango."

"It does," he agreed.

"I can't believe I gave in to you."

"Me either," he said and laughed. "Holy shit." I bumped my shoulder into his.

"Tristan!"

He was still Tristan to me. He would always be Tristan to me. I leaned over against him and he draped his arm around me.

"Eric and I are separating for the summer." He squeezed my shoulder.

"Just the summer?"

"I think we all know it won't be just for the summer."

"I can't say that makes me unhappy."

"It was amicable."

"That's good." I turned to him.

"So, I am no longer married. You don't have to feel guilty anymore." He laughed and held up my left hand.

"No rings?"

"Nope."

"Sorry to tell you this," he said. "But, technically, you are still married."

"But it makes me feel better to think about it this way." He shook his head, laughed again.

"Okay."

"Long Island?" I asked.

"What about Long Island?"

"Is that where you're from?"

"Yes. Well, it was."

"How did you end up here? I mean, Virginia."

"School. I went to VCU on a music scholarship. I did Music Theory but then I took a Criminal Justice class and I loved it, so I ended up doing both. I know it sounds like an odd combination."

"Yeah, kind of."

"Anyhow, I never intended on doing what I'm doing now but I got interested in it so once I graduated I went through training and so on and so forth - you get it." I nodded again.

"At least now I know when I thought you looked older than you said you were I wasn't losing my mind."

"No."

"Can," I stopped because I wasn't sure I wanted to know. "Can I ask you how old you are?"

"You may," he replied. "I'm twenty-six. I'll be twenty-seven in August."

"Are you kidding me?" I asked. I bowed my head and put my hands over my face. He chuckled.

"Do you want to see my driver's license?"

"Is it your real driver's license or your fake one?"

"Both." He laughed, then more seriously, "A lot has happened these pasts few months, Lilah."

"Yeah," I agreed.

"Hey," he said pulling me closer to him. He took my chin in his fingers. "Look at me."

I did. I wanted to be stubborn, but my heart overrode my feminine logic.

"Hi."

"Hi." My voice broke and he lowered his eyes.

"I want to introduce myself." I sucked in my breath. "I'm Adrian Bennett." Tears rolled down my cheeks.

"Hey," he said again. "I'm still that guy. The one who kissed you in the kitchen?"

I pressed my lips together and closed my eyes. The tears didn't stop. He wiped them away with his thumb.

"The one who helped you paint your living room?" I sniffed.

"The one who let me write notes for him, so he wouldn't get unexcused absences from school?" He laughed.

"Yep."

"Very clever. You really had me going there."

"I hope so. It's how I make a living." He gave me that playful smile.

We were quiet for a moment.

"By the way," he said. "I'm also the guy who let your son beat the hell out of him. I could have put him in the hospital, just so you know." I shook my head.

"Oh, my gosh. I'd forgotten about that. I'm so sorry."

"Don't be sorry. It was inevitable given the circumstances. Although I can't tell you the last time I had a busted lip." He hesitated. "Or if I've *ever* had a busted lip."

"I'm sorry," I said again.

"You could make it up to me."

"I'm almost afraid to ask how."

"Let's re-live *that* night."

"We're sitting," I pointed out. He chuckled.

"You're right."

"You know what they say about sex on the beach?" He pulled the bottom of my sundress up as his hand caressed my thigh. He leaned over.

"Can I kiss you before you tell me?" I nodded.

"Yes." He took my face in his hands and kissed me softly. Once. Twice. Three times. Chill bumps erupted over my skin.

"What do they say?"

"Sand in your crack," I whispered. He laid back on the sand behind me and put his hands under his head.

"Is that true? Because I've never had sex on the beach."

"You grew up on Long Island and you've never had sex on the beach??" He grinned.

"I was a late bloomer."

I looked at the little sliver of skin between his shirt and shorts, ran my finger across it. He shivered as I slipped my fingers underneath the button. I'd been wanting to unbutton his pants for a month. It was deeply satisfying.

"I'm about to introduce you to sex on the beach," I said as I leaned over him. He lifted his head and kissed me quickly.

"Then I should have brought a blanket," he responded.

"Yeah, you should've."

I laid down beside him and he rolled over against me. I tried to pull the skirt of my dress up between us as we kissed. He laughed.

"Wait," he said as he pulled away. He sat up and I sat up beside him. "There has to be a better way."

He moved further away and leaned back, unzipped his shorts. I got up onto my knees. As I raised the skirt of my dress, he reached over and untied the strings of my bikini bottom. He grabbed me by my waist and lifted me over into his lap. I shifted my hips and pulled up the bottom of his shirt. I wanted to feel his skin next to mine. I put my arms around his neck, leaned into him.

"I'm not even going to pretend there is a possibility I can sustain this," he said as he laid back onto the sand again.

"It's okay."

Honestly, it didn't matter to me. Having him that close was all I needed. He took a deep breath and let it out slowly as I moved against him. His hands went to my waist and I put mine over them. He took one of my hands in his, entwined our fingers together. He closed his eyes, squeezed my hand. His body tensed and relaxed beneath me. I leaned down and kissed him, and he drew in his breath.

"I love you," he said against my lips.

"I know."

I laid my forehead on his shoulder, felt his heart beating fast against mine. I turned my face into his neck, inhaling his scent. Still bubblegum and cookies. He squeezed my fingers tightly.

"You're going to break my fingers," I whispered in his ear.

He mumbled something into my hair, but I couldn't understand him, and he didn't let go of my fingers. His body trembled, and he held his breath. When he finally let go of my hand I wrapped my arms around him.

"I'm sorry," he whispered as he ran his hands over my shoulders and down my back.

"It's okay," I said as I sat up. He took my hand in his and brought it to his face, kissed my fingers.

"Are any of these dislocated?" I laughed.

"I don't think so."

"I swear I will fix this later."

"My fingers?" He smiled and shook his head.

"No. You."

"You will?"

"Yes. I promise." I laid back down onto his chest.

"Can you please never do that to me again?" He murmured into my ear.

"What?"

"Leave me indefinitely."

"You're the one who left," I reminded him.

"Yeah, but I had to watch Family Feud because they blocked the porn channel at the hotel." I sat up and slapped him on his chest.

"I can't believe you just admitted that to me." He laughed.

"This is what you get when you leave me alone without porn."

"Get up," I said as I moved off him. He sat up and looked over to me.

"Ugh," he said. "Sand everywhere."

"I told you," I said and laughed.

He leaned back and buttoned his shorts, ran both of his hands through his hair to shake out the sand. He reached over and picked up my bikini bottom off the sand beside him and threw it at me.

"You might want these later." Surprisingly enough, I caught them.

"Thanks." I offered him my hand and he took it.

"Please don't let me forget the blanket next time," he said as he stood up.

"How about since you've had your sex on the beach experience we hang it up and use a bed? Like normal people."

"Or a kitchen chair," he said and smiled.

"Okay," I said. "I like that idea."

An hour later, we walked back into a darkened beach cottage. The only light was from a small lamp sitting on the kitchen counter. Tristan sat his bag down in a kitchen chair and I went to the refrigerator to get us a drink. He walked up behind me as I gazed inside.

"Orange juice," he said so I took it out and poured us two short glasses.

There was a note on the kitchen counter addressed to him. He picked it up, read it and handed it to me. It said: 'We are going to have a serious talk in the morning.' I huffed and rolled my eyes.

"She's not kidding," I said.

"I know."

"She obviously doesn't know what I know."

"I know." He leaned up against the counter.

"Are you going to tell her?"

"No," he said. "I can't." I walked over to him.

"I can't keep this secret. How am I supposed to do that? Isabel is going to rake me over the coals for taking you back and make me feel like shit."

"Well, she shouldn't be able to make you feel like shit. You know the truth."

"Somehow that doesn't make me feel any better. I can't lie to Isabel."

"I never said you had to lie." I sat my empty juice glass in the sink.

"Well, what then? She's going to ask me a million questions if she thinks I'm keeping something from her."

"Then tell her."

"I can't tell her!! You said we couldn't tell her!" He took a drink of his juice.

"I never said you couldn't tell her," he said. "I said *I* couldn't tell her."

"So, I can tell her?"

"That's up to you."

"Will it cause problems for you if I tell her?"

"No. She's not going to tell anyone because of you and she's good at keeping secrets. She's kept our secret and however many other affairs she's had over the years." He downed the rest of his juice and sat his glass in the sink with mine. "She's harmless." I laughed.

"You talk like she's a bug."

"If the shoe fits. Let me see your hand."

"What?"

"Give me your hand." He took my right hand in between both of his. "Look at me." I looked up to him. "I will tell you who isn't harmless," he said standing in front of me. And don't ask me to tell you anything else because I can't."

I bowed my head because I knew what he was going to say. I already knew it in the back of mind, but I constantly tried to push it away. I was hoping somehow if I didn't say it out loud it would go away. Now Tristan was going to say it out loud for me.

I tried not to lose it completely. I didn't want to hear him say it. I wanted to say it, to get it out of my subconscious into a deliberate thought – one I could reconcile. I managed to whisper "Bret" before I fell into him. He wrapped his arms around me.

"Yeah," he said. He kissed my forehead then put his hands on either side of my neck, looked down at me.

"But I'm going to fix this. Okay?" I nodded, tears rolling down my face. "I won't let anyone hurt Vonnie." I bowed my head, rested it against his chest. My body shook. "Lilah? Did you hear me?" He grabbed my shoulders and stepped back from me.

"Lilah?" I looked up to him. "Did you hear me?" I pressed my lips together and closed my eyes. Fresh tears spilled onto my cheeks and I leaned into him. His arms instinctively went around me and held me tightly.

"I am going to keep your little girl safe," he said into my hair. "I promise. And if I can't do it myself, I will find someone who can. Trust me, okay?" I nodded against him.

"Do you trust me?"

I felt the calm flow from his body into mine.

"Yes," I whispered.

Later after we had showered, I laid in bed with my head on Tristan's chest, in awe he was tangibly there, and I could feel his body against mine. I couldn't stay still. He tightened his arm around me, his voice sleepy.

"What is wrong?" he whispered. "I know you're upset but you need to relax. Everything is going to be okay. I promise."

"I know but I can't."

"Why not?" He leaned up and kissed the top of my head. "Aren't you tired? I'm tired. I drove nine hours today. Go to sleep. I'm not going anywhere."

I looked up to him, twisted my leg over his. He sucked in his breath and groaned, shifted in bed.

"I need you." He rubbed my arm.

"You've got me." Then, "Seriously?"

"I missed you," I explained, kissing his chest. "Didn't you miss me?"

"Well, yeah," he said. "But, you know, we just..."

"No," I interrupted. "You did." When he didn't say anything, "You promised." He groaned again.

"I didn't necessarily promise it tonight."

"That's a technicality." He turned on his side toward me and kissed the tip of my nose.

"You're gonna call me on a technicality?"

"Uh-huh."

"The things I do for you. This is really an inconvenience."

"It wasn't an inconvenience earlier."

"No," he said. "It was a necessity."

"Ha." He nuzzled his face into my neck, kissed me there.

"It makes me feel safe," I admitted. He pulled back, rubbed a piece of my hair between his fingers.

"Does it?" I nodded. "Do I?"

"Yes."

"I can do that," he whispered as he kissed my cheek. When he moved over me I immediately shoved his boxers down over his hips with my hands then the rest of the way down with my foot.

"Not wasting any time. Are you?" he asked.

"I don't want to play games."

"Are we playing games?" he teased, and I felt his lips graze my collar bone. "What game are we playing?"

"I just want you. I don't need a bunch of kissing or anything like that."

"Wow. Okay."

He held himself up on his elbows above me. His damp hair fell into my face, so I reached over to the nightstand to grab one of my hair bands. I grasp his hair in my hands and pulled it back, securing it behind his neck.

"Ow..."

"Sorry," I said. "It's in the way."

He lowered his face and pressed his lips against mine. I loved his lips. They were full and soft and around them was always clean shaven and smooth. He hovered over for me for a moment.

"I love you, Lilah. You get that, right?"

"Just do it," I said as I squirmed beneath him. His shook his head back and forth.

"Why do I feel like a sex object right now?" he asked but without hesitation he shoved his hips into mine.

The warmth of him overcame me. It was a complete and utter feeling of serenity. A kind of peace that comes only with limitless trust. That's not something you can create instantaneously, by the way. It takes time and effort and kept promises. I didn't think there was anything other than this kind of love that could solve life's problems. Except maybe a frozen shot of tequila. He moved against me. On second thought, no. Scratch the tequila.

One of the things I loved about Tristan was his unconventionality. I had never considered sex an opportunity for conversation but in a typical Tristan-style approach, he had changed my mind concerning the matter.

“Depending on how you want this encounter to go,” he said.

“Encounter?”

“Uh, meeting, rendezvous. Let’s see.” He leaned over and grabbed his phone off the nightstand. “Let me summon my synonym app.” He pretended to look at it then laid it back on the table. “Tryst, date.”

“This is a date?”

“I know. I’m easy.” He lowered his face to my neck and whispered in my ear. “I have no morals.”

“Stop it.” He kissed my ear.

“I might be able to maintain this for a while. That was supposed to be my point. Is that what you want?”

“I thought you were tired. Didn’t you drive nine hours today?”

“Is that what you want?” he asked me again.

“What do you think?” I answered.

As soon as I said it he rolled over and pulled me on top of him. He grabbed me by my waist and my legs somehow twisted around him as we sat up together. I gasped because he moved me around so quickly and effortlessly. He was sitting in the middle of the bed with me in his lap.

“I had to pretend I didn’t know how to do this before, remember?” I smiled, and he kissed my forehead then my lips. “Guess what?”

“Hmm?”

“I know how to do this.”

“I see.”

He lifted me up by my waist and slowly moved me up and down over him. This took no effort on my part and I relaxed against his arms. He pressed his face into my breastbone as he moved me against him. He sat me down for a moment and pulled my nightgown over my head, running his hands back down my arms as he threw it to the side. They came to rest on either side of my ribcage and he lowered his face to my chest, his lips teasing me. He raised me above him, the pleasure building gradually.

"Tristan…oh, my God…"

"I think that's the first time I've heard my name and God's in the same sentence," he breathed. "Except it's not my name."

"It also wasn't a sentence," I said. He chuckled.

"What are you? The grammar police?"

He brought me back down onto him, grabbed me by my waist again and flipped me over onto my back, laid me down gently on top of the sheets. I held my breath, not sure what he would do next but feeling secure in his hands.

"Relax," he said. "Let me do it."

'Let me do it.' Was he kidding? I would let him do it every day, every minute of every day until I could no longer walk, or even function at all. He slid his body down mine, kissed my stomach, lingered on my hip for a moment. I put my hands gently on his shoulders and he lifted my hips in his hands, pulled me down the bed toward him, away from what I thought was going to happen. He traced his tongue up my breastbone and I exhaled, his fingers barely touching my sides. I tried to control my breathing, but I couldn't.

"Please," I said. "Just do it." He looked up to me.

"Do what?" I blushed and felt the warmth creep over my skin. I don't know why or how after all the times we'd been together.

"You know."

"Do I?" he asked as he ran his fingers over my stomach. I sucked in my breath, my body trembling in anticipation. "Relax." His hands went back to my hips.

"Is this what you want?" he asked as he moved downward, his tongue trailing across my thigh. I cried out, a small moan escaping my lips, entirely unintentional, without any thought of being heard. It must have been louder than I thought.

"Shhhh…be patient."

Ha. Patience.

You know that feeling you get when you've been nervous or tense about something for hours? When you feel like all you need is a warm bath and a neck massage to relax again? Think about that except think about it like it's a good thing, knowing the relief you need is going to flood through you at any moment. It wasn't like, can you move a little to the left? It was perfect pressure in the perfect place, a warm tingling sensation that made my body tense and release.

"Stop," I said. He looked up to me.

"Stop? Really?" I put my hands on the bed beneath me.

"Not stop," I breathed. "Stop teasing me."

He smiled. I didn't know this about him, the control he could create over me within minutes. I felt the warmness of his mouth against me again and I cried out. He reached up with his hand to shush me, brushing his fingers lightly across my wrist.

It came suddenly, the cresting of the roller coaster hill, the ride down the other side, except there was no bottom - at least not for a while - and I twisted beneath him. He held onto my hips with his hands, not letting me move. I may have levitated off the bed.

"Stop," I managed as I put my hands on his shoulders. "Stop." I couldn't breathe. He moved up me and wiped his hand over his mouth.

"The hair band worked out well," he teased as he pressed himself into me.

I couldn't speak. I thought I might hyperventilate. He stopped moving against me, tucked my hair behind my ear.

"Relax. Take a deep breath." My lips quivered. He ran his thumb over my cheek. "Lilah, relax."

I raised my legs up around his waist and that feeling, the expectancy of release rolled over me again. I lifted my body up off the bed and he wrapped one of his arms around my back and held me tightly against him. My body tensed as he kissed my lips. I didn't kiss him back, of course, because I still couldn't breathe.

"It's okay," he whispered. "I'm holding you. Let go."

I wrapped my arms around his shoulders, buried my face into his neck, his scent enveloping me as I inhaled and let the wave course through me. He held me tighter, his arm encircling my entire body, his fingers firmly holding onto my ribcage on the other side. When I relaxed against him he lowered me back down onto the bed. I reached up to touch his lips and ran my fingers over them. He opened his mouth and my fingers slipped inside. When I pulled them out, he took my hand and kissed my palm.

Have you ever had anyone kiss your palm? Because it is an intimate act. It doesn't sound like it is, but it is. There must be special receptors on the palm of your hand that tell you heaven is real.

"Are you done?" he asked and gave me his playful smile. I nodded. "Are you sure? Because I can keep doing this until you're unconscious if you want."

"Mm..."

"Okay," he chastised. "But we're gonna talk about this later."

He moved against me slow and steady until I heard his breath catch in his throat. I could see him through the moonlight in the window. He pressed his lips together, lowering his face to my shoulder. I felt every muscle in his body flex and I held onto him. He pulled his head up, looked down at me, locking his eyes with mine. I lifted my head toward him, pressed my lips against his and he breathed into them. He turned his head to the side for a moment to catch his breath. He looked back to me.

It didn't have to be 'I love you,' but it was. He pressed his forehead against mine. One of my hands went to his shoulder, the other one found his hand and entwined our fingers together. He squeezed. Not tightly like before but firm with anticipation. I didn't look away. He closed his eyes for a moment, those long dark eyelashes against the darkness of his skin and lowered his face to that little hollow in my neck.

"This is your last chance," he said as he exhaled.

"No. You," I managed.

He shoved his hips into mine one last time and held himself there. I could feel the sweat beading on his back and the cool air from the fan above us as it wafted across my damp skin. He drew in his breath. I think for a moment he stopped breathing altogether.

"Damn, Lilah," he said afterward. I laughed "Please tell me I fixed it." He tried to catch his breath. "Or don't and in about fifteen minutes we can do it again."

"Fifteen minutes??"

"Okay," he joked. "Twelve. Maybe ten." I leaned up and kissed him, ran my thumb across his cheek. "Tell me I'm good at it."

"Are you claiming clairvoyance?" I asked. He shifted onto his side as I turned toward him.

"Instinctual may be a better word although I'm not sure you deserved it."

"I did too deserve it! You want to talk about all the things I've done for you in the past?? You're welcome." He smiled and shook his head back and forth.

"Lilah," he whispered as he leaned toward me.

"Hmm?"

He rubbed his lips against mine. It was that thing he did when he kissed me but didn't. Tantric kissing. Was there such a thing? He placed his warm hand on my waist and I kicked the twisted sheets away from us.

"I love you." He closed his eyes and leaned back against the pillows. He took my hand in his and massaged my fingers.

"You mentioned that earlier."

"Say it," he said, his eyes still closed. "Because I know you do." I bit my lip. "Say it."

"I love you," I said, giving in. He lifted his head and looked over to me.

"Say my name." My breath had finally calmed.

"Which one?" He looked at me and when he said nothing I said, "Adrian."

It felt weird. He wasn't Adrian to me. He was still Tristan.

"Say it together," he breathed.

"Tristan! I can't."

"You can. Say it."

"I love you."

"Together," he said again. I took a deep breath and he rolled over toward me.

“I love you…Adrian.”

He kissed me. An actual kiss this time.

“It wasn’t that hard. Was it?”

“Kinda.”

“Then say it again.” I shook my head back and forth and smiled. “Do it.”

“I love you, Adrian.” He nestled his face into my neck.

“Next time I’m going to make you say it before I let you…” I slapped his arm playfully and he raised up to look at me.

“You wouldn’t,” I said, appalled.

“I would,” he whispered, and he kissed my forehead. “It might help you remember it.”

The next morning, I awoke to Tristan softly kissing my lips. He was *still* Tristan to me, but I was trying.

“Hi,” he whispered.

“Mm…”

“I’m sorry I had to wake you. You looked so peaceful.”

“Mm…”

“I didn’t want you to wake up and not be able to find me.” I glanced over at the clock on the bedside table. It was six a.m. I had slept so soundly.

“Where are you going?” I asked groggily.

“I’m going for a run on the beach,” he said, and I nodded. “Go back to sleep.” He kissed my cheek. “I’ll be back in a little while.”

I tried to fall back asleep, but I couldn't so after a restless hour I got up to take a shower. The master bathroom had a double shower with two shower heads. I didn't even like to think about what my mother and Daddy did in it. I was rinsing the conditioner out of my hair when Tristan stepped inside. His hair was pulled back and up off his neck.

"Man bun?" I said. He laughed and pulled the hair band out as he stepped under the water on the other side.

"I only do it out of necessity."

"I like it better down anyway," I said as I walked toward him. He held up his hand.

"Nope," he said. I went to hug him anyway.

"No!" He said backing away. "I'm gross and sweaty."

"I don't care."

"You do," he said still holding me at arm's length while he rinsed his hair. "Trust me."

"Okay. Fine. I'm getting out." He smiled and grabbed my arm.

"Hey," he said. "I have something I want to tell you. I thought about it while I was running."

"What?" I said as I leaned in to kiss him. He pulled back, the water cascading over his head.

"No," he said as he wiped his hand over his face. "Stop it. I want to tell you about Lorelei."

"Who?"

"Lorelei." He said it like Lora-lay, not Lora-lie, the way you were supposed to pronounce it. "She was my first girlfriend. In eleventh grade." I raised my eyebrows.

"Oh yeah? Was she hot?"

"She was," he said. "Not as hot as you, but hot."

"Right."

"I spent the whole summer before my senior year with Lorelei. I thought she was the best thing that had ever happened to me."

"Was she?"

"Up until then, yes." I leaned up against the shower wall as he washed his hair. "But her Dad didn't like me so much."

"How come?"

"Because I wasn't good enough for her. Apparently, not having parents wasn't acceptable."

"That's a little small-minded."

"He wasn't a reasonable man."

"So, what happened?" I handed him the soap.

"He sent her away to boarding school."

"Because of you??"

"Yes. I always thought she'd come back to me one day. I wrote her letters, but she never answered them. When I called her, it said her number had been disconnected."

I leaned into him. This time he let me.

"I'm sorry," I whispered as I stood on my tiptoes. I kissed him. He slipped his arms around me.

"No one has ever made me feel the way Lorelei made me feel. Until you." I leaned my head against his chest and his fingers caressed my backbone. "You know when this is all over I'll have another assignment." I looked up to him.

"I feel like I should have already known that, but I didn't." Water dripped from his lashes onto his cheeks.

"I may not be able to tell you where I am or what I'm doing. I don't know right now." He hesitated. "I want to make sure you know without a doubt I will always be thinking about you – that I love you more than you can ever imagine. Do you understand that?" I looked down and he put his chin on top of my head.

"Yes." He pulled back and took my face into his hands.

"You are the love of my life," he said. "I will always come back to you, Lilah. I promise."

I leaned my head against his chest again. I hope so, I thought.

It was hard to say how many ***Lavender Martinis*** Isabel had the night before, but she didn't descend the stairs the next day until noon. I was sitting in a wicker chair with my legs tucked beneath me. Tristan – Adrian (I had convinced myself I would eventually get used to his real name) was reclined on the sofa, his bare feet propped on the ottoman in front of him.

We were trying to be as quiet as possible so as not to awaken the wrath we knew awaited us upstairs. He was throwing paper airplanes at me with little notes on them that said things like, 'I love you;' 'I'm hungry;' 'I can see your panties;' 'Come over here.'

"Why are you still here?" Isabel asked as she clumped down the stairs and headed toward the coffee pot. "Why is the coffee pot not on?"

"Because it's noon," Tristan said.

"Shut up, Tristan."

"Put it in the microwave," I suggested as Tristan wrote out another note. He threw it at me. I shook my head.

"Stop," I mouthed.

The note read, 'I want to strangle her.'

Isabel came over and sat on the opposite end of the sofa as Tristan. She hadn't combed her hair and she still had on her bathing suit from the day before with her nightgown over it.

"Why do you have little paper airplanes everywhere?" she croaked.

"Tristan keeps throwing them at me." She looked over to him, cradling her coffee in her hands.

"What are you? Twelve?"

I put my hands over my face and rubbed my eyes. Either she didn't see me, or she was ignoring me out of sheer loathing. One was just as likely as the other.

"So, I'm guessing the two of you had your little tête-à-tête last night on the beach."

Neither Tristan nor I said anything.

"Well, I hope you're proud of yourself," she said to Tristan. "For continuing to screw up Lilah's life when I finally thought I might be getting her over you. I hope you're not planning on going to back to Woodlawn unless you want your girlfriend to go to jail." She looked over to me. "You *are* going to jail. You realize that, right?"

"She's not going to jail," Tristan said.

"You have no idea what you're talking about."

Isabel sat up straighter and in the process, some of her coffee spilled over the edge of her cup. She wiped at it, but a little red splotch appeared on her chest. Tristan took it and sat it on the table in front of her.

"You should let that cool a little more." She grabbed it and picked it back up.

"What are you? My mother?"

"Can we cut to the chase?" Tristan asked me. "Because I'd like to go out on the beach at some point today."

"If I could poison you and get away with it, I would. I still might," Isabel warned.

"Stop it," I said. "Sit your coffee down."

"Why?"

"Because I'm about to tell you something that will shock you."

Isabel looked at me like I'd lost my mind. I got up and walked into the kitchen, opened the junk drawer where I had hidden Tristan's business card. I walked back over to Isabel.

"You should sit down," Tristan joked as I handed it to her.

"I am sitting down, you idiot." She looked at the card. "What is this?" Tristan cleared his throat, rubbed his hand across the back of his neck.

"I'm going upstairs," he said. "Change into my bathing suit." Isabel glared at him then looked back to me, down at the card again.

"What is this?" I sat down beside her. "What?" she asked. "You're starting to scare me. I would think it had something to do with Vonnie but if that were the case we'd be driving back home by now... and we're not."

"That's Tristan," I said softly. She held the card up.

"This? This is Tristan?" I nodded.

"Adrian." She stared at the card then looked up to me.

"Wait a minute. Let me get this straight. You're telling me Tristan is an undercover policeman?" She looked down at the card again. "Drug Enforcement?"

"Yes."

"Like narcotics?" I nodded.

"Does he have a gun?" I laughed.

"I'm sure he does."

"Have you seen it?"

"No."

"Holy shit." She held up her pointer finger. "Give me a minute. I need to process this." I smiled.

"I know."

"That's why we had the drug search right before the end of school," she said.

"Yes."

"That's why he told me Bret was a bad guy after he told me he didn't know anything." She looked up at me. "I thought I had coaxed it out of him or he made it up because of Vonnie."

"Why would he make it up because of Vonnie?" She took a deep breath.

"Because at one point I thought something might have been going on with the two of them."

"Wait. Tristan and Vonnie?"

"Yeah and he could've been lying to me to get Bret out of the picture."

"What?!? Why would you think something was going on between Tristan and Vonnie?"

"Because I saw her get into the hot tub with him one day when everyone else was in the pool. She whispered something in his ear then sat down beside him and kissed him."

"On the lips??" Isabel shook her head.

"No. On the cheek and I went around the building at school to smoke a cigarette one day and they were back there together. Talking. But they stopped as soon as they saw me."

"Why didn't you tell me this?" I asked. "Why on earth would you not tell me this??"

"Because I didn't want to tell you something that wasn't true, something I only suspected. I wanted to have proof of it before I told you." I put my head in my hand then looked back up to her.

"Jeez, Isabel. Didn't you think I'd want to know something like that?"

"Well, yeah but there was no reason to upset you about something I didn't even know was true or not."

"I'm not a child," I said.

"Well, it doesn't matter now anyway."

"What was she whispering to him?" Isabel shrugged.

"I don't know.

"Why didn't you ask him?"

"What am I supposed to do? Walk up and say, 'Hey, I saw you and Vonnie in the hot tub together. What were you talking about?'"

"Yes," I said. "You say anything else you want to him. You threatened to poison him a few minutes ago, if you don't remember."

"I remember."

Tristan walked down the stairs in his swim trunks, a beach towel thrown over his shoulder.

"Are we good?" he asked as he motioned over his shoulder. "Because I can go back upstairs." I stood up.

"What were you talking to Vonnie about?" I asked. He came to the bottom of the steps.

"Um, in what context are we speaking?"

"In the hot tub at Isabel's?" He walked toward me.

"I'm sorry. I don't remember that." I frowned at him. "I don't. I seriously don't."

"What about the day you were talking to her behind the building at school?" Isabel asked.

"When you walked around the corner?"

"Yes."

"I can't tell you that." I walked over to him.

"You *will* tell me that," I said angrily. "She's my daughter. I have a right to know. Tell me."

"I'm not going to tell you," he said straight-faced.

I slapped him. It was the second time I had done it within twenty-four hours. He rubbed his cheek.

"YOU WILL TELL ME," I yelled. "Tell me now!!" He took a deep breath and looked away from me. Isabel came over and stood behind me.

"You should tell her," she said.

"I'm not going to tell either one of you," he said calmly.

The fact that he said it so casually made me so mad I couldn't see straight. I wanted to stomp my foot like a little girl who wasn't getting her way, but I decided to slap him again instead. He instinctively grabbed my wrist.

"Stop it." And when I tried to maneuver my arm away from him, "Just stop."

"You," he said to Isabel. He did not let go of my wrist. "Go upstairs and get dressed." He looked her up and down. "Take a shower, brush your teeth, whatever you need to do to go out to the beach." Isabel just stood there. "Go!"

Unbelievably, Isabel walked past him and started up the stairs. I had never heard Tristan talk with such authority. No wonder him and my mother were getting along so well. Isabel stopped.

"I can hear everything you say," she said to him over her shoulder. He didn't turn around.

"Scary," he said. "Go upstairs, Isabel." She huffed but went just the same.

"Lilah, we had this talk last night," he said as he loosened his grip on my wrist. "You know I can't tell you. I told you I would take care of Vonnie and I will."

"Tell me nothing is going on between the two of you." He let go of my arm.

"Like what?"

"Like, you know." I looked away. "Like you were having a fling with her or something." He stepped back, crossed his arms over his chest.

"Like sleeping together??" I nodded.

"Are you nuts??" he asked. "What the hell is wrong with you? She's a kid."

"You were supposed to be a kid," I said.

"Except I wasn't and even if I had been, you think I would've done something like that? To you?"

"I don't know." He came back closer to me and took my hands in his.

"You don't know?" he asked. "Look at me." I looked up to him.

"I don't know what I have to do to prove to you how much I love you but whatever it is, I'll do it." He hesitated. "But don't ask me to go against my oath of honor because you know I can't do that."

"I would never ask you to do that."

I'm not sure what made me think of it at the time, maybe because we were talking about honor, I also thought about morals – which Isabel and I have always said we had none, but we did.

It wasn't as easy now as it had been earlier in our lives to keep up with our scandalous behavior. We wanted it to be, but once you get older you start to realize what the truly important things are in life and it's not how many men you can sleep with before the summer is over. We had a contest to do that one summer. Isabel won because she's a lot cuter than me. I tried not to take it personally.

In the process of professing our laissez-faire attitude toward men Isabel had lost the man she loved, and I had lost my dignity - because that is what you lose when you try to second guess your happiness. Now I had another chance for that happiness and I wasn't going to waste it away by pretending I couldn't care one way or the other - because I did care. More than I would ever be willing to admit to anyone except myself.

"I love you," I said unprompted, which was totally out of character for me. It also broke every rule I'd ever had about men in general.

He grabbed ahold of my waist, hoisted me up and locked his arms underneath me. I rested my hands on the tops of his arms. You know, the ones his t-shirt barely contained? I felt his muscles tighten beneath my hands. He loosened his grip on me and I slid down his chest stopping long enough to kiss his lips.

"Really? Do you mean it? Should I believe you?" I smiled.

"Yes."

"Should she believe *you*?" Isabel said from the top of the steps. "Because I find it a little hard to believe when you have another girl's name tattooed across your back." Tristan put me down.

"Kyrie Eleison? You think that's a girl?" he asked.

“Yeah,” she said. She walked down the stairs. “What is she? Swedish or something?” He laughed.

“You amaze me sometimes, Isabel. You’re so smart yet you’re so…”

“Clueless?” she asked, a glimmer in her eye.

“She already knows it’s not a girl.” He looked over to me. “She does. She looked it up online. Things like that drive her crazy.”

Isabel sat her beach bag down on the floor and walked past him into the kitchen.

“All I want to know is how religious you have to be to put something like that on your back.”

“I’m not really that religious,” Tristan replied.

“But obviously you believe in God,” she said.

“I do.”

“Well, then you need to go to confession.” He laughed.

“Yeah. Probably.”

“No. Definitely. You have to mean it. Do you mean it when you go?”

“I’m not Catholic.” Isabel opened the cabinet above the sink and pulled out several bottles of various liquors.

“Oh, you confess directly to God wherever you are.” She looked over to me. “Like Lilah.”

“Something like that,” he said as he playfully pinched my waist.

“Forgiveness,” she said. “Now there’s a concept.”

“All you have to do is ask,” Tristan said.

“To who?” Isabel asked. “Because so far in my life asking forgiveness has gotten me nowhere.” Tristan pointed upward and we all looked at each other knowingly.

"Yeah," he said and shrugged. "The only part of my story that is true. My twisted spiritual history."

"I was being sarcastic," Isabel replied. He smiled.

"I know."

"Do you have a gun?" she asked. He looked down to the floor.

"Yes."

"Where is it?"

"Isabel! Maybe he doesn't want you to know where it is."

"Oh, I don't care," he said. "It's not like either one of you are capable of shooting me." Isabel and I looked at each other.

"You'd be surprised," she said looking back to him.

"No. I wouldn't be surprised because it isn't loaded right now."

"Well, what kind of cop are you that you don't have a loaded gun?"

"Isabel!!!" I exclaimed. "Stop it."

Tristan walked over to the counter in front of her.

"Isabel," he said. "I'm going to tell you this once and then we're never going to talk about it again. Okay?"

"Whatever."

"I can load that gun before you'd even realize it was in my hand."

"Well, where is it?" she asked as she chopped up limes for our drinks.

"You don't have to tell her that," I said.

"It's fine," he said to me. "It's on top of the dresser in Lilah's bedroom."

"It is??" I asked. He chuckled.

"Yeah," he said turning to me. "I never conceal my gun unless it is absolutely necessary."

"Where are the bullets?" Isabel asked. I hung my head and Tristan shook his in disbelief.

"That, you do not need to know. Nor will I ever tell you so don't ask me again."

"Fine," she said.

"Are we going out to the beach?" Tristan asked.

"I guess," Isabel said. "Just so you know, I haven't changed my mind about you. I can't flip a switch like Lilah does." She started pouring a little of each liquor into three different shakers. "I don't care what you do for a living."

"Okay," Tristan acknowledged.

"But I need to see your driver's license."

"Isabel!" Her audacity amazed me sometimes.

"Hold on," he said, and he ran over to the stairs taking two at a time.

"What is he doing?" Isabel asked me.

"Going to get his driver's license, I guess."

He came back down and handed a driver's license to Isabel. It wasn't the real one. She looked at it and smiled.

"You're not even old enough to drink," she said smartly. "What are we going to do about this?"

"That *is* me," he said seriously. He propped himself up with his hand on the counter. "You realize this?"

"Yeah," she said. "I got it. You're Tristan. But that doesn't mean I have to like you."

"It does not," he said. "In fact, I would prefer you didn't like me. That way, you see, I can return the favor."

"Fuck you then." Tristan was unmoved by her show of affection. He gestured toward the three cocktail shakers sitting on the counter.

"How will I know I'm not going to die by drinking that?" he asked her.

"You're good at solving mysteries," she replied. "I'm sure you'll figure it out." She pulled a bag of ice from the freezer and poured it into the cooler.

"Oh? Is it the oleander bush out front?" She laid her hands flat on the counter and leaned toward him.

"I didn't really want to give that away," she said trying not to smile. "But now that you've asked me a direct question I have no choice."

"I'm good at things like that," he said. "Because, you know, I solve mysteries for a living."

"I did, however, write ***'You've Been Poisoned'*** on the bottom of your cup," she confessed. He laughed, and she looked over to me and winked.

"But by then, of course, it would've been too late."

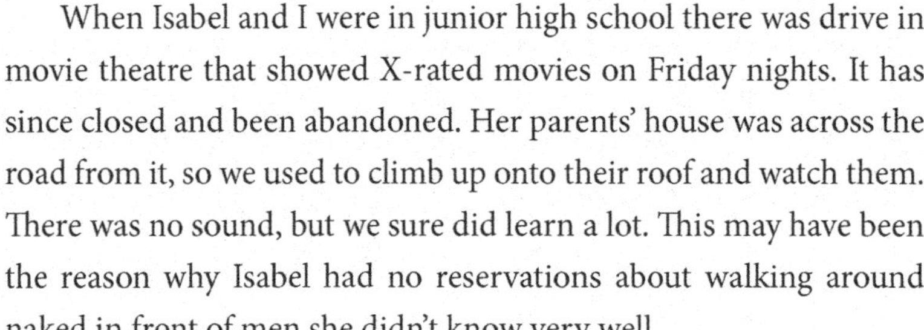

When Isabel and I were in junior high school there was drive in movie theatre that showed X-rated movies on Friday nights. It has since closed and been abandoned. Her parents' house was across the road from it, so we used to climb up onto their roof and watch them. There was no sound, but we sure did learn a lot. This may have been the reason why Isabel had no reservations about walking around naked in front of men she didn't know very well.

I'm sure in Tristan's line of work there wasn't much he hadn't seen but his mouth still fell open when Isabel walked in off the side deck bikini-less with an invitation for all of us to get into the hot tub together. We quickly sat up and tried to compose ourselves. She was drunk, of course.

"I have an idea," she said.

"What is it?" Tristan asked. "Because my top is already off." Isabel ignored him. She had never appreciated his sense of humor.

"We're all adults, right?"

"The last time I checked," he said. "Lilah? Are we all adults?" I rolled my eyes. Just because Isabel was my best friend did not mean she never got on my last nerve.

"Let's all get in the hot tub together," she said. "I was in there all by myself thinking how much fun it would be if we were enjoying it together." I looked over to Tristan.

"Is this against your oath of honor?" He chuckled and ran his hand over his mouth.

About fifteen minutes later, Tristan and I had settled into the hot tub with our drinks. He held up his glass for a toast with the drink Isabel called, ***A Happy Ending***.

"Not that some of us haven't already had enough of these," I said as he touched his glass to mine.

"Wrong. Just wrong," he replied. He took a cautious sip.

"Where does she gets all these drink ideas?"

"She has a book," I explained. "But most of them she just makes up in her head."

"Ah…well that explains her chemistry degree."

"No one has ever accused Isabel of not using her expertise for the betterment of mankind." He laughed.

"Okay," Isabel said as she waltzed out of the French doors onto the deck. She held one of those toy eight balls – the ones kids used to answer, 'life's most important questions.' "This should be fun."

"Where did you get that?" I asked.

"Your mother." I narrowed my eyes at her. "It was on the bookcase in the living room."

She threw her leg over the side of the hot tub and sank down inside it. She was still naked. I think at this point Tristan was used to it because his mouth was no longer hanging open. She handed him the eight ball.

"You first." Tristan looked to me.

"What should I ask it?"

"Whatever you want, I guess," I replied.

"Does Isabel believe I'm an adult?" He shook it lightly then turned it over. He laughed. "Reply hazy."

"See? It tells the truth," she said.

"Liquor is what tells the truth," I commented.

I downed the rest of my martini. There was nothing like adding a little milk to the rest of the liquid diet you had consumed over the course of the day. It was one of those nights when you knew the next day was going to be hell, but you just didn't care.

I was still semi-sober at that point but not for long. After the Happy Ending martinis, Isabel made a batch of what she called ***Isabel's Beach Punch.*** Let me tell you right now that mixing red Kool-Aid, red wine and vodka is not a good idea. I reasoned I had come to the beach to get away from the complications of my life, which was still true despite the change of events. I considered the situation with Tristan a fortunate coincidence although I knew Isabel didn't feel that way. Not even a little bit. But now that she was drunk off her ass there was the possibility, not as distinct as you might think because we're talking about Isabel, I would have to share Tristan with my best friend.

Isabel took the eight ball from him. She looked over to me before asking her question, so I knew right away she was about to ask it something that would more than likely piss me off. She held the ball in her hands and closed her eyes, giggling.

"Will Lilah get mad if I kiss Tristan?" she asked as she turned it upside down. "Ha, ha, ha."

"What? Let me see."

I reached for it but before I could make out what it said Isabel crawled over into Tristan's lap. She straddled him, took his face in her hands, and placed her mouth over his. It was a soft and sensuous kiss and Tristan placed his hands on her hips under the water as she kissed him. I looked down at the eight ball.

"Better not tell you now," I read out loud.

I don't think either one of them heard me.

Isabel

Tristan didn't come back to Woodlawn. Lilah wouldn't tell me whether she knew where he was, but I could only gather she did since she hadn't committed herself to "The Ward" over the last few weeks. There is no way she would be sane and fully functioning if she wasn't in touch with him somehow.

It was nearing a hundred degrees when the air conditioning at my house decided it didn't want to turn on anymore. Well, that's a lie. The fan would turn on but there was no cold air. It didn't surprise me one bit when the air conditioning company who installed it said they weren't available to do repairs until the following week. That's what they called a limited warranty. Hence, the kids and I packed up and went to Lilah's house. Lilah's house is not as big on the inside as it looks on the outside.

With the humidity percentage above eighty percent, convincing the kids to do anything outside was out of the question. I couldn't blame them. Fortunately, Lilah had the basement, which is where we made them all stay until we figured out sleeping arrangements. Our kids were getting to the age where secluding them to one spot in the house to save our sanity was no longer a workable solution.

They were restless. Plying them with wine coolers was not out of the question.

"How many do we have?" I asked.

"I don't know," she said as she unpacked the groceries I had brought. "But I can go to the store and buy more."

"We can't still give them Benadryl. Can we?" Lilah laughed.

"I don't think so."

Once I had unpacked I met Lilah in the kitchen for happy hour. She insisted she treat me to one of her personal favorites: ***Liquid Candy.*** Let me be honest and say I hate the drink Liquid Candy. I am not a candy person. Neither is Lilah which made me wonder which one of her boyfriends over the years had introduced her to it.

"This is not going to be enough for me," I said as I sat down at the kitchen table with her. "I need something stronger."

"This is all liquor, Isabel. You can't get any stronger than this."

"Okay. Well, I'll need more than one."

We were mixing up the second batch when there was a knock at Lilah's front door. No one knocked at Lilah's front door. She looked over to me and I shrugged. Both of us got up. When Lilah opened the front door to find two policemen standing on her porch was when I realized I was still holding my drink in my hand. I knew neither one of them.

"May I help you?" Lilah asked.

"Good afternoon, Ma'am."

"Hi," I said. "Can we help you?"

"Are you Mrs. Trenton?" I pointed to Lilah.

"She is."

"Mrs. Trenton, I'm sorry to bother you this afternoon. It's awfully hot. Isn't it?" We both just stared at him.

“Is your daughter home?

“Vonnie?” Lilah asked. I could hear the alarm in her voice. The officer looked down at his paperwork.

“Veronica?”

Lilah turned to look at me as if to ask whether she should admit Vonnie was downstairs in the basement. I nodded. It’s not like we could hide her for long. She looked back to the officer.

“Um, she’s downstairs.”

“Would it be alright if we came in, Ma’am?” The other officer asked. I stepped forward.

“Wait a minute,” I said holding up my hand. I sat my drink down on the foyer table. Under normal circumstances, Lilah would have fussed at me for not using a coaster. “What is this about?”

“Are you related to Miss…” he looked down at his paper again. “Trenton?”

“No,” Lilah said giving me the evil eye. “She’s just a friend.”

“Well, I’m afraid I can’t talk to you,” the officer said.

“What is this about?” Lilah asked.

“May we come in?” he asked again.

“I want to know why first. What for?” The officer shifted from one foot to the other.

“We have a search warrant, Ma’am.”

“What the hell for?” I asked.

“Isabel!” Lilah said without turning around.

“We have reason to believe there are drugs at this location.”

“What??” we exclaimed at the same time.

While it was true there was a possibility of marijuana being at my house, the possibility of it being at Lilah’s house was almost non-existent. For one, Isaac was the pot smoker and secondly, Eric could smell drugs. Who couldn't smell pot? He would never have tolerated them being in his house. Lilah had never disagreed with him so there was no reason to believe this had changed because Eric had moved out.

"What kind of drugs?" Lilah asked.

See? I would have never thought to ask that question. I would have automatically assumed it was pot.

"To be honest with you Ma'am, I don't think that is the point here. May we come in?"

Lilah took a deep breath as she opened the door further and I stepped back into the foyer. In a completely neurotic effort she picked up my cocktail glass and wiped off the table with the bottom of her t-shirt. She handed it back to me and we followed the policemen into the living room.

"I don't believe this requires further explanation," he stated. "But if you would retrieve Miss. Trenton I would be appreciative."

"I'll get her," I said as I placed my hand on Lilah's arm. I gestured toward the policemen. "Please, sit down."

They looked at each other as if they were confused but that was typical with the Woodlawn police department. They were always confused. They employed Roy, for God's sake. I went to the top of the basement stairs. I thought about yelling for Vonnie like I normally did then reconsidered. I descended the steps and looked around.

"Where's Vonnie?" I asked Isaac.

"She left," he said, and he pointed to the outside basement door.

"What do you mean she left?" I asked. "Where did she go?" He shrugged.

"I have no idea," he said. "I thought you guys wanted to get rid of us." I put my hand to my forehead.

"What is it?" Ben asked. Michael turned down the television.

"Nothing," I said as I turned around. "Stay down here until I come back." Maria ran over and grabbed my legs. "I'll be right back, honey."

"Vonnie left with Curtis," she said.

"What?" I asked. I looked down to her. "Who is Curtis?"

"Curtis is one of Bret's friends," Ben explained. "He's always coming to pick up Vonnie because Bret says he has no gas."

"How convenient," I said as I turned and ran up the stairs. Isaac followed me, and I turned around.

"Stop." I held up my hand.

"What is going on?"

"Just stay down here with Maria, please."

"Okaay. Are you alright?"

"I'm fine." I headed back up the stairs.

By the time I got to the top I was panting for breath. Not because I am out of shape but because I was out of my element, and given the officers had a search warrant I didn't think my uncle could save us. What was I going to tell them? I had no choice but to tell them what I knew, which was nothing. Once I admitted I knew nothing, Lilah would go into crisis mode and then I would be dealing with two police officers and a crazy woman. Oh, and not to mention the six children. I briefly wondered where I had put my Liquid Candy.

"I'm sorry," I said as I walked into the living room. Everyone turned to me in expectation. "Vonnie isn't here." Lilah stood up.

"What do you mean she isn't here?"

"Apparently, she left," I said.

"Left?" Lilah asked. "Where did she go?"

"I don't know," I said. "Isaac only said she left."

"And Isaac is?" one of the officers asked.

"My son," I explained. "No relation to Vonnie."

"We're all just friends," Lilah said.

"I'm really sorry, Ma'am but we'll need to go down and look for her ourselves. There are some questions that need to be answered and we'll need to search the rest of the house as well." He looked to me. "Can you take me downstairs, please?" I held up my hand.

"Wait. We have six other children down there. Can I at least bring them up here first? Or take them outside?" Lilah looked at me, grateful.

"Sure," he said. "Take them outside. We'll go down and you can bring them back in up here. I understand."

"Thank you."

Lilah still says she thinks I went into a slight case of shock at that point because I can't remember ushering the kids out of the basement and bringing them back in through the front door. The police car was sitting in the driveway so there was no denying the officers were inside the house. I'm not sure how I justified it, only that I did.

I don't know how much cocaine the police found in Vonnie's room once they came back upstairs. I only know they tore it apart. There was nothing extraordinary about it. It was like they were looking for a lost earring and when they were satisfied there were no more lost earrings, they left. Four state police officers showed up before it was over. Vonnie didn't or wouldn't or maybe couldn't answer her cell phone. I didn't like thinking about the couldn't possibility. She wouldn't answer Ben or Isaac's texts either. It was after eight when all the officers left that night.

I poured Lilah two shots of spiced rum in a short glass and handed it to her then made one for myself. Lilah sat in her favorite chair in front of the fireplace, her feet tucked underneath her.

"Light a fire," she said to me.

"Why?" I asked. "It's a hundred and fifty degrees outside."

"It's cold in here," she replied. "And I like looking at it. It relaxes me."

I wasn't going to argue with her at a time like this, so I had Ben bring in a few logs from the shed out back. I got the lighter from the hallway table drawer. It took me about fifteen minutes to light it. I wasn't good at making fires.

"You should call Tristan," Ben said to me after I lit it. I looked over to him in surprise.

"Why on earth would I call Tristan?"

"Mom," Ben said but Lilah didn't acknowledge him. He called a little louder. "Mom!"

"Yes?" She didn't take her eyes off the fire.

"Call Tristan."

As out of it as she seemed she still had enough wherewithal not to acknowledge she knew anything at all about Tristan. I was proud of her. Proud she could keep composure at a crazy time like this.

"Why?" she asked. Ben glanced over to me then back to his mother.

"Because if anyone knows where Vonnie is, it will be him."

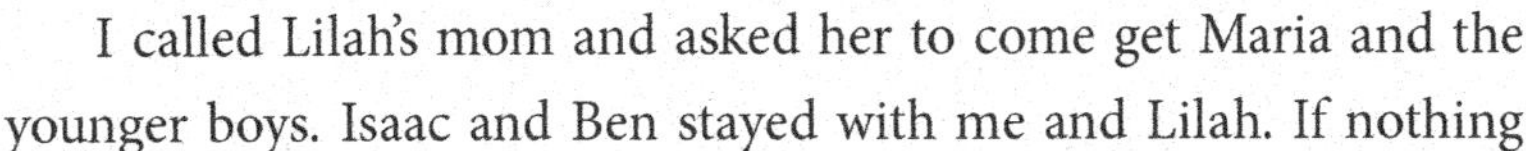

I called Lilah's mom and asked her to come get Maria and the younger boys. Isaac and Ben stayed with me and Lilah. If nothing else, I needed them for moral support. I felt as if I was preparing for a hurricane although I didn't know from which direction it was coming.

Tristan didn't answer his phone. At least he didn't answer the number I had, and Lilah said he had a different number now. She said she had written it down somewhere, but couldn't remember where she'd put it. When I asked why she hadn't put it in her phone she said she didn't want to take the chance of someone finding it in her contact list. When I asked her why she didn't put it under someone else's name she screamed at me.

"I don't know, Isabel!! I don't know!"

Ben and Isaac turned the house upside down looking for it in places I already knew it wasn't, but it gave them something useful to do. I searched the places I knew were an actual possibility – Lilah's jewelry box, her bedside table drawer, her favorite books. You would be surprised if you knew the kind of things Lilah put in her books. Grocery lists, school project dates for her kids, things she needed to do before the end of time, a love letter Eric had written when Maria was born. I found several other men's phone numbers but not Tristan's. I even found a lock of Vonnie's hair wrapped in a piece of tissue paper. The entire time we were all searching Lilah sat in front of the fireplace watching the fire with an afghan her mother had made stretched over her legs.

"They'll find her," she kept saying. "They'll find her."

I wanted to call Eric, but I didn't expect him to do anything when he was halfway across the country. Lilah told me he was at some "show." I didn't know what that meant and didn't really care, but I later found out it was an IT convention in L.A. Ben told me it was an excuse to party for the weekend. I left Eric seven messages to call me on his voicemail.

Now I don't know about you, but if my wife's best friend left me seven messages I would begin to wonder if everything was okay - with her, with my children, if maybe my house had burned down. But apparently Eric felt Lilah was in control of everything at home and I was being a pesky drama queen. After the last time he called me a pesky drama queen I told him his wife had tried to kill herself with fourteen hydrocodone and when she didn't "feel" anything tried to slit her wrists. Eric had no emotions that I could tell. He put money in Lilah's checking account every week and didn't ask any questions.

I wanted to find Bret and rip his eyeballs out of his head, maybe after I cut off all his fingers one by one and tried to drown him in a septic tank. Neither Ben nor Isaac knew where he lived but that was probably a good thing. Lilah told me Bret lived in the East End. That meant nothing to me. That was like saying, if you get in your sleigh with eight tiny reindeer and drive into the blizzard, you'll eventually see Santa's toy shop on the left.

One of the differences between me and Lilah is that Lilah has the patience of Job. And not in a good way. She will wait indefinitely before she starts to "worry." At that point she will go into a dead panic and expect someone else to do something. I, on the other hand, have no patience -with stupid people, with stupid situations, with lies, threats or any other kind of thing that makes no logical sense. If it doesn't make logical sense it doesn't exist. Well, apart from God. He wasn't logical, but I knew He was up there somewhere.

I reasoned Vonnie must have needed Lilah and I a lot more than we'd thought. By being the only girl growing up in a sea of boys she had developed an air of superiority around her most people found intimidating. She seemed self-sufficient. I had no doubt she was smarter than any of the boys. Every study I'd read revealed girls' brains developed faster than boys' brains. In all honesty, I didn't think boys' brains *ever* caught up with girls' brains. I know for a fact

I am smarter than any man I've ever had in my bed. In case you're wondering, that is a lot of men.

Vonnie was indisputably cleverer than any of our boys but that did not attest to her moral fiber. Vonnie kept score and when you least expected it, she returned fire. It was one of the reasons her and Lilah fought so much. Lilah saw a little bit of herself in Vonnie and it scared her.

Sometimes people see the truth right in front of their eyes but subconsciously ignore it because they don't want to admit what it means. I knew long before that night something dangerous was going on with Vonnie. Now I silently condemned myself for trying to protect Lilah from it. A mother should never be protected against the plight of her own child. Maybe if I had said something none of this would be happening right now. Maybe we would know where Vonnie had gone. Maybe she would have never gone there in the first place.

The house phone rang, and I nearly jumped out of my skin. Ben ran to grab it off the side table and answered it before I could get across the room. He tried to hand it to Lilah and she turned her head slowly to look over her shoulder, but she didn't reach for it.

"It's the state police," he said nervously. I said a silent prayer. She took the phone from Ben.

"Yes?" A moment of silence while she listened. The expression on her face did not change. "Okay. Yes. Thank you." She stood up.

"They have Vonnie," she said. "At the station in the East End." She turned to Ben. "Where are my car keys?"

"You're not driving," I said immediately. "I will take you." No arguing. No resistance at all.

"Okay."

I made Isaac and Ben stay at the house even though Ben begged to go with us. It took Lilah and I an hour to get to Richmond because of the summer vacation traffic. It took me another twenty minutes to find the state police station. The air conditioning at the station hit me in the face as we walked inside the door. It may have been colder than Lilah's house. I shivered and rubbed my arms. Lilah walked up to the window.

"I'm here to see my daughter, Veronica Trenton."

Within minutes an officer had come out of a side door from the back of the office to retrieve Lilah. He didn't question my presence or say I couldn't go with them, so I followed Lilah through the doorway. He led us to a small room with a very cold metal bench that left red indentions on my legs when I stood up. Another officer brought Vonnie out in handcuffs, but he unlocked them as soon as he closed the door. When he did Vonnie ran to her mother. The scent of her Victoria's Secret perfume that always filled whatever space she occupied flooded the room. She buried her face into Lilah's shoulder, her long dark hair cascading over her back. She kept crying and whispering, "I'm so sorry, Mama. I'm so sorry." She whispered something else, but she said it so softly I couldn't hear.

The policeman had to pry her away from Lilah after a time and it broke my heart. Watching him put the handcuffs back on Vonnie and lead her away brought Lilah to her knees and she fell on the cement floor and sobbed. I went over and pulled her back to a standing position.

"Come on sweetie," I whispered. "You can't do this. Don't let Vonnie see you this way. Be strong."

Another officer came out of the same door they had taken Vonnie moments before and handed Lilah his business card. He shook her hand.

"Mrs. Trenton?" Lilah nodded. "I'm Mike Hobbs. I'm a detective with the state police. How are you?"

"I'm okay," she said though it was obvious she wasn't okay. She wasn't anywhere close to being okay.

"I wanted to come out and tell you that you are more than likely going to be able to take your daughter home tonight." Lilah looked up suddenly, a look of surprise and hope on her face.

"I am?"

"Yes," he said. "Her drug test came back clean and it appears the drugs the officers found in her room belonged to someone else. It doesn't mean there won't be charges but she'll be free to go home."

"Who?" Lilah asked ignoring everything else he'd said.

"I'm sorry Ma'am but I can't give you that information."

"Bret," I muttered. They both looked my way but said nothing.

"It might be a few hours before they're done with the interrogation."

"Interrogation?" Lilah asked.

"It's standard procedure," he replied. "Don't worry." He looked over to me. "You might want to go get some coffee or a bite to eat while you wait."

"Did they post bail?"

"No, Ma'am. They don't consider her a flight risk." He turned to Lilah. "I'm sorry you had to see her in handcuffs, Mrs. Trenton. I know it must have been very upsetting to you."

"Thank you." The officer stood up.

"Do you have a cell phone number where I can reach you?"

I rattled off Lilah's number and he wrote it on a tiny slip of paper he pulled from his pocket. I'd seen other police officers do the same thing. Did they all walk around with tiny pieces of paper in their pockets just for these types of occasions?

"I'll call you if we're done before you return." He reached out to shake Lilah's hand again and she took it. He looked to me. He knew Lilah was in no state to drive.

"I assume you are taking care of her?" he asked.

"Yes," I said. "Always."

Lilah and I went to the corner café down the street. We didn't drive. It was less than a block and despite it not being in a very good part of town I didn't see the point in moving the car. The waitress came over at once with a pot of coffee and two coffee cups in her hand. She filled them without asking whether we wanted any or not. I couldn't help but think she must have seen a lot of people wasting time while they waited for someone at the police station.

"Can I get you girls something else?" she asked. I looked over to the pie cabinet behind the counter.

"I'll have a piece of the coconut pie and she'll have the lemon." I could tell by the way she looked at me that people didn't usually order anything.

"Sure," she said.

"I can't eat anything," Lilah said blandly. "How can you eat?"

"Well, I can't have a drink, so I figured I'd ply myself with sugar." She didn't smile but she did look up at me from the table.

"You never cease to amaze me, Isabel."

"What did Vonnie whisper to you?" I asked as I put sugar in my coffee. She seemed surprised I'd noticed. I notice everything. I had to pay attention because Lilah never did.

"She said Tristan was there." I nearly jumped up out the booth.

"What?!" I must have said it a lot louder than I thought because everyone in the restaurant turned to look at me. Lilah showed no emotion.

"She said Tristan was there."

"Where? At the police station?" Lilah shook her head and shrugged.

"I don't know. She only said Tristan was there."

"So, somewhere else?"

"I think so."

"Where?"

"I don't know."

She reached into the pocket of her shorts and pulled out a small card. I thought it must have been the business card the officer had given her just moments ago, but it was crumpled and folded into a million pieces.

"Vonnie gave me this," she said. "She pushed it into my hand before the officer took her away." I took the card from her and read it silently.

THE PERSON WHO GAVE YOU THIS IS A

UNDERCOVER

POLICE OFFICER

DO NOT PANIC

YOU ARE UNDER POLICE SURVEILLANCE – DO NOT MAKE ANY SUDDEN MOVES – WE DO NOT WISH TO INJURE YOU, SO LISTEN CAREFULLY TO THE OFFICER'S INSTRUCTIONS AND COMPLY IMMEDIATELY

I looked up to Lilah.

"Tristan gave her this?"

"I'm assuming."

"Do the officers at the station know she had this??"

"I'm sure they do. I imagine they searched her."

"What else did she say?"

"Nothing," she replied. "Nothing at all."

They released Vonnie two hours later. We were all silent on the way home. Well, I was silent. Vonnie and Lilah cried the entire time. We ran out of napkins from the glove compartment, so I ended up giving them a couple of old tissues I found in the bottom of my purse.

When we got back home and after I had given Vonnie a speech about what I wanted to do to Bret, I gave her another speech about what would happen if I ever found out she went anywhere near him again. Lilah told me I was being too hard on her.

"You haven't seen hard," I said. "If she were mine it wouldn't have only been a speech. I would've beaten her with a wooden spoon. She might not even be alive."

"Oh, Isabel."

"You noticed she didn't say anything back to me. Did you notice that?"

"Yes. I noticed."

"You know why? Because she knows if she had I would have smacked her across the room. I've always looked for a reason to smack her anyway."

"She's upset," Lilah said.

"She's upset??" I shouted. "She shouldn't be upset. She should be deciding whether she wants the top or bottom bunk."

"I know."

After my speech Vonnie had gone directly downstairs to the basement where Isaac and Ben had been camped out since we'd left to go get her. It was four in the morning. At the time, I wasn't aware Vonnie had told the police she was in love with Bret. If I had, the speech would have been a lot worse.

Vonnie's current situation was what happened when you fell in love with a jackass – and when I say jackass, I mean someone who cares only about themselves. They are the type of people who will say or do anything to get you to do whatever they want to help *themselves* – not you. Some women think this is love because those men will convince you what they want should be what you want, too. Vonnie wasn't old enough to know that type of behavior is called control.

In this case, what Bret wanted from Vonnie was for her to believe hiding his drugs was for *her* benefit because she didn't want him to go to jail, did she? Didn't she love him? I'm sure it was also to get into Vonnie's pants but that wasn't something I liked to think about in any capacity. It made me want to do other things to Bret that probably weren't legal in some states.

While Lilah went downstairs to check on everyone I took down a bottle of whiskey and some butterscotch schnapps and made a couple of Breakfast Shots. Four o'clock in the morning is when you have a ***Breakfast Shot.*** Especially when you've had a night like we'd had. When Lilah came back up she rounded the corner from the back stairs and stopped at the edge of the counter. She looked like she'd seen a ghost. I waited for her to say something, but she didn't.

"What?" I asked.

"Tristan is downstairs," she said but before I could digest what she was saying he had come up the stairs behind her. She jumped when he touched her arm.

"Vonnie just left," he said. "I'm sorry."

"What!?!" I yelled. "What do you mean she just left?"

"I was talking to her about everything that's happened," he said with complete composure. "She wanted me to do something to help Bret and when I told her I wouldn't she told me to go to hell and left."

"Why did you let her leave?" Lilah screamed at him. A look of sheer devastation came over her face. "Where did she go?"

"I don't know," he said.

"What do you mean you don't know?" Lilah asked. "Why don't you know?"

Tristan pulled her against him and put his arms around her. She struggled to get away from him, but he wouldn't let her go.

"What did I tell you?" he asked softly.

"Let me go!"

"Tell me what I promised you first." He tightened his arms around her. She finally gave in and fell limp against his chest.

"That you'll take care of Vonnie," she cried.

"Yes," he said as he laid his hand on top of her head and brought it down over her hair. "I don't break my promises and I'm going to take care of Vonnie just like I said I would. You have to trust me." He pulled her further into his chest. It was such an intimate moment between them I felt as if I shouldn't have been there. I looked away.

"I need you to get Ben and Isaac out of the house," Tristan said to me as he held Lilah close to him. "Take them to your house. Where is everyone else?"

"With Loretta."

“Good. Can I trust you?” he asked. I pointed to my own chest.

“Me?”

“Yes. You.”

It was the first time in my life anyone had asked me if they could trust me when it wasn’t an accusation, but a request – a need.

“Yes,” I said. “You can. Absolutely.”

Bret

It's not about anything except how much I can get out of it. I mean, you know. She was gorgeous. With a body like that you would pretty much sell your soul. Except there were certain things I wouldn't put up with – competition, being one – which was why from the beginning Vonnie needed to understand that she was mine. Not like 'we're gonna date for a little while' or even 'we're gonna be friends with benefits. I would have done that, by the way, but there were other things that were more important.

You see, first off, getting my money was the number one thing. Because if I couldn't get my money I got my ass kicked. And I didn't particularly enjoy getting my ass kicked. Luther could be brutal if he didn't get his part.

It's not like I didn't let Vonnie get with any of my guys. Not because she wanted to but because they wanted to, and she knew that was part of the deal. It didn't hurt that she looked like that type of girl, the one who would agree to have a fucking tattoo put on her back, just because she thought that would make you love her more. Vonnie was good at sex. No doubt about that.

When Tristan showed up I knew there was something weird going on, so I never liked him in the first place. He acted like he was a part of everything. Luther thought he was so obviously so did I. Vonnie kept telling me Tristan was all about her Mom and he wasn't interested in me or anything I did. She said he couldn't care less about me which pissed me off in an entirely different way.

My dad once told me Lilah lived near Richmond – the one girl who wouldn't give him what he wanted but that he still loved. I understood that on some level because I thought one day I might be able to love Vonnie that way.

I was impressed the first time I let Vonnie shoot my gun. She was pretty good at it and she liked to shoot. She told me I didn't need to teach her anything. She knew how to shoot a pistol. I only had to teach her about the other guns.

She was a party girl. She loved to dance with the other guys. They were always blowing or doing rails and they loved to do belly button shots with her. I mean, who wouldn't? I didn't really give a rat's ass if at the end of the night she was mine. And she was always mine.

I finally figured out who Tristan was and where he came from – that guy from Long Island. What's his name? I don't even remember now but I knew he was after me and that was enough. I wasn't going to let him win, though. I was in control of this game and I was in control of Vonnie. I didn't give a fuck who her mother was.

Lilah

"This is not crisis mode," Tristan reassured me quietly as we sat on the sofa in the living room.

Everyone else was gone. There was a movie playing but I can't remember what it was now. It wouldn't be long before the sun would be up.

"I don't understand," I cried. "How can you be so calm when we have no idea where Vonnie is or what is happening?"

"I know what's happening," he said. "Trust me." He took my hand and stood up. "Come on." I stood up beside him.

"Where are we going?"

"Well, first off, we're going to get some of the coffee I made and then we're going to go down to the pond and watch the sunrise."

"Oh, I don't want to watch the sunrise. I don't even want be alive right now and you hate coffee."

"I don't hate coffee," he said. "I just don't drink it very often."

"You're so weird," I said. "You're a cop who doesn't drink coffee." He chuckled.

"You should know by now I never follow the rules."

"You and Isabel."

He tried to lead me to the kitchen, but I stopped him and pulled on his arm.

"Do you know where Vonnie is?" I asked. "Can you tell me? Please?" He turned to me.

"I don't know where Vonnie is for sure, Lilah. I have a lot of ideas, but I can't be certain."

"Why aren't you doing something?" I began to cry again. "I don't understand." He clasped my hands between his own.

"Lilah, listen to me. Do you think I'm the only police officer on the face of the earth?" I shrugged.

"Something *is* being done," he comforted. "I'm just not the one doing it. I'm here. With you. In case Vonnie comes home. I'm exactly where I'm supposed to be."

I sighed and pressed my lips together. I had learned it was one of the only things that could keep me from crying anymore – that and holding my breath.

"Come on," he said. He looked at his watch. "The sun is going to rise in thirty-two minutes."

"Seriously? Thirty-two minutes?"

"Mm-hmm."

We walked into the kitchen together and he took down two coffee cups from the rack under the cabinet.

"I'm drinking mine black," he said. "But I'm thinking you want about six teaspoons of sugar and a half a cup of cream in yours." I smiled weakly.

We walked down the hill in the dark to the edge of the pond. Ben had moved the Adirondack chairs we normally sat in the last time he'd cut the grass. I looked around to see if I could find them, but they were nowhere. What the hell had he done with them?

"It doesn't matter," Tristan said. "We can sit on the ground. Relax."

"What if Vonnie *does* come home? And we're not up there?"

"If Vonnie is coming home…I promise you, I will know before she gets here."

"How?"

"Lilah. Please."

He took my coffee cup from me and we laid back in the grass to look at the stars. I guess he thought he needed to distract me. He should've known that wasn't possible. Despite that, it was a beautiful, clear night.

"Have you ever read a sky chart?"

"Uh, no."

"See that?" he asked. "That's the Big Dipper. You've heard of that, right?"

"Yeah."

"Now look to the left. See that bright star?"

"Yeah."

"That's Polaris."

"I've never heard of that."

"Like the North Star?"

"The one the wise men followed?"

"No. The Star of Bethlehem was in the East."

"How do you know that?"

"I just do." He pointed to the left. "Now, look there. "That's Cassiopeia."

"If you say so." He turned to face me, propped his head in his hand.

"Look Lilah, I know you're completely freaking out right now, but I need you to have faith in me. What you think, how you feel, means everything to me. Do you believe me?"

"Yes." He rubbed his thumb across my cheek.

"I may even love you more than you love me."

"Oh, I doubt it. Ask Isabel how much I love you. She had to put up with me while you were gone." He leaned over me and kissed me softly. Once. Twice. Three times. His hair tickled my face.

"Your hair," I said pushing it behind his ear. "It drives me crazy."

"I put it up sometimes," he said.

"Not very often."

"It's sexier down." He smiled mischievously.

This was one of the things Tristan did for me. He could always make me smile whenever I was overwhelmed with everything going on in my life – which was often.

"You want me to cut it?" he asked. "I will."

"No."

"I thought it drove you crazy."

"Only when it's hanging in *my* eyes." He rolled over onto his back and pulled me on top of him.

"How's that?" He smiled. "Better?"

I laid my head on his shoulder and let the calm he always exuded surround me. If I could fell his heart beating against mine I knew I was still alive. He put his arms around me.

A quiet noise. A crackle of leaves. I pulled away from Tristan to listen. He laid perfectly still but I could tell he was listening, too. He put his finger over his lips to tell me to be quiet then put his hands on my waist. He grasped my hips in his hands and lifted me above him, slowly sliding from beneath me. He laid me back down gently on the ground, like a puppet he could easily maneuver any way he wanted.

He brought his finger to his lips again and I nodded. He rolled onto his side, his hand going inside the back of the waistband of his jeans. I sucked in my breath as he pulled out his gun. I knew he had the gun, but I didn't know he had it on him. He not only had the gun. He'd already loaded it. I should have known.

He slowly brought himself to a squatting position and took the safety off the gun, both of his hands on the handle. He motioned with his head for me to get over behind the tree beside us but before I could shots rang out. Not his. It was so loud everyone within a five-mile radius must have heard it. I put my hands over my ears. I crouched at the foot of the tree, holding onto it like it was a person.

Then, perfect stillness. Absolute silence. Not a sound. Tristan knelt close to the tree keeping his gun drawn. He searched the woods in front of him, the light on his gun shining across the brush and trees.

Suddenly there were red and blue lights behind me, coming across my backyard and…Vonnie. Not behind me but in front of me – in Tristan's line of sight - with Bret. Bret shot again and Vonnie fell to his feet, holding onto his leg.

"Stop," I heard her screaming. "Bret! Stop!"

"Shut up," he yelled at her.

There were cops behind me. Beside me. Coming down the hill toward the pond, backing Tristan up. I was up on all fours.

Without thinking I yelled, "Vonnie! Run to me, baby." I knew at once I shouldn't have. Bret fired again.

"No! Vonnie!" Tristan shouted. "Stay there!"

But Vonnie ran and before Tristan realized she had he returned fire toward Bret. The bullet hit her with such force it threw her to the ground. I stumbled to my feet and started to run to her. Tristan grabbed the back of my shirt with one hand, holding his gun in the other. He pulled me backward and I fell on the ground in front of him.

"No!" I fought him.

"Stop it!" he yelled. "Get down."

Finally, he shoved me further to the ground and when I fell onto my stomach he put his knee across my back, held me there.

"Vonnie!" I cried. "Vonnie!"

Other police had arrived. Bret was no longer in sight, but he was still firing, or someone was firing. I saw Vonnie crawling across the ground between us. I couldn't tell where she'd been shot but I heard her screaming, crying.

"Tristan!" she sobbed. "Come…get…meee."

"Stay there Vonnie," he yelled back. "Stay down."

I looked to heaven. That was all I had left. Dear God, I prayed. Please help us.

I saw Bret by the beam of the spotlights behind us. He was so visibly nervous the gun shook in his hands.

"Drop it," an officer behind me called.

"Put down your weapon," Tristan said calmly. "Now."

Bret stood, his arms extended, pointing his gun directly at Tristan. There must have been twenty cops behind us, weapons drawn.

"Put down your weapon," Tristan said again. "Or I will shoot."

"Shoot!" Bret yelled. "Shoot me, you son of a bitch."

"I…won't…miss," Tristan yelled back.

Bret ran toward Tristan, dropping the gun beside Vonnie. I don't know if it was intentional or an accident. Shots rang out around me. Vonnie grabbed Bret's gun off the ground and without hesitation, shot it.

Something your kid must know: how to shoot a gun.

The shot hit Bret in the back. He fell forward, his feet swept out from under him like an ocean current. Two officers ran to him, pulling his arms behind his back. The other officers scattered into the woods in front of us, around us, protecting us from every angle.

Tristan left me, stuffing his gun back into the waistband of his jeans and ran to Vonnie. She dropped the gun at once and he dropped to his knees, opened his arms. One of his arms held her, the other hand guiding her head to his shoulder, her tank top covered in blood and now soaking through Tristan's t-shirt.

I hope you never see your child covered in blood. That is a memory you will never forget and a fear you will never overcome. The fact Tristan held her was only a temporary respite.

"It's okay sweetheart," he said. "I've got you. I've got you, Vonnie. Everything is going to be okay now." Vonnie clung to him and he laid her down gently on the ground in front of him.

"No!" she screamed, reaching for him. By the sound of her voice I knew she was terrified. "Tristan! Don't leave me!"

Medical personnel surrounded her, and she fought them.

"Honey," one woman said. "Let us look at your shoulder."

"No!" She sat up, saw Tristan squatting on the ground in front of her. Tristan laid his hand on her ankle. I watched in shock, unable to move.

"Come on, Vonnie," he said. "Let them take care of you."

"No!" she screamed again, and she was up on her knees. She fell into Tristan and he caught her.

"Vonnie," he said holding her against him. "You're safe." She clung to him. "I promise. Take a deep breath. Let these guys help you. Okay? I'm not leaving you."

Tears rolled down my cheeks. Tristan looked up and motioned for me to come over to him. I tried to stand up, but I fell. A guy from the rescue team grabbed my arm before I hit the ground and helped me over to Vonnie.

"Mommy," Vonnie called when she saw me.

Tristan had lowered her to the ground, but she still wouldn't let go of him. He pulled her close, his hand covering her wound as he held her arm tightly against her. One of the rescue men handed him a piece of thick gauze and he quickly put it under his hand to stop the flow of blood. I took Vonnie's hand in mine.

"Mommy," she sobbed. "I'm…I'm…sorry." I knelt next to her, ran my hand across her cheek and leaned over to kiss her forehead. There were splatters of blood across her face.

"I know, baby…."

The sun had begun to rise behind us.

"She's okay," Tristan said as I laid my head against him and wept. He put his free arm around me and kissed the top of my head. "She's okay, Lilah," he comforted. "Your little girl is okay. She's safe now. I promised she would be. Remember?"

He pulled me into him.

Kyrie Eleison. Lord, have mercy.

He did.

But God's mercy is great, and he loved us very much.

Ephesians 2:4 (NCV)

EPILOGUE

Six Months Later

Isabel

For Valentine's Day Lilah and I went to dinner together – alone. It was a rare occurrence not to have at least one child with us but Vonnie had volunteered to babysit Maria and everyone else had their own plans. It was a quiet restaurant, perfect for winding down with a glass of wine after a busy day. Afterward we decided to go back to my house for a nightcap. As we walked across the yard I noticed the lights were on in the living room.

"Vonnie must be in there playing her drums," I said.

"She's supposed to be babysitting Maria."

"She can do that here," I said and smiled. Lilah rolled her eyes.

I unlocked the front door but instead of hearing the drums I heard the piano. Lilah and I stood in the foyer and listened as we took off our coats. A soft, unhurried melody, each note flowing deliberately into the next. Not a song either of us recognized. We were quiet. Lilah followed me down the hall to the French doors that opened into the living room. We stood outside of them in the hallway.

Adrian. He never ceased to amaze us. Every time we thought we knew it all he revealed something else. Maria sat on the bench beside him. Lilah looked through the panes of the windows and sucked in her breath, her hand going to her mouth. Adrian played with such fluidity it seemed his fingers never touched the keys. Vonnie sat at her drums, listening, her sticks in her hand. Her head moved with an imaginary beat but then she began playing alongside Adrian. Tiffany and Isaac walked up behind us, Abe following behind them.

"Is that Vonnie?" Isaac asked. Lilah nodded.

"Who is playing the piano?" Abe asked quietly.

"That would be my brother," Tiffany answered, and Abe's mouth dropped open. Matt came out of his room and walked down the hall. He looked over to me for an explanation and I pointed through the doors.

We watched them play. Adrian looked over to Vonnie and she smiled. They played seamlessly, perfect together. This wasn't the first time they had played this song although I wondered when they could have played together before now.

The front door opened, and I looked around the corner. We were still standing outside the French doors. Ben and Michael came over and stood behind me. Ben put his hands on my shoulders, mesmerized like the rest of us.

The tempo picked up and in a matter of seconds Adrian had turned the piano sound into an electric vibe that synthesized the music. He played with such veracity I was stalled for a reaction. This was the kind of talent rarely appreciated by the everyday musician. This music was not being played by ear. It was being played with a vast amount of knowledge and even more intuition.

Vonnie leaned back as the rhythm intensified. It had always been spellbinding to watch her play and seeing her play with Adrian was no exception. Music had the ability to change her back into the girl we loved, the girl we knew was still there but had somehow been lost.

“What is this song?” Isaac asked. I shook my head.

“I have no idea,” I said.

“It’s Bruno Mars,” Ben said. We all turned to look at him. He shrugged. “It is. It’s Rianne’s new favorite song.”

I opened the French doors and when Maria saw Lilah she jumped down off the piano bench and ran to her. She grabbed Lilah’s legs and Lilah leaned over and kissed the top of her head. She turned around and ran back to the piano, jumped back up onto the bench with Adrian. Adrian and Vonnie looked up but they didn’t stop playing. Adrian smiled and shrugged his shoulders. He nodded toward Vonnie and she smiled, too.

“It’s good, right?” Vonnie asked her mother over the music.

Lilah looked as if she were about to pass out. She was in awe. I think we all were. She walked over to Adrian and put her hands on his shoulders, her diamond glistening in the chandelier above her.

“Yes,” Lilah said. “It’s *really* good.”

Adrian winked at me. We thought he must have broken through Vonnie’s wall somehow. I’ve never seen her glow the way she did that night.

Special thanks to:

Susan Janette – for dreaming with me

Eric Avensbo – for drinking with me

Angela Corrine and Rebecca M. – for teaching me there really are friends like Isabel

And

The City of Richmond, Va. – for helping me make "those" memories

Lilah and Isabel's Happy Hour Cocktails

Snowy Night – ½ oz. Dark Rum. ½ oz. Kahlua, 1 oz. Vodka, 1 oz. Heavy Cream. Fill glass with ice. Add Rum, Coffee Liqueur, and Vodka. Pour the cream over the back of a spoon into the drink.

A Peaceful Acquisition - Fill glass with ice. 1 oz. Gin, ½ oz. Grand Marnier, 1 oz. Sour Mix. Shake. Strain into chilled glass.

A Sophisticated Lady – Fill glass with ice. 1 oz. Vodka, 1 oz. Midori. Top with Pineapple Juice.

Bumblebee - Fill glass with ice. 2 oz. Bourbon, 1 tsp. Honey. Top with Grapefruit Juice.

Mojitos - Fill glass with ice. 2 oz. Light Rum, 1 tsp. Sugar, Dash of Lime Juice. Fill with Soda Water. Garnish with Lime and Mint.

Vodka Tonic *(Lilah's version)* - Fill glass with ice. 2 oz. Citron Vodka. Top with tonic water and a lime slice.

Death in a Glass (French Martini) – Fill champagne glass with ice. 1 ½ oz. Vodka, ½ oz. Chambord. Shake. Strain into chilled glass. Top with Champagne.

Mint Julep – Muddle together in a glass: 10-20 mint leaves, 1 tsp. brown sugar, 2 Tbsp. water. Fill with crushed ice and Whiskey. Garnish with Mint Leaves.

Frozen Tequila – "Freeze" shot glasses. "Freeze" Tequila. Pour "frozen" tequila into "frozen" shot glasses.

Happy Hour – Fill glass with ice. 1 ½ oz. Vodka, ½ oz. Chambord, ½ oz. Grand Marnier or Orange Juice, Dash of Lime Juice. Strain into chilled glass.

Bubble Gum – Fill glass with ice. 1 oz. Vodka, 1 oz. Whiskey, 1 oz. Banana Liqueur, Dash of Grenadine, 1 oz. Cream. Shake. Strain into chilled glass. Garnish with Bubble Gum Stick.

Electric Lemonade – A glass of homemade Lemonade, enough Vodka to convince you it might not be just lemonade.

Fairy Nectar – Fill glass with ice. 1 oz. Rum, ¾ oz. Lime juice, 1 oz. Grapefruit Juice, ½ oz. Maraschino Cherry Liqueur, 1 tsp. Absinthe. Shake. Strain into chilled glass.

Isabel's Sangria – ½ cup Brandy, ¼ cup Lemon Juice, 1/3 cup Frozen Lemonade Concentrate, 1/3 cup Orange Juice, (1) 750ml. bottle of DRY Red Wine, ½ cup Triple Sec, (1) Lemon, (1) orange and (1) Lime – all sliced into rounds, ¼ sugar, (8) maraschino cherries, Club Soda. Combine all ingredients in a large pitcher. Add Fruit. Add Club Soda just before serving.

Lemon Drop Martini *(Isabel's version)*– Moisten rim of martini glass with Lemon Juice and dip in Sugar. Squeeze of lemon juice. Fill with Citron Vodka. Garnish with lemon wedge

Manhattan – Fill glass with ice. 2 oz. Whiskey, ½ oz. Sweet Vermouth. Stir. Add maraschino cherry.

Cherry Kool-Aid and Vodka – Uh…self-explanatory.

Southern Sunset – Fill glass with ice. 2 oz. Coconut Rum. Top with Orange Juice. Pour ½ oz. Grenadine down side of glass.

Mountain Dew Me (Sprite Me) – Fill glass with ice. 2 oz. Midori, 1 oz. Triple Sec, 1 oz. Pineapple Juice. Shake. Strain into chilled glass. Fill with Mountain Dew (or Sprite).

Blood Clot – 1 ½ oz. 151-Proof Rum, Dash of Grenadine. Float ¼ oz. Cream on top.

A Jaded Woman – Fill glass with ice. 1 oz. Coconut Rum, 1 oz. Spiced Rum, 2 oz. Pineapple Juice. Shake. Strain into chilled glass.

Lavender Martini – Fill glass with ice. 1 ½ oz. Vanilla Vodka, ½ oz. freshly squeezed lemon juice, ¼ oz. lavender syrup. * Shake. Strain into chilled glass. Garnish with lavender flower or lemon slice.

*You can buy Lavender syrup at some liquor stores, but you can make your own by making simple sugar syrup and steeping with sprigs of lavender.

You've Been Poisoned – Fill glass with ice. 1 oz. Vodka, ½ Dark Rum, ½ Spiced Rum, ½ oz. Coconut Rum, ½ oz. Amaretto, 1 oz. Orange Juice, 1 oz. Pineapple Juice. Shake. Strain into chilled glass. (Oleander is optional.)

A Happy Ending– Fill glass with ice. ½ oz. Vodka, ½ oz. Triple Sec, ½ oz. Amaretto, ½ oz. White Crème De Cacao, ½ oz. Banana Liqueur. Shake. Strain into chilled glass. Fill with Milk or Cream.

Isabel's Beach Punch – Mix 1 gallon of Cherry Kool-Aid with 1 liter of Cheap Red Wine and (1) 750ml bottle of Vodka.

Liquid Candy - 1 oz. Whiskey, 1 oz. Butterscotch Schnapps, ½ oz. Tuaca. Shake with ice. Strain into short glass.

Breakfast shot – ½ oz. Irish Whiskey, ½ oz. Butterscotch Schnapps, 1 oz. Orange Juice. Shake Whiskey and Schnapps in cocktail shaker with ice.

Pour into one shot glass. Pour the Orange Juice into a separate shot glass. Shoot the liquor and chase with juice.

Other Creative Cocktails from Isabel's Collection

Sweet Fantasy – Fill glass with ice. 1 ½ oz. Dark Rum, ¾ oz. Grand Marnier, ½ tsp. Sugar, ½ Egg White. 1 oz. Sour Mix. Shake. Strain into chilled glass.

Chocolate Chip Cookie Martini - About 10 chocolate chips, 4 or 5 chocolate chip cookies (of course, homemade are best), 1 ½ oz. Vanilla Vodka, 1 oz. Godiva Chocolate Liqueur, ½ oz. Butterscotch Schnapps, Milk to fill. Crush chocolate chips and cookies. Dip rim of glass in milk and coat with crushed chips/cookies. Refrigerate glass while you make the cocktail. Combine Vodka, Chocolate and Butterscotch Liqueurs and shake. Strain into glass. Top with ½ oz. milk.

Six Minutes – Fill glass with ice. 1 ¾ oz. Bourbon, ½ oz. Crème de Mure, 2 oz. Apple Juice. Shake. Strain into chilled glass. Garnish with a strawberry and blackberries.

Desire – Fill glass with ice. 1 ½ oz. Whiskey, ¼ oz. Triple Sec, ½ oz. Dubonnet Rouge, ¼ oz. Pernod. Shake. Strain into chilled glass. Garnish with lemon and/or orange twist.

Kiss - Fill glass with ice. 1 ½ oz. Vanilla Vodka, ½ oz. Godiva Chocolate Liqueur, ¼ oz. Cherry Brandy, ¾ oz. Milk. Shake. Strain into chilled glass.

Starless Sky – Fill glass with ice. 1 oz. Vodka, 1 oz. Coconut Rum, 1 oz. Crème du Mure, Dash of Grenadine. Fill with equal parts Orange and Pineapple Juice. Shake. Strain into chilled glass. Garnish with maraschino cherry.

A Backless Dress – 1 ½ oz. Gin, ¼ oz. Dry Vermouth, ¼ oz. Sweet Vermouth, ½ tsp. Blue Curacao, ¾ oz. Orange Juice. Shake. Strain into chilled glass. Garnish with orange slice.

Liquid Marijuana – Fill glass with ice. ½ oz. Spiced Rum, ½ oz. Blue Curacao, ½ oz. Coconut Rum, ½ oz. Midori, Splash of Sour Mix. Fill with Pineapple Juice. Shake. Strain into chilled glass.

Playing with Fire – 1 ½ oz. Fireball, ½ oz. Licor 43, Cream Soda to taste. Fill with Crushed Ice. Garnish with Atomic Fireball Candies.

Aladdin - Fill glass with ice. 2 oz. Spiced Rum. Fill with equal parts Pineapple, Cranberry, and Orange Juice. Top with ½ oz. Midori.

Ripped Jeans - Fill glass with ice. 2 oz. Vodka, ¼ oz. Blue Curacao. Shake. Strain into chilled glass.

A Transatlantic Deal – Fill glass with ice. 2 oz. Whiskey. Fill with water. Stir.

Perfect, Perfect, Perfect - Fill glass with ice. ¾ oz. Rum, ½ oz. Allspice Dram. Fill with Champagne. Stir.

Cheap Date – Fill glass with ice. 1 ½ oz. Cucumber Vodka, ¾ oz. Dry Vermouth. Shake. Strain into chilled glass. Garnish with cucumber.

Bad Rumor – Fill glass with ice. 1 oz. Vodka, 1 oz. Apricot Brandy. Fill with equal parts Sour Mix and Orange Juice. Shake. Strain into chilled glass.

French Kiss – Fill glass with ice. 1 oz. Whiskey, 1 oz. Dry Vermouth, ½ oz. Dubonnet Rouge, ¾ oz. Orange Juice. Shake. Strain into chilled glass.

Study Hall – 1 oz. Frangelico, 2 tsp. Sugar. Fill with hot black coffee.

Answered Prayer – Fill glass with ice. 1 ½ oz. Dry Gin, ½ oz. Grand Marnier, ½ oz. fresh Lemon Juice, ½ oz. fresh Orange Juice. Shake. Strain into chilled glass.

A State Slightly South of Rapture – Fill glass with ice. 1 oz. Vodka, ½ oz. Peach Schnapps, ½ oz. Chambord, Dash of Cranberry Juice, Dash of Pineapple Juice. Shake. Strain into chilled glass. Top with Champagne.

Waterfall – In a Blender: 1 cup Ice, 1 ¼ oz. Rum, 1 oz. Blue Curacao, 3 oz. Orange Juice, 3 oz. Pineapple Juice, 3 or 4 drops of Lime Juice. Blend on low speed for 3-5 minutes.

Busted Lip – Fill glass with ice. 1 oz. Scotch, ¾ oz. Cherry Brandy, ½ Sweet Vermouth, 1 oz. Orange Juice. Stir. Strain into chilled glass.

Little White Lie – Fill glass with ice. 1 oz. Gin, 1 oz. Rum, ½ oz. Triple Sec, ½ oz. Lemon Juice or Sour Mix. Shake. Strain into chilled glass.

Tristan (In A Bottle) - Fill glass with ice. 1 oz. Vanilla Vodka, ½ oz. Wild Rose Liqueur, ½ oz. Allspice Dram, ¼ oz. Absinthe. Shake. Strain into chilled glass.

Bleach Blonde Bunny – Fill glass with ice. 1 ½ oz. Gin, ½ oz. Grenadine, 2 oz. Pineapple Juice. Shake. Strain into chilled glass.

Easy Lover – Fill shaker with ice. 1 oz. Limoncello, 1 oz. Vodka, 1 oz. Orange Liqueur. Shake for 20 seconds. Pour into champagne glass. Top with Prosecco. Add a dash of Grenadine for color.

Stick Shift – Fill tall cocktail glass with Glow-in-the-Dark Ice Cubes (Amazon). Pour all at once: 1 oz. Rum, 1 oz. Apple Pucker, 1 oz. Blue Curacao. Add 1 oz. Coconut Rum. Top with Ice. Pour 1 oz. Sprite over ice. Top with Soda Water.

Come and Get Me – Fill glass with ice. ½ 151 Rum, ½ oz. 100 Proof Bourbon, ½ oz. 100 Proof Peppermint Schnapps, ½ Grenadine. Shake. Strain into chilled glass.

Visceral Passion – Fill glass with ice. ¾ oz. Amber Rum, ¾ Peach Schnapps, ¾ oz. Grand Marnier, 2 oz. Orange Juice, 2 oz. Cranberry Juice. Shake. Strain into chilled glass.

Cleansing Breath – Fill glass with ice. 1 ½ oz. Brandy, ½ oz. Peppermint Schnapps. Stir. Strain into chilled glass.

I Can't Wait – Fill glass with ice. 1 ½ oz. Gin, ½ oz. Sour Mix, 1 tsp. Powdered Sugar. Shake. Strain into chilled glass.

Three Blank Pages – Fill glass with ice. 2 oz. Vodka, 1 oz. St. Germain, ¾ oz. White Cranberry Juice, ½ oz. Lime Juice. Shake. Strain into chilled glass.

Consequences – Fill glass with ice. 1 oz. Green Chartreuse, 1 oz. 100 proof Peppermint Schnapps. Stir.

Magic – Fill glass with ice. 1 ½ oz. Gin, 1 tsp. Blue Curacao, ½ tsp. Lemon Juice, ½ tsp. Grenadine. Shake. Strain into chilled glass.

Restricted – Fill glass with ice. 2 oz. Gin, Dash of White Crème De Menthe, Dash of Bitters, 2 oz. Sour Mix. Shake. Strain into chilled glass. Garnish with Cherry.

Homeless Hooker – ½ oz. Coffee Liqueur, ½ oz. Honey Liqueur, ½ Orange Liqueur. Shoot it and hold in your mouth as long as possible before swallowing. (Isabel always wins this "game.")

Silver Ring – Fill glass with ice. 1 oz. White Crème De Cacao, 1 oz. White Crème De Menthe. Stir.

Devil in Sheep's Clothing – Fill glass with ice. ½ oz. Vodka, ½ oz. 151 Rum, ½ oz. Yukon Jack, ½ oz. Cinnamon Schnapps. Stir. Strain into chilled glass.

Lip Gloss – Fill glass with ice. 2 oz. Rum, 1 oz. Brandy, ½ Lemon Juice, 2 dashes Grenadine, (1) egg white. Shake. Strain into chilled glass. Garnish with cherry.

Love Hate Relationship – Fill glass with ice. ½ oz. Gin, ½ oz. Rum, ½ oz. Brandy, ½ oz. Triple Sec. Fill with Sour Mix (leaving ½ inch from top). Top with Lager.

Inner Judgement - Fill glass with ice. ½ oz. Vodka, ½ oz. Cognac, ½ oz. Banana Liqueur, 1oz. Sour Mix, 1 oz. Orange Juice. Shake. Strain into chilled glass.

Root of All Evil - In Blender: ½ cup ice, 1 oz. Light Rum, 1 oz. Gin, 1 oz. Brandy, 1 oz. Orange Juice, 1 oz. White Wine, 1 oz. Lemon Juice, ½ oz. Crème De Noyaux. Blend until smooth. Float ½ oz. Dark Rum on top.

Veronica - Fill glass with ice. 2 oz. Gin, 1 Egg White, 1 oz. Orange Juice. Shake. Strain into chilled glass. Top with ½ oz. White Crème De Curacao.

A Good Time – Fill glass with ice. 1 ½ oz. Gin, ½ oz. Apricot Liqueur, ½ Lemon Juice, 1 tsp. Grenadine, Dash of Bitters. Shake. Strain into chilled glass.

Outer Banks – Fill glass with ice. 1 ½ oz. Vodka. Fill with Grapefruit Juice. Rub rim of second glass with Lime. Dip rim in kosher salt. Pour contents on first glass into salted glass. Garnish with lime.

Neon Pink Bikini – Fill glass with ice. 2 oz. Pink Vodka, 2 oz. Triple Sec, ¼ oz. Grenadine. Shake. Strain into chilled glass.

Stingray – Moisten rim of martini glass with lime juice and dip in coarse sugar. Place in freezer while you make drink. ¼ cup Cranberry Juice, 1 oz. Citron Vodka, 1 oz. Blue Curacao, ½ oz. Lime Juice. Shake. Strain into glass.

Long Island Iced Tea – Fill glass with ice. ½ oz. Vodka, ½ oz. Gin, ½ oz. Rum, ½ oz. Tequila, ½ oz. Triple Sec, 1 oz. Sour Mix. Top with Cola. Garnish with lemon.

Sex on the Beach *(With Tristan)* – Fill glass with ice. ½ oz. Vodka, ½ oz. Whiskey, ½ oz. Peach Schnapps, ½ oz. Apple Schnapps, ½ oz. Orange Liqueur, ½ oz. Orange Juice, ½ oz. Cranberry Juice, ½ oz. Milk. Shake. Strain into chilled glass.

No Morals – Fill glass with ice. 1 oz. Vodka, ½ oz. Amaretto, ½ oz. Coffee Liqueur. Fill with Pineapple Juice. Shake. Strain into chilled glass.

Loaded Gun – Fill glass with ice. Coat rim of second glass with Paprika Sea Salt Spice. 1 ¾ oz. Blue Agave Tequila, 1 oz. Lime Juice, ½ oz. Orange Liqueur, 1 oz. Chili Liqueur. Shake. Drain over fresh ice.

Eight Ball – Fill glass with ice. 1 ½ oz. Vodka, ½ oz. Blackberry Brandy. Fill with Sour Mix. Shake. Strain into chilled glass.

Drama Queen – Fill glass with ice. Fill with equal parts Red Wine and Diet Cola.

Belly Button Shot – Find an attractive, desirable belly button. Ask permission to use it. If yes, lay owner on their back (completely nude, if possible). Fill belly button with your favorite straight liquor (be careful not to spill). Place your lips over belly button and slurp drink out as loudly as possible. Take turns with your friends. Repeat.

North Star – Fill glass with ice. 1 ½ oz. Black Vodka, 1 ½ oz. Cherry Juice, 1 oz. Orange Juice, ½ oz. Maraschino Cherry Juice, Edible White Pearl Dust (can be found in your local craft store in the cake decorating aisle). Shake. Strain into chilled glass.

DIDN'T GET ENOUGH OF LILAH AND ISABEL?

Join them in Renay Jordan's new upcoming novel

Amityville Magic

"I think I'm going to Long Island for the summer," I said to Isabel as we sat by the pool. It was nearly eighty degrees, but she hadn't taken off the cover yet. Well, she hadn't made the kids take off the cover yet.

"What? Why?" She shook the cocktail shaker over her head then poured it into two chilled martini glasses. It was black.

"Black? What is this?"

"It's the ***Color of my Soul.***" I laughed.

"That's a good name for it."

"It is," she agreed. She settled on the chaise lounge beside me.

"So, Adrian is taking you away from me for the entire summer? Awesome." I turned to her.

"I want you to go."

"I can't go to Long Island for the entire summer, Lilah." She took a sip of her drink.

"Why not?" I asked. "School will be out in a few weeks. It's not like you have to work. This drink would give a hell of a hangover. It tastes like pure sugar and blackberries."

"Where would I stay?" she asked ignoring my comment because every drink Isabel made gave a hell of a hangover. "I can't afford to rent a house and pay this mortgage at the same time."

"You'd stay with me."

"Do I want to know where that is?"

"Adrian's grandmother left her entire estate to him and Tiffany. So, there." She didn't seem surprised.

"Is there a house?"

"No," I said shaking my head. "We're going to pitch tents on the beach."

"What??"

"I'm kidding, Isabel. Of course, there's a house."

"What kind of house? Because there are seven children between us. It would have to be one big ass house."

"It's an old Victorian on the beach. 1906. Amityville." She widened her eyes.

"As in the Amityville Horror?" I laughed.

"Well, not THAT house. That village." I rolled up the bottom of my shorts to get a little more sun.

"It's a village?"

"So, Adrian says."

"How big is the house?"

"6000 sq. ft."

"Are you fucking kidding me?" I smiled.

"Nope." She looked over to me and grinned mischievously.

"What would *we* do in an old Victorian beach house for an entire summer?"

"Well, for one, work our asses off. I need a refill." I got up and walked over to the bar.

"Why?" she asked turning around.

"Because I'm not drunk yet."

"No, goofball. Why will we be working our asses off?"

"Because it used to be a Bed & Breakfast when Adrian was little, and he wants to restore it." I poured a little more ice into the shaker.

"Well, now I know why you want me to go." She took another sip of her martini, slurped the sugar out of the bottom.

"It will be fun," I said.

"Hmm…"

"We'll have the kids," I reassured her. "We can drink and direct traffic like we usually do."

"Ha."

"Please." I walked back around the edge of the bar toward her.

"I'll think about it."

"That means yes, doesn't it?"

"Maybe."

"That's good." I sat down beside her. "Because I told Adrian I wasn't going unless you did."

"Oh, wow. What did he say to that?" I laughed.

"He said Amityville will never be the same."

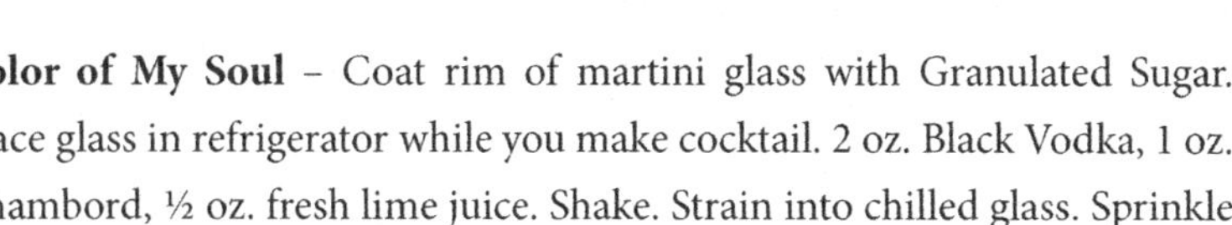

Color of My Soul – Coat rim of martini glass with Granulated Sugar. Place glass in refrigerator while you make cocktail. 2 oz. Black Vodka, 1 oz. Chambord, ½ oz. fresh lime juice. Shake. Strain into chilled glass. Sprinkle with Confectionary Sugar. Garnish with blackberries.